THE GUYANA QUARTET

Wilson Harris was born in New Amsterdam, British Guyana, in 1921, of mixed parentage (Amerindian, European, African). He was educated at Queen's College, Georgetown, and studied land surveying in 1939, subsequently qualifying to practise. He led many survey parties into the heart of the British Guyanan rainforests and from 1955 to 1958 was the Senior Surveyor for Projects for the government of British Guyana.

He came to London in 1959 where he still lives with his wife. As well as writing, he has taught in universities throughout the world. In December 1984 he received an honorary doctorate from the University of the West Indies.

His most recent novel is *Carnival*.

by the same author

ff

WILSON HARRIS

The Guyana Quartet

faber and faber

LONDON · BOSTON

This collection first published in 1985
by Faber and Faber Limited
3 Queen Square London WC1N 3AU

Palace of the Peacock first published in 1960
The Far Journey of Oudin first published in 1961
The Whole Armour first published in 1962
The Secret Ladder first published in 1963

Phototypeset in Great Britain by Wilmaset Birkenhead
Printed in England by Clays Ltd, St Ives plc

A CIP record for this book is available
from the British Library
ISBN 0-571-13451-3

2 4 6 8 10 9 7 5 3

CONTENTS

Some years ago I attempted to outline the possibility of validating or proving the truths that may occupy certain twentieth century works of fiction that diverge, in peculiar degrees, from canons of realism. I sought such proof or validation by bringing the fictions I had in mind into parallel with profound myth that lies apparently eclipsed in largely forgotten so-called savage cultures.

The nature of such eclipse is a haunting dimension; and now across many years when I find I may read *The Guyana Quartet* as if it were written by another person, it is possible to conceive how the fiction validates itself through buried or hidden curiously live fossils of another age.

None of this incurs complacency. Far from it. For proof of fiction's genesis or fiction's truths, in the spirit I seek, leads one into the enigma of violence and forces resembling yet other than violence. Proof penetrates every mask of complacency we tend to erect. Proof like Doubt must seek the hidden wound in orders of complacency that mask opportunist codes of hollow survival.

A great magical web born of the music of the elements is how one may respond perhaps to a detailed map of Guyana seen rotating in space with its numerous etched rivers, numerous lines and tributaries, interior rivers, coastal rivers, the arteries of God's spider. Guyana is derived from an Amerindian root word which means "land of waters". The spirit-bone of water that sings in the dense, interior rainforests is as invaluable a resource in the coastal savannahs which have long been subject to drought as to floodwaters that stretched like a sea from coastal river to coastal river yet remained unharnessed and wasted; subject also to the rapacity of moneylenders, miserable loans, inflated interest.

To plunge into the *Quartet*. Carroll's music in the last stages of *Palace of the Peacock* slices through every character-mask, "mixing blind joy and sadness and the sense of being lost with the nearness of being found" (page 114) to intimate distances that cannot be measured in the body of the crew, distances that breed a gateway or intangible architecture when El Dorado, or the city of gold, secretes a resemblance to the city of God. In such resemblances lie profoundest self-judgements converting music into terrifying vision.

Donne, the master of the El Doradonne crew, hangs upon a scaffolding to which he is secured by "the unflinching clarity with which he looked into himself and saw that all his life he had loved no one but himself. He focused his blind eye . . ." (page 107) in surrender to the folk constellated in the stars he had exploited and the woman Mariella of the moon and the sun, the rapids and the forests, he had abused.

Let me confess that my apprehension of Carroll's music is peculiar and "primitive": *primitive* in that it consumes anthropomorphic objects, marching boots akin to enemy rocks, rainbows and butterflies akin to sails on a wave of savannah: all this to invoke *depth* in space, oceanic/forested space, *sound* and *sounding*. Carroll's music is not "pure" nor is it engaged in a sophisticated divorce from fictile morsel or construct. Rather the intention is to imbue Caribbean shell and pottery with the metaphor of an organ or vision of substance. Upon each horizon of music that issues from the organ, sound matches an illumination of land and sea to imply a paradise in which the infernal deeds of the El Doradonne crew are so ingrained that nothing has apparently changed since the hanged/shot/drowned horseman appears to fall in the opening phases of *Palace* and to foreshadow more than one death for the crew, more than one encounter with genesis, a genesis of the imagination. "I dreamt I awoke with one dead seeing eye and one living closed eye" (page 19).

Nothing has changed in Carroll's paradise save for "the second death" that re-opens or re-visits every blind deed in the past and begins a ceaseless penetration of objects as surrogates of original volume, original sound, original capacity or comprehension of limits, genuine change within and without.

This bitter ground of ecstasy, the second death, change yet changelessness, implies a fiction that seeks to consume its own biases through many resurrections of paradoxical imagination and to generate foundations of care within the vessel of place. That "original vessel" on which *Palace* rests validates itself, in my judgement, through vestiges of the Carib/ cannibal bone-flute in the soil of place though I was unconscious of this when I travelled in the heartland of Guyana and when, after discarding three novels, I struck what I knew at last was the right note with which to commence the *Quartet*.

I do not wish in this preface to say more than is strictly necessary on the Carib bone-flute. In essence it validates, as I have implied, the intuitive diet and metaphysical consumption of bias in Carroll's music. I became aware of the bone-flute some years after I had written *The Guyana Quartet* and upon reading an appendix to the *Marches of El Dorado* by Michael Swan. This led me to research the articles of Walter Roth, an Australian anthropologist, who travelled in British Guyana and whose work began to appear in 1909 from the Bureau of Ethnology, Washington, DC. I had heard of Roth in the 1940s when I began my survey expeditions into the primeval rainforests of Guyana but never read him until long after when I was fortunate in the late 1960s and the 1970s to have the opportunity for research in specialist libraries in Canada and the United States.

The Carib flute was hollowed from the bone of an enemy in time of war. Flesh was plucked and consumed and in the process secrets were digested. Spectres arose from, or reposed in, the flute. Swan identifies this flute of soul with "transubstantiation in reverse". In parallel with an obvious violation ran therefore, it seems to me, another subtle force resembling yet differing from terror in that the flute became the home or curiously *mutual* fortress of spirit between enemy and other, an organ of self-knowledge suffused with enemy bias so close to native greed for victory.

Wishrop is curiously sliced in two – *webbed* enemy-in-other, webbed other-in-enemy – within the shadow of Carroll's music in which the bone converts into spider cosmos as Wishrop consumes "a diet of nerve and battle to induce him to find his changeless fortress and life" (*Palace of the Peacock*, page 115).

The spider metamorphosis is Daedalian, I think, but it is also native to Afro-American bridges in space and thus it enhances the mixed blood, the mixed metaphysic, of the crew, the dangers, the potentialities. The "changeless fortress" or bridge arching across worlds is a surrogate of paradise, the bone of spirit turns fine and elongated, half-visible, half-invisible.

I mention all this in order to stress the convertible imageries in the narrative of the entire *Quartet*, the paradoxes of emphasis born of necessity as sliced being revolves nevertheless into a new configuration or complex evolution, complex regeneration, sound yet sight woven together.

Now to *The Far Journey of Oudin*. It is upon the spirit-bone of the river that Beti, an illiterate East Indian woman, vomits web or paper. She is pregnant with her dead husband's, Oudin's, child. She must save it from the devil of a moneylender Ram with whom Oudin has signed a mysterious contract that terrifies her since it may give the devil power over her unborn child. When Oudin dies she extracts the paper from his fingers and eats it. How much would Ram – an impotent man despite his hold upon others – give for a son and an heir!

The Far Journey of Oudin subsists in significant part on Oudin's struggle with Ram. That struggle mirrors a "covenant" or rehearsal of truth. It is a rehearsal in which "doubles" appear to invoke the dead and the living who revisit or re-play the deeds of the past in a new light of presences woven closely into the tapestry of past action. Oudin appears to be the moneylender's slave and agrees to track down Mohammed's unmarked calves and put Ram's brand upon them. When he arrives at Mohammed's house Muhra – Mohammed's wife – is overcome by Oudin's resemblance to her husband's half-brother whom Mohammed, Hassan, Kaiser and Rajah had murdered when they learnt that their dying father, Rajah's uncle, had intended to make the "outside child" his heir.

Oudin's coming as a slave (yet the substance of a dream-covenant to bind or overthrow Ram), a servant (yet the double of Mohammed's murdered half-brother) weaves parallel forces backwards and forwards in conspiratorial time through which one sees Mohammed plotting again with his dead brothers in an underworld of "masks and bones of death".

> "Oudin had succeeded in lighting the tall reflective fire at last, which was to illumine the constructive and relative meaning of the time, as if the seed-water in the flood of the river, where Beti . . . had vomited, now rose into a . . . spirit-fire . . . Oudin had risen early and collected . . . the masks and bones of death Mohammed plotted with . . . It was the knowledge one shares with a trembling leaf and phantom from a smouldering heap and fire stinging one's nostrils as one steps back upon another's unexpected foot."
>
> (*The Far Journey of Oudin*, pages 164–5)

In a peasant, religious society – such as the enigmatic Oudin visits – that seems at times secure, though inwardly ravaged by flood and drought, and by legacies of conquest and indenture, the genesis of fiction may lie in part in one's intuitive rapport with densities of conspiratorial time that deepen over the generations into potential for, yet deprivation of, sensibility. Family authority, like the rule of law, loses

11

its sacred premium, and as that happens deprivation of the senses of soul becomes a curious rot or *seed* in the soil of age. The paradox is that a new covenant with fate and freedom – or emergent fiction of truth in "tall reflective fire" – begins to grow from that seed.

In *The Secret Ladder* the paradoxes of a covenant with Being are nowhere better illumined in *The Guyana Quartet* than in the averted rape of Catalena Perez, the Portuguese wife of a member of Fenwick's crew. With the tragic death of great Poseidon, the descendant of seventeenth-century African runaway slaves, the followers of the god go mad and would haul down the stars and bring time to an end if they could. Poseidon is their fortress of soul and his death at the hand of a member of Russell Fenwick's crew leaves them bereft of hope.

Catalena is suddenly aware, prostrate on the ground and still untouched, of a nameless presence above her who promises to save her. She focuses with all her strength on that presence. When she thinks she sees it nothing is there except the faces of two of her enemies. They are framed in its place. They have run a long way to alert their fellow conspirators to imminent danger from the jungle police who, they believe, are on their trail. They come into the clearing and stand above Catalena at the very moment she is conscious of the nameless, majestic presence overshadowing her. The plot of rape collapses as dead Poseidon's followers flee. Was she saved by a rot or seed in the soil such as we saw in Oudin's world, rot or seed growing into "tall reflective fire"? Did that fire blow with multiple faces, the hideous faces of rape withdrawn but in parallel with the spark of a wholly different protective Being? *Catalena alone was conscious of what had happened.* Such aloneness bears, I believe, upon a capacity for innermost vision within the individual person in times of singular ordeal or singular ecstasy. And I wonder: is such vision an initiation into well-nigh unbearable beauty or saving presence *through* masks of terror?

The ancient jaguar or tiger of South America – whose flayed

hide Cristo wears in *The Whole Armour* – is another costume and initiation mask. The stripes on Cristo's carnival body like the stars on the peacock's tail lend themselves to different interpretations and explications. The tiger comes out of the vastness of a continent and is older than the Carib bone-flute though it is possessed by music nevertheless, by chords or stripes of genesis-drum that are painted sometimes by the moon in the depths of the forest.

The jaguar runs off into the Bush of the Pomeroon "with a neighbour's child" (*The Whole Armour*, page 309).

The stress on painted drum sounds the note of "mate of all generations . . . devouring the umbilical *chord* of a stolen life" (*The Whole Armour*, page 311).

Umbilical chord and cord sound also between Magda, the terrible mother, and Cristo, her epic son. A simultaneous cord of peril, as of something stolen yet implicitly newly severed, binds them together.

In what degree, one wonders, is epic rooted in the lost infancy of a people and their need to compensate that loss through various trials, complicated jealousy, guilt, passion, innocence?

New research – at Edinburgh University, for instance – claims that the perceptual intelligence is in play much earlier in childhood than we used to think: indeed from within a few days of birth when the infant child may reach out purposefully to show forth an inherent capacity to unravel the masquerade of appearances. By and large that wonderful eye or capacity tends to fade or lose its magic within a few years.

This, I find, throws some light on the intuitive thrust of *The Whole Armour*. The newly severed/devoured umbilical cord bears upon the universal theft of vision by the artist from the "lost child" within the tapestry of the jaguar. Inimitable play, belonging to the infancy of Mankind, fades into the fixations of later culture but stolen life or umbilicus becomes the navel of recall to breach what is lost. That breach – however apparently terrifying in some of its aspects – may be transformed into a series of initiations/penetrations/visualizations of the roots of play. Cristo, the "dead man", returns to establish his innocence of a crime for which he is accused.

I surveyed the Pomeroon river – the setting of *The Whole Armour* – in 1950 and was conscious even then – many years before I commenced *The Guyana Quartet* – of the uncertain economic fate of the society, its need to deepen its insights into the soil of place in which ancient masquerades exist to validate the risks a community may take if it is to come abreast of its hidden potential.

In the same token, the people of the Canje river – the setting of *The Secret Ladder* – face the encroachment of new technologies. Fenwick, the engineer/surveyor, clashes with Poseidon who fears that he may lose his long-established home within a projected irrigation reservoir for rice and sugar estate lands.

"This was Poseidon's asylum and home. It had acquired . . . the stamp of a multiple tradition or heritage . . . Had he not the right to defy all the sciences of the earth in the blessed name of his humanity?" (*The Secret Ladder*, page 411).

He pays with his life; and his death goads his blind followers to threaten the entire fabric of a society blind itself to innermost ambiguity and to a clash of cultures it needs to transform through the very "multiple heritage" to which Poseidon appeals if it is to bridge the divide between "blessed name of humanity" and the indifferent objects or goals of science.

WILSON HARRIS
August 1984

14

PALACE OF THE PEACOCK

For Margaret, Nigel and Sydney

It ceases to be history and becomes. . .
fabricated for pleasure, as moderns say,
but I say by Inspiration.

William Blake

And after the earthquake a fire; but the
Lord was not in the fire: and after the
fire a still small voice.

I Kings 19 : 12

BOOK ONE

HORSEMAN, PASS BY

Cast a cold eye
On Life, on death.
Horseman, pass by.

W. B. Yeats

I

Cabalgan ficción e historia

Imágen de la conquista

s. XVI

A horseman appeared on the road coming at a breakneck
stride. A shot rang out suddenly, near and yet far as if the
wind had been stretched and torn and had started coiling and
running in an instant. The horseman stiffened with a devil's
smile, and the horse reared, grinning fiendishly and snapping
at the reins. The horseman gave a bow to heaven like a
hanging man to his executioner, and rolled from his saddle on
to the ground.

The shot had pulled me up and stifled my own heart in
heaven. I started walking suddenly and approached the man
on the ground. His hair lay on his forehead. Someone was
watching us from the trees and bushes that clustered the side
of the road. Watching me as I bent down and looked at the
man whose open eyes stared at the sky through his long
hanging hair. The sun blinded and ruled my living sight but
the dead man's eye remained open and obstinate and clear.

I dreamt I awoke with one dead seeing eye and one living
closed eye. I put my dreaming feet on the ground in a room
that oppressed me as though I stood in an operating theatre,
or a maternity ward, or I felt suddenly, the glaring cell of a
prisoner who had been sentenced to die. I arose with a violent
giddiness and leaned on a huge rocking-chair. I remembered
the first time I had entered this bare curious room; the house
stood high and alone in the flat brooding countryside. I had
felt the wind rocking me with the oldest uncertainty and
desire in the world, the desire to govern or be governed, rule
or be ruled for ever.

Someone rapped on the door of my cell and room. I started

19

on seeing the dream-horseman, tall and spare and hard-looking as ever. "Good morning," he growled slapping a dead leg and limb. I greeted him as one greeting one's gaoler and ruler. And we looked through the window of the room together as though through his dead seeing material eye, rather than through my living closed spiritual eye, upon the primitive road and the savannahs dotted with sentinel trees and slowly moving animals.

His name was Donne, and it had always possessed a cruel glory for me. His wild exploits had governed my imagination from childhood. In the end he had been expelled from school.

He left me a year later to join a team of ranchers near the Brazil frontier and border country. I learnt then to fend for myself and he soon turned into a ghost, a million dreaming miles away from the sea-coast where we had lived.

"The woman still sleeping," Donne growled, rapping on the ground hard with his leg again to rouse me from my inner contemplation and slumber.

"What woman?" I dreamed, roused to a half-waking sense of pleasure mingled with foreboding.

"Damnation," Donne said in a fury, surveying a dozen cages in the yard, all open. The chickens spied us and they came half-running, half-flying, pecking still at each other piteously and murderously.

"Mariella," Donne shouted. Then in a still more insistent angry voice – "Mariella."

I followed his eyes and realized he was addressing a little shack partly hidden in a clump of trees.

Someone was emerging from the shack and out of the trees. She was barefoot and she bent forward to feed the chickens. I saw the back of her knees and the fine beautiful grain of her flesh. Donne looked at her as at a larger and equally senseless creature whom he governed and ruled like a fowl.

20

I half-woke for the second or third time to the sound of insistent thumping and sobbing in the hall outside my door. I awoke and dressed quickly. Mariella stood in the hall, dishevelled as ever, beating her hand on my door.

"Quiet, quiet," I said roughly shrinking from her appearance. She shuddered and sobbed. "He beat me," she burst out at last. She lifted her dress to show me her legs. I stroked the firm beauty of her flesh and touched the ugly marks where she had been whipped. "Look," she said, and lifted her dress still higher. Her convulsive sobbing stopped when I touched her again.

A brilliant day. The sun smote me as I descended the steps. We walked to the curious high swinging gate like a waving symbol and warning taller than a hanging man whose toes almost touched the ground; the gate was as curious and arresting as the prison house we had left above and behind, standing on the tallest stilts in the world.

"Donne cruel and mad," Mariella cried. She was staring hard at me. I turned away from her black hypnotic eyes as if I had been blinded by the sun, and saw inwardly in the haze of my blind eye a watching muse and phantom whose breath was on my lips.

She remained close to me and the fury of her voice was in the wind. I turned away and leaned heavily against the frail brilliant gallows-gate of the sky, looking down upon the very road where I had seen the wild horse, and the equally wild demon and horseman fall. Mariella had killed him.

I awoke in full and in earnest with the sun's blinding light and muse in my eye. My brother had just entered the room. I felt the enormous relief one experiences after a haze and a dream. "You're still alive," I cried involuntarily. "I dreamt Mariella ambushed and shot you." I started rubbing the vision from my eye. "I've been here just a few days," I spoke guardedly, "and I don't know all the circumstances" – I raised myself on

21

my elbow – "but you are a devil with that woman. You're driving her mad."

Donne's face clouded and cleared instantly. "Dreamer," he warned, giving me a light wooden tap on the shoulder, "life here is tough. One has to be a devil to survive. I'm the last landlord. I tell you I fight everything in nature, flood, drought, chicken hawk, rat, beast and woman. I'm everything. Midwife, yes, doctor, yes, gaoler, judge, hangman, every blasted thing to the labouring people. Look man, look outside again. Primitive. Every boundary line is a myth. No-man's land, understand?"

"There are still labouring people about, you admit that." I was at a loss for words and I stared blindly through the window at an invisible population.

"It's an old dream," I plucked up the courage to express my inner thoughts.

"What is?"

"It started when we were at school, I imagine. Then you went away suddenly. It stopped then. I had a curious sense of hard-won freedom when you had gone. Then to my astonishment, long after, it came again. But this time with a new striking menace that flung you from your horse. You fell and died instantly, and yet you were the one who saw, and I was the one who was blind. Did I ever write and tell you" – I shrank from Donne's supercilious smile, and hastened to justify myself – "that I am actually going blind in one eye?" I was gratified by his sudden startled expression.

"Blind?" he cried.

"My left eye has an incurable infection," I declared. "My right eye – which is actually sound – goes blind in my dream," I felt foolishly distressed. "Nothing kills *your* sight," I added with musing envy. "And your vision becomes," I hastened to complete my story, "your vision becomes the only remaining window on the world for me."

I felt a mounting sense of distress.

"Mariella?" There was a curious edge of mockery and interest in Donne's voice.

"I never saw her before in my dream," I said. I continued with a forced warmth – "I am glad we are together again after so many years. I may be able to free myself of this – this –" I searched for a word – "this obsession. After all it's childish."

Donne flicked ash and tobacco upon the floor. I could see a certain calculation in his dead seeing eye. "I had almost forgotten I had a brother like you," he smiled matter-of-factly. "It had passed from my mind – this dreaming twin responsibility you remember." His voice expanded and a sinister under-current ran through his remarks – "We belong to a short-lived family and people. It's so easy to succumb and die. It's the usual thing in this country as you well know." He was smiling and indifferent. "Our parents died early. They had a hard life. Tried to fight their way up out of an economic nightmare: farmers and hand-to-mouth business folk they were. They gave up the ghost before they had well started to live." He stared at me significantly. "I looked after you, son." He gave me one of his ruthless taps. "Father and Mother rolled into one for a while. I was a boy then. I had almost forgotten. Now I'm a man. I've learnt," he waved his hands at the savannahs, "to rule *this*. This is the ultimate. This is everlasting. One doesn't have to see deeper than that, does one?" He stared at me hard as death. "Rule the land," he said, "while you still have a ghost of a chance. And you rule the world. Look at the sun." His dead eye blinded mine. "Look at the sun," he cried in a stamping terrible voice.

II

The map of the savannahs was a dream. The names Brazil and Guyana were colonial conventions I had known from childhood. I clung to them now as to a curious necessary stone and footing, even in my dream, the ground I knew I must not relinquish. They were an actual stage, a presence, however mythical they seemed to the universal and the spiritual eye. They were as close to me as my ribs, the rivers and the flatland, the mountains and heartland I intimately saw. I could not help cherishing my symbolic map, and my bodily prejudice like a well-known room and house of superstition within which I dwelt. I saw this kingdom of man turned into a colony and battleground of spirit, a priceless tempting jewel I dreamed I possessed.

I pored over the map of the sun my brother had given me. The river of the savannahs wound its way far into the distance until it had forgotten the open land. The dense dreaming jungle and forest emerged. Mariella dwelt above the falls in the forest. I saw the rocks bristling in the legend of the river. On all sides the falling water boiled and hissed and roared. The rocks in the tide flashed their presentiment in the sun, everlasting courage and the other obscure spirits of creation. One's mind was a chaos of sensation, even pleasure, faced by imminent mortal danger. A white fury and foam churned and raced on the black tide that grew golden every now and then like the crystal memory of sugar. From every quarter a mindless stream came through the ominous rocks whose presence served to pit the mad foaming face. The boat shuddered in an anxious grip and in a living streaming hand that issued from the bowels of earth. We stood on the threshold of a precarious standstill. The outboard engine and

24

propeller still revolved and flashed with mental silent horror now that its roar had been drowned in other wilder unnatural voices whose violent din rose from beneath our feet in the waters. Donne gave a louder cry at last, human and incredible and clear, and the boat-crew sprang to divine attention. They seized every paddle and with immortal effort edged the vessel forward. Our bow pointed to a solid flat stone unbroken and clear, running far into the river's bank. It looked near and yet was as far from us as the blue sky from the earth. Sharp peaks and broken hillocks grew on its every side, save where we approached, and to lose our course or fail to keep our head signified a crashing stop with a rock boring and gaping open our bottom and side. Every man paddled and sweated and strained toward the stone and heaven in his heart. The bowman sprang upon the hospitable ground at last followed by a nimble pair from the crew. Ropes were extended and we were drawn into a pond and still water between the whirling stream and the river's stone.

I felt an illogical disappointment and regret that we were temporarily out of danger. Like a shell after an ecstasy of roaring water and of fast rocks appearing to move and swim again, and yet still and bound as ever where the foam forced its way and seethed and curdled and rushed.

The crew swarmed like upright spiders, half-naked, scrambling under a burden of cargo they were carrying ashore. First I picked and counted the daSilva twins of Sorrow Hill, thin, long-legged, fair-skinned, of Portuguese extraction. Then I spotted old Schomburgh, also of Sorrow Hill, agile and swift as a monkey for all his seasoned years. Donne prized Schomburgh as a bowman, the best in all the world his epitaph boasted and read. There was Vigilance, black-haired, Indian, sparkling and shrewd of eye, reading the river's mysterious book. Vigilance had recommended Carroll, his cousin, a thick-set young Negro boy gifted with his paddle as if it were a violin and a sword together in paradise. My eye fell on Cameron, brick-red face, slow feet, faster than a snake in the forest with his hands; and Jennings, the mechanic, young, solemn-featured, carved out of still wood it seemed, sweating still the dew of his tears, cursing and reproving his whirling engine and toy in the unearthly terrifying grip in the water. Lastly I counted Wishrop, assistant bowman and captain's understudy. Wishrop resembled Donne, especially when they stood side by side at the captain's paddle. I felt my heart come into my mouth with a sense of recognition and fear. Apart from this fleeting wishful resemblance it suddenly seemed to me I had never known Donne in the past – his face was a dead blank. I saw him now for the first faceless time as the captain and unnatural soul of heaven's dream; he was myself standing outside of me while I stood inside of him.

The crew began, all together, tugging and hauling the boat, and their sing-song cry rattled in my throat. They were as clear and matter-of-fact as the stone we had reached. It was the best crew any man could find in these parts to cross the falls towards the Mission where Mariella lived. The odd fact existed of course that their living names matched the names of a famous dead crew that had sunk in the rapids and been drowned to a man, leaving their names inscribed on Sorrow Hill which stood at the foot of the falls. But this in no way interfered with their lifelike appearance and spirit and energy. Such a coincidence we were beginning to learn to take in our stride. Trust Donne to rake up every ghost in his hanging world and house. Mariella was the obsession we must encounter at all costs, and we needed gifted souls in our crew. Donne smiled with a trace of mockery at my rank impatience. His smile suddenly changed. His face grew younger and brutal and impatient too. And innocent like a reflection of everlasting dreaming life.

The sun was high in the heavens. The river burned and flamed. The particular section, where we were, demanded hauling our vessel out of the water and along the bank until we had cleared an impassable fury and obstruction. The bright mist lifted a little from my mind's eye, and I saw with a thumping impossible heart I was reliving Donne's first innocent voyage and excursion into the interior country. This was long before he had established himself in his brooding hanging house. Long before he had conquered and crushed the region he ruled, annihilating everyone and devouring himself in turn. I had been struck by a peculiar feeling of absence of living persons in the savannahs where he governed. I knew there were labouring people about but it had seemed that apart from his mistress – the woman Mariella – there was no one anywhere. Now she too had become an enigma; Donne could never hope to regain the affection and loyalty he had mastered in her in the early time when he had first seduced her above the doom of the river and the waterfall. Though he was the last to admit it, he was glad for a chance to return to that first muse and journey when Mariella had existed like a shaft of fantastical shapely dust in the sun, a fleshly shadow in his consciousness. This had vanished. And with his miraculous return to his heart's image and lust again, I saw – rising out of the grave of my blindness – the nucleus of that bodily crew of labouring men I had looked for in vain in his republic and kingdom. They had all come to me at last in a flash to fulfil one self-same early desire and need in all of us.

I knew I was dreaming no longer in the way I had been blind and dreaming before. My eye was open and clear as in the strength of youth. I stood on my curious stone as upon the reality of an unchanging presence Donne had apprehended in a wild and cruel devouring way which had turned Mariella into a vulgar musing executioner. This vision and end I had dimly guessed at as a child, fascinated and repelled by his company as by the company of my sleeping life. How could I escape the enormous ancestral and twin fantasy of death-in-life and life-in-death? It was impossible to turn back now and leave the crew in the wild inverse stream of beginning to live again in a hot and mad pursuit in the midst of imprisoning land and water and ambushing forest and wood.

27

The crew – all of us to a man – toiled with the vessel to lift it from still water and whirlpool. At last it stood on the flat stone. We placed round logs of wood beneath it, and half-rolled, half-pushed, until its bow poked the bushy fringe on the bank. This was the signal for reconnoitre. A wild visionary prospect. The sun glowed upon a mass of vegetation that swarmed in crevices of rocky nature until the stone yielded and turned a green spongy carpet out of which emerged enormous trunks and trees from the hidden dark earth beneath and beyond the sun.

The solid wall of trees was filled with ancient blocks of shadow and with gleaming hinges of light. Wind rustled the leafy curtains through which masks of living beard dangled as low as the water and the sun. My living eye was stunned by inversions of the brilliancy and the gloom of the forest in a deception and hollow and socket. We had armed ourselves with prospecting knives and were clearing a line as near to the river as we could.

The voice of roaring water declined a little. We were skirting a high outcrop of rock that forced us into the bush. A sigh swept out of the gloom of the trees, unlike any human sound as a mask is unlike flesh and blood. The unearthly, half-gentle, half-shuddering whisper ran along the tips of graven leaves. Nothing appeared to stir. And then the whole forest quivered and sighed and shook with violent instantaneous relief in a throaty clamour of waters as we approached the river again.

We had finished our connection, and we began retracing our steps in the line to the starting point where our boat stood. I stopped for an instant overwhelmed by a renewed force of consciousness of the hot spirit and moving spell in the tropical undergrowth. Spider's web dangled in a shaft of sun, clothing my arms with subtle threads as I brushed upon it. The whispering trees spun their leaves to a sudden fall wherein the ground seemed to grow lighter in my mind and to move to meet them in the air. The carpet on which I stood

28

had an uncertain place within splintered and timeless roots whose fibre was stone in the tremulous ground. I lowered my head a little, blind almost, and began forcing a new path into the trees away from the river's opening and side.

A brittle moss and carpet appeared underfoot, a dry pond and stream whose course and reflection and image had been stamped for ever like the breathless outline of a dreaming skeleton in the earth. The trees rose around me into upward flying limbs when I screwed my eyes to stare from underneath above. At last I lifted my head into a normal position. The heavy undergrowth had lightened. The forest rustled and rippled with a sigh and ubiquitous step. I stopped dead where I was, frightened for no reason whatever. The step near me stopped and stood still. I stared around me wildly, in surprise and terror, and my body grew faint and trembling as a woman's or a child's. I gave a loud ambushed cry which was no more than an echo of myself – a breaking and grotesque voice, man and boy, age and youth speaking together. I recovered myself from my dead faint supported by old Schomburgh, on one hand, and Carroll, the young Negro boy, on the other. I was speechless and ashamed that they had had to come searching for me, and had found me in such a state.

Schomburgh spoke in an old man's querulous, almost fearful voice, older than his fifty-odd seasoned years. Words came to him with grave difficulty. He had schooled himself into a condition of silent stoical fear that passed for rare courage. He had schooled himself to keep his own counsel, to fish in difficult waters, to bow or steer his vessel under the blinding sun and the cunning stars. He spoke now out of necessity, querulous, scratching the white unshaven growth on his chin.

"Is a risk everyman tekking in this bush," he champed his mouth a little, rasping and coughing out of his lungs the old scarred broken words of his life. I thought of the sound a boat makes grating against a rock. "Is a dead risk," he said as he

29

supported me. "How you feeling son?" he had turned and was addressing me.

Carroll saw my difficulty and answered. "Fine, fine," he cried with a laugh. His voice was rich and musical and young. Schomburgh grinned, seasoned, apologetic, a little unhappy, seeing through the rich boyish mask. Carroll trembled a little. I felt his work-hardened hands, so accustomed to abnormal labour they always quivered with a muscular tension beyond their years; accustomed to making a tramp's bed in the bottom of a boat and upon the hard ground of the world's night. This toughness and strength and enduring sense of limb were a nervous bundle of longing.

"Fine, fine," he cried again. And then his lively eyes began darting everywhere, seeking eagerly to forget himself and to distract his own thoughts. He pointed – "You notice them tracks on the ground Uncle? Game plenty-plenty."

Old Schomburgh scratched his bearded chin. "How you feeling?" he rasped at me again like a man who stood by his duty.

"Fine, fine, right as rain Uncle," Carroll cried and laughed. Old Schomburgh turned his seasoned apology and grin on Carroll – almost with disapproval I felt – "How come you answer so quick-quick for another man? You think you know what mek a man tick? You can't even know you own self, Boy. You really think you can know he or me?" It was a long speech he had made. Carroll trembled, I thought, and faltered a little. But seeing the difficulty I still had in replying, he cried impulsively and naively taking words from my lips – "He fine-fine Uncle, I tell you. I know – "

"Well why he so tongue-tied?"

"He see something," Carroll laughed good-naturedly and half-musingly, staring once again intently on the ground at the tracks he had discerned.

Schomburgh was a little startled. He rubbed away a bit of grey mucus from the corners of his eyes. His expression grew animal-sharp and strained to attention. Every word froze on his lips with the uncanny silence and patience of a fisherman whose obsession has grown into something more than a normal catch. He glared into my eye as if he peered into a stream and mirror, and he grumbled his oldest need and desire for reassurance and life. He caught himself at last looking secretive and ashamed that he had listened to what Carroll had said. I too started suddenly. I felt I must deny the vague suggestion – given as an excuse to justify my former appearance and stupefaction – that I had seen something. I was about to speak indignantly when I saw the old man's avid eye fixed shamefully on me, and felt Carroll's labouring hand tremble with the longing need of the hunter whose vision leads him; even when it turns faint in the sense of death. I stifled my words and leaned over the ground to confirm the musing foot-fall and image I had seen and heard in my mind in the immortal chase of love on the brittle earth.

III

It took us three days to take to the river again and launch our boat after hauling it through the open line we had cut. The rapids appeared less dangerous before and after us. It was Vigilance who made us see how treacherous they still were. We had been travelling for several hours when he gave a shrill warning cry, pointing with his finger ten yards ahead of the bow. I detected a pale smooth patch that seemed hardly worth a thought. It was the size of the moon's reflection in streaming water save that the moment I saw it was broad daylight. The river hastened everywhere around it. Formidable lips breathed in the open running atmosphere to flatter it, many a wreathed countenance to conceal it and half-breasted body, mysterious and pregnant with creation, armed with every cunning abortion and dream of infancy to claim it. Clear fictions of imperious rock they were in the long rippling water of the river; they condescended to kneel and sit, half-turning away from, half-inclining and bending towards the pale moon patch of death which spun before them calm as a musical disc. Captain and bowman heeded Vigilance's cry turning to momentary stone like the river's ruling prayer and rock. They bowed and steered in the nick of time away from the evasive, faintly discernible unconscious head whose meek moon-patch heralded corrugations and thorns and spears we dimly saw in a volcanic and turbulent bosom of water. We swept onward, every eye now peeled and crucified with Vigilance. The silent faces and lips raised out of the heart of the stream glanced at us. They presented no obvious danger and difficulty once we detected them beneath and above and in our own curious distraction and musing reflection in the water.

32

It was a day of filtered sunshine, half-cloud, half-sun. Wishrop had been bowing for old Schomburgh. He retired to the stern of the vessel to relieve Donne who looked the strangest shadow of himself, falling across the boat into the water, I suddenly thought. The change in Donne I suddenly felt in the quickest flash was in me. It was something in the open air as well, in the strange half-sun, in the river, in the forest, in the mysterious youthful longing which the whole crew possessed for Mariella and for the Mission where she lived above the falls. The murdered horseman of the savannahs, the skeleton footfall on the river bank and in the bush, the moonhead and crucifixion in the waterfall and in the river were over as though a cruel ambush of soul had partly lifted its veil and face to show that death was the shadow of a dream. In this remarkable filtered light it was not men of vain flesh and blood I saw toiling laboriously and meaninglessly, but active ghosts whose labour was indeed a flitting shadow over their shoulders as living men would don raiment and cast it off in turn to fulfil the simplest necessity of being. Wishrop was an excellent steersman. The boat swayed and moved harmoniously with every inclination of his body upon the great paddle. A lull fell upon the crew, transforming them, as it had changed Donne, into the drumming current of the outboard engine and of the rapid swirling water around every shadowy stone. All understanding flowed into Wishrop's dreaming eternity, all essence and desire and direction, wished-for and longed-for since the beginning of time, or else focused itself in the eye of Vigilance's spirit.

In this light it was as if the light of all past days and nights on earth had vanished. It was the first breaking dawn of the light of our soul.

BOOK TWO

THE MISSION OF MARIELLA

. . . the widow-making unchilding unfathering deeps.

Gerard Manley Hopkins

IV

Our arrival at the Mission was a day of curious consternation and belief for the colony. The news flew like lightning across the river and into the bush. It seemed to fall from the sky through the cloudy trees that arched high in the air and barely touched, leaving the narrowest ribbon of space. The stream that reflected the news was inexpressibly smooth and true, and the leaves that sprinkled the news from the heavens of the forest stood on a shell of expectant water as if they floated half on the air, half on a stone.

We drove at a walking pace through the brooding reflecting carpet unable to make up our minds where we actually stood. We had hardly turned into the bank when a fleet of canoes devoured us. Faces pressed upon us from land and water. The news was confirmed like wild-fire. We were the news. It was ourselves who were the news. Everyone remembered that not so long ago this self-same crew had been drowned to a man in the rapids below the Mission. Everyone recalled the visits the crew had paid the Mission from time to time leading to the fatal accident. They recalled the event as one would see a bubble, bright and clear as the sun, bursting unexpectedly and knitting itself together again into a feature of sheer consternation, mingled gladness and fear. Or into a teardrop, sadness and unexpected joy running together, in the eye of a friend or a woman or a child.

They did not know how to trust their own emotion, almost on the verge of doubting the stream in their midst. Old Schomburgh looked as timeless as every member of the crew. Carroll, Vigilance, Wishrop, the daSilva twins. The wooden-faced, solemn-looking Jennings stood under the

37

disc and toy that had spun the grave propeller of the world. Where there had been death was now the reflection of life.

The unexpected image of Donne awoke a quiver of sudden alarm and fright. A heavy shadow fell upon all of us – upon the Mission, the trees, the wind, the water. It was an ominous and disturbing symptom of retiring gloom and darkened understanding under the narrow chink and ribbon of sky. They shrank from us as from a superstition of dead men. Donne had had a bad name in the savannahs, and Mariella, to their dreaming knowledge, had been abused and ill-treated by him, and had ultimately killed him. Their faces turned into a wall around her. She was a living fugitive from the devil's rule. This was the birth and beginning of a new fantasy and material difficulty and opposition.

We had barely succeeded in tying our boat securely to the bank than they had left us alone. We could see their houses – set down in little clearings – through the trees. The small thatched walls and sloping roofs were made of cocerite palm – a sure sign of goodness and prosperity. The flesh of the cocerite fruit was succulent and dreamy and white, and the tree only appeared where there was promising land.

The young children playing and scrambling near the cocerite houses had vanished with the entire population, and the Mission now looked abandoned.

"We sleeping in a funny-funny place tonight," Wishrop said wonderingly.

"Them Buck folk scare of dead people bad-bad," Cameron laughed, chewing a sweet blade of grass. "They done know all-you rise bodily from the grave. Big frauds! that is what all you is." He spoke with affection.

His face was brick-red as the first day we had set out, his hair close and curling and negroid. His hands moved like a panther boxing and dancing and quick, and in a moment he had slung his hammock between the trees near the river's edge. He sat in it and tested it, rocking awhile. His brow and expression endorsed the sureness and the life in his hands.

They bore an air of patience and experience, a little tired and cynical almost one would imagine when he smiled and his face wrinkled a little: a timeless long-suffering wrinkle of humour and scepticism and native poetry that knew the guts of the world wherein had been invested and planted the toughest breed of sensibility time had ever known.

Cameron's great-grandfather had been a dour Scot, and his great-grandmother an African slave and mistress. Cameron was related to Schomburgh (whom he addressed as Uncle with the other members of the crew) and it was well-known that Schomburgh's great-grandfather had come from Germany, and his great-grandmother was an Arawak American Indian. The whole crew was one spiritual family living and dying together in a common grave out of which they had sprung again from the same soul and womb as it were. They were all knotted and bound together in the enormous bruised head of Cameron's ancestry and nature as in the white unshaven head of Schomburgh's age and presence.

It was this thread of toughness and guts that Cameron understood and revelled in more than any other man. It gave him his slowness and caution of foot (in contradistinction to the speed in his hands): he stood like a melodramatic rock in mother earth, born from a close fantasy and web of slave and concubine and free, out of one complex womb, from a phantom of voluptuousness whose memory was bitter and rebellious as death and sweet as life; every discipline and endurance and pain he felt he knew. But this boast sprang from a thriftless love of romance and a genuine optimism and self-advertisement and self-ignorance.

Cynicism and ribaldry were the gimmick he adopted. Courage was native and spontaneous. Stoicism and shame played a minor part in fashioning his consciousness of himself and his adopted wrinkle and mask. He was never a cunning fisherman like Schomburgh, straining his attention upon the fish that swam in the river, only to delude himself after a while about the nature of his catch. Cameron knew in as plain and literal terms as hell fire itself what it was he actually wanted and had never been able to gain.

He wanted space and freedom to use his own hands in order to make his own primitive home and kingdom on earth, hands that would rule everything, magical hands dispensing life and death to their subjects as a witch doctor would or a tribal god and judge. This was a gross exaggeration of his desires and intentions, an enormous extension and daydream to which hard and strong and tough men are curiously subject though they fear and seek to reprove themselves for thinking in such a light. In fact it was the only unconscious foreboding (in the midst of his affections and laughter) Cameron ever experienced, the closest he came to Schomburgh's guilt and imagination he dimly felt to lie beyond his years. So it was, unwitting and ignorant, he had been drawn to his death with the others, and had acquired the extraordinary defensive blindness, ribald as hell and witchcraft, of dying again and again to the world and still bobbing up once more lusting for an ultimate satisfaction and a cynical truth.

There was always the inevitable Woman (he had learnt to capitalize his affairs) – the anchor that tied him down for a while against his will and exercised him into regaining his habitual toughness to break away again for good. Still he could never scrape together enough money – after every grotesque adventure – to buy the place he wanted. That was the taste of death and hell: to make do always with another unintelligent and seedy alternative, while the intelligent and fruitful thing remained just beyond his grasp.

"A miss is as good as a mile," he sang aloud impishly. "I must scrape together some real capital – " he winked his eye at the company. "The soil here good," he spoke stoutly. "Right here in this Mission is the start I always seeing in view. Donkey's years I seeing it I tell you. I never seem to quite make it you know. Maybe I'm silly in the upper mental storey of me house," – he tapped his head humbly. "Not smart and obliging enough. Fact is we don't speak the same language that is God's truth. They speak shy and tricky – the Mission folk. I speak them hard bitter style of words I been picking up all me life. Is the way I make me living." He scowled and looked at the world for approval, like a man who conceals his dread of his mistress turning into his witch and his widow. "I got to keep making these brutal sounds to live. You realize these Mission folk is the only people who got the real devil of a title to this land?" He opened his hands helplessly. "If only the right understanding missy and mistress would come along sweet and lucky and Bucky and rich, Ah would be in heaven, boys." He let his foot drag on the ground crunching the soil a little. His head swung suddenly, in spite of himself and against his will, turning an envious reflective eye on the image of Donne – a superstitious eye almost, fearing the evil within himself as the Mission folk had feared Donne within them.

"You think you really want this ghost of a chance you fishing for?" Schomburgh interrupted. "Maybe you don't understand you can drive and scare the blasted soul of the world away and lose your bait for good." It was a speech for him. He had his fishing-rod in his hands and was adjusting the line, rubbing his itching unshaven chin on his shoulders as the gloomy words broke in his chest like an ancient cough. Cameron trembled a little with a sense of cruel unwanted cold, the meaningless engagement with and stab of death that he – with the entire crew – had not yet shaken off. It was a wind blowing on the water, a knife and chill they recognized like tropical fever that blew out of the Mission in an ague of fears, shaking the leaves of the dreaming forest.

V

Night fell on curling flames, on our hammocks curling too like ash and ghost, and the trees turning black as charcoal. Fugitive green shone on the leaves nearest us in the illumination of the camp fire, turning black a little farther away on the fringe of the brittle glaring shadow reflected in the river at our feet.

The fire subsided slowly, spitting stars and sparks every now and then and barking like a hoarse dog. The burning logs crouched and settled and turned white as fur still burning all the while underneath their whiteness redly and sombrely.

The white fur greyed to hourly ash as the night aged in the trees and the fugitive fiery green of dreaming leaves turned faintly silver and grey in anticipation of the pale shadow of dawn.

It was the first night I had spent on the soil of Mariella. So it seemed to me in a kind of hallucination drawing me away from the other members of the crew. Every grey hammock around me became an empty cocoon as hollow as a deserted shell and a house.

I felt the soul of desire to abandon the world at the critical turning point of time around which curled the ash and the fur of night. I knew the keen marrow of this extreme desire and desertion, the sense of animal flight lacking true warmth, the hideous fascination of fire devoid of all burning spirit.

A dog rose and stood over me. A horse it was in the uncertain grey light, half-wolf, half-donkey, monstrous, disconsolate; neighing and barking in one breath, its terrible half-hooves raised over me to trample its premature rider. I grew conscious of its closeness as a shadow and as death. I made a frightful gesture to mount, and it shrank a little into

42

half-woman, half-log greying into the dawn. Its teeth shone like a misty rag, and I raised my hand to cajole and stroke its ageing, soulful face. I sat bolt upright in my hammock, shouting aloud that the devil himself must fondle and mount this muse of hell and this hag, sinking back instantly, a dead man in his bed come to an involuntary climax. The grey wet dream of dawn had restored to me Mariella's terrible stripes and anguish of soul. The vaguest fire and warmth came like a bullet, flooding me, over aeons of time it seemed, with penitence and sorrow.

This musing re-enactment and reconstruction of the death of Donne ushered in the early dawn with a grey feeling inside. The leaves dripped in the entire forest the dewy cold tears of the season of drought that affected the early tropical morning and left me rigid and trembling. A pearl and half-light and arrow shot along the still veined branches. The charcoal memory of the hour lifted as a curtain rises upon the light of an eternal design. The trees were lit with stars of fire of an unchanging and perfect transparency. They hung on every sensitive leaf and twig and fell into the river, streaking the surface of the water with a darting appearance crimson as blood. It was an illusory reflection growing out of the strength of the morning light on my closed eyelids and I had no alternative but to accept my eye as a shade between me and an inviolate spirit. It seemed to me that such a glimpse of perfection was a most cruel and distressing fact in that it brought me face to face with my own enormous frailty. It grew increasingly hard to believe that this blindness and error were all my material fantasy rather than the flaw of a universal creation. For manhood's sake and estate I saw there must arise the devil of resistance and incredulity toward a grotesque muse which abandoned and killed and saved all at the same time with the power of indestructible understanding and life.

How stupid and silly to lose the cruel expectation and

stronghold of death. It was the surest gamble I had known in my life; I was mad to believe I had seen an undying action and presence in the heartfelt malice of all mystery and seduction.

How could I surrender myself to be drawn two ways at once? Indeed what a phenomenon it was to have pulled me, even in the slightest degree, away from nature's end and wish, and towards the eternal desire and spirit that charged the selfsame wish of death with shades of mediation, precept upon precept in the light of my consciousness which was in itself but another glimmering shadow hedging the vision and the glory and the light.

I awoke now completely and fully. I tried to grapple again with my night-and-morning dream; it all faded and vanished. I recognized a curious sense of inner refreshment. The old innocent expectations and the journey – Donne's first musing journey to Mariella – returned with a rush. The eccentric emotional lives of the crew every man mans and lives in his inmost ship and theatre and mind were a deep testimony of a childlike bizarre faith true to life. It was as if something had snapped again, a prison door, a chain, and a rush and flight of appearances jostled each other – past, present and future in one constantly vanishing and reappearing cloud and mist. I rubbed my eyes. Old Schomburgh was carefully cleaning the fish he had caught the night before. Cameron was poking and lighting the fire, assisted by a young man with high pale cheeks – one of the daSilva twins.

"Cammy," the young man was saying in a confidential rather duncified tone, "an old woman knocking about one of them houses. I see she since foreday morning." He pointed.

"Only she come back?" Cameron was incredulous.

"Looking so," daSilva said.

"Well what in hell really going on. . . ."

"Have you chaps seen Donne anywhere?" I interrupted from my hammock.

44

"He and me brother gone for a lil look-see walk," daSilva said somewhat heavily. His voice had a moody almost stupid drawl out of keeping with the slight active life of his hands and limbs.

I rose and began dressing.

"You don't think is Donne scare them away?" daSilva spoke to me confidentially.

"I dunno," I said, vaguely stirred by sleeping memories. "They're funny folk."

"But you *know* is he," daSilva insisted, repeating a brutal time-worn lesson.

"They fear *you* too," I waved my hand as vaguely as ever around.

"Yes, I s'pose so," daSilva consented heavily. "But is a different-different thing," he argued, struggling with an emotional tide. "I been to this Mission before and I can't remember me doing harm to anybody. Don't laugh, Cammy. I know I mek a chile with one of the women. I see you laughing. . . ." He stopped and gave a coarse heavy bray astonishing for his frail chest and shoulders. "You mean to say" – he argued – "a man wife and chile going run from he?"

Cameron replied by laughing soundlessly.

"You got a bad name, Cammy," daSilva said, wishing to arouse in his companion a sense of shame – "such a bad name you is a marked man. All the trips you been mekking to the Mission and you just can't pick a pepper." It was his turn to laugh lugubriously and derisively.

Cameron sobered a little. "Where's there's life there's hope, Boy." He tried to jeer daSilva by giving his words a ribald drawling twist. "You lucky bastard – you." He poked daSilva in the chest. "What's in hell's name keeping you from settling right here for good?"

"You don't know what?"

"Naw Boy, I don't."

"I ain't marry to she," daSilva confessed.

"Ah see," Cameron laughed like a man who had at last dismissed his fool.

"'Pon this Mission," daSilva explained in a nettled voice, "you know as well as I the law say you must marry the Bucks you breed. Nobody know is me chile."

"Is it a secret?" Cameron roared and laughed again.

"Well is an open secret," daSilva said in his heavy foolish way. "Last year when the boat hit moonhead – remember? – was the first and last time for me – I see real hell. Like if the chile real face and the mother real face all come before me. Like if even as I deading in the waterself something pulling me back. Ah mek up me mind then to do the right thing by she. . . ."

"You skull crack wide open, daSilva. Still," he sighed and mocked in one breath, "every new year is a fool's new paradise. I wish I could mek the grade meself Boy. A rich piece of land like this! And is now everybody gone and vanish."

"Is a true thing you seeing. Just vanish."

Schomburgh gave one of his hoarse brief chuckles. "They bound to vanish. They don't *see* dead people really, do they? Nor dead people seeing them for long."

"I ain't dead," Cameron cried. "I can prove it any day." He sniffed the air in which had risen the delightful smell of cooking fish.

"Uncle thinking of his epitaph", daSilva said with his slow heavy brand of humour, "'pon Sorrow hill. You must be seen you own epitaph sometimes in your dreams, Cammy? Don't lie." He winked at Cameron impressing upon him a conspiracy to humour the old man. Schomburgh intercepted the wink like a man who saw with the back of his head.

"I see you, daSilva," he croaked out of intuitive omniscience. He bent over the fire and the meal he had started preparing, half-ashamed, resenting the uneasy foundations of knowledge he possessed. His uncertainty in the rescue and apprehension of being, started tears in his eyes like smoke and fearful belief all mingled together. He stood up abruptly, losing all appetite.

"Come, come, Uncle," Cameron roared and scowled. "You must try some of this ripe nice fish. Breakfast! lads! Uncle. It's good fish not the devil himself you catch."

VI

Donne and the other daSilva twin returned as I put the last
petrified morsel in my mouth. They were accompanied by the
old woman whom the first daSilva had spoken of, and whom
I too felt I knew in a mixed futuristic order of memory and
event. It suddenly occurred to me that I was premature in
thinking she had come of her free will. I suddenly saw – what
I had known and dreaded from the very beginning – she was
under arrest. Donne had made her come just short of the
coarsest persuasion and apprehension he would exercise in
the future, hoping to gain information from her about the
whereabouts of the rest of the fearful frightened folk.

I shook my head a little, trying hard to free myself from this
new obsession. Was it possible that one's memory and
apprehension of a tragic event would strike one's spirit before
the actual happening had been digested? Could a memory
spring from nowhere into one's belly and experience? I knew
that if I was dreaming I could pinch myself and wake. But an
undigested morsel of recollection erased all present waking
sensation and evoked a future time, petrifying and painful,
confused and unjust.

I shook my head violently, trying harder than ever to
picture the deathless innocence and primitive expectation that
had launched our inverse craft. Had we made a new
problematical start – a pure and imaginary game, I told myself
in despair – only to strip ourselves of all logical sequence and
development and time? and to fasten vividly on our material
life as if it were a passing fragment and fantasy while the
curious nebulosity of ourselves stood stubborn and permanent? and as if every solid force and reason and distraction
were the cruel stream that mirrored our everlastingness? I felt

48

I was caught in a principle of never-ending anxiety and fear, and it was impossible to turn back.

I saw that Donne was ageing in the most remarkable misty way. It was something in the light under the trees I said to myself shaking my head. The day had grown sultry and darker than morning and a burst of congealed lightning hung suspended in the atmosphere, threatening to close the long drought and the dry season of the year.

Thirty or forty seasons and years had wrenched from him this violent belt of youth to shape a noose in the air. A shaft from the forest and the heaven of leaves aged him into looking the devil himself. The brownness of his skin looked excessive pallor. He stooped in unconscious subjection I knew to the treachery and oppression in the atmosphere and his eyes were sunken and impatient in rage, burning with the intensity of horror and ambition. His hands opened and closed of their own will, casting to the ground everything save the feeling of themselves and of the identity they wished to establish in the roots of their mortal and earthly sensation. He was an apparition that stooped before me and yet clothed me with the very frightful nature of the jungle exercising its spell over me. I could no longer feel myself shaken: dumb with a morsel of terror.

He started suddenly addressing the company in the lurid storm but it was as if he spoke only to himself. The whole crew were blasted and rooted in the soil of Mariella like imprisoned dead trees. I alone lived and faced him. Words came as from a frightened spiritual medium and translation. Meaning was petrified and congealed and then flashing and clear upon his rigid face and brow hanging in his own ultimatum and light.

The storm passed as quickly as it had begun. Every man came to life again. Donne was free of the hate he had shown, I thought, and a smile had been restored to him ingenuous as youth. He drew me aside leaving the old Arawak woman encircled by the crew.

"Why you're looking haggard as hell," he said to me in solicitude. "Put on ten years overnight, old man," he spoke with a knowledgeable air beneath his apparent freshness and youth. "It's the trip all the way from the coast I suppose. How do you feel? Up to another strenuous exercise and excursion? Afraid I've been deserted by every labouring hand I had, and I've got to go on the trail to find them. Think you would relish coming?"

I shook my head quickly and affirmatively.

"Do you know" – he was in a better mood than I could ever remember – "there's something in what you've been telling me, old chap." He tapped me on the chest significantly, "You do see the situation sensibly and constructively. I grant I have been cruel and harsh. . . ." he paused reflectively.

"Yes," I prompted him.

"I have treated the folk badly," he admitted. "But you do know what this nightmare burden of responsibility adds up to, don't you? How gruesome it can be? I do wish", he spoke musingly, "someone would lift it from my shoulders. Maybe who knows" – he was joking – "you can. Your faith and intuition may be better than mine. I am beginning to lose all my imagination save that sometimes I feel I'm involved in the most frightful material slavery. I hate myself sometimes, hate myself for being the most violent taskmaster – I drive myself with no hope of redemption whatsoever and I lash the folk. If they do murder me I've earned it I suppose, and I don't see sometimes how I can escape it unless a different person steps into my shoes and accepts my confounded shadow. Some weight and burden I confess frankly," he laughed as at an image – alien to himself – he was painting. "Still I suppose", he had grown thoughtful, "there's a ghost of a chance . . ."

"Ghost of a chance of what?" I demanded, swept away by his curious rhetoric.

"Changing my ways," he spoke mildly and indifferently. "Not being so beastly and involved in my own devil's schemes any more. Perhaps there's a ghost of a chance that I can find a different relationship with the folk, who knows? Nothing to lose anyway by trying. I suppose it's what I've always really wanted." He spoke absentmindedly now, stooping to the fire and helping himself to a plate of fish. "God," he said to himself, eating with sudden awareness and appetite, "I am damnably hungry" – brooding a little as he ate, his face growing severe as of old, spoilt, hard, childish with an old obsession and desire. He tapped me on the chest turning ruthless and charming and smiling. "Of course I cannot afford to lean too far backwards (or is it forwards?) can I? Balance and perspective, eh, Boy? Look what's happened now. Nearly everybody just vamoosed, vanished. They're as thoughtless and irresponsible as hell. I was lucky to find even this old bitch" – he pointed to the old Arawak woman – "still hanging around. You can never trust these Bucks you know but she seems harmless enough. Isn't it a fantastic joke that I have to bargain with them and think of them at all?" He spoke bitterly and incredulously. "Who would believe that these devils have title to the savannahs and to the region? A stupid legacy – aboriginal business and all that nonsense: but there it is. I've managed so far to make a place for myself – spread out myself amply as it were – and in a couple of years I shall have firm prescriptive title myself. If", he spoke bitterly again, "these Indians start to kick up the world of a rumpus now it could be embarrassing and I may have to face costly litigation in the courts down there" – he pointed across the wrinkled map of the Arawak woman's face in the vague direction of the Atlantic Ocean as towards a scornful pool in heaven – "to hold my own, not to speak of forfeiting a cheap handsome source of labour. It's all so blasted silly and complicated. After all I've earned a right here as well. I'm as native as they, ain't I? A little better educated maybe whatever in hell that means. They call me sir and curse me when I'm not looking." He licked his lips and smiled. "The only way to survive of course is to wed oneself into the family. In fact I belong already." His brow wrinkled a little and he pointed to his dark racial skin.

"As much as Schomburgh or Cameron or anybody." He could not help laughing, a sudden set laugh like a mask.

"We're all outside of the folk," I said musingly. "Nobody belongs yet. . . ."

"Is it a mystery of language and address?" Donne asked quickly and mockingly.

"Language, address?" I found it hard to comprehend what he meant. "There is one dreaming language I know of . . ." I rebuked him . . . "which is the same for every man . . . . No it's not language. It's . . . it's" . . . I searched for words with a sudden terrible rage at the difficulty I experienced . . . "it's an inapprehension of substance," I blurted out, "an actual fear . . . fear of life . . . fear of the substance of life, fear of the substance of the folk, a cannibal blind fear in oneself. Put it how you like," I cried, "it's fear of acknowledging the true substance of life. Yes, fear I tell you, the fear that breeds bitterness in our mouth, the haunting sense of fear that poisons us and hangs us and murders us. And somebody," I declared, "must demonstrate the unity of being, and *show* . . ." I had grown violent and emphatic . . . "that fear is nothing but a dream and an appearance . . . even death . . ." I stopped abruptly.

Donne was not listening to my labour and expression and difficulty. He already knew by heart my unpredictable outbursts and attacks and inmost frenzy. Old Schomburgh and the Arawak woman stood at his side.

"What does she say?" he demanded. "You know the blasted Buck talk."

Old Schomburgh cleared his throat. He disciplined his voice to reply with the subservience of a shrewd labouring man. "They reach far away by now," he said awkwardly. "They moving quick and they know the trails."

"We must follow and overtake them," Donne said promptly.

"They accustom to move at this season, sir," Schomburgh spoke like a man making an obscure excuse. "Some kind of belief to do with the drought – once in seven year it bound to curse the land. . . ." He paused and cleared his throat again.

"What's this to do with me Schomburgh?" Donne demanded.

"By Christmas when the hard time blow over they come back." Schomburgh spoke brokenly. "They gone to look for rain to plant easy-easy younder." He pointed. "By Christmas they come back." He stopped and I saw the light of uncertainty in his eye. "Perhaps we best to wait right here for them to come back, sir?" he pleaded.

"Are you mad, Schomburgh?" Donne cried. "Listen Uncle," it was his turn to plead and throw all stiffness to the winds, "find out – you know the Buck lingo – how we can catch up. I must have help in a month's time at latest, and that's long-long before you dream to see them back. Why the drought nearly done, and I got to have labour for my estate, my new rice planting, my cattle, everything. The folk just all can't bloody well run away. It's a hell of a superstitious unreasonableness. O Christ, don't look so sad man, ask her."

"She tell me already," Schomburgh cried awkwardly. "If we follow the river we going catch up in seven day time at a place where they bound to ford the water. . . ."

"Why in hell you didn't say so before?" Donne laughed and cried.

"Look, you going to you death," Schomburgh shouted and threatened suddenly. "To you death I say. I know. The river bad like a devil topside of this Mission. I know." It was an involuntary croaking outburst of which he grew instantly ashamed.

Jennings, the mechanic, wiped his hands nervously on his pants. "Is true, sir," he addressed Donne. "Is a dangerous time of the year to venture higher. Look what a bad time we had already."

"You fellows losing your fire or what?" Donne shot at him. "I thought this was a *crew* when we started."

"I vote to go," the daSilva twin exclaimed who had helped Cameron.

Jennings turned furious. "You potagee fool," he cried, "shut you mouth for a change. I is a young married man, two kiddy, and an old sick mother to mend. . . ." He was no longer wiping his hands on his pants but pointing a black angry finger in daSilva's face.

"I thought you knew all of that at the beginning," Donne shouted cold and sharp. "Look here, did you, or did you not, tell me you joined us because you were fed up – anything for a clean break? You wanted the water-top again you said. I pointed out how dangerous a season it was and you said you knew. You had had a narrow escape before, you had escaped by the skin of your teeth, you said. But it hadn't frightened you, you said. In fact when you felt you were dying you knew what a cowardly waste your life was. Anything was better you promised yourself than living again with a harridan and a shrew. Those were your words. Now tell me, Jennings do you wish us to stay right here and rot?" His voice had grown wretched and powerful. He knew he had to hold the crew to his side or he was lost.

"I know," Jennings said surlily. All of a sudden he grinned and began wiping his hands again on his grease-stained engineer's pants. "The truth is – you done know it already, so why pretend? – the folk I come from – me wife and me mother and me two child – believe I dead," he said. "Good for them and good for me. I like it right here under the trees. I vote to stop." He glared at the fateful propeller in the water as if that were the cause of all his trouble.

Cameron scowled at Jennings. "Shit," he said. "Let's move. We got to keep turning. I vote like daSilva to go." He adopted a belligerent air but he too was heartily uncertain and afraid.

Carroll had begun laughing and the fresh ringing sound of his voice made everyone forget himself and turn in involuntary surprise. The laugh struck them as the slyest music coming clear out of the stream. It was like a bell and it startled away for one instant every imagined revolution of misery and fear and guile. It was an ingenuous sound like the homely crackle of gossiping parrots or of inspired branches in the leaves, or the slicing ecstasy and abandonment of the laughing wood when the hunter loses and finds his game in the footmark he has himself left and made.

Carroll laughed because he could not help himself. He saw that the omens and engines of grace and salvation were so easily turned again into doom. He felt – without clearly understanding why – that the entire crew had been drawn together almost against their will it seemed now and that their living desire was ambivalent and confused as the origin of the first command they dimly recalled and knew in the grave of memory. Something had freed them and lifted them up out of the deeps, a blessing and a curse, a reverberating clap of thunder and still music and song. The sound was jubilant and obscure and tremulous in their ear like a dreaming sword that had cut them from the womb.

Wishrop and Vigilance stood silent listening to the sound of the sword and the bell in the stream. Wishrop was a man of about forty, I dreamed, scanning his features with the deepest attention. A strong aquiline face it was, and still delicate and retiring in mood. I remember how he balanced himself and stood with the promise of a dancer on the prow of the boat when it moved in midstream. He spoke infrequently and as brokenly and whimsically as his labouring companions. His desire for communication was so profound it had broken itself into two parts. One part was a congealed question mark of identity – around which a staccato inner dialogue and labouring monologue was in perpetual evolution and process. The other half was the fluid fascination that everyone and everything exercised upon him – creatures who moved in his consciousness full of the primitive feeling of love purged of all murderous hate and treachery.

He sought to excuse his deficiency and silence by declaring that he knew better Spanish than English. It was a convenient lie and it carried the ring of truth since he had lived for many years on the Guyana, Venezuela border. A look of unconscious regret and fear would flash when he spoke as if he feared he had already said too much. The crew knew what his guilt signified. He had whispered to them at various half-crazy times that he was dead for the record. He had told them secretly he would be a wanted man now, wanted for murder if it was known he was living. And so he wished to stay dead, he shouted, though he was perfectly alive.

He was mad they all knew. And yet harmless as a dove. They could not conceive of him as a real murderer. They preferred to accept his story as myth. He was an inspired vessel in whom they poured not only the longing for deathless obedience and constancy (which they read in his half-shadowed face) but the cutting desperate secret ambition he swore he had once nourished – the love that became its colder opposite – the desire they too felt, in their vicarious daydream, to kill whatever they had learnt to hate. This dark wish was the deepest fantasy they knew mankind to entertain.

As deep as the nameless fish Schomburgh sometimes hooked whose flat beady eyes and skulls made him shiver and fling them back into the river. Electric eels for example. His hands twitched with shock in the presence of these playful absurd monsters as before a spirit of innocent malady and corruption he knew in his blood and bone. Old as the hills it was, this electrification and crucifixion of the mind.

Wishrop had dared to kill what he had learnt to hate. That was his mythical recommendation. He had dared to purge himself free – to execute what troubled him, to pluck from a phantom body both its arm and its eye of evil.

The boon companions with whom he lived at the extremity of the known world were thieves. And the women were whores. They slaved for gold and diamonds, the most precious thing they knew. Wishrop did not feel himself superior to anyone. He was honest because of a native inborn fastidiousness like a man who loved wiping and cleaning himself for no earthly reason. He never wanted to conceal diamonds in his mouth and lodge them between the toes of his feet after a day's work in the pits. Yet since everyone did it he accepted the principle and the practice. At that moment he started hating the phantom that was himself.

He saw himself reflected intimately in one of the women, dreamt he was in love with her, and unable to resist the challenge and the destiny of hate, married her and set her up to prove himself and his gods. The catechist who performed the ceremony sniggered behind his book. Wishrop marked him and never forgave him, swearing he was married now for good to the devil's country, and that he had started courting hell and disaster.

He came upon his wife in bed with another man, and suddenly swept by a cold hard virginal joy and pleasure, knew abruptly, here was what he had waited upon to begin; he shot the couple in the head through the eye. He repaired to the drinking saloon cold and mad in his pride. The boon companions were riddled, astonished and surprised, waving their hand vaguely to the blind bullet.

He shot the catechist stone-dead and sniggering under a couple of whores on the pathway leading to church. Lastly himself.

That was the end save that Wishrop woke to find himself still alive; and crawling out of the fracas into the bush he met the inevitable Arawak woman (this was the crew's ancestral embroidery and obsession) who nursed him to life. In the mortal hullaballoo that followed the muse reported that she had seen Wishrop crawling like a spider into the river where he had been tangled in the falls. Days after she pointed out his curious skeleton picked clean by perai, and that was the last of dead Wishrop.

The living Wishrop awoke overwhelmed by a final spasm of murderous fury and he shot the poor Arawak woman, his muse and benefactress. The curtain vanished upon this last act removing the web of death within himself. An eternity dawned. His victims had never perished, constantly moving before him, living and never dying in the eternal folk.

His faith and optimism endeared him to the crew and they fed upon his brief confessions and ravings as the way of a vicarious fury and freedom and wishful action they had known, not believing a word in the improbable tale he told of a harmless lover and lunatic: nevertheless they pledged themselves anew to the sense of their indestructibility.

BOOK THREE

THE SECOND DEATH

I tune the instrument here at the door,
And what I must do then, think here
before.

John Donne

VII

The crew came around like one man to the musing necessity in the journey beyond Mariella. We set out in the rising sun as soon as the mist had vanished. We had in our midst a new member sitting crumpled-looking, like a curious ball, old and wrinkled. Her long black hair – with the faintest glimmer of silvery grey – hung in two plaits down to her waist. She sat still as a bowing statue, the stillness and surrender of the American Indian of Guyana in reflective pose. Her small eyes winked and blinked a little. It was an emotionless face. The stiff brooding materiality and expression of youth had vanished, and now – in old age – there remained no sign of former feeling. There was almost an air of crumpled pointlessness in her expression, the air of wisdom that a millennium was past, a long timeless journey was finished without appearing to have begun, and no show of malice, enmity and overt desire to overcome oppression and evil mattered any longer. She belonged to a race that neither forgave nor forgot. That was legend. In reality the legend and consciousness of race had come to mean for her – patience, the unfathomable patience of a god in whom all is charged into wisdom, all experience and all life a handkerchief of wisdom when the grandiloquence of history and civilization was past. It was the subtlest labour and sweat of all time in the still music of the senses and of design.

Her race was a vanishing one overpowered by the fantasy of a Catholic as well as a Protestant invasion. This cross she had forgiven and forgotten in an earlier dream of distant centuries and a returning to the Siberian unconscious pilgrimage in the straits where life had possessed and abandoned at the same time the apprehension of a facile beginning and ending. An unearthly pointlessness was her true manner, an all-inclusive manner that still contrived to be – as a duck sheds water from its wings – the negation of every threat of conquest and of fear – every shade of persecution wherein was drawn and mingled the pursued and the pursuer alike, separate and yet one and the same person. It was a vanishing and yet a starting race in which long eternal malice and wrinkled self-defence and the cruel pursuit of the folk were turning into universal protection and intuition and that harmonious rounded miracle of spirit which the world of appearances had never truly known.

Before the sun was much higher we were in the grip of the straits of memory. The sudden dreaming fury of the stream was naught else but the ancient spit of all flying insolence in the voiceless and terrible humility of the folk. Tiny embroideries resembling the handwork on the Arawak woman's kerchief and the wrinkles on her brow turned to incredible and fast soundless breakers of foam. Her crumpled bosom and river grew agitated with desire, bottling and shaking every fear and inhibition and outcry. The ruffles in the water were her dress rolling and rising to embrace the crew. This sudden insolence of soul rose and caught them from the powder of her eyes and the age of her smile and the dust in her hair all flowing back upon them with silent streaming majesty and abnormal youth and in a wave of freedom and strength.

The crew were transformed by the awesome spectacle of a voiceless soundless motion, the purest appearance of vision in the chaos of emotional sense. Earthquake and volcanic water appeared to seize them and stop their ears dashing the scales only from their eyes. They saw the naked unequivocal flowing peril and beauty and soul of the pursuer and the pursued all together, and they knew they would perish if they dreamed to turn back.

"Is War Office," Schomburgh screamed but his voice was silent and dead in his throat. And then the full gravity and climax of our predicament came home to us. We had entered the War Office rapids, a forbidden passage, deceived by the symbols in the inhuman drought of the year, and by the bowing submissive rock that guarded the river. We should have kept to the other bank in this season of nature. To turn back now and ride the stream was to be swept so swiftly and unpredictably along we were bound to crash and collide and collapse. The only course was to fight, glued to the struggle, keeping our bow silent and straight in the heart of an unforgiving and unforgivable incestuous love. This fantasy had descended upon us like a cloud out of the sun. Everyone blamed everyone else for being the Jonah and for having had an evil intercourse with fate. Donne had arrested the witch of a woman and we had aided and abetted him. A murderous rape and fury filled our heart to an overburden, it seemed, nevertheless balanced and held in check by our voiceless impossible wrestle and struggle in the silent passage in the lava of water. We were screwed to boat and paddle in sending the vessel forward inch by inch. The spinning propeller spun in Jennings' head and beneath our graven feet. The great cloud sealed our eyes again and we saw only the spirit that had raped the old woman and invoked upon us our own answering doom in her daemonic-flowing presence and youth. We began to gripe and pray interminably and soundlessly. Carroll – the youngest in the crew   stood up quickly as though he had been inspired to behold Schomburgh's straining difficulty at the bow and Wishrop's helpless engagement with Donne at the stern. He had hardly made a step when he appeared to slip and to fall with a cry into the water. He disappeared silently and completely. The crew set up a further cry which was as helpless as a dream. The old woman bent over the water, suddenly rolling a little in her seat. She looked old as ever, old as she had looked fantastically young and desirable before. The crew were filled with the brightest-seeming clarity of tragedy, as cloudless as imperfectly true as their self-surrender to the hardship of the folk they followed and pursued: the cloudy scale of incestuous cruelty and self-oppression tumbled from their eye leaving only a sense of disconsolate flying compassion and longing. Their ears were unstopped at last and they heard plainly Vigilance's pointing cry as well as their own shout penetrating their ears with the grief and the musical love and value in the stricken fall and sacrifice of youth. In an instant it were as if we saw with our own eyes as well as heard with our own ears an indestructible harmony within the tragedy and the sorrow of age and the malice and the nature of youth. It was Carroll's voice and head that turned to stone and song, and the sadness of the baptismal lamentation on his lips which we heard in the heart of the berserk waters was our own almost senseless rendering and apprehension of the truth of our art and our perfection in the muse.

The boat seemed to gain momentum as though every effort we made carried a new relationship within it. The water heaped itself into a musing ball upon which we rolled forward over and beyond the rapids. The stream grew wide and gentle as a sheet, and with a sigh we relinquished our paddles – save at stern and bow – and allowed ourselves to be propelled forward by Jennings' engine.

I knew that a great stone of hardship had melted and rolled away. The trees on the bank were clothed in an eternity of autumnal colour – equally removed from the green of youth as from the iron-clad winter of age – a new and enduring spiritual summer of russet and tropical gold whose tints had been tenderly planted in the bed of the stream. The sun veined these mythical shades and leaves in our eye. Old Schomburgh had been relieved by Vigilance and he sat silent and wondering and staring in the water. No one had dared broach Carroll's name out of some strange inner desire not to lose the private image and thought within us which at the moment bore our gratitude and our mature joy and sadness more deeply than seasonal words.

Carroll was one of the old man's beloved nephews.

Schomburgh knew him first as a lad arriving from a distant mission, a little inquisitorial, but much more shy and wistful than dogmatic he had appeared after dawdling his time away in idleness and speculation far from Sorrow Hill where Schomburgh lived. He was seventeen, and a shocking long time it was, Schomburgh said, he had been idle. Now at last he had deigned to think of looking for a real job on the watertop (when he had already wasted so much time) Schomburgh scolded his nephew. He remembered it all now with a shock as he sat staring from the bow of the boat – the intimate cold shock of old that had served to bait the guilt he had already felt and known even before his new nephew came. There had always been a thorn in acknowledging his relationships – an unexplored cloud of promiscuous wild oats he secretly dreaded. His family tree subsisted in a soil of entanglement he knew to his grief in the stream of his secretive life, and Carroll's arrival brought the whole past to a head before him. Still Carroll proved himself in the fits and starts of the older man's dreaming adventures to be superior to the ambivalent ominous creature he first looked to be. He was tough, tougher than expectation. He slept easy as an infant on the hardest ground. His bones were those of a riverman, hard and yet fluid in emergency, and his senses grew attuned to musical footmarks and spiritual game. Many an evening he borrowed Cameron's guitar and his painstaking light-hearted predisposition to melody emerged and touched the listening harp in every member of the crew. No one knew where or what it was. Schomburgh felt the touch of harmony without confessing a response when in the midst of his evening recreation with rod and line in the stream he listened deeply to the stirrings within himself. He would suddenly catch himself and declare he had found the hoax that was being played upon him.

And still he knew it was impossible to abandon an inexplicable desire and hope, the invisible pull in his fingers, a tautness and tension within, around which had been wrapped all doubtful matter and flesh like bait on a fisherman's hook. A long bar of secret music would pass upon the imbedded strings and his flesh quaked and shook. The nervous tension of the day – that had now rooted him in the bow – had broken every barrier of memory and the tide came flooding upon him. He felt the fine stringed bars of a universal ecstasy tuning within him beyond life and death, past and present, until they neither ceased nor stopped.

He was a young man again – in the prime of maturity – meeting his first true invisible love. She had appeared out of the forest – from a distant mission – far from Sorrow Hill. She was as dark as the curious bark of a tree he remembered, and round and promising like sapodilla. Schomburgh was a stranger to her it seemed (she had not yet discovered his name) fair-skinned, older by wiser years, athletic and consc- ious in his half-stooping, half-upright carriage of an ancient lineage and active tradition amongst the riverfolk.

What a chase it was. He cornered her and poured upon her his first and last outburst of frenzied self-forgetting eloquence until he felt the answer of her lips. She smelt like leaves growing on top the rocks in the sun in the river, a dry and yet soft bursting smell, the dryness of the hot scampering sun on the fresh inwardness of a strong resilient plant. She smelt dry and still soft. The vaguest kerchief of breath had wiped her brow after her exertion running with fear and joy.

He had hardly found her when she had gone. So incredible it was he rubbed his eyes again as he sat staring into the water. He set out after her but it was as if a superior fury – insensible and therefore stronger and abler than he – had propelled her away. It dawned upon him – like an inward tremor and voice – that she had learnt his name – from what source and person he did not know since she had spent such a very short time at Sorrow Hill – and this had engineered her suspicion and flight. Dread seized his mind, the dread of sexual witchcraft. He drew at last to the distant door of the Mission where she lived, and the dubious light of the fantastic wheel of dawn strengthened and sliced his mind. It was an ancient runaway home of his father's he had reached. His father had settled here late in life – with a new mistress – and founded a separate family. Some said he guillotined his birthright for a song, a flimsy strip of a thing, beautiful as a fairy. All was rumour and legend without foundation. Even as a boy Schomburgh had known the truth and dismissed the exaggerated fairy-tale. His father was dead. That was the living truth. And yet he could not stir one step beyond where he now stood. He stood there it seemed for the passage of months until he grew greyer than the ghost of the stars and the moon and the sun. She was waiting for him he told himself, like any young girl – frightened in a first indiscretion and affair – nevertheless waiting for love to enter and take her everlastingly. Her folk and parents would kill the fatted calf and welcome him like a son. He shuddered, and the vibration struck him inwardly, a lamentation in the wind, fingers on the strings of his spirit, the melancholy distant sound of a raining harp. His fear and horror lifted a little as he heard it – riveted to the ghostly threshold and ground of his life. It no longer mattered whether Carroll was his nephew or his son or both. He had heard clearer than ever before the distant music of the heart's wish and desire. But even now he tried to resist and rebuke himself for being merely another nasty sentimental old man.

Vigilance bowed for Schomburgh, his paddle glancing and whirling along the gunwhale, equally alert and swift on both sides when the occasion demanded. His penetrating trained eye saw every rock, clothing it with a lifelikeness that mirrored all past danger and design. His vision of peril meant an instantaneous relationship to safety. He offered himself to the entire crew – as he bowed – a lookout to prove their constant reality – and he hid his tears from everyone. The truth was Carroll was his stepbrother. Vigilance had introduced him to Uncle Schomburgh, and the old man had stared at the ultimate ghost he both dreaded and loved.

Vigilance had been a boy of thirteen when his father had taken Carroll's mother into his house as his wife, the boy Carroll, her only child, being four or five years old then. Vigilance was the eldest of seven, and their mother had died a couple of months ago in her last childbirth. Carroll's mother thus became the adoptive mother of the Vigilance brood who were lucky to get such a young woman and stepmother for the large family, the youngest of whom was an infant two months old.

She was lucky too to find the protection of the Vigilance family for her child whose father no one had ever seen. The name the child bore was little-known in those parts. Her husband bore her no malice and wished her son to take his name as a final safeguard. This she resisted. She felt it would do no good – the name Carroll was as innocuous and distant a name as any she could choose. She did not wish to attract upon her head and the head of her new family the hoax of sin in an implacable future. Vigilance could not remember ever addressing his stepbrother as anything else but Carroll. In fact this habit of using the surname was the curious custom amongst most families in the enormous dreaming forest who dreaded mislaying and losing each other. After a time everybody believed Carroll's name was a true one. It were as if they had a long and a short memory at one and the same time so that while they forgot the name Carroll's mother had borne (as one is inclined to forget maiden names) they helped to invent and forge a name for her son which established distant ties they only dimly dreamt of. Carroll was one burning memory and substance for his mother and another dimmer incestuous substance and myth for his uncertain and unknown father folk. He had become a relative ghost for all as all ultimately became a ghost for everyone.

It was a strange and confusing tradition beyond words. Vigilance saw that Schomburgh had been overwhelmed in some unnatural way that fractured his vision and burdened him with a sense of fantasy and hoax. It was the darkest

narcissism that strove with him and fought against accepting
Carroll's name as Carroll, against relinquishing paternity to
some one who was still untouched by and unknown to the
spirit of guilt. He wished to give the boy his own name but
the desire frightened and killed him. No one knew and
understood better than a mother what a name involved. It
was the music of her undying sacrifice to make and save the
world. Sometimes he accepted and grew enamoured of the
thought that Carroll was his nephew and nothing else. Often
times he lived in the flight of mortal gloom and fear Carroll
was nothing to him at all, a bastard memory from a bastard
hellish tribe and succession and encounter. Who and what
was Carroll? Schomburgh had glimpsed, Vigilance knew with
an inborn genius and primitive eye, the living and the dead
folk, the embodiment of hate and love, the ambiguity of
everyone and no one. He had recognized his true son,
nameless out of shame and yet named with a new distant
name by a muse and mother to make others equally nameless
out of mythical shame and a name, and to forge for their
descendants new mythical far-flung relationships out of their
nameless shame and fear.

Vigilance read this material hoax and saw deeper than
Schomburgh to the indestructible element. It was a simple
lesson for him since he was born to discern and reflect
everything without the conscious effort of speech.

His eyes were brighter than ever after their fit of crying. The
past returned to him like pure fictions of rock he had never
wearied spying upon since childhood. Sometimes they stood
in columns, or they embraced each other in groups, or in
couples, or they stood solitary and alone.

Donne was the only one in their midst who carried on his
sleeve the affectation of a rich first name. Rich it seemed –
because none of his servants appeared at first to have the
power to address him other than obsequiously. The manner
of the crew could change, however, one sensed, into
familiarity and contempt. It was on their lips already to

declare that their labouring distress and dream was the sole tradition of living men.

He had come from a town on the coast they knew to found and settle, be baptized again, as well as to baptize, a new colony. He was careless of first name and title alike they saw. All were economic names to command and choose from (as one chose to order one's labouring folk around). All were signs of address from a past dead investment and history with its vague pioneering memories that were more their burden than his.

They knew he had once dreamt of ruling them with a rod of iron and with a ration of rum. His design was so brutal and clear that one wondered how one could be so cheap to work for him. There was nothing he appeared to have that commended him. Save the nameless kinship of spirit older (though he did not yet apprehend it) than every material mask and label and economic form and solipsism. Vigilance had seen clear into the bowels of this nameless kinship and identity Donne had once thought he had abused as he wished, and in one stroke it had liberated him from death and adversity.

He recalled as he bowed that his father had built a new house after the second marriage. The three-roomed cabin – his first home – remained; a stone's throw away stood the new rough-hewn spacious five-roomed cottage into which the family had moved.

It was natural to Vigilance to perceive what was going on wherever he lived. He was always *there* when his parents spoke, or he always seemed to *see* something through a half-open door or window or crack. It was a habit of fortune he possessed, ingrained and accidental as all remarkable coincidences are.

The new house was a year old, and his father was away that afternoon for a couple of days on a wood-cutting mission. The rest of the family were busy far afield outdoors.

Carroll and his mother had just come in. He saw them in

the next room through an open door. They were so flustered-looking and inwardly disturbed that they had no eyes for him.

"She lose the baby, she lose me baby, she lose she baby," Carroll was crying to his mother, all his shyness and charm fractured and gone. Vigilance knew instantly they were speaking of his sister; she happened to be a couple of years younger than Carroll who had just attained his seventeenth birthday.

"O love," Carroll's mother cried to him. "Is lucky," she nearly bit her lips, broken in their emotion. "No, no, not lucky. I wrong. But I mean is just as well. Think what your stepfather would say." She wrung her hands.

"I can marry her. She's not my blood-sister," Carroll spoke glumly and half-dementedly.

"No, no," his mother cried. "She too young to marry. I going take care of her." She smoothed Carroll's unhappy brow. He jerked away a little. "Why, why?" he cried. "Why?"

"You got to travel and see the world," his mother said sadly, looking at him as if she dared not touch him again. "You don't know what is a wife feeling yet. You don't know anything. You got to make your fortune. Look," she wrung her hands again, "from the day you born to me I see you were different. You were a problem. I feel as if you was not even me child. A strange funny child in me hands. As if you didn't belong to me at all, at all. If you stay here is only trouble going come under this roof. And you stepfather is a good kind man I love," she suddenly grew quiet and spoke softly. Then she cried – "Mek yourself into a man and *then* come back. Is a different story then."

Carroll's eyes flashed and he moved further away from her still – "I is not as soft as I look. I can live and work hard. I can mek me way to the ends of the earth. I born to go far." He was boasting and still sad. "Like you don't know me at all."

His mother was sadder still. "Is best you go," she said. Her lips were torn and they looked burnt with the sun.

"I don't want to leave she," Carroll cried. "I can tek she with me and tek care of she and she tek care of me." He cried to her louder than ever.

"Your stepfather would forbid it," his mother said passionately.

"I can carry she and look after she," Carroll said sullenly.

"You think life so simple?" his mother pleaded with him. "You got to earn you fortune, lad. Sometimes is the saddest labour in the world."

"You mean if I mek a million dollar and come back I can claim she as me wife?" Carroll said.

"If you mek a million dollar you think you can fool the living and bring the dead alive?" His mother spoke strangely. "Is not money make me flesh and fortune."

"I can mek it all up to she. She suffer bad-bad. She had a fall. We did plan to run and marry soon as she start to show big. She was a child yet." His voice broke.

"Everything going be all right," his mother tried to soothe him. "Everything going be right as rain. Right as a song. Make you fortune and come back." She spoke sadly as if she knew his fortune was the despair of mere flesh and blood.

"We been playing a year ago," Carroll said musingly. "Suddenly we lose we way in the trees. We think we never find home. We started hugging, a frighten sweet-sweet feeling like if I truly come home. I wasn't a stranger no more. She cry a little and she laugh like if she was home at last. And she kiss me after it all happen. . . ."

"How you know she was with baby?" his mother asked after a long silence.

"One day I hear a heart, clear-clear . . . I wanted to tell somebody. But I was afraid even to tell you. Until today when she fall and she cry in she pain I was so afraid . . ." he cried and his voice sounded like hers. "Did you hear anything?" he said a little wildly, looking out of the window. "Was a terrible fall. You hear anything?"

"Impossible," his mother rebuked him. "You couldn't have

72

heard that infant heart beating so small and long ago . . .
three or four months ago. . . ."

"I hear it," Carroll insisted and his voice fell and broke into
two again.

His mother smiled as if she had forgotten him. "Maybe is
true," she said, "I hear it too." She rubbed herself gently on
her belly.

"You," Carroll shot at her.

"Yes," she caught herself. His eyes probed hers deep. She
spoke like one seeking forgiveness. "I am with child for your
stepfather too," she expressed herself awkwardly. Her voice
broke into two like his. "My first child under his roof after so
long and I getting old. . . ."

Carroll nodded his head dumbly. "Is the child as old
as. . . ?" he choked with alarm and fear.

"Yes," she nodded.

"A boy or a girl?" he asked foolishly.

"Was a boy," she said. "I saw." They were at cross
purposes. "If you go and come back you will find the child,"
she sighed.

"His child borning and mine dead," he spoke passionately,
forgetting to whom he spoke.

"No," his mother said sharply. "Is all one in the long run.
You can make peace between us. . . ."

"And go?" he demanded. He was crying. Suddenly he
knew he did not want the child in her to live. A heart-rending
spasm overwhelmed him, all ancestral hate and fear and
jealousy.

"You are my child always," his mother spoke softly. Her
lips twisted again. "You must live and go. Is your own will if
you stay to rot and die since you will start to imagine foolish
things. Go I tell you." She spoke softly again.

Carroll ran out of the house blindly towards the cabin in the
woods where Tiny, the Vigilance sister, lay. She looked old
and sad lying there he thought, wrinkled in his imagination.
He saw her as an old woman in the future, wrinkled and

wise, the memory of her mythical incestuous child come again – living and strong as life. It was as if he came to his spiritual mother at last, and the effect of his child's death had sealed and saved the maternal pregnancy and womb beyond all jealousy and fear and doubt.

Carroll's mother looked up suddenly with a sense of unexplored and inexplicable joy. She was startled when she saw Vigilance. "You here?" she cried. "How long you been listening?"

Vigilance nodded dumbly. He did not know what to say. He knew that the child she carried for his father would live, and bear the eyes of the living and the dead. He felt drawn towards it as towards a child of his own.

"You are free to go too, and this time take him with you for ever when you go," his stepmother addressed him with a curious blessing smile.

VIII

We stood on the frontiers of the known world, and on the
selfsame threshold of the unknown.

Schomburgh was dead. He had died peacefully in his
hammock and in his sleep.

The old crumpled Arawak woman had advised us the
evening of the day before where to stop and camp for the
night. It was too late she said (Schomburgh interpreting) to
venture into the nameless rapids that seethed and boiled
before us.

We buried Schomburgh at the foot of the broken water
whose agitation was witness of the forces that lay ahead.

Carroll was dead. Schomburgh was dead. One death, a
cross for father and son. They had been ghosts to each other
in the limited way a man grasped reality. Schomburgh often
inhabited Carroll's shoes running from and towards his love
the day it was born and had died. Carroll often listened,
almost worshipping the hoax of death and age and sin in
Schomburgh's boots, like a child prematurely stricken and old
with the passage of mortal conception and thought. It had
been an enormous endless growing pain and fantasy – rich
with the wealth of unexplored possibilities – all over and done
with and secure. They had sown and won a great liberal
fortune for the whole world though the full fruitage and
inheritance lay yet in the future and time.

Everyone paid silent tribute in the breakfastless empty
morning. None dared to say anything yet knowing their
common speech was the debased coinage and currency of the
dreaming folk. Silence seemed golden now and superior to
the universal mask and ironic disavowal of principle in the
nameless indestructible soul. The broken speech of the crew

died awhile on their lips though in their affections they still heard themselves speak in the old manner of distortion and debasement. It was the inevitable and unconscious universe of art and life that still harassed and troubled them.

DaSilva broke the golden silence and expressed his misgivings aloud. "Is how much further we got to go?" He spoke to himself, forgetting his destination and turning helplessly to the old Arawak woman. There was no interpreter now Schomburgh had gone. A wrench had uprooted the instrument of communication he had always trusted in himself. And yet he knew it was a mortal relief to face the truth which lay farther and deeper than he dreamed. This deathblow of enlightenment robbed him of a facile faith and of a simple translation and memory almost.

"Is how much farther we got to go?" he cried in his helpless dull way. "The Buck woman can't speak a word."

Donne started unrolling his plan quickly. The country ahead was mysterious and little known he said. A long series of dangerous rapids marked the map in his hands. The neighbouring country was mountainous and crude, the trails secret and hidden. One day had passed since they left Mariella. And today – the second of the allotted seven before them – had started with an omen of good fortune, strange and shattering as it seemed. They were on the threshold of the folk. They must cling to that knowledge since – he had never seen it so clear before – it was all they had.

He felt the clearest keenest perception of their need and security. Remember – he said – when they entered the world ahead – the world of the second day – they had passed the door of inner perception like a bird of spirit breaking the shell of the sky which had been the only conscious world all knew. In the death of their comrades, the cross of father-and-son, Donne said pedantically and sorrowfully, they had started on the way to overcoming a sacred convention of evil proprietorship and gain.

The crew drew around as he turned to practical issues in

hand. "Today we will reach *here*," he pointed to a little indentation where he proposed to camp next. "Tomorrow . . ." his voice droned on and on.

"One shear pin snap in that water and all gone," Jennings sang out. He was frowning. He pushed his way until he stood face to face with Donne. "All this is a lot of balls," he said.

"You can stay here if you wish," Donne said calmly. "I will drive the motor, Vigilance will bow and Wishrop – on whom I feel I can lean more than ever – will steer. The three of us alone will go if need be, come what may. And as a matter-of-fact the daSilvas and Cameron are still with us I believe? We can do with their help." He turned to the crew. They nodded a little.

Jennings was partly taken aback. "O, you want to leave me here, you do?" he shouted.

"Matter entirely for you," said Donne.

Jennings laughed. Fine lines of sweat – customary to him – stood out again. His laugh resounded like a trumpet. Clearly – it came like a revelation – whatever the beads on his brow – he was without fear. A stubborn nameless streak rose and sweated him into a man who wanted a fight. Irritation and resentment boiled within him against all authority and responsibility. He saw too clearly and harshly the strength of his mechanical arm and position and the farce and guile and deception he had always experienced. The knowledge burned him and invigorated him at the same time with the honey of justification and leisure and laziness in palate and nostril. He was as good as any man he knew. "You can't fool me no more," he said. "All of you *bastards* – high and mighty alike. If I come with all you is of me own sweet will. You can't *fool* me no more." His voice brayed like a resurrection trumpet over the dead.

"Who want to fool you?" said Cameron. His heart was suddenly beating fast and loud. A shaft of nameless misery had entered and wounded him. He had never felt this sensation before. Jennings loomed upon him now with a terrifying jeer and gibe on his lips.

"Who want to fool you?" Cameron cried again. He listened closely to his own voice. It was the voice of dread: the voice of dread at the thought that nothing existed to fool and terrorize anybody unless one chose to imagine one was bewitched and a fool all one's life. The terrible sound and vision struck him a blow, sharp and keen and intimate as a knife bursting into a drum. The ground felt that it opened bringing to ruin years of his pride and conceit.

"Who want to fool *you*?" Cameron shouted in rage and indignation. He wished desperately the oracular grave under his feet would close for ever and disappear and he could cherish once again his old pagan desire and ambition. It struck him like an acute dismemberment and loss and injustice.

Jennings jeered – "You silly dope, Cameron you," he laughed. "I shit on devils like you. By the time you fall out of one scrape you land in another. Who is you to ask me a thing?"

"What I want to know – " Cameron was in a greater rage than ever – "who trying to fool who?"

"O buzz off" – Jennings laughed. "You is just anybody's plaything and wood, Cameron, a piece of what I call flotsam and jetsam" – he spoke jeeringly and a little sententiously, advertising his phrases and words. "Me?" he cried. "I is me own fucking revolution, equal to all, understand? I can stand pon the rotten ground face to face with the devil. And I don't gamble pon any witch in heaven or hell. I lef' that behind me long long ago." His voice grew wicked and chiding – "You is one of them old time labouring parasite, Cammy boy, you is such a big grown man but you still hankering for a witch and a devil like a child in a fairy-tale Cammy, boy. You must be learning more sense than that by now! You mean to say you ain't seeing daylight yet Cammy, me boy?"

Cameron saw red. His arm shot out and burst Jennings' mouth. Jennings' look lost its jeering ease and smile in a startled flash of surprise. He wiped his mouth, even as he

78

tasted the salt on his lips, and he spied the blood on his hand. He sprang. Cameron took the over-eager blow on his shoulder, ducking where another deadly wild fist crashed to his skull. Jennings went mad and Cameron felt an onslaught such as he had never dreamed to face in his life. He defended himself, retaliating with the swiftest flying fists in the world. An overpowering sense of injury smote the air again and again in their joint nameless breath.

"Stop," Donne shouted. "Stop." The voice was so terrible and full of suppressed turbulence and demonic authority, it halted them like an overflow of scalding self-confidence and self-knowledge.

"Stop."

They were turned to stone stung to the bitterest attention by what they knew not. Jennings remained powerful, thrusting, the air of a primitive republican boxer upon him, and Cameron stood, heavy and bundled like rock, animal-wise, conscious of a rootless superstition and shifting mastery he had once worshipped in himself and now felt crumbling and lost. Donne stood pointing at them with an air of aristocratic fury beyond words. His eyes were liquid and misty and dark. It was a picture to be long remembered in an age that stood at the door of freedom though no one knew yet what that truly meant. It was a grave of idols and the resurrection of an incalculable devouring principle.

Once again the crew came around to the musing necessity in the second day's journey into the nameless rapids above Mariella. They had hardly entered the falls when they knew their lives were finished in the raging torrent and struggle. The shock of the nameless command and the breath of the water banished thought and the pride of mockery and convention as it banished every eccentric spar and creed and wishful certainty they had always adored in every past adventure and world.

They felt naked and helpless, unashamed of their nakedness and still ashamed in a way that was a new experience for them. They saw and heard only the boiling stream and furnace of an endless life without beginning and end. And the terror of this naked self-governing reality made them feel unreal and unwanted for ever in dreaming themselves up alive. They wished the man who stood before them, or next to them, was real and true and capable of exercising the last power of banishment over them by dismissing their own fiction and unreality and life.

The monstrous thought came to them that they had been shattered and were reflected again in each other at the bottom of the stream.

The unceasing reflection of themselves in each other made them see themselves everywhere save where they thought they had always stood.

After awhile this horrifying exchange of soul and this identification of themselves with each other brought them a partial return and renewal of confidence, a neighbourly wishful fulfilment and a basking in each other's degradation and misery that they had always loved and respected. It was a partial rehabilitation of themselves, the partial rehabilitation of a tradition of empty names and dead letters, dead as the buttons on their shirt. It was all well and good they reasoned as inspired madmen would to strain themselves to gain that elastic frontier where a spirit might rise from the dead and rule the material past world. All well and good was this resurgence and reconnoitre they reasoned. But it was doomed again from the start to meet endless catastrophe: even the ghost one dreams of and restores must be embalmed and featured in the old lineaments of empty and meaningless desire.

A groan rose from their lips to silence their half-hopeful half-treacherous thoughts that oscillated over their predicament as the sky dreams indifferently over the earth. The vessel had struck a rock. And they saw it was the bizarre rock and vessel of their second death. The life they had clung to and known before was turning into a backward incoherent dream of the first insensible death they had experienced. Even so a groan rose to their lips and a longing to re-establish that first empty living hollowness and brutal habitation. Surely ignorance was better than their present unendurable self-knowledge and discomfort. Their lips however were smothered and silenced in the hunger of spray.

The boat struck and glanced into the foaming current on the edge of overturning. Wishrop danced at the bow. His paddle hooked and caught a sharp point an inch beneath the belly of the vessel's wood. He hurtled into the air like a man riding a wheel. A nameless gasp riddled and splintered the crew. He vanished.

The boat appeared to right itself miraculously. And Jennings' machine – which Cameron kept a sturdy hand upon when Jennings had sprained his wrist in the struggle – sent a hideous strangled roar out of the water. It had lost its vulgar mechanical fervour and its enthusiasm was dwindling into an indefatigable revolving spider, hopeless and persistent.

Hopeless to dream of finding Wishrop in the maelstrom. He too had dwindled in a moment. They had seen his hands aloft two times quickly after his immersion for all the world like fingers clinging to the spokes and spider of a wheel. The webbed fingers caught and held for an instant a half-submerged rock but the crouching face was too slippery and smooth and they had slipped and gone. The wheeling water lifted him spread-eagled once again for an instant. He disappeared from their view. But rose still again – a skull on whom the hair had been plastered for a changeling demon. It was impossible to say. Anything was everything in the whirling swift moment and in the fantasy of their shattered boat and life. All rose and were submerged a hundred feet or yards apart or ages.

The boat still crawled, driven by the naked spider of spirit. Wishrop's flesh had been picked clean by perai like a cocerite seed in everyone's mouth. They shuddered and spat their

81

own – and his – blood and death-wish. It had been forcibly and rudely ejected. And this taste and forfeiture of self-annihilation bore them into the future on the wheel of life.

The water moved past with reflective backward strokes as the vessel went forward. The old Arawak woman stirred a little, a sudden wind fluttering her sleeves. She had been sleeping all the while but now that the danger was past she had awakened. The river was familiar ground to her, it was plain. High precipitous cliffs and walls had appeared on either hand and bank. She blinked a little, pointing her aged and active fingers. Vigilance saw trees growing out of the cliffs overhead parallel to the river and he wondered whether any man could climb and clamber there. He rubbed his eyes since he felt he saw what no human mind should see, a spidery skeleton crawling to the sky. It danced and gambolled a little, clutching the vertical floor that seemed to change in a shaft of cloudy sun into a protean stream of coincidence where every mechanical revolution and image was the inscrutable irony of a spiritual fate.

Vigilance could not make up his bemused mind whether it was Wishrop climbing there or another version of Jennings' engine in the stream. He shrank from the image of his hallucination that was more radical and disruptive of all material conviction than anything he had ever dreamt to see. The precipitous cliffs were of volcanic myth and substance he dreamed far older than the river's bed and stream. He seemed to sense and experience its congealment and its ancient flow as if he waded with webbed and impossible half-spidery feet in the ceaseless boiling current of creation. His immateriality and mysterious substantiality made him dance and tremble with fear a little as Wishrop danced. It was incredible that one had survived. He saw into the depths of the deathless stream where the Arawak woman pointed. A flock of ducks flew, their wings pointed like stars. They were skeletons fixed from ancient geological time unmoving as a plateau. The sudden whirr of their wings awoke him as they flew living and wild across the river. The Arawak woman laughed. Vigilance drew himself up like a spider in a tree. He stood over an archway and gate in the rock through which swarmed and streamed a herd of tapirs, creatures half-donkey and half-cow. They were seething with fear as they ploughed into the river.

"Look – chased by the folk," Donne said. He spoke from the bow of a skeleton craft Vigilance discerned in the stream of the rock. "Look one has been wounded and is dying. We are close as hell to the huntsman of the folk." His deathless image and look made the Arawak woman smile. Vigilance winced a little and rubbed his eyes where he climbed and clung to the cliff wondering at the childish repetitive boat and prison of life. What an enormous spiritual distance and inner bleeding substance lay between himself and that crust and shell he had once thought he inhabited. He could hardly believe it. He tried to convey across the span and gulf of dead and dying ages and myth the endless pursuit on which Donne was engaged.

"Rubbish," Donne said. "That herd is a good sign. The folk are not so far away. We can catch up and repair our fortunes. They'll lead us home safely and we'll cultivate our fields and our wives." He spoke out of a desire to hearten himself and the crew. The truth was he no longer felt himself in the land of the living though the traumatic spider of the sun crawled up and down his arms and his neck and punctured his sides of rock.

Vigilance was sensible to the fantasy of his wound and alive, the sole responsible survivor save for the Arawak woman who clung with him to the wall of rock. He dreamed she had kept her promise, her stepmotherly promise, and had saved him from drowning. Donne's boat had righted itself, he dreamed, in the volcanic stream and rock and the crew were all there save Wishrop's spider and transubstantiation: wheel and web, sunlight, starlight, all wishful substance violating and altering and annihilating shape and matter and invoking eternity only and space and musical filament and design. It was this spider and wheel of baptism – infinite and expanding – on which he found himself pinned and bent to the revolutions of life – that made his perception of a prodigal vessel and distance still possible. Darkness fell and the banks were too steep for the crew to land. The river had grown smooth and this was a great good fortune. The stream sang darkly and the stars and harmony of space turned into images of light.

The sun rose on the third day of their setting out from Mariella. The cliffs appeared to rise higher still on both hands and the river seemed to stretch endlessly and for ever onward. The water was as smooth as a child's mirror and newborn countenance.

Nevertheless the crew were downcast and dejected. They had forgotten the miraculous escape they had had and recalled only fear and anxiety and horror and peril. This was hard-hearted nature they contemplated without thinking they may have already suffered it and endured it and re-lived it. Rather it seemed to them only too clear that the past would always catch up with them – when they least expected it – like a legion of devils. There was no simple bargain and treaty possible save unconditional surrender to what they knew not. Call it spirit, call it life, call it the end of all they had once treasured and embraced in blindness and ignorance and obstinacy they knew. They were the pursuers and now they had become the pursued. Indeed it looked the utmost inextricable confusion to determine where they were and what they were, whether they had made any step whatever towards a better relationship – amongst themselves and within themselves – or whether it was all a fantastic chimera.

They stared hopelessly into the air up the high walls and precipice that hung over their head – an ancient familiar house and structure – and as hopelessly into the bright future and sun that streamed. It was all one impossible burden and deterrent they could neither return to nor escape.

They felt themselves broken and finished in the endless nightmare and they slouched and nodded in the stream. Vigilance alone preserved the vessel straight ahead, steering with spider arm and engine. The water grew still and quiet and clear as heaven. The Arawak woman pointed. A dense flock of parrots wheeled and flew and a feather settled on Vigilance's cheek with a breath of life. They wheeled closer and·nearer until he saw the white fire of feathers – around their baiting eye, giving them a wise inquisitive expression and look – and the green fire on their bubbling wing as they rose from the stream and the cliff and the sun.

Vigilance had been wounded by a nameless shaft from the enormous unpredictable battlements he dreamed he stormed – cliff and sun and rock and river all set with their ceaseless pursuing trap as if he were the most precious remarkable game in all the world. Nevertheless he was the one most alive and truly aware of everything. He saw differently and felt differently to the way the herd slept in the innocent stream of death. All blind lust and obfuscation had been banished from his mind. Indeed the living life that ran within him was a unique and grotesque privilege and coincidence because of the extraordinary depth and range he now possessed. Vision and idea mingled into a sensitive carnival that turned the crew into the fearful herd where he clung with his eye of compassion to his precarious and dizzy vertical hold and perched on the stream of the cliff. The light of space changed, impinging upon his eyeball and lid numerous grains of sound and motion that were the suns and moons of all space and time. The fowls of the air danced and wheeled on invisible lines that stretched taut between the ages of light and snapped every now and then into lightning executions of dreaming men when each instant ghost repaired the wires again in the form of an inquisitive hanging eye and bird.

The feather on his face pricked him like a little stab of fear as though he had not yet become reconciled to his understanding. He felt himself drawn again into the endless flight that had laid siege to the ambivalent wall of heaven and every spidery mis-step he made turned into an intricate horror of space and a falling coincidence and wing. The parrots wheeled and flew around his head on the cliff and the Arawak woman pointed again to a close silver ring that girdled one flying foot. Vigilance rubbed his eye in vain. It was strange but there it was.

"That bird got a ring on he foot," said daSilva, opening one sudden leering dreaming eye, his face all puffed and unnatural in awkward sleep. One could see he was struggling with all the might of his mind to recall something. "I sure-sure I see that bird long ago, sure as dead." He stared fixedly at the creature and shook his head.

"In the London Zoo," Cameron jeered and snored. "Is there you see it and now it fly all the way to Brazil with its pretty ring on its foot to look at you and me. We is a sight for sore eyes. But is where this ring you seeing? I can't see no ring on no bird foot. Is how many ring and vulture you counting in the sky?" He laughed a little, unable however to hide his fear of the beak of death that had been born in his sleep.

"I never been to London or to a zoo," daSilva yawned lugubriously. "And I didn't tell you nothing about vulture. Is parrot Ah seeing and one got a ring on she foot. O God you think I blind or what? How you can't see it I don't know. You mean is another dream Ah dreaming?" He turned wooden and still, speaking almost to himself in the lapping whispers water made against the boat when the wind blew. "Ah been dreaming far far back before anybody know he born. Is how a man can dream so far back before he know he born?" He looked at Cameron with conviction and enquiry in his eye.

"Because you is a big fool," Cameron cried. "A fool of fools. Look at you. You face like a real dead man own. I hungry." He tried to laugh and his tongue was black. "I going nail and drop one of them vulture bird sure as stones. . . ." The novel idea seemed to wake nearly all of the crew from boredom and they stared in encouragement as Cameron felt in the bottom for a rock.

"I is a fool yes, a foolish dead man," daSilva puffed, "but I seeing me parrot. Is no vulture bird. . . ."

"What in heaven name really preying on you sight and mind, Boy?" Cameron suddenly became curious. "I only seeing vulture bird. Where the parrot what eating you?"

"Ah telling you Ah dream the boat sink with all of we," daSilva said speaking to himself as if he had forgotten Cameron's presence. "Ah drowned dead and Ah float. All of we expose and float. . . ."

"Is vulture bird you really feeling and seeing," shouted Cameron. His voice was a croak in the air. DaSilva continued – a man grown deaf and blind with sleep – "Ah dream Ah get another chance to live me life over from the very start. Live me life over from the very start, you hear?" He paused and the thought sank back into the stream. "The impossible start to happen. Ah lose me own image and time like if I forget is where me sex really start. . . ."

"Fool, stop it," Cameron hissed.

"Don't pick at me," daSilva said. "The impossible start happen I tell you. Water start dream, rock and stone start dream, tree trunk and tree root dreaming, bird and beast dreaming. . . ."

"You is a menagerie and a jungle of a fool," Cameron's black tongue laughed and twisted.

"Everything Ah tell you dreaming long before the creation I know of begin. Everything turning different, changing into everything else Ah tell you. Nothing at all really was there. That is", he grew confused "that is nothing I know of all me life to be something . . ." He stopped at a dead loss for words open mouthed and astonished as if he had been assaulted by the madness and innocence of the stream.

"Tek a batty fool like you to dream that," said Cameron. "A batty fool like you . . ."

"Is a funny-funny dream," daSilva said slowly, recovering himself a little. "To dream all this . . ." he pointed at the wall of cliff behind him – "deh pon you back like nothing, like air standing up. . . ."

"You got a strong-strong back," Cameron croaked and his hands brushed the water with beak and wings.

"Is true," daSilva sulked. His mind grew suddenly startled and punctured as the stream. "I know is who bird now," he gasped and shouted. "I remember clear." He pointed at the parrot and the silver ring with such swamping eagerness and enthusiasm the words drowned on his lips . . . "Is me . . . is mine . . ."

The crew rippled and laughed like water so loud and long that Donne awoke to their merriment.

"What? what is it?" he said.

"Laugh good," daSilva warned. "You going laugh good again like a guest at me true marriage and wedding feast. . . ."

"Must be in heaven," Cameron croaked and roared in Donne's ear.

"Is me lady bird," daSilva insisted. "It must be fly away from she for a morning outing. Them people ain't deh far," he cried in a burst of inspiration. "The lil bird tekking a morning outing . . . I know it. Last year when Ah been with she in the Mission Ah feed it meself often. It used to eat from me lip. Tame Ah tell you. Is me mistress bird." He whistled.

"It's good news then," said Donne. "Yesterday we witnessed the huntsman's promissory wound and today daSilva's promissory ring. . . ." he laughed. "The folk are close at hand to save us." He did not believe a word he said in his heart and he added a warning note – "Of course you chaps mustn't bank on anything too much. A bird like that can fly a hundred miles in an hour. Still we must hope for the best." He smiled stiffly, waving his hand darkly to greet the air.

"I feed it often from me lip," daSilva said whistling loud. "Me pretty lady bird. She and me was one flesh. I going

88

marry she this time. Ah tell you. Look she leg slender. Slender like . . . like . . ." he stared unseeingly . . . "a branch . . ." he was uncertain.

"Like poison," said Cameron.

"Slender branch," said daSilva as if he was drunk. "And she taste sweet. Me mistress breasts like sweet cocerite. She got sweet-sweet honey lip too. And she hair long and black like midnight feathers. Ah kiss she eyes fast and thick till she nearly dead in me hand. . . ."

"What a vulture of a bird you are," Cameron grinned in derision. "You never speak a truer word than when you say you got everything mix up in you head. . . ." He had hardly stopped speaking when he flung a stone and bird past Jennings' head. Aimlessly. The crew gave a sudden answering cry. The stone had cut air and flesh and it fell. But on fluttering upon the water it recovered itself instantly and wings flashed and soared. The whole flock rose in swelling protest higher and higher until all dwindled in the sky at the top of the wall.

"Miss," Cameron cried.

"You wounded it," Donne said quietly. "We have given ourselves away as their huntsman gave them away. O never mind I'm sure I'm talking nonsense. I can't see a thing."

"I used to feed it from me lip," daSilva whimpered.

"O shut up," Cameron waved. "What do you mean – give ourselves away?" he asked.

"O well," said Donne speaking without conviction, "the bird may return bleeding with a mark upon it. The folk may take it in their heart to start hunting us. We can never outwit them now. Our strength is gone. Three of our best men finished. No ammunition. Nothing remaining. Everything overboard. We can only throw imaginary stones in the air to frighten and alarm ourselves and make imaginary rings in the water. . . ."

"Better we stop and turn back," said Jennings sombrely.

"Impossible. Where can we land? If we turn back we're lost. How can we run the rapids in our condition? We do need help more than ever to locate a safe ground trail if we succeed in escaping these walls. . . ." he waved his hands at the cliff. "O it's a hellish business and trial and responsibility I never foresaw. If one of us – " he stared at them with a glassy eye – "gets across he'll carry the mark of a beast or a bird I tell you. It's a wounding dream and task. . . ." he began to ramble and rave. "Let's hope there'll be someone there to meet us and heal us in the end whatever we are. It's all that counts. . . ."

"Ah used to feed she with me lip," daSilva said.

"O shut up," Cameron cried. "Who cares?"

"Why did you pelt it?" daSilva cried.

"Wait you going on like if is you I pelt. Aw shut up, I hungry."

"I ask you why you pelt the ring of me flesh. . . ."

"O Christ, shut up," said Cameron. "I didn't pelt *you*. I didn't see no precious ring. You is bewitched . . . that's what. . . ."

DaSilva muttered wildly – "I tell you when you pelt she you pelt me. Is one flesh, me flesh, you flesh, one flesh. She come to save me, to save all of we. You murderer! what else is you but a plain vile murderer? She ain't no witch. . . ." His face was mad.

"Who say she is a witch . . ." Cameron began to protest.

DaSilva jumped. Cameron's hands flashed. For the first time in his life he missed. The truth was he had no footing in the water: he groaned and fell, his face grinning and splashing surprise. The crew were dumb. They bore him up unwittingly. He was dead and his blood ran and encircled their hand.

DaSilva shook like a leaf. The knife and blade fell from his fingers as flesh from bone turning clean and silver in the stream.

"O God," said Donne in voiceless surprise and horror as at himself. "What have you done daSilva to a brother friend?"

DaSilva did not hear and understand. He too was deaf and dumb. He saw Cameron in the stream and in the sky where

their joint flesh had flown and darted above the fantasy of
their carnal death. He looked around foolishly, telling himself
Cameron had attacked him in some idle and faithless fashion.
It all seemed blind and empty now like the air and stream that
jostled them.

The Arawak woman pointed and Vigilance, straining his
mind from the volcanic precipice where he clung, looked and
saw the blue ring of pentecostal fire in God's eye as it wheeled
around him above the dreaming memory and prison of life
until it melted where neither wound nor witch stood.

IX

The Arawak woman rolled like a ball on the cliff, clinging to tree and stone and Vigilance was able to follow. The river crept far beneath them, and above them – beyond the wall they were climbing – lay safety and freedom. Vigilance knew that every step he made was a miracle of survival. It was incredible he had escaped after the wreck of the boat and succeeded in climbing so far and high. Millions of years had passed he knew until now he felt bruised and wounded beyond words and his limbs had crawled and still flew. He had slept in a cradle of branches and in a cave overlooking the chasm of time. However strange it was the fact remained he was living after all. The memory of the conventional crew was a dead eccentric belief that still continued to haunt him every now and then whenever he thought he had fallen and died in the primitive moments of a universal emptiness and fear.

The fantasy of the fourth day dawned – the fourth day of creation – since they had all set out from Mariella. From his godlike perch he discerned the image of the musing boat in which they had come. They had found a cave the previous nightfall and they had stretched their limbs until morning.

It was a close fit lying there – too close for ease and normal sleep – and everyone stirred when Vigilance moved. They could not help turning their dull eye upon the vessel they had managed to anchor at their ghostly side in the stream and it was as if they sought a long lost friend and soul. Everyone stirred and woke, all except Cameron. He was dead with a stab wound in his back. In their enormous fatigue the night and day before they had kept him at their side as they would an idol and companion.

They hurriedly abandoned him in the cliff, turning the room in which they had slept into his grave alone, and were soon travelling fast in the river when Jennings deliberately shut off the engine and the boat swung in the stream, lodging its bow in a fresh hollow of stone.

"Ah got an idea," he announced. He spoke with hopeless obstinacy. His face was no longer the same as before: it had changed into a dream, the dream of an unnatural unshaven dead man's beard and growth. The cheeks were hollow as the caves in the wall and the blackness of his skin had grown lighter and greyer into an older drier mask and presence lying within. The lust and soul of rebellion had been killed abruptly in a manner that left him suddenly empty. He felt now only the loss of an opposition and true adversary within himself. His eyes had lost all rude fire and in their blindness and loneliness they spun deeper than nature's darkness and light. It was the strangest abstract face Vigilance had ever seen – the abstraction of a shell afloat over a propeller and a machine with the consistency of a duty rather than of a desire and a spirit. Indeed it reminded him of a coconut shell he had once observed beached against the river; someone had brought it a long way from its natural grave on the seacoast and deposited it here dry and desiccated and foreign in the midst of the river's stone and vegetation. He had held the husk in his hand and it had given a dry brittle harp's cry of relief, mummified and mystical and Egyptian, melting at the same time into an inner 'dust that crumbled to an ancient door of life.

It was the oldest soulless expression of self-surrender he had ever seen – the dutiful mask of resurrection and the engineer of death.

"Ah got an idea," said Jennings again. His voice was meaningless. "Let we look for the hole where the wild tapir pass through the cliff. Was when? Yesterday? Or day before yesterday? Let we pass through the same door to the land . . . This is dead man river . . . We can't stay here any more. . . ."

93

DaSilva shook his head. "Ah dream you done dead already Jennings," he tried to crack a joke. "And the hole close up for good for you a million year ago. You is a prehistoric animal." His chest brayed foolishly. "Where Cameron?" he asked.

No one replied.

"Where Cameron?" he asked again. A sickly smile that reflected everyone's condemnation wrinkled his lips. "Ah dream Cameron dead too," he confessed, "and yet he swim and float next to me trying to hug and kiss me. Is he pull me down. Is a sight to feel a drowning man clinging to you," he pleaded and confessed. "I had to stab at he to mek he loose me. And still he hold on. Don't mind how ugly you find it . . ." he shuddered and hiccoughed in a sentimental bloated fashion of goodwill . . . "is still the dream of love floating everywhere . . . I forgive he . . . even if he mek me dream bad that a bewitched whore killed us both . . . grabbed hold us in the water . . . pulled us down . . ." He spoke with the blind innocence of a clown floundering in the blank of memory in the shattering of his life.

Jennings turned his abstract face towards him indifferently as if he knew another version. "Yes is common knowledge you kill poor Cameron daSilva. Is common knowledge in the world you encourage he to mek this trip and that you quarrel stupid-stupid with he in the end. Nobody know the reason 'cept was jealousy or love. Is he probe at me till he enrage me to lef' the shit I been living in. I was always a stay-at-home not like wutless Cammy." A grotesque tear opened his cheek.

DaSilva chuckled gaining a flash of an old rumour of fellowship in winning this ugly tear and response – "He butt me like if he was mad. I dive and pull away from he . . . But I didn't mean to hurt he. Not Cammy. How could I ever hurt Cammy? Was me last memory and hope of happiness in this world. I remember feeling surprised that I had seconds of drowning life and fight lef' in me while poor Cammy was bewildered and dead and didn't feel a thing. . . ."

"You believe a drown-man skin got no feeling in it and

can't make out friend or foe pon his back?" Jennings mumbled his rhetorical senseless question and his face cracked open a little more. He knew it was all invention, da Silva's erratic memory and story, all the crude prevarication and sentiment of life they debated and that it was pointless and pretentious for one dead man (which was the only feeling he felt inside himself) to address another on non-existent spiritual and emotional facts. No one could truly discern a reason and a motive and a distinction in anything. It was as bad as talking of two sexes and of blind love all in the same breath in his wife's mother's sitting-room. The old harridan! she had helped to drive him from his hell and his home. The shock of memory and of a duty to fight to rescue himself drove him again to address himself to the thought of another frightful revolution and escape he had to engineer however soulless and devastating the thought of a living return to the world was.

"If we find the door where the wild tapir pass we can land and live. . . ." He spoke without conviction and with dread at the thought of embarking again for a place he hardly relished and knew. It was better to stay just where he was and crumble inwardly he said like a man who had come back to his shell of nothingness and functional beginning again.

"What tapir?" mocked daSilva. "I tell you I remember no tapir. You recall any?" He turned in a foolish mocking way to his twin brother.

Vigilance was startled. He had forgotten this particular twin and brother. He recalled seeing him last with Donne tracking the old woman in the Mission while the other one remained with Cameron at the campfire. He had completely forgotten him until now when he saw him in the mirror of the dreaming soul again – an artifice of flight that had been summoned rather than a living man and way of escape. His reflection was the frailest shadow of a former self. His bones were splinters and points Vigilance saw and his flesh was newspaper, drab, wet until the lines and markings had run fantastically together. His hair stood flat on his brow like ink. He nodded precariously and one marvelled how he preserved his appearance without disintegrating into soggy lumps and patches when the wind blew and rocked the pins of his bones a little. He shook his head again but not a word blew from his lips. DaSilva stared at the apparition his brother presented as a man would stare at a reporter who had returned from the grave with no news whatsoever of a living return.

Now he knew for the first true time the fetishes he and his companions had embraced. They were bound together in wishful substance and in the very enormity of a dreaming enmity and opposition and self-destruction. Remove all this or weaken its appearance and its cruelty and they were finished. So Donne had died in the death of Wishrop; Jennings' primitive abstraction and slackening will was a reflection of the death of Cameron, Schomburgh had died with Carroll. And daSilva saw with dread his own sogging fool's life on the threshold of the ultimate stab of discredit like one who had adventured and lived on scraps of vulgar intention and detection and rumour that passed for the arrest of spiritual myth and the rediscovery of a new life in the folk.

Vigilance dreamed and felt all this; he recognized the total exhaustion of his companions like his own superstitious life and limbs. And he rested against the wall and cliff of heaven as against an indestructible mirror and soul in which he saw the blind dream of creation crumble as it was re-enacted.

BOOK FOUR

PALING OF ANCESTORS

This piece-bright paling shuts the spouse
Christ home, Christ and his mother and all his
  hallows.

Gerard Manley Hopkins

X

The daSilva twin and scarecrow of death had vanished in the dawn of the fifth day. Donne rubbed his eyes in astonishment. He did not feel inclined to search every cave and indentation in the wall, and after a lusty shout and halloo brought no reply, he decided to set out again and go on. Furthermore Vigilance and the old Arawak woman had also disappeared. Donne rubbed his eyes again wondering whether on leaving Cameron in the cave the previous day he had lost count of the living crew as well. An idea flashed upon him and he scanned the smooth cliff as if he followed a reflection. He saw nothing, however. And a wave of hopelessness enveloped him: everyone in the vessel was crumbling into a door into the sun through which one perceived nothing standing – the mirror of absolute nothingness.

An abstraction grew around him – nothing else – the ruling abstraction of himself which he saw reflected nowhere. He was a ruler of men and a ruler of nothing. The sun rose into the blinding wall and river before him filling the stream and water with melting gold. He dipped his hand in but nothing was there.

He felt it was certainly better to move than remain where he was, and he started the engine, pointing the boat up-river for the fifth morning and time. Jennings' wrist was aching and swollen. Donne sent him to serve as look-out at the bow while daSilva remained between them, in the middle, smiling foolishly at nothing.

The river was calm as the day before, innocent and golden as a dream. The boat ran smoothly until the stream seemed to froth and bubble a little against it. A change was at hand in the sky of water everyone sensed and knew. The vessel seemed to hasten and the river grew black, painted with streaks of a foaming white. The noise of a thunderous waterfall began to dawn on their ear above the voice of their engine. They saw in the distance at last a thread of silver lightning that expanded and grew into a veil of smoke. They drew as near as they could and stopped under the cloud. Right and left grew the universal wall of cliff they knew, and before them the highest waterfall they had ever seen moved and still stood upon the escarpment. They were plainly astonished at the immaculate bridal veil falling motionlessly from the river's tall brink. The cliffs appeared to box and imprison the waterfall. A light curious fern grew out of the stone, and pearls were burning and smoking from the greenest brightest dwarfs and trees they remembered.

Steps and balconies had been nailed with abandon from bottom to top making hazardous ladders against the universal walls. These were wreathed in misty arms blowing from the waterfall.

Donne looked at the engine and felt its work was finished. They needed only their bare hands and feet now to climb the wall. He unscrewed it from its hold and wedged it at the foot of the stairway. Jennings and daSilva assisted him also in hauling the boat out of the water and upon a flat stone. In a couple of months it would start to rot in the sun like a drowned man's hulk in the abstraction of a day and an age. As he bade goodbye to it – as to another faithful companion – he knew there was some meaning in his farewell sadness, something that had duration and value beyond the years of apparent desertion and death, but it baffled him and slipped away from him. All he knew was the misty sense of devastating thoroughness, completion and endless compassion – so far-reaching and distant and all-embracing and still remote, it amounted to nothingness again.

He shook himself into hands and feet of quicksilver and

100

dream and started his ascent of the ladder, followed painfully by Jennings and daSilva.

As he made the first step the memory of the house he had built in the savannahs returned to him with the closeness and intimacy of a horror and a hell, that horror and that hell he had himself elaborately constructed from which to rule his earth. He ascended higher, trying to shake away his obsession. He slipped and gasped on the misty step and a noose fell around his neck from which he dangled until – after an eternity – he had regained a breathless footing. The shock made him dizzy – the mad thought he had been supported by death and nothingness. It flashed on him looking down the steep spirit of the cliff that this dreaming return to a ruling function of nothingness and to a false sense of home was the meaning of hell. He stared upward to heaven slowly as to a new beginning from which the false hell and function crumbled and fell.

A longing swept him like the wind of the muse to understand and transform his beginnings: to see the indestructible nucleus and redemption of creation, the remote and the abstract image and correspondence, in which all things and events gained their substance and universal meaning. However far from him, however distant and removed, he longed to see, *he longed to see* the atom, the very nail of moment in the universe. It would mean more to him than an idol of idols even if in seeing it there was frustration in that the distance between himself and *It* strengthened rather than weakened. The frustration would disappear he knew in his sense of a new functional inspiration and beginning and erection in living nature and scaffolding.

The wind rushed down the cliff so strong he almost fell again but it turned and braced him at last and he continued ascending as a workman in the heart and on the face of construction. He fastened on this notion to keep his mind from slipping. The roaring water was a droning misty machine, and the hammer of the fall shook the earth with the misty blow of fate. A swallow flew and dashed through the veil and window. His eyes darted from his head and Donne saw a young carpenter in a room. A light shone from the roof and the curtains wreathed slowly. Donne tried to attract the young man's attention but he did not hear and understand his summons. He hammered against the wall and shook the window loud. Everything quietly resisted. The young carpenter nevertheless turned his face to him at last and looked through him outside. His eyes were darker than the image of the sky and the swallow that had flown towards him was reflected in them as in window-panes of glass. Donne flattened himself against the wall until his nose had been planed down to his face. He wanted to see the carpenter closely and to draw his attention. He saw the chisel in his hand and the saw and hammer lying on the table while the ground was strewn with shavings resembling twigs and leaves. A rectangular face it was, chiselled and cut from the cedar of Lebanon. He was startled and frightened by the fleshless wood, the lips a breath apart full of grains from the skeleton of a leaf on the ground branching delicately and sensitively upward into the hair on his head that parted itself in the middle and fell on both sides of his face into a harvest. His fingers were of the same wood, the nails made of bark and ivory. Every movement and glance and expression was a chiselling touch, the divine alienation and translation of flesh and blood into everything and anything on earth. The chisel was old as life, old as a fingernail. The saw was the teeth of bone. Donne felt himself sliced with this skeleton-saw by the craftsman of God in the windowpane of his eye. The swallow flew in and out like a picture on the wall framed by the carpenter to breathe perfection.

He began hammering again louder than ever to draw the carpenter's intimate attention. He had never felt before such terrible desire and frustration all mingled. He knew the chisel and the saw in the room had touched him and done something in the wind and the sun to make him anew.

Fingernail and bone were secret panes of glass in the stone of blood through which spiritual eyes were being opened. He felt these implements of vision operating upon him, and still he had no hand to hold anything tangible and no voice loud enough to address anyone invisible. But the carpenter still stood plain before him in the room with the picture of the swallow on the wall perfectly visible amidst all and everything, and there was no earthly excuse why he could not reach him. He hammered again loud to attract his attention, the kind of attention and appreciation dead habit taught him to desire. The carpenter still looked through him as through the far-seeing image and constellation of his eye – clouds and star and sun on the windowpanes. He hammered again but nothing broke the distance between them. It was as if he looked into a long dead room in which the carpenter was sealed and immured for good. Time had no meaning. The room was as old as a cave and as new as a study. The walls – whether of glass or stone or wood – were thicker than the stratosphere. All sound had been barred and removed for ever, all communication, all persuasion, all intercourse. It was Death with capitals, and when he saw this he felt too that it was he who stood within the room and it was the carpenter who stood reflected without. This was a fantasy, this change of places, and he hammered again loud. The image of Death in the carpenter stared through him, the eyelids flickered with lightning at last in the midst of the waterfall. He raised his hammer and struck the blow that broke every spell. Donne quivered and shook like a dead branch whose roots were reset on their living edge.

The carpenter turned to another picture he had framed on the wall. An animal was bounding towards him through the prehistoric hole in the cliff Jennings had dreamed to find. It had a wound in its side from a spear and its great horns curved into a crescent moon as if the very spear had been turned and bent.

The animal was so lithe and swift one had no eye for anything else. It bounded and glanced everywhere, on the table, on the windowsill with the dying light of the sun, drawing itself together into a musing ball. It danced around the room swift as running light, impetuous as a dream. It was everywhere and nowhere, a picture of abandonment and air, a cat on crazy balls of feet. It was the universe whose light turned in the room to signal the approach of evening, painting the carpenter's walls with shades from the sky – the most elaborate pictures and seasons he stored and framed and imagined. The room grew crowded with visions he planed and chiselled and nailed into his mind, golden sights, the richest impressions of eternity. It was a millionaire's room – the carpenter's. He touched the dying animal light at last as it ran past him and it turned its head around towards him, a little startled by his alien fingers and hand, remembering something forgotten. The alert dreaming skin – radiant with spiritual fear and ecstasy – quivered and vibrated like the strings of a harp where the mark of the old wound was and it tossed the memory of the spear on its head, trying to recall the miracle of substance and flesh. It stood thus – with the carpenter's hand upon it – with a curious abstract and wooden memory of its life and its death. The sense of death was a wooden dream, a dream of music in the sculptured ballet of the leaves and the seasons, the shavings on the ground from the carpenter's saw and chisel. His finger had touched an ancient spear point and branch and splinter and nail, whose nervous vibration summoned a furious portrait to be framed by the memory of creation. The windowpane clouded a little with the mist of falling evening and water and one had to press one's face and rub with all one's might to see through. The animal light body and wound – upon which his hand lay – turned into an outline of time followed by its own wild reflection vague and enormous as the sky crowding the room. The bulb shining from the roof turned green as water, weird and beautiful as the light-colour from long-dead twinkling stars and suns millions of years old. The room became a dancing hieroglyph in the illumination of endless pursuit, the subtle running depths of the sea, the depths of the green sky and the depths of the forest. It was the mist on the windowpane of the carpenter's room, and one had to rub furiously to see.

One saw a comet tailing into a flock of anxious birds before the huntsman of death who stood winding his horn in the waterfall. The sky turned into a running deer and ram, half-ram, half-deer running for life. A ball of wind was set in motion on the cliff. Leaves sprang up from nowhere, a stampede of ghostly men and women all shaped by the leaves, raining and running against the sky.

They besieged the walls of the carpenter's room, clamouring and hammering with the waterfall. He leaned down and removed the shaft once again from the side of the hunted ram – as he had moved it an eternity before – and restored the bent spear of the new moon where it belonged. The signs of tumult died in the animal light and cloud and the stars only thronged everywhere. So bright they framed his shape through the misty windowpanes. The carpenter looked blind to the stumbling human darkness that still trailed and followed across the world. He closed his window softly upon Donne and Jennings and daSilva.

Jennings cried slipping suddenly in the dark upon a step in the cliff. His wrist gave way too with the shaft of his engine snapping at last as a branch in the flight of the stream. They both answered him but their voices were drowned in the waterfall and they saw nothing save the ancient winding horn of the moon falling from the sky like the bone of his metal and wood.

They shook with the primitive ram again, scanning the endless cliff in fear and ecstasy, feeling for the bodily image of themselves.

Darkness still fell upon the cliff and the horn of the new moon vanished in the end behind the window of the wall as into a long-feared shelter in the earth rich with the frames of humility of God's memory and reflection. The stars in the sky shivered as they crawled once more up the fantastic ladder and into the void of themselves. They wondered whose turn would be next to fall from the sky as the last ghost of the crew had died and they alone were left to frame Christ's tree and home.

As they climbed upward Donne felt the light shine on him reflected from within. He had come upon another window in the wall. The curtains were drawn a little and after he had rubbed the windowpanes he began to make out the interior of the room. He looked for the carpenter but at first he saw no one. And then it grew on him a woman was standing within. A child also stood at her feet seeming hardly above her knee. The room was an enormous picture. It breathed all burning tranquillity and passion together – so alive – so warm and true – Donne cried and rapped with the world of his longing. He felt a glowing intimacy as he knocked but the distance between himself and the frame stood as the distance between himself and the stars.

The room was as simple as the carpenter's room. Indeed as he looked he could not help reflecting it was simpler still. Bare, unfurnished, save for a crib in a stall that might have been an animal's trough. Yet it all looked so remarkable – every thread and straw on the ground, the merest touch in the woman's smile and dress – that the light of the room turned into the wealth of dreams.

The woman was dressed in a long sweeping garment belonging to a far and distant age. She wore it so absent-mindedly and naturally, however, that one could not help being a little puzzled by it. The truth was it was threadbare. One felt that a false move from her would bring it tumbling to the ground. When she walked, however, it still remained on her back as if it was made of the lightest shrug of her shoulders – all threads of light and fabric from the thinnest strongest source of all beginning and undying end.

The whole room reflected this threadbare glistening garment. The insubstantial straw in the cradle, the skeleton line of boards made into an animal's trough, the gleaming outline of the floor and the wall, and the shift the child wore standing against the woman's knee – all were drawn with such slenderness and everlasting impulse one knew it was richer than all the images of seduction combined to the treasuries of the east. Nothing could match this spirit of warmth and existence. Staring into the room – willing to be blinded – he suddenly saw what he had missed before. The light in the room came from a solitary candle with a star upon it, steady and unflinching, and the candle stood tall and rooted in the floor as the woman was. She moved at last and her garment brushed against it like hair that neither sparked nor flew. He stared and saw her astonishing face. Not a grain of her dress but shone with her hair, clothing her threadbare limbs in the melting plaits of herself. Her ancient dress was her hair after all, falling to the ground and glistening and waving until it grew so frail and loose and endless, the straw in the cradle entered and joined it and the whole room was enveloped in it as a melting essence yields itself and spreads itself from the topmost pinnacle and star into the roots of self and space.

Donne knew he was truly blind now at last. He saw nothing. The burning pain he felt suddenly in his eye extended down his face and along the column of his neck until it branched into nerves and limbs. His teeth loosened in their sockets and he moved his tongue gingerly along them. He trembled as he saw himself inwardly melting into nothingness and into the body of his death. He kept sliding on the slippery moss of the cliff and along columns and grease and mud. A singular thought always secured him to the scaffolding. It was the unflinching clarity with which he looked into himself and saw that all his life he had loved no one but himself. He focused his blind eye with all penitent might on this pinpoint star and reflection as one looking into the void of oneself upon the far greater love and self-protection that have made the universe.

The stars shivered again as they climbed. The night was cold, ice-cold and yet on fire. His blindness began melting and soon had burned away from him, he thought, though he knew this was impossible. He had entered the endless void of himself and the stars were invisible. He was blind. He accepted every invisible light and conceived it as an intimate and searching reflection which he was helping to build with each step he made. His unique eye was a burning fantasy he knew. He was truly blind. He saw nothing, he saw the unselfness of night, the invisible otherness around, the darkness all the time, he saw the stars he knew to be invisible however much they appeared to shine above him. He saw an enormity of sky which was as alien to him as flesh to wood. He saw something but he had not grasped it. It was his blindness that made him see his own nothingness and imagination constructed beyond his reach.

This was the creation and reflection he shared with another and leaned upon as upon one frame that stood – free from material restraint and possession – as the light and life of dead or living stars whom no one beheld for certain in the body of their death or their life. They were a ghost of light and that was all. The void of themselves alone was real and structural. All else was dream borrowing its light from a dark invisible source akin to human blindness and imagination that looked through nothingness all the time to the spirit that had secured life. Step by step up the support grew and contained everything with a justness and exactness as true to life as a spark of fire lived, and with an unyielding motive that crumbled material age and idolatry alike.

They were exhausted after a long while, and they leaned in a doorway of the night hammering in blindness and frustration with the fist of the waterfall. They had been able to lay hold upon nothing after all. It was finished and they fell.

The door they hammered upon was the face of the earth itself where they lay. It swung wide at last with the brunt of the wind. The dawn had come, the dawn of the sixth day of creation. The sun rose in a cloud hinged to the sky. DaSilva stood within the door in the half-shadow. He looked old and finished and beaten to death after his great fall. Donne stared at him with nervous horror and fascination and in his mind he knew he was dead. He could see nothing and yet he dreamt he saw everything clearer than ever before. DaSilva was opening the door again to him: hands stiff and outstretched and foolishly inviting him to step into the empty hall. His mouth gaped in a smile and his teeth protruded half-broken and smashed. The high bones still stood in his face as when he had signalled their downfall. The early sun climbed a little higher and the world beneath the cliff became an aerial portrait framed in mist. The river shone clear as glass and a pinpoint started glittering in the bed of the stream. The mist rolled away from the cliff and the sun curled and tossed a lioness mane that floated slowly up into the sky over the dead. The resurrection head was uplifted and the great body rolled over in a blanket. DaSilva was shivering and shaking cold as death. Indeed he had never been so bitterly cold. He had woken to find himself inside the house and Donne hammering away outside almost in a heap together at the bottom of the wall. He had fumbled for the catch and release in the door, trembling and astonished at himself. The great cliff sprang open like the memory of the lion's spring he had made tumbling him smashed and broken on the ground. Every bone seemed to break and he wrapped himself in the misery of death. But the wind that had sprung upon him flew out again shaking him from his blanket on the ground.

It was strange to wake to the world the first morning he had died he told himself a little foolishly. Donne was standing on the threshold staring blind and mad. DaSilva smiled crookedly because he felt that Donne thought he was dead. He knew better and he stretched out his hand. Donne mumbled to him like a man saying a prayer. . . .

"It is better to be a doorkeeper in the house of the Lord . . ." he mumbled foolishly. He stepped over the eloquent arms that reached to him in a fixation of greeting. DaSilva was dead he knew. He entered the corridor over the dead body and stood himself at strict attention by the lion door. He had stopped a little to wonder whether he was wrong in his knowledge and belief and the force that had divided them from each other – and mangled them beyond all earthly hope and recognition – was the wind of rumour and superstition, and the truth was they had all come home at last to the compassion of the nameless unflinching folk.

XI

It was the seventh day from Mariella. And the creation of the windows of the universe was finished. Vigilance stood at the top of the sky he had gained at last following the muse of love, and I looked over his dreaming shoulder into the savannahs that reached far away into the morning everywhere. The sun rolled in the grasses waving in the wind and grew on the solitary tree. It was a vast impression and canvas of nature wherein everything looked perfect and yet at the same time unfinished and insubstantial. One had an intuitive feeling that the savannahs – though empty – were crowded. A metaphysical outline dwelt everywhere filling in blocks where spaces stood and without this one would never have perceived the curious statement of completion and perfection. The work was truly finished but no one would have known it or seen it or followed it without a trusting kinship and contagion.

The eye and window through which I looked stood now in the dreaming forehead at the top of the cliff in the sky. The grave demeanour of cattle and sheep roamed everywhere in the future of distance, lurking in pencils and images of cloud and sun and leaf. Horsemen – graven signs of man and beast – stood at attention melting and constant like water running on a pane of glass. The sun grew higher still and the fluid light turned and became a musical passage – a dark corridor and summons and call in the network of the day. We stood there – our eye and shoulder profound and retiring – feeling for the shadow of our feet on the ground. The light rolled and burned into quicksilver and hair shining in the window of my eye until it darkened. I found the courage to make my first blind wooden step. Like the step of the tree in the distance.

My feet were truly alive I realized, as were my dreaming shoulder and eye; as far flung and distant from me as a man in fever thinks his thumb to be removed from his fingers; far away as heaven's hand. It was a new sensation and alien body and experience encompassing the ends of the earth. I had started to walk at last – after a long infancy and dreaming death – in the midst of mutilation and chaos that had no real power to overcome me. Rather I felt it was the unique window through which I now looked that supported the life of nature and gave it a full and invisible meaning and perfection in the way I knew my hands and feet were formed and supported at this instant.

I had never before looked on the blinding world in this trusting manner – through an eye I shared only with the soul, the soul and mother of the universe. Across the crowded creation of the invisible savannahs the newborn wind of spirit blew the sun making light of everything, curious hands and feet, neck, shoulder, forehead, material twin shutter and eye. They drifted, half-finished sketches in the air, until they were filled suddenly from within to become living and alive. I saw the tree in the distance wave its arms and walk when I looked at it through the spiritual eye of the soul. First it shed its leaves sudden and swift as if the gust of the wind that blew had ripped it almost bare. The bark and wood turned to lightning flesh and the sun which had been suspended from its head rippled and broke into stars that stood where the shattered leaves had been in the living wake of the storm. The enormous starry dress it now wore spread itself all around into a full majestic gown from which emerged the intimate column of a musing neck, face and hands, and twinkling feet. The stars became peacocks' eyes, and the great tree of flesh and blood swirled into another stream that sparkled with divine feathers where the neck and the hands and the feet had been nailed.

This was the palace of the universe and the windows of the soul looked out and in. The living eyes in the crested head were free to observe the twinkling stars and eyes and windows on the rest of the body and the wings. Every cruel mark and stripe and ladder had vanished. I saw a face at one of the other constructions and windows from my observation tower. It was the face of one of the crew that had died. Carroll, I said, nudging my shoulder, as one would address an oracle for confirmation. Carroll was whistling. A solemn and beautiful cry – unlike a whistle I reflected – deeper and mature. Nevertheless his lips were framed to whistle and I could only explain the difference by assuming the sound from his lips was changed when it struck the window and issued into the world. It was an organ cry almost and yet quite different I reflected again. It seemed to break and mend itself always – tremulous, forlorn, distant, triumphant, the echo of sound so pure and outlined in space it broke again into a mass of music. It was the cry of the peacock and yet I reflected far different. I stared at the whistling lips and wondered if the change was in me or in them. I had never witnessed and heard such sad and such glorious music. I saw a movement and flutter at another window in the corner of my eye like a feather. It was Schomburgh's white head. He too was listening rapt and intent. And I knew now that the music was not an hallucination. He listened too, like me. I saw he was free to listen and to hear at last without fearing a hoax. He stood at his window and I stood at mine, transported beyond the memory of words.

The dark notes rose everywhere, so dark, so sombre, they broke into a fountain – light as the rainbow – sparkling and immaterial as invisible sources and echoes. The savannahs grew lonely as the sea and broke again into a wave and forest. Tall trees with black marching boots and feet were clad in the spurs and sharp wings of a butterfly. They flew and vanished in the sky with a sound that was terrible and wonderful; it was sorrowful and it was mystical. It spoke with the inner longing of woman and the deep mastery of man. Frail and nervous and yet strong and grounded. And it seemed to me as I listened I had understood that no living ear on earth can truly understand the fortune of love and the art of victory

113

over death without mixing blind joy and sadness and the sense of being lost with the nearness of being found. Carroll whistled to all who had lost love in the world. This was his humorous whimsical sadness.

I was suddenly aware of other faces at other windows in the Palace of the Peacock. And it seemed to me that Carroll's music changed in the same instant. I nudged the oracle of my dreaming shoulder. The change and variation I thought I detected in the harmony were outward and unreal and illusory: they were induced by the limits and apprehensions in the listening mind of men, and by their wish and need in the world to provide a material nexus to bind the spirit of the universe.

It was this tragic bond I perceived now – as I had felt and heard the earlier distress of love. I listened again intently to the curious distant echo and dragging chain of response outside my window. Indeed this was a unique frame I well knew now to construct the events of all appearance and tragedy into the vain prison they were, a child's game of a besieged and a besieging race who felt themselves driven to seek themselves – first, outcast and miserable twins of fate – second, heroic and warlike brothers – third, conquerors and invaders of all mankind. In reality the territory they overwhelmed and abandoned had always been theirs to rule and take.

Wishrop's face dawned on my mind like the soul of all. He was obviously torn and captivated by Carroll's playing that lifted him out of his mystical conceit. I felt the new profound tone of irony and understanding he possessed, the spirit that allowed him to see himself as he once lived and pretended he was, and at the same time to grasp himself as he now was and had always been – truly nothing in himself.

The wall that had divided him from his true otherness and possession was a web of dreams. His feet climbed a little and they danced again, and the music of the peacock turned him into a subtle step and waltz like the grace and outspread fan of desire that had once been turned by the captain of the crew into a compulsive design and a blind engine of war. His feet marched again as a spider's towards eternity, and the music he followed welled and circumnavigated the globe. The sadness of the song grew heart-rending when he fell and collapsed though his eye still sparkled as a wishing glass in the sun – his flashing teeth and smile – a whistling devil-may-care wind and cry, a ribald outburst that wooed the mysterious cross and substance of the muse Carroll fed to him like the diet of nerve and battle to induce him to find his changeless fortress and life. It was a prodigal web and ladder he held out to him that he climbed again and again in the world's longing voice and soul with his muted steps and stops.

XII

The windows of the palace were crowded with faces. I had plainly seen Carroll and Wishrop; and now as plainly I saw Cameron, the adversary of Jennings. I saw as well the newspaper face and twin of the daSilvas who had vanished before the fifth day from Mariella after making an ominous report and appearance. The music Carroll sang and played and whistled suddenly filled the corridors and the chosen ornaments of the palace; I knew it came from a far source within – deeper than every singer knew. And Carroll himself was but a small mouthpiece and echo standing at the window and reflecting upon the world.

In the rooms of the palace where we firmly stood – free from the chains of illusion we had made without – the sound that filled us was unlike the link of memory itself. It was the inseparable moment within ourselves of all fulfilment and understanding. Idle now to dwell upon and recall anything one had ever responded to with the sense and sensibility that were our outward manner and vanity and conceit. One was what I am in the music – buoyed and supported above dreams by the undivided soul and anima in the universe from whom the word of dance and creation first came, the command to the starred peacock who was instantly transported to know and to hug to himself his true invisible otherness and opposition, his true alien spiritual love without cruelty and confusion in the blindness and frustration of desire. It was the dance of all fulfilment I now held and knew deeply, cancelling my forgotten fear of strangeness and catastrophe in a destitute world.

This was the inner music and voice of the peacock I suddenly encountered and echoed and sang as I had never heard myself sing before. I felt the faces before me begin to fade and part company from me and from themselves as if our need of one another was now fulfilled, and our distance from each other was the distance of a sacrament, the sacrament and embrace we knew in one muse and one undying soul. Each of us now held at last in his arms what he had been for ever seeking and what he had eternally possessed.

THE FAR JOURNEY OF OUDIN

For Margaret, Ivan and Anne

A magic spell for the Far Journey

Wandering in Heaven, one eats the spirit-power of the receptive.

I no longer know at what place the house of my spirit and my crucible are.

The Secret of the Golden Flower
(translated by Richard Wilhelm)

BOOK ONE

THE COVENANT

I

The stars shone faint in the stream on the windy night and they penetrated a flying cloud. The lights shining far across the river were uncertain and distant, close to the ground and one with glimmering heaven. The shape of a cow loomed on the opposite bank, so enormous it blotted out the lights and invisible windows of the far scattered settlements: it loomed like a cloud, shapeless and massive in the dreaming faint light, slithering down the bank suddenly into the water, washing the stars away as it swam across the night.

He awoke with a drowning sensation in his mouth as unlike the memory of creek-water as rum tastes like *padi*. The tasteless dawn shone through the window; a dim radiance of ancient pearl and milky rice washed the ground and settled in his eyes, moving stealthily, circulating within the room until he saw in the image of his limbs the dry brown stalks of harvest. He had been reaped and he lay staring and dead as a naked cliff, or as a window that had fallen from its house to rot on the earthen floor until there sprouted forth the solitary relics of grass.

Oudin knew it was still a dream, the dream of the heavenly cycle of the planting and reaping year he now stood within – as within a circle – for the first time. He felt his heart stop where it had danced. It was the end of his labour of death. The night and the day were finished as the starlight and the lantern-light of every dying human settlement and flame.

It was a new freedom he now possessed. He roused himself to stand on his dry feet, and to swallow his saliva over and over again. There was a shot of rum on the shelf in the room and he poured it out into a cup as a miser counts the change he hoards – stealthily as a ghost swallowing the last drop.

The vague harvested bundles lying on the floor of the room began to stir.

Oudin's hut stood against the river, looking dressed and drenched in dew on a high round mound in the savannahs. The early light circled it with a spray of vapour, as when the sea encounters an ancient foreshore and clothes the first sentinel and tree. The tide beneath the mound and house was dark: yet it seemed white on the surface, still and lifeless, and only the mist of the dawn appeared to drift.

The hut emerged suddenly, ordinary and dead as day. The vague eternity and outline vanished. There was no mystery in the poverty of its naked appearance – a few planks nailed together and roofed by bald aluminium.

Oudin saw it in the corner of his eye as if for the first time: so clearly he might never have seen it before. The stark light in which he beheld it was a mystery to him, the first real mystery and power of apprehension he possessed.

The dark surface of the river cleaned suddenly, showing in the running tide a deeper spirit and across the track of spiritual reflection stood the hanging head of horses and cows. The day cleared in the new light of his eye and the land was a wilderness on which had fallen the curious naked spoil of his conquest and death. He possessed it all now as one would a matchbox world surrounded by its models and furniture, their head still outstretched to crop the ground beneath every windless and breathless tree. Oudin held it all in the corner of his eye. And it seemed to him that the first outcry from within the hut – the wailing voice of his wife and child – had happened in the depth of time long before the vain echo of the announcement could be heard in the still air he had ceased to breathe.

"Oudin dead, Oudin dead. Oudin dead."

It was a senseless outcry and it ran over him as water from a duck's back and became part of the flimsy scaffolding of the world.

Beti ran and stood half-wailing, half-breathless outside the door. She had the refined emaciated face of an East Indian and Guyanese woman that looked older than it was, bearing the stamp of a well-known ornament.

Destiny had fulfilled itself in dividing Oudin and herself after thirteen years together in the blind eye of the world. They had never known each other in reality as far back as they knew. Oudin saw this now – as it had always been – in a new way of self-possession that overcame the folly of grief and lent him an image of transparency and compassion.

She wore her long unbelted dress; her elbows were pressed hard against her stomach and her hands outstretched beseechingly, intent on making an awkward catch. Her black hair escaped on all sides from the cloth over her head and her wrists and ankles were adorned with reflective bracelets. The cry she raised was as involuntary as a bird's or animal's. She always relished standing in this light advertising a mournful need and curiosity, waiting for something to happen and fall into her hands. Her cry and wail were the oldest expression and tradition of inviting and deceiving everyone, and herself into the bargain, so that there stood upon her now the stamp of timeless slavery, rather than selection and freedom, and of belonging to someone and something living and dead, like a commodity everybody instantly recognized. She was Oudin's wife and she cried both hopelessly and hopefully – "Oudin dead."

Oudin understood how she was the representation of a slave despite her secret longing and notion to be free.

"Beti, Beti, is what happen? Oudin can't be dead. You talking foolish. Me and he had a lil drop yesterday. He did send he boy-picnie to the road for a bottle. Remember? Oudin been strong-strong then I tell you. Beti is what happen? Oudin and me got pressing business and contract on hand. . . ."

Beti shrank from the man who had approached and questioned her as from a sudden unwelcome visitor. His house was near to Oudin's and he had been cleaning his teeth and had come running in his singlet and old pyjamas, still chewing the stem of sage bush he used as a brush. He turned to implore the child – standing beside his mother – whom Oudin had sent yesterday for a bottle of rum to seal the contract – "Is where you daddy, picnie? where you daddy?" The child bowed his head to the ground without a word. He saw the hard grey toenails staring up at him from the man's feet where they protruded from the pyjamas. He was fascinated and repelled: they reminded him of his father's nails and feet, grey and hard as stone. Ram looked down at the boy's bent head and neck and he feared the unwelcome silence.

He regretted now running across to Oudin so quickly and standing chained to the ground where Oudin had over-powered him, holding him firmly in the corner of a dreaming eye. His shadow crossed the door entering the hut with the rising sun, fearful of this involuntary bondage and servility.

"Oudin really dead?" he asked himself under his breath. He was frightened, frightened of the gliding shadow of the sun and a prospect of calculation circulating around him, his cattle and ricefields. The news of Oudin's death had come to him as such a sudden and unexpected reversal of fortune that it struck him as a trick possessing and activating everyone and everything.

The empty rum bottle stood on the shelf, and he looked reproachfully and accusingly at the body lying on the floor. Oudin had been able to buy this with Ram's money and not a drop now remained, though Ram was sure last night they had not consumed all of it.

Oudin was smiling at the superstitious conceit like an observant host who knew every desire in the craftiest reflection.

Oudin dead? Ram's mind was once more assaulted by an incredible image of possession and dispossession. A crowd of voices had started outside the house. He felt he must bar them out until he had cornered the impossible smiling thing. He scanned the room frantically and blindly, knowing it was

126

full to bursting with a rich secret: his miserly instincts were frustrated and aroused. Oudin dead? The gliding thought that Oudin was *alive* and in process of catching him – rather than being caught – filled him with panic. He trembled, unable to discern the wall and the shadow of the sun he wished to corner and possess with every grain of rice he harvested in the present and the future, and every acre of land he acquired from his tenants who had mortgaged their labour and their world to him.

II

Ram returned to Oudin after the funeral – a man making many steps and still not moving one from the blazing eye of the rising sun bright and tropical. Oudin dead and buried? Ram blinked, wondering whether the blinding shock he had felt when he first heard the wailing impossible cry (a million dreaming years ago it was) had burst his inner tube to flatten him and rob him of air, and fill him with a drowning sensation he had never had before. He seized the empty rum bottle to plunge it into the river outside but stealthily replaced it.

Beti forced herself to address him: "Is who you want, Mr Ram?" She thrust her hands to him, helplessly inviting and warding him off – "Oudin gone, Mr Ram."

Ram stared at her. He knew she was in league against him as she shrank from him. In league with whom? Everyone in the savannahs dreaded him, and it made him cold and uncomfortable all of a sudden to see her watching him intently. There was a time when he would not have known the slightest misgiving and discomfiture. What was it that made him see himself as a foul obnoxious shadow against the world? His heart plunged with the force of a cricket ball falling in a stream of air and emptying him of concentration. Emptying him like a fieldsman who stared into the sun at a blind catch. Oudin was encircling all and dispossessing him.

"I looking for a piece of paper," Ram blurted out softly and unseeingly. "Oudin tek it from me the same-same night before he dead. . . ." His voice was a pleading whisper.

Beti glared at him in terrible astonishment. She was stunned by the plea and the subservience. And she felt that such awful confidence called for a whisper in return so that she would not be overheard. Overheard by whom? Oudin had vanished from the hut. Her outstretched hands writhed and struggled to seize a spirit that had always eluded her and the heart of Ram stared, hanging on her breath.

"You see it?" he cried hopefully. "You see it? You know where it is?"

Beti was startled and the spell of the moment slipped from her mind. "I dunno is what you mean," she said falling back.

Ram was disappointed and enraged. "Suppose is me life Ah sign away and you drop and lose it?" he cried accusingly. "You *stupid*." He turned to the shelf in the room where the empty rum bottle stood, picking up a pen and rusty nib still smeared with ink. "Is this Ah use to sign. *Stupid*. Where the ink gone?" he demanded. "It been next to the rum."

"Mr Ram, Ah don't know nothing," Beti wailed and shouted. All of a sudden she was conscious of the dreadful menace she addressed; she recalled his notorious power and his avarice that had faded a little from the field of her recollection a moment ago in the light of intuition.

"Mr Ram, Ah don't know nothing."

"Hush woman," Ram said rebuking her for her outcry.

They both stood and listened.

The wind blew upon the hut and shook the roof just over their head. Every window had been closed to conform with the rule in a dead man's house. Half-light and vision circulated through the space of the door and along lines in the walls where the rough-sawn boards had been nailed blind together.

Ram crinkled his eye, looking along the sights of an imaginary gun and peering through a slit outside. He saw Oudin's boy chasing a cow. It was a fleeting glimpse that looked distant and still as a rolling game and a dream.

"The picnie deh far," he said turning to Beti. "He can't hear we."

A curious frightened intimacy enveloped them once again, the intimacy of perhaps belonging to no one and nothing and yet of being overheard and caught by someone and something.

129

The Far Journey of Oudin

They were growing conscious of a presence whose apparent nothingness was more real and penetrating and commanding than anything they had ever known.

Ram suddenly remembered and looked on another shelf on the opposite wall. "Ink," he said. "Ah sign me name with this ink."

"Look paper," Beti said. She tore him a scrap of old newspaper sensing his need and desire. It had been lying crumpled on the floor. Ram smoothed it carefully. "Ah sign like this," he said. He scratched his name with precision. The paper had acquired a thin film of dung as it lay on the ground and the nib disturbed the flake as Ram wrote upon it until the smell rose into his nostrils. "Is dog dung," he cried in disgust, flinging the pen from him.

He opened his mouth wordlessly and his tongue curved into a plunging wave turning up the ragged burnt edge of one of his teeth that appeared like floating planks in their sockets.

"I only know to mek me mark on paper," Beti cried half-fearfully, half-craftily observing him. "I never learn to read and write clever like you, Mr Ram." She felt herself drawn closer to him than ever in fresh surprise at his insecure humanity. "No paper with *you* writing been in here when Oudin dead." She spoke in artless wonder, bringing an intonation of vehement secrecy into her voice. "I swear I don't know and I never see it. Look," she started undressing before him as if to prove she was as naked as the walls around her.

Ram stared at her with a sense of dreadful hallucination and assault and intimacy. He wanted to feel that she was still part of – and belonged to – Oudin's boarded walls. The listening catching spirit in the room drew him to her – in his evil curiosity to plumb the depths of appearance – as to a worthless abandoned place and shelf or to a priceless mystery in which had been hidden the contract he had made a couple of days ago with Oudin. He felt he dared not speak aloud to her or the husband of silence might reply and crush him. It was impossible to plead with a presence he could neither seize nor possess. He saw her cruel nakedness and the injustice of her position like a man who had made a blinding covenant with a ghostly phenomenon and life.

"The only place lef' to look, Mr Ram", Beti said at last, "is under the floor in the bowel of the earth." Ram felt that she had begun to despise him – in the intimacy of self-knowledge – now that his assault on her had served to yield nothing.

"Oudin put you up to this," he raved, "you bitch."

Beti's smile trembled, scorning his self-evident powerlessness and defeat.

III

Ram had no alternative but to follow the enormous blind vigil he had started. He must watch Oudin's hut in the impossible hours of sleeping and waking to see who entered and who departed. He had spies and obsessions to warn him if anyone visiting or leaving contemplated a trip down river to the public road on Beti's behalf. He felt he must confront every appearance she made until he had willed her to gain no help to spell and read the lines he had signed and written. It was a gesture of control he made over himself, and the world he used to govern, speaking inwardly and indefatigably to himself. The truth was – and this he never uttered aloud even in the silence of his heart – it was her contempt for him that conceived an indifference to his power and possessions. This, he sensed – remembering the time he had searched her, squirming under her scorn – was his salvation. His contract was pointless in her eye and what use learning the contents now? It was Oudin's dead business and desire, not hers. Ram was drawn to this conclusion and it helped to comfort him in the misery of impotency and understanding.

Still it was a secret he must wrest from Oudin's property he told himself, or he would never sleep for fear of Beti taking it into her head to do something after all.

Oudin was no longer available and responsible Ram knew in essential chagrin. Every process would have been normal and regular then. He had disappeared like a thief leaving behind him a naked wall and legacy. It was unprincipled and grotesque in the extreme that Ram should be excluded from finding what belonged to him in a way he had never bargained for or realized in the nature of the contract.

Ram learnt to approach the door of the hut in the dark. From afar off he could see the flickering light through the invisible curtain and wall, blowing it seemed to him in the wind, as if it was nowhere at all and the whole thing was the reflection of a star. He followed it: his eye was drawn by the thin silver radiance across the dark earth to the hidden treasure of his life.

The door was never securely barred, only tied he knew by filthy string that had been wound through a hole and around a post.

Ram learnt to retire at last with the coiled twine in his eye, and he knew in his dreams, when he snatched a couple of hours of sleep before dawn, the slightest interference with the coil on the door would start him cruelly awake in his bed. The twine, he was aware, would uncoil before him, so that stretched taut at last it drew him forward as Oudin walked backward into the distance like a sleepwalker, till their vision met in a way that shattered him to the core. He tried to shout across the distance his gratitude and his horror all at once that his vigil was so fixed and established. It was his stupefaction and sense that Oudin had not really deserted him. Oudin knew not only what he wanted but was intent as well on overthrowing every misconception and inferior relationship in their contract, the fulfilment of which had become a matter of spiritual conscience to him. Ram was filled with fear as he was drawn from his waking sleep to Oudin's unsleeping watch, until it seemed he no longer understood whether the covenant lay with a reality beyond him or an appearance of life and death within and around him.

IV

Beti put out two large helpings of rice – shaped like truncated cones – on the plates before her. She was about to serve a third smaller heap for the boy when she caught herself and realized Oudin was no longer there to eat his portion and she might as well divide his share. The curry stood in a separate steaming pan, humped vegetables and traces of small green leaves floating on a thick surface. She stared at it unseeingly and yet with a bird's-eye view of Oudin's savannahs cooking in the sun.

Beti felt little appetite in a mind and spirit of absence that made her forget to stop laying the extra place and providing the extra helping. A grain of rice filled her in the shadow of recollection and earth and it crossed her mind how she had grown to accept the dread shattering figure she always thought she saw patrolling the house after dark. It would approach and rattle the door with the wind shaking the roof, but when she peeped outside she beheld no one but the stars and they had been parted into the broken mound of rice Oudin deliberately scattered when she absent-mindedly laid his place.

It was as if noon – the time for the meal of rice – had become the stars of a new universal spiritual night in which the fear of Ram had begun to vanish.

Beti rose from the scattered rice on the low table where the child ate innocently and greedily. Outside the sun shone and devoured the blinding heavens and she made her way to the riverside. A couple of planks jutted out from the bank touching the water and Beti squatted beside a bundle of clothing with a flat wooden spade in her hand. The rhythmic thud, thud, thud became an interminable undivided pulse that beat in the depths of the river's smoky reflection where it waved up and down with Beti's rising and falling arm and sliced forwards and backwards where her heels shook the planks and broke the water-top.

The sun was furious and hot and she grew a little tired. The feeling passed in a moment and in its hollow place there came a beating fullness in her breasts and in the region of her heart, as if the pulse in the river had begun to flog her blood. She stopped in the act of beating and washing and listened, straining her mind and attention, until the see-saw reflection subsided. A faintness had risen to her lips and she was sick to death.

It was the sickness of pregnancy, she told herself, without realizing the force and significance of her words, a late morning sickness, she said, that would pass. She clung desperately to her plank of living emotion seeing a crumbling vision and image in the mirror within her. A darting stream of fish had risen to the surface of her mind and it nibbled and divided the bait she had vomited until everything shone clean where the vanishing floating trailers of soap still lingered.

Beti was startled and transposed and amazed. "You mean to tell me is a child in me Oudin lef'?" She spoke to no one and yet knew she addressed someone. A strangeness rose up in her, a strangeness that made her see herself unexpectedly. Her eyes were round and black in the river, almost falling from her head, and the smoothness of her skin was an intent and naked particle of freedom like one who had been stripped in truth at last. The unexpected face she saw was guarded and protected in the glass of the river and it stood beyond a touch where no material impact could break it, vulnerable as it looked. The fish darting beneath the glass and upon it were torn scraps of paper Beti dreamed she had sliced and eaten and vomited. She had swallowed it the night and morning of Oudin's death – in a wave and spasm and panic – for any kind of mysterious paper and appearance was to be swallowed, she knew, and given a chance to be digested. It was the oldest crumb of fear and habit binding the illiterate world of reflection around her. Pro-notes, transports on property, invaluable documents and contracts had been concealed in the belly from time immemorial, and fortunes were thus overthrown or mysteriously razed to the ground, cruel promises broken and repudiated. Beti saw in the superstitious scrap of paper Oudin held, like the fish swimming before her eye, a passport to the depths of hell. She extracted it from his fingers, ate it and swallowed it before Ram arrived as she knew he would. Whatever unholy bargain had been consummated she had shattered in her breast.

This was all a fantasy, Beti knew, rousing herself to reassure herself. Midnight sunstroke, pregnancy and hallucination had overpowered her. She had swallowed nothing. She had seen nothing in Oudin's dreaming hand, neither passport nor fortune, she told herself.

"You mean to tell me is only a child in me Oudin lef'?" She spoke aloud again to stir herself into a practical move.

"Beti, is what happen, you sick?" Ram stood on the bank of the river watching her. Beti's naked pointed face vanished as she scrambled upright hiding her transparent flesh and blood. Ram stared with his suspicion and curiosity aroused as never before in the blind days and nights and weeks he patrolled.

"I see like you fall forward and I come running," he cried. "I just passing. When Ah run up Ah hear you talking to youself. You got something secret-secret and momentous 'pon you mind." He spoke sternly and yet ingratiatingly and wistfully.

She gathered up her washing, ignoring him as she had learnt to do, and made for the clothes' line beside the hut.

Ram remained staring into the water and stepping forward he looked for something he felt she had hidden in an empty rum bottle or jug. He saw himself instead, waving up and down as he trod on the shaking planks, slicing and waving almost endlessly until the slices and fragments were drawn together on a loose sailing thread. He could make out very little as he peered into the river's obsession and depth, save that a banner had been unfurled over the grave of Oudin, one of those waving flags anonymous processions hold over their head when they celebrate a victory or resolution and triumph. A public banner and epitaph everyone knows it is, and yet a most private symbol of rebirth and death, since the face on the banner represents an absent hero whose sliding proportions are the mask of timeless spirit rather than Ram's fading personality.

Ram felt this alien motive in himself making for public presence and fantastic participation in a unique way and ceremony. It bewildered and alarmed him. He was afraid of becoming something other than he had always known himself to be. It was an unfair advantage to find himself in this curious suspension in which everything he possessed was gathered and adopted by someone other than himself. He was a soldier of fortune whose revolutionary uniform clinging to a dissolving piratical appearance – in the invalid ward and world to which he had been confined – distinguished an immortal being as well as a child of fantasy, rather than a dying and insecure man.

V

Ram hitched his trousers that had become slack and disordered around his waist, like Oudin's trousers Beti was hanging on the clothes' line in the savannahs. The wind and the sun felt as if they drained him too of every sweating furious drop until the beads had accumulated into the river's margin and pool, and the pool contained the unearthly beginning of his life.

Ram knew the motion of the river by heart, like one who had never moved from the same place where he had always stood. He had always followed with his eye – seeing and yet blind to the light in the depth – the dark bed and journey of the water past the far-strung cracks and windows and settlements of the brooding land, towards the brittle dams and villages on the public road, and farther still, through foreshore and masses of defensive *courida*, into the sea.

He stood on the relative margin of the ocean, he knew, and within the span of his life he had seen the water come past the road twice, he recalled, and the river's flood rise six feet deep, where he stood now, into a grave over the ground.

Survival was a miracle, a miraculous ascendancy upon the flux of death, cows and horses already bloated and floating with a bobbing frisky coconut like the head of a child. The drums of festival were silent before death and flood, Hindu and Moslem alike, and the sound of church bells alone came across the miles of dreaming water, reminding him of the passing upright face of time that measured and calculated and undermined the rain and the tides.

Ram saw the pitiful procession of the bride and groom reflected in the floods of memory. The groom was decked out in a magnificent head-dress with the tiniest tinkling bells,

138

whose mimicry of the universal call of time was that of a mosquito in the *courida* jungle to an aeroplane in the sky. The bride was less fanciful, and the *pundit*, plainest of all. They had been launched on the flood, that had risen and rained overnight on the eve of drums and preparations, and were setting out at noon with a skeleton disconsolate key of guests and relatives to the village on the road, where the dams would ensure safety and ceremonial and a yard's damp space to kindle the holy fire in the middle of the land.

Ram recalled the procession (ten years and more it was) of Oudin and Beti. It was the year of the great flood, surpassing the previous one of his childhood recollection, and he recalled it as if what he had seen then was the dream and reflection of misery, and what he saw now was the launching and freedom of a release in time.

And still he could not yet accept the evolution and change in appearance; the wedding procession passed mournfully, poling its way to keep in the main river and not to wander over the flooded banks where occasional trees stood, like watching poles themselves, stretching from nowhere to nowhere.

Oudin's dark face was enigmatic and musing. An inexplicable fantastical creature, and yet a child-like man he was, Ram knew. Ram wondered what difference the marriage and Beti would make and whether he would feel safe as ever in the whimsical fleeting way he cherished Oudin.

Oudin was the vessel in which Ram poured his hunger and ambition and hatred and contempt. A couple of drinks ordinarily made him Ram's eager correspondent and listener and slave.

Ram had been in desperate need – before he met Oudin – of an accomplice, and a submissive cornerstone as well, upon which to found a conception of empire. Oudin had materialized – to fulfil this reflective need – no one knew from where and when. He may have come from the sand-hills a long way off topside but this was unlikely since he was not of

Amerindian stock, neither trace nor ghostly feature was his. Or he may have crawled from under the eastern horizon – Berbice and Dutch Guyana way. The Dutch were known to be queer and ancient settlers and to have a far-seeing eye. Yet still he may have come from the west – though this looked as unlikely as every other alternative – across the Demerara swamps in search of a new start and life. The truth was no one knew whom he represented or where he had sprung from.

Ram adopted him and christened him a Mussulman, whatever that meant. Brand Mohammed's calves, he said, and he would let him have the shed on the mound, in which he could live.

It was an ugly bastard deal, Ram knew, to invite Oudin to venture upon Mohammed's property, where he could be shot like a dog of a cattle-thief, an outcast and nameless adventurer who had trespassed upon the settlers' hospitality.

Mohammed was violent, Ram confided to Oudin, but a careless hard-drinking stick of a man who converted his substance into running and driving cars and buses on the road and in the villages. An absentee landlord, Ram chuckled, confiding the sinful irresponsible secret into Oudin's receptive ear.

The calves were sitting ducks, Ram exploded, and Mohammed was not the only one whose cattle dropped young ones everywhere in the wide spaces of the careless land, unknown and unobserved for months. Ram saw the mating years and seasons unroll before him – as he cajoled and wooed Oudin – and every original pillar and proprietor converted into his lasting fence and world and market. He wished to undermine all and everyone, he confessed, looking at Oudin and yearning for a far-flung reflection and mark.

Oudin consented to stake his life on the initial mission and to capture Mohammed's unbranded cattle if it meant chasing them down into the sea. Ram could hardly believe his ears. He despised Oudin and yet he admired him all at once. He

140

had never expected such capitulation and consent. Oudin was a dream, a fantasy and an obedient servant who had come to him at last across an incredible divide of time and reality. Ram recalled suddenly the first awful occasion he had addressed someone miles away on the telephone. He had been fearful of the instrument and had longed to escape the box on the public road, where he stood, and return to the trackless reaches of the savannahs. Later, familiarity and submission bred contempt, and he learnt to despise the enigmatic ear and instrumental mouth-piece, as he involuntarily despised Oudin now for his unthinking reply and consent. He knew the distance and the divide was there between himself and the other ear and speaker, but his own reflection rose and deceived him until everything seemed nearer and narrower than it actually was.

BOOK TWO

THE HUSBANDMEN

A certain man planted a vineyard, and let it forth to husbandmen, and went into a far country for a long time.

Luke 20 : 9

VI

Beti met Oudin for the first time in the middle of the *courida* on the foreshore that always awoke her apprehension, the trees were so gnarled and twisted in their extremity. His face was new and strange to her and yet he seemed like someone she had seen before.

She was walking on the middle dam when she saw him in the bush alongside the open high earth-mound on which she stood. It was Mohammed's middle-walk dam to the sea, and Beti was carrying a bundle of light firewood on her head, and had just turned to retrace her steps from the foreshore to the public road.

The donkey-cart Mohammed used for domestic chores such as collecting firewood, and picking a dozen or two of the dry coconuts that lay on the ground, where they often fell and wasted and rotted because of poor labour and management and attention, was waiting for her outside, to drive her up the dam a half-mile inland from the road, to the rambling house Mohammed had bought a couple of years ago.

Mohammed was her father's cousin, and when death had quickly orphaned her, he adopted her like a poor relation, whose bundle could hold in the pair of socks and the handkerchief he had worn at her father's funeral. He took her in and brought her out of the savannahs.

The change, however, had come to signify nothing save extreme servitude and frustration. She had never crossed a school door all her life, and she met no one who could show her anything save the border of mystery and blind apprehension.

Mohammed and his wife lived with their three children, all growing up in illiteracy, as women were left to do in the labouring, bargaining world. Only the men chose to marry and to read and to write. Beti was past sixteen, she knew herself in a vague way, and the daughters of Mohammed were one, two, three years younger than she was. They were all relative servants in Mohammed's eye, the servants of his blood.

Beti realized that even if the household had faced the road she would have seen no one in the dust of tramping feet and rolling traffic. They were three and a half miles from the nearest village. Red dust from the burnt-earth country highway had painted the trees on each hand. On the sea side the foreshore of the estate was overgrown with *courida*, and the soft crab-holed ground sang with mosquitoes. On the land side a coconut plantation had been massed going towards secretive windows of distance on the savannahs. Mohammed's house emerged from coconut-palms in a clearing that misted and smoked the trees, out of cleverly banked fires, to drive away mosquitoes.

Beti balanced the precarious brittle bundle on her head – brushing herself vaguely all the while with a horsetail fan – and staring at the apparition of Oudin that seemed to accompany her all the way, like the sun dark on her shoulder, in the hallucinated trees. Oudin's extremities – hands and feet – had turned to mud. He had crawled and crept far. He had risen to his feet to follow her, but he carried with him rings around his ankles, and islands off the foreshore, and it was with difficulty he still uprooted and extricated himself. She had seen him once before she was certain now. *He* was the man who had rapped on their door, in the savannahs, seeking employment, shortly before her father died. He had looked like a bundle of death then – as wild and terrible as he looked now – and her father had thrown him out, swearing he wanted none of him.

She had felt at the time confused and sorry, in the midst of her father's violence that exceeded all bounds, as though the creature represented a passionate and ancient feud, and the same ambiguous reason – made of half-childish dread, half-childish compassion – made her cry in her sleep on seeing him patrolling the world near her, the desperate image and author of freedom.

She felt a great wrong had been done but it was all childish and confused in her mind. The brittle dream fell from her head and scattered on the ground, encircling her with a game of firesticks. The clattering naked sound startled and washed the dry floor of her bed and awoke her.

She rubbed her eye involuntarily and stealthily, looking towards the misty space and light of window and door. The dream was so clear and vivid it matched the darkest reality. She saw the invisible partition and wall that divided her from the dead world of sleep in the rest of the house. Every whisper and breath alerted her and made her want to run as far as she could, though it dawned on her, wherever she ran, she would never escape a close alignment and reckoning and a spirit of inviolable trespass and longing in privacy. She knew that an awkward word and sound would bring Mohammed with his gun, in the same way her father would have responded to a misdemeanour and a thief, as though he lived in mortal pain, and acute anxiety all his life.

Mohammed brought Oudin in and Beti's heart rose into her mouth. She felt sick with horror, imagining his shout of address was the echo of some – almost forgotten – urgent call. The event and call had occurred a long time ago and their echo struck a faint response within her.

"Muhra, Muhra," he shouted. Mohammed's wife came running to him as she had run before in answer to the identical tone and summons.

"Is who you bring? O God, who?" Beti felt she knew Aunt Muhra's cry by heart. The words were abstract as the womanhood Beti had not yet fathomed, though inevitable as birth and death to the mind of a child.

Muhra's eye fastened on Oudin's face and she trembled into protest and chaos wishing to refashion her settled past and part. "O God, not again. Ah warning you, Mohammed. This time is no accident but is plain and brutal murder you going commit. I too old now to be bamboozled. I is not a child no more to look on and say nothing and accept everything. All-you plan you nasty story well and proper, and you carry it through like a set of demons in hell. And what you gain from it? Not a blind cent in the long run. All your buddy dead poor and not a boy-picnie self lef' to represent them. . . ." Beti saw she was crying . . . "like savannah rat all of them dead, and as for your precious cousin – he dead the baddest of all – not a grain of repentance to the last end – O you poor loving child. . . ." She had turned to find Beti trembling and astonished – "I must be going out of me wits, I didn't see you there or I wouldn't have talk ill of your father. Forgive me, child, me mouth run far with me. Ah get such a terrible shock this morning when Ah set eye on . . ."

"Muhra, you gone mad? You want me to *beat* you? He name *Oudin*. Ram send he." Mohammed was shouting loud to drown the insurrection.

Muhra let her arm fall slowly and weakly from around Beti's waist. The shock of recognition subsided a little. Nevertheless she still felt all the turbulence of emotional hope. She riveted her eye upon Oudin, wanting to know whether this was a chance – a ghost of a chance – to convert and restore her life into the warmth and protective meaning it should have had. She wanted to shed the false colouring – the colouring of a fabulous kind of beast of burden, ageing prematurely into Mohammed's shaky spirit and idol and contrivance. She was a tiny witch of a woman against his tall overmastering presence and angular frame. She had always been compelled to hide her robust manner and image in a voluminous pretence and dress, so that her ardent rustling knees turned to paper in their envelope. Her shoulders had begun to droop and follow her hands that were heavily burdened and ringed, though she never forgot to lift them in meditation in search for space to rub naked surfaces together, until they rustled like ghostly leaves in a natural tree and abandonment. The occasional startling metallic *clink* woke her ear to an unrealistic joint.

Mohammed turned on his side, leaned his body on his elbow; his eye caught the light circulating in the room through a crack. He sat up suddenly and heavily. The strike of a cutlass on a stone moved him and he recalled the dream he had had, yawned, stretched and groaned, and stumbled to the door.

His eye met the road, grey and remote in the dawn; everything was dead and still, and he wondered where the clinking life of cutlass had come from. Then he saw Oudin with a bucket and a cutlass, tapping the road every now and then and measuring his work as he wet and soaked all around him. He had been up now for a little while, Mohammed detected, from the dark wet riband that ran before the house and separated the light approaches of dryness.

He shivered a little. Certainly this was *not* Oudin. Who was *Oudin*? Where had the name sprung from? The man he beheld on the road – who looked like the spirit of Oudin – was his half-brother. His feeling hardened, hating the thought of the true relationship, wanting the unknown to be real – since he might be able to banish that – and the actuality to be a fable.

Alas! he wished one did not have to face the actual truth. Grey-clad and industrious before him, the man was damping down the dust of the day, pestilence and paint. It was a super-human task – on which to be so early engaged – as extraordinary as the obsession he had witnessed in the crumbling insurrection of his lot. He felt now he had not slept a wink, and the figure watering and paving the way was an essential link in a chain and a plot directed at his heart's ambition and lust.

It was a recurring and unwelcome vision he seemed unable to interpret and stop, of subversion and opulence, misery and well-being resting upon no one and nothing. The frustration and meaninglessness goaded him and frightened him until he wanted to remain blind to the womb of all, since it resembled the features of death, looking outwards and inwards in the dreaming conspiracy of time and history and migration, with a threat to convert him, and everyone else, into the relative image of a child.

He jumped at the clatter of sticks sounding like children playing hop-scotch or rounders against the partition of the room. He knew he must rouse himself to overcome the disturbance, as well as every other symptom and approach of an enemy, who insisted in attacking all his senses.

The ominous clink of a drawn sword, sounding right inside his ear, drove him to his feet. Muhra was sleeping, and her rings of defiance and hostility retired and began to fade into stillness.

He smiled stiffly, half-placated and still anxious and troubled. He recalled the great L-shaped house – before which they had stood – when he had shouted and she had come running. One day he knew he would build this identical palace for himself. Not next to the road like now – where the present cottage was – but half a mile inside the coconut walk. He had seen and marked the exact spot where he would clear the undergrowth. Five–ten years' time he visualized, would do the trick. A new building and rehabilitation programme would have been launched on the sugar plantations of Demerara, and a lot of old-fashioned overseers' frames would be going dirt-cheap then for anyone who saw himself becoming a new kind of ruler.

Of course it must have different windows to spy from to please a man like himself, windows that would thwart the fierce eye of the sun, like coloured glass stuck in a church or mosque, blue, green, purple. He was not sure why he felt this, whether his intention was to accustom his eye to a settlement of darkness within, or to veil the world with a living darkness without. Mohammed reflected on his windows in astonishment, remembering how in his image of time the family lived in the same illusion of dark space they had always occupied and rented. They had the same room or rooms, as in the cottage where they were in the present, while the remainder of the dreaming mansion of the future was bare and unlived in, and unoccupied as ever, and altogether too big, he knew.

Muhra and he slept in the same room, and on the other side of the thin dividing wall he was conscious of his three daughters. Everything was the same except that everyone was older. Muhra was old, older than five or ten years should have made her. His daughters were grown up, and approaching the age when he would have to lay out miserable dowries for them. They were good working girls in the bargain. The eldest one looked about sixteen, nearly as ripe as her cousin Beti, who lived permanently with the family like a fourth daughter. This puzzled him but as he pondered he remembered with a stab: Beti's father was dead!

What nonsense, he nearly burst with relief. This comical pass surely had shattered the duel and spell of the dream and restored the time. Beti's father was exceptionally well and alive, and Beti herself hardly more than a child of ten. She had come with her father to visit Mohammed. An important family gathering and occasion it was.

Beti had squeezed in with his daughters. Her father was sleeping downstairs, in the bottom-yard space and compartment, which he shared with Mohammed's brothers. Mohammed had two full blood-brothers, as well as the odious half-demented half-brother. Nobody wanted and counted him.

The warning significance of the dream returned and struck, clear and vivid, with full force, wiping out all, save the imbecile brother and the useless women of the family.

Mohammed replied with an angry incredulous snort. He was stale-drunk, and he imagined unpleasant things in his naked bed and trough, a real hand-to-mouth case he was, since scraping together every penny to repair an ancient bus he had bought, and even mortgaging a piece of land. It didn't matter, he knew it would pay.

But rum and gasolene never mixed, and he miscalculated in boarding a dozen extra beseeching passengers in a glow of charity and courage that defied the number and stipulation in the law. He was blind and the police pounced. He was lucky to escape with his licence and a fine. A heavy unsympathetic fine; he was compelled to borrow to pay, having exhausted his capital. Ram was the money-lender. Where did the devil get it from? No one could fathom the source of his supply. And it was *he* who had sent the spirit of Oudin to torment him in the mask and motive of a crime Mohammed felt both in the dreaming past and future of his limbs, as if he occupied two places and situations at the same time, a mansion and a cottage. He shivered a little, excusing himself.

Should he – even though indebted to the devil – have refused the veiled request and the fantastic command to feed his dead brother?

What a nightmare rhetoric of greed and mental dissociation the sleeping world was. Mohammed was still half in the mists of sleep and he saw that Ram had offered Oudin a coffin's mound and tree and it was now a question of the hungry bastard stretching himself to earn a penny or two, for a fortnight or so, as crab-catcher and cattle-hand. And was it not a fact that Mohammed did need the surreptitious labour and the flitting spirit of his living half-brother, if the estate was to be saved from going to rot? Mohammed was away for much of the day, remember, plying his drunken commerce and traffic on the road. One blood-brother was his partner and relief and conductor, while the other had just started a gasolene station and pump. Their first cousin was an invaluable conspirator and member of the clan but his hands were already loaded, growing rice in the fifth depth of the estate, and in the savannahs, far away from the sea and the road. Indeed the place was falling into what appeared at times to be a deliberate and an absurd and a fanciful neglect, and who was there to remedy and overcome it?

Mohammed slapped himself hard for being a helpless fool and a drunkard in spawning an ubiquitous shadow and image, and brother. He woke as the sun was rising and filling him with horror and relief.

"You slap me hard in you sleep, Mohammed," Muhra cried. Mohammed groaned, stale-drunk. He heard the stifled sound of the four children next door, and the ominous click of cutlass and bucket grating on the road.

"Ah dream Ah mekking a man-child at last, Mohammed. No more girl-picnie. He going to be the apple and rule of you eye," Muhra tried to hold his attention. She spat helplessly into a utensil at the side of the bed, and saw the misery and redemption in her reflection sailing on the flood tide of rebirth and hope.

VII

Mohammed descended the steps and opened the latticed door of the bottom-yard. His brothers were sitting up, clad in their singlet and underpants; his cousin was still stretched out, though wide-awake, on a sugar-bag cot, and he yawned and cried when Mohammed appeared – "That madman start wetting the road before a bird-wife wake. Is what you going do 'bout he at all, Mohammed?" He frowned and his brow wrinkled like brown paper while his chin opened into a menacing tuft and brush.

"A nightmare business you asking me 'bout, Rajah," Mohammed yawned and replied. "He stopping the burn-earth from painting we face red at least. Give he that. . . ." The rattle of a van confirmed and smothered his words. It was the milk-van and its trailing dust subsided when the wheels rolled over the watered road before the house.

"I suppose so," the cousin, Rajah, grumbled. "Though he mek me jump when he cutlass hit the bucket in the foreday morning. Was like alarm bell. Ah lef' like I wide awake for good."

"Is who then I hear snoring and snorting like a pig in he trough under the floor?" Mohammed guffawed.

"Was me," one of his brothers spoke absent-mindedly, picking corns on his toes.

"Kaiser is a snoring devil," Rajah laughed.

Kaiser abandoned his corns and looked up. He was a shorter, thinner version of Mohammed and could have passed for a twin. "So the old man at death's door at last," he said seriously. "Is true-to-God story this time, Moham-med? Ah lef' the pump last night late as soon as Ah get you word to come. Ah don't even think you did hear me

154

creep in bottom-house here. Mosquito been tearing ass. . . ."

Mohammed's eyes were bloodshot and red from the liquor he drank. "Is true-to-God story, Kaiser. False alarm after false alarm been ruling, but the doctor mek no bones yesterday. When Ah leffing the hospital he gie we daddy two day at the most. . . ."

"He lose consciousness yet?" Kaiser asked.

"The old man keeping conscious to the end. But he losing all pain. He lying there like a king. He beard white-white like snow Ah never see Ah tell you. And his face still black-black with the sun. Is not the old man I worrying 'bout no more. I going match he soon in the end. He had he *long* day. He come in this country with he daddy – we grand daddy that dead before we born – from India. And we got to forgive he for the strict unfathomable way he got of looking at we like if he grieving for a language. Is ancient scorn and habit at the hard careless words we does use. But is who fault if the only language we got is a breaking-up or a making-up language? At least nobody pretending they is anybody high-schooled and polite 'cept they got hard cash to rule. Is a parable we meaning all the time every time we can't help twisting we tongue when we speak the truth. Ah know he dying there despising all of we proper. He last word to me yesterday . . ." Mohammed lowered his voice. "He last word was he want to born heself over again. And when he see me looking drunk and stupid-like and ignorant-like he turn over 'pon his side. Not another word. Wasn't me fault if I didn't understand." Mohammed stopped and there was a short silence.

"Is not we daddy I worrying over though. I going match he," said Mohammed softly. He approached the latticed door gingerly and peeped out. "What worrying me," he announced, "is that one. . . ." He pointed along the road. "The old man put he prominent in the will, boys. We got we work cut out. Soon as we daddy breathe he last we got to move. . . ."

"What?" Rajah sat up. "You been seeing you daddy regular and you allow he to put you in a boat?" He sprang to his feet:

"I wouldah been worrying me head off 'bout this long ago. Who you fooling you ain't worrying and how you going match he when the damage done-done? Is what you saying at all?"

"I ain't saying I not worrying. What I mean is – the only course was to humour we daddy all along. But when he breathe he last all the monkey story got to end right there. . . ."

"Let me mek me story plain-plain," Rajah cried. "You see Kaiser been picking he toe just now? Well if I was to start on me corn I would never end. Nothing does broke you foot up worse than ricefield work. I been slaving in that back-dam now more than anybody – is how long? Think good. And I had an undertaking from you Mohammed. As soon as the estate come into you and you brothers' hand, you going to give me machinery. Tractor and such like. Everything now I telling you is *hand*, hand I working with. But you give me that undertaking. And unless all-you get control to give me what I want – well buddy-boy I done. I done, you hear me? You daddy did declare he want no machine 'pon he land, and is how is I to know that half-mad idiot, with he little water-can 'pon the road in the foreday morning, seeing further than he nose?"

"Take it easy, Rajah." It was a cool soft voice, speaking for the first time, the last brother to join in. He was the one who worked with Mohammed on the bus. A round-faced man he was. Sometimes he was mistaken for a rather outlandish Indian priest because of his round thoughtful simplicity and a kind of secretive-looking wisdom and detachment. He had risen as he spoke and had begun putting on his white trousers, caked with dust, as well as his long hanging white shirt, that reached to his knee, and was stained with a rust-like film of curry. He always wore these impractical and filthy white garments.

Rajah waited for him to say something more, but seeing he was returning into silence, he prompted him: "How you mean tek it easy? I want to hear *you*, Hassan."

Hassan walked softly to the door and peeped out.

"Don't worry," Rajah cried impatiently, following him. "Nobody hearing we. I see he walking up the coconut walk just now. . . ."

"Mohammed right when he tell you we had to humour the old man," Hassan declared softly. "No use making a royal fuss. Would have put his back up and make him suspect us. What chance then to disappear his will from under his very eye?"

"Talk, Hassan, talk, man."

"He sleeping with it in an envelope under his pillow. . . ."

"You allowing that?"

"At least he think is the same will and paper he sign two fortnight ago. He had it careful drawn up long before he fall so sick and enter hospital. He must have ponder over a year before he really decide to sign. Then on the spur he show we the contents, signed, and call two perfect stranger as witness. Was like a bombshell to Mohammed and me. We never guess the old man did make a fresh will. I believe he been keeping it secret even from God. And whether he bring it to us in the end, out of a kind of malice, to show us how far we falling from grace, I don't know. Is the one over-confident slip he make. And what Mohammed didn't tell you is how we succeed in breaking up we daddy spectacle. . . ."

"What?" Kaiser cried. "O God Hassan, all you going too far. . . ."

"Yesterday," Hassan said solemnly, "I let the spectacle fall hard on the floor like if is a real accident and it break. Then in the confusion with the old man trying to raise heself to see – I slip an identical sealed envelope under the pillow with plain paper fold up inside. He can feel that everything safe but even if he want to open and see he can't see no more without he spectacle. Everything seal up and address to the Registrar of Wills in care the hospital when he dead. Is better it left so and then everybody going wonder if the old man been dreaming and if he tear up his will, or if he was going out of his head in the end. Either the old true will he make in favour of *us* going come to light or he dead intestate," Hassan declared triumphantly.

"And what 'bout the spectacle?" Kaiser asked anxiously.

"Mohammed take it for repair. It going take two-three day to done and by then. . . ."

"I hope to God we daddy dead and don't find out," Kaiser cried out. "I shame for all of we. . . ."

"Don't be a fool, Kaiser," Hassan cried sharply, losing his retiring look. He turned his full moonface on his brother like an open eclipse and threat. "Is the only way to keep the estate in the right hands. You know what the old man want to do in his madness? All the first, second and even the third depth left to that idiot boy. . . ."

There was a sibilant and involuntary sigh and exclamation of rage from both Kaiser and Rajah, who, though they had expected an ultimatum of this kind from Mohammed's early remarks, were appalled when it was actually delivered. It was a heresy they found difficult to endure, and the astonishing thing was how close they had come to losing all.

"Well to me God," Kaiser cried, feeling at a loss for another word.

"To think if he did do his business and show you not a word! . . ." Rajah too was dumbfounded. "Is close-close call."

"Ah don't know what come over the old man at the eleventh hour to show we what been up he sleeve for so long," Mohammed whispered, peeping through the latticed door. "*That* alone convince me he wasn't righted in his head. You mean to say he really think we would lef' it to go like that? Ah can't understand."

"Over-confident," Hassan said. "He believe we all really gone soft, driving car, and getting so Englishified in all our style. You know what I mean. Year after year you throw away every tradition the old man prize. When he show us the will, was like consulting a dead post he could ignore. He didn't believe we would *dare* to do a thing. He felt he had all of us *crushed*. Was the final blow he deliver to hand over nearly all he had to a slaving spirit of a bastard."

"Gone crazy," Mohammed agreed. "Look it. Who *is* this half-brother of we? All you ever ask youself the question?"

Rajah stared at Mohammed seeing something for the first time. "Mohammed", he said slowly, "I seeing a lot-lot question mark in you mind. Tell me, you think is possible the old man tell *he* anything? After all he tell *you*. . . ."

There was a silence.

"Is that what worrying me, Rajah," Mohammed confessed. "You hit the nail on the head at last. . . ."

There was another silence.

Mohammed began to probe: "All you ever question youself who this half-brother is?" His bloodshot eyes were intent on inflaming his listeners.

"Well, since a child you hearing one thing, another thing, sometimes you seeing one thing, another thing. Was always a kind of mystery to me," said Kaiser.

"The old man get a six for a nine," Mohammed cried.

"You tekking an overlot 'pon youself, Mohammed. We can't know the truth for sure. . . ."

"But I know it," Mohammed cried. "I know more than you. I was the far oldest and biggest of all-you. I see and I hear and I remember things before everything hush up and die down."

"What you mean exactly?"

"Is like this. Tek it from me is a bad thing when husbandman lose he head for a slut. . . ."

There was an uproar, on this offensive remark, that drowned Mohammed's voice. "Is we mother very words I repeating," Mohammed justified himself.

The uproar subsided and everyone's attention was riveted upon him. "The old man did want to bring the boy in as we full blood-brother," Mohammed began unravelling the mystery. "The outside woman he had – God know how he tek up with she (she must be give he some kind of food to eat one day in the ricefield and pasture) – *dead* in childbirth. We daddy wrap up the boy – close-close. Was a rainy noon." Moham-med's bloodshot eyes were steady. Hardly a breath stirred. Everyone was listening intently. "The rain did pouring 'pon the tent. Is under there everything happen. To start with, the woman did foolish to come out from she house at all. She was big-big, and she still leaving she home and walking with she saucepan of *roti* and curry to the ricefield to give the old man, though he always lef' his house in the morning with his rightful midday meal from we mother in he hand. She tek in sudden 'pon the dam on she way. Them overseer and government public work man did have the tarpaulin slung up there. They did digging some communal drain and four-foot. She tek in right there. And is then the rain decide to start! Is then the rain going loose it belly and burst. Rain fall to kill. And the child born in a lightning flash under the tent. We daddy and all them man run from the ricefield. She breathe she last 'pon the dam, and only the child live. The woman was too weak. Bad woman always weak like straw." Mohammed's lips were set. The thought flickered on his mind that he had gone too far. "Well is a figure of speech," he excused himself, a little uneasily. "All women weak. You know what I mean."

"Tell the story and never mind," Hassan said softly.

"A strange thing happen in that tent. We daddy start to cry like a child. All them hard-back man look ashamed. They had do their miserable best when they cut the navel string. We daddy start wrapping the lil picnie up . . . and then . . . you remember that black-skinned coolie man who use to drive the bad bull along the road here? the same bad bull that race all-we down the dam one day? remember? Well is that man's father Ah telling you about. The boy know a lil smattering of the story. One day Ah question he clever 'pon the road about his father who run from where he been working near we daddy in the next section of land, and claim our half-brother was *his own begotten son too*."

"What!" Kaiser gasped, "it sounds mad."

160

"Yes, was uproar. We daddy threaten to shoot." Moham- med stopped to reflect, a little overcome. "When the story broadcast – you know black man and coolie mouth never lazy – we mother (who would have take the picnie, grieved as she was) say no. He must board the outside lil one out. . . ."

"What about the other man, who lay claim he was the baby's father, whom we daddy threaten to shoot?" Hassan smiled softly and rhythmically as if he saw and knew the reply.

"He calm down after and say he sorry, was a mistake. He thought was he outside woman, the resemblance so true. What I believe", Mohammed explained, "he did clearly see his child was in good hands in we father hands." He spoke bitterly.

There was silence, the silence of a curious exhaustion, and Mohammed began to wonder whether he had said too much. He felt that something he had dimly foreseen and ap- prehended, was happening in a way that made him uncertain of himself and of everyone. Life was becoming too big and challenging, and death was encamping in the room and in the house. He knew in a twinkling intuition and moment his father was dead, blind and dead, and that a certain page and time in the book of the world was finished. Mohammed was filled with fearful, cringing wonder. Why had he translated their little life into such grand terms? It baffled him. There was a simple natural explanation for everything he knew, and it was the exhaustion in the apparent motive and reason in nature that drew him to dwell on a hazy world-spirit and symbol, signifying the ultimate expression and the vague renewal of all.

Something small and secure had been broken beyond repair. It was a unity of faith and family, a unity and a structure of particular loyalties to which they had always paid lip-service, even if in their hearts they had doubted that the meaning and the value lay in a fixity of appearance. They had never dared to overthrow completely – until now – the secret participation and magic of ancient authority and kinship, father, brother, daughter, etc. This faith and loyalty had been their diamond and breath and body, their true province and relationship to withstand a sameness and a misery in life, and an unchanging role in experience akin to the acceptance of holy poverty.

Mohammed knew the page had been written and finished, and its consumption and perusal were shattering. They had come one step too far to stifle the seed of inquiry and ambition they had drawn and sown into the life of the mind. Every word of meaning within them was rotting. It had been rotting for long decades and time. Their partial neglect of the land was contained in the seed. Their disfiguring and vulgar quest for new ways of making money, the new dreaming architecture and house, the acquisition of sordid power, were all a beginning and a rot in the womb of subversion, and the turning towards a wider changing window and world. It was an end and also a beginning in themselves, the death and dying of a province, and the new wedding of esoteric ascendancy over technical greed and accumulation and flood. All this held and baffled Mohammed, as it baffled and controlled everyone else. They were conscious of it, in their consciousness of a hideous body of rot, and in their self-destructive seed and lot.

"It flash on me mind all of a sudden the old man dead," Mohammed said at last. "He do, he do, and he had he day. Is we turn now." He tried to impart a vigour and hope into his remarks.

"Look it," Rajah said. "We must find out how much *he* know, the boy you daddy leave nearly all the estate to."

"Yes," said Hassan quietly, and he caressed the moon of his face, staring with unseeing eyes.

"He still in the coconut walk looking about. Must be counting his fortune," said Kaiser, trying to crack a joke. No one smiled or laughed.

"I going to the hospital to check up," said Mohammed suddenly. "Hassan better drive the bus today and put a man to relieve you at the pump, Kaiser."

"Yes," Hassan said gently.

"What I want you to do is this. You and Rajah . . . you listening, Kaiser?"

"Ah listening."

"You and Rajah must go with we half-brother to the backdam. All-you going to round up cattle. Understand? That is you excuse. Find out tactful as you can, whatever you can. Sleep out in the savannah tonight. Find out everything. Tomorrow morning we going make the final decision and plan of campaign. Is a world at stake boys, all-you do you best."

"Yes," Hassan said, secretively and softly, like a priest who superintends an ordeal and a travail in the blind eye and scorn of every dreaming ancestor.

VIII

Oudin clinked his cutlass upon his bucket and looked up at Mohammed's L-shaped house with its sombre eye-shades and spectacles and windows. He was conscious that the figure he cut on his arrival had brought consternation into the household of Mohammed and Muhra and Beti, and of the three childish daughters of Mohammed. He wondered whether Mohammed had sensed Ram's object, which was to give Oudin a first-hand opportunity to brand Mohammed's cattle under the owner's very eye. This was, however, nightmare suspicion and stupidity, Oudin knew, since Mohammed would have killed him in broad daylight, if he had dreamed of such a thing. The truth was, he was under an obligation to the devil, Ram, whose request he feared refusing, and whose grace he saw himself in need of, in regard to the interest on the loans he had been granted on a couple of occasions, as well as in respect of the capital repayments he wished to postpone for a year.

Oudin saw, however, as in the smoke between the trees, a deeper and fantastic compulsion overriding every binding hope of release that had prompted Mohammed. The murdered one was walking again on living smoke and feet, and behind a living face that trailed and resembled his. That was why Muhra was terrified of the past, whose ageing plot she knew like a premature wrinkle. And why Mohammed seemed to writhe in a paralysis of will, alone, without aid and succour, and his flaming sense of desertion slapped heaven, and sought to descend to every brother and shade in hell, whose blind conspiracy and wisdom were succumbing to Oudin's far-sightedness.

Oudin had succeeded in lighting the tall reflective fire at

last, which was to illumine the constructive and relative meaning of the time, as if the seed-water in the flood of the river, where Beti had beaten her soapsuds and vomited, now rose into a dreaming spirit-fire at Ram's feet. Oudin had risen early and collected a bucketful of coconut husks and damp chips of wood like the masks and bones of death Mohammed plotted with and wished to find. In the distance, blind with a mood of smoke, he heard the faint rumble of a transport lorry on the road passing before the site where Mohammed's cottage had stood, when his old father died in hospital six to seven years ago. Whether Ram whispered this to him where he stood in the reflection of fire – or whether he had gleaned the idea from scraps and a mound of debris – was a mystery to to him. He simply accepted what he knew as one drinks in the stifling brooding atmosphere of a dream. It was the know-ledge one shares with a trembling leaf and phantom from a smouldering heap and fire stinging one's nostrils as one steps back upon another's unexpected foot.

"Sorry", Oudin mumbled, turning around in Ram's ubi-quitous shoe, "didn't know you been there."

Beti had come up silently with a message from her uncle. She always thought of her father's cousin, Mohammed, in this way, as if he were a closer relative. She lost her tongue now and stared at Oudin mesmerized, unable to address him in any fashion whatsoever. After all *he* was a perfect stranger, neither cousin nor uncle. She felt she loathed him, there was something so ragged and unkempt about him. Nevertheless he was free and could return to a world outside Mohammed's compound. His strangeness was actually a dreadful likeness to the same man who had been rudely thrown out on the night he had come begging at the door, and her father had been struck by the resemblance to someone he insisted was dead, who appeared to stand before her again now. He was an intimate portrait, and yet she had never known him in any permanent sense, save only in the knowledge that he eluded her because of her abysmal ignorance. She could neither read nor write nor draw, and yet her mind was often besieged by a word and a line and a face she dreamed she had sketched and made. She dreaded Oudin because of this obscure and terrible recurring spirit and reason, but she was drawn to him as to the ultimate heir and bridegroom to fire one's freedom and imagination in the midst of one's pitiful shell and dowry and fate.

She found her voice at last as though she spoke in a secret language from a great distance.

"Uncle say you must collect dry coconut today."

Oudin prodded the fire at his feet, shaking his head and nodding. Beti's eye followed the magic of sparks in the blaze. A shell suddenly dislodged itself from the burning smoke and rolled towards her, losing its fire and turning into a black ball. It was like an eclipse and cloud of memory darkening the sky.

Hassan was the first of the brothers to die, at the zenith of life, after the plot and conspiracy that eliminated their imbecile half-brother. He told Mohammed and Kaiser and cousin Rajah shortly before he fell down with a stroke – when he had had an intuition of his sudden end – that he would not rest in his grave, unless his corpse was fired on a pyre, in the ancient way of his ancestors, before they had dreamed to cross the ocean to Demerara.

Mohammed secured permission from the police. A precedent existed – to support the application – in a mound erected to an eminent Hindu landowner, and King's Counsel to boot, whose funeral pyre had startled his little world.

The rules were that the ceremony must be conducted on the distant foreshore in the heart of a private estate, a good mile or two from the nearest public road and village, and that the ashes of the casket and the dead were to be buried immediately the blaze had cooled and died down.

Beti was thirteen when the event occurred, the age when childhood turns into the curse and potency of womanhood. The burning mystery was an unfathomable running stream within her that died in order to rise again. Rajah had insisted on bringing her from the savannahs to the road, and she had run unnoticed from Mohammed's cottage – with a flowing procession of villagers and farmers – along the middlewalk dam to the seashore.

It was low tide and the sea was retiring an enormous distance from the *courida* fringe and from the narrow bank and crest of sand dividing the *courida* growth from a smooth open drift of mud, like glass, reflecting the clouds.

A thoughtful clearing had been made in the *courida* trees and earth had been dug up and mixed with sand to form a temporary roadway and space leading to the pyre which towered above everything.

The crowd that had poured forth to witness the conflagration could hardly stand on the footing the middlewalk dam offered, or upon the narrow ribbon of sand and the clearing and roadway that had been plastered and cemented to approach and abandon the spirit of the dead. They were forced largely to slip knee-deep and waist-deep in the soft ground of the *courida* and the melting fluid of the foreshore.

It grew worse when the time came near, and everyone within the pathway and the clearing of the mound of Hassan was forced out.

The torches were lit and the last ladders hastily removed by troops abandoning their siege.

A faint wind blew and died, followed by a drift of rain like tears of mist. The fire was stubborn and it seemed for a while it had been extinguished. And then a tongue darted like a snake and poised. The crowd was unaccountably startled and their alarm drowned the intoning voice of the outlandish priest, whose speech had somehow been forgotten and taken for granted so that no one noticed and heard it.

The snake retired a little, scrutinizing the wind that had almost vanished, and writhing its body where the fine needles and arrow-points of rain struck. Man had abandoned the siege but the elements were still undecided.

The first spiritual snake to defy all was soon followed by many others that stood and clambered until their reflection ran on the glassy foreshore and earth and encircled the spectators who now desired to run. They ran without danger of entanglement amidst the snakes, gathering the heart of every witness into an undivided longing whole.

The tide had begun to rise and return, and from far out came the first muffled angry roar and voice of a still greater crowd than any that had gathered, and fled from the occasion. No one knew whether it spoke its anger for the shedding of innocent blood in the past and the present family of man, or whether it resented the defeat of a mob, and the self-surrender of Hassan, and the fire of his prayer for release from the rotten crime and conspiracy of death.

The spirit of the wind that had died blew. The misty rain cleared, and guns appeared to explode in a new salute and furnace. A cloud of dense smoke rose from the uppermost level of the pyre which had been dampened by the early rains. It rose into the football of the sun, trembling in a dark ecstatic fall and wave.

Beti and Rajah returned to the savannahs, and the two brothers – Mohammed and Kaiser – thought of putting their heads together now that Hassan was gone. The time was ripe for review. They had set aside money to buy the machinery Rajah needed in the ricefields. Their commerce on the road – the bus and the gasolene station and pump – was prospering. It added up to a profit on paper. The fact was, however, their gains had been eaten and swallowed, and they had incurred new debts.

Mohammed had deposited a large sum on the frame of his overseer's mansion, and he hoped to move it to his site and to rebuild soon.

Kaiser had extended his station and started a hardware shop behind.

Hassan's sudden death, and the fulfilment of the ancestral

mound and fiery epitaph, had drained away another large sum.

The promised land of plenteous return stood in view before them but a still greater sacrifice had to be endured before they would free themselves of bondage.

Mohammed was a superstitious man, and from the time of Muhra's miscarriage he had become a confirmed victim of a partial system – half material hope, half spiritual despair – composed of a guilt nothing could shake away, and the difficulty in overcoming the context of appearance around him.

The miscarriage of Muhra's last child killed his motive for advance, though his life's ambition for wealth and prosperity seemed unaffected, and he continued to make daring and feverish plunges and speculations.

Muhra had fallen headlong down the steps of the cottage and when they raised her up she was lifeless. She opened her eyes nevertheless and said: "Mohammed you see how your black crime fall 'pon me head? O God I in pain and I done lose you boy-picnie."

Mohammed cried like a child, knowing how helpless and impotent he was to restore life. Muhra had to be taken to hospital where she lay ill for months. It was a more serious fall and blow than they had first understood and Mohammed had had to borrow to meet both rum-shop and doctor's bills. He began to drink like a fiend, and he confided everything to Kaiser, who had heard it all from his lips half a dozen times already.

"A curse there 'pon we Kaiser," Mohammed said. His eyes were like red fire. "Is who next?"

"If you don't look out going to be your turn, Mohammed. You drinking too hard and you can't stop dwelling in the past." Kaiser spoke warningly and he looked sad. "Thank God the two of we still there, and you still got three girl-picnie, and the future can always be bright. We got fortune coming to we, I know."

"You right as rain, Kaiser." Mohammed felt a dryness on his lips. "Let we get a big bottle and talk things over good and proper."

"I suppose so," Kaiser said, but his consent was unhappy and disapproving. "Is good money you throwing 'way all the time," he spoke warningly again.

As they made their way to the rum-shop, Kaiser found himself experiencing, for the first time, a positive dislike of Mohammed. The feeling rose upon him with so much force that he was startled. It amounted almost to a wave of hate, and it was alarming. Why? Why? Here was a man he had always accepted as the leader of his family, even during his father's lifetime, and whom he had genuinely loved as a brother and twin. Why this fullness so startling and so terrible, like a ripe fruit contradicting the harmonious rooted memories of the past?

Some of it sprang from Mohammed's persistent and heavy withdrawals from their mutual gains in business. Kaiser knew that if he could sever the business connection now, he would begin to retain lasting profits for himself alone and his bank balance would grow by leaps and bounds. Mohammed had become a cancer in the body politic, whatever that signified. It was an expression he had picked up in the newspapers that day while engaged in his painful deciphering of badly proofed and written material. Nothing that he harvested and gained was the reporter's intention or fault. It was the miracle of a raw schooling and where the blame or praise truly lay was beyond a critical comprehension. The time was violently right to break from Mohammed he saw and read, and to change their future relationship and life, and while Kaiser realized that the economic writing and reason was a powerful mad incentive, and the burden of carrying Mohammed was growing beyond his endurance, he was still not satisfied that these conditions alone accounted for the unexpected wave of hate that had engulfed him.

He was actually glad to feel the sudden emotional tide

beginning to retire and subside, almost bringing a return of
the old ground of fellowship, and leaving him free to ponder
– with detachment almost – the bitter invasion and attack he
had known from an incalculable and obscure source.

For a couple of moments at least he had hated in all
bitterness the man he had always loved. It would be idle to
deny that now, even if the old establishment of trust had
come back. The truth was, nothing could be the same
between them again.

The rum-shop stood where the village started on the bank
of the river. They entered the swinging doors to be greeted by
the blast and hush of many voices. The lull lasted for a few
seconds while everyone turned and stared, taken in the
flashbulb of their own consternation and astonishment. It was
rare that they revealed themselves like this, but the two
brothers had entered so unexpectedly, without a warning
voice and view coming across the bridge over the river, that
nobody in the rum-shop had had time to compose the casual
studied greeting.

They stood against the counter, and in knots and lines
against the wall, or sitting at table, glass in hand. The strong
smell of Demerara rum and of high wines was in the air, and
everyone was still and transported into creatures who had
been embalmed and preserved in a timeless flash.

Kaiser and Mohammed stopped too, seeing the reflections
in the mirror that stretched behind the long counter, amidst
variegated spirits and paraphernalia.

They knew intuitively – as if in response to a lightning
greeting – what this focus and exposure signified in every
remote shade and corner. They were the acknowledged
representatives of a dark deed in the region and the estate and
the world. Kaiser had learnt the expressive cue as a boy of
twelve when the Allamans – a family of ambiguous Hindu
and Moslem and African descent – had borne the role and
part that was now his and Mohammed's. He recalled seeing
them often the centre of a drama of curiosity and longing and

wonder such as this. They were the husbandmen of the time whose deed was whispered about, and dreamed of, by every man and woman and child. They were known to be the true hot-blooded and violent folk. They had *killed*, killed the heir, it was rumoured, in a remote part of the estate, and left him hanging from a tree in such a way as to resemble suicide. Even the police had been thwarted, for the Allamans were legendary cattle barons and landowners far above the law. It was a tale, Kaiser knew, but real as anything, real as he was and Mohammed.

The extraordinary feeling and admiration the world knew for the family of the dark deed was something no one could explain in simple terms. It had been so, generation after generation, a recurring myth and a particular fable that fired the land and exposed the features of reflection and subversion. It was the naked recognition of themselves, and the stripping away of an ancient veil and masquerade in the light of a spirit – too technical for understanding – that shone and entered the darkest chamber of hope and regeneration they admired because it contained themselves in their abortive incestuous greatness and fascination and treachery.

The flash of recognition exploded in a cork from a bottle. The harsh voices resumed their current and pitch. Mohammed and Kaiser made their way to the bar amidst the crowd's animation that grew more boisterous than ever in an attempt to deny their startled witness of the new arrivals.

It was market noon and a Friday in the bargain, and this was responsible for the large number ostensibly selling and purchasing livestock and paddy. Naked feet padded on the floor, and hands were raised in demonstration and preliminary debate that were unnecessarily fierce for matters that needed the simplest open-air bargain and negotiation.

Kaiser felt all this and it surprised him, because he had never seen the people in this fierce inner light and contradiction before. He had been blind to their alarming incongruity and had accepted an inborn and humourless condition of things. Now, it dawned on him, he was losing his fixed unreflective submersion and participation in all. Perhaps it had been crumbling for a long time without his knowing. Remember he had been consuming less and less, a ghostly drop here and there, and losing a crude appetite, while retaining a cold-water face and irrational sobriety in the hottest drinking hours when everyone bought and bargained. Whether this change, from absence of reflection to alien presence and thought, had been indeed evolving secretly all the while, was a matter for difficult speculation and argument. The actual and crucial event to reckon with was a full awareness of the stages of private distinction he now saw, and public divorce he experienced. It might have started with the question of violent economic hate he had known for Mohammed half an hour ago, turning into a drawn twine and thread of dreaming spirit, a tension and distance coiling within himself and stretching into ordinary nature. He tried to dismiss it and explain it as a laughable distress and tiredness coming from a long hard walk under the hot riddling sun, followed by an abrupt entry into a negative dark room and unexpected visionary sign. He was turning into an old wandering man, Kaiser said wryly to himself. He must watch the sun. He was getting too nervous and jumpy, he warned himself. His shoulders contracted involuntarily – as if he cowered in response to this judgment he had made – and his blood flushed like fireworks within him starting on the nape of his neck and processing down his back and spine.

"Ghost walking over me grave," he rebuked his pointless and helpless extravagance.

"A big bottle of blue label," Mohammed called. "You say something Kaiser?"

"No, nothing. Just thinking Ah could do with a seat. We can't talk easy in this crowd."

Mohammed signalled to the barman, who pointed to room No. 3. They entered a small room overlooking the river.

173

"Ah don't feel too good today," Kaiser said musingly and apologetically. "Ah must be catching a cold or something."

Mohammed gave a great thump on the wall, and the barman came running, setting before them, on a round table, a bottle of rum, two glasses and a bowl of ice.

"Tek a drink," Mohammed prompted. "You going feel miles better."

"Ah getting old before me time and Ah seeing things Ah would like to get to the bottom of," Kaiser laughed with a secret unhappy jeer.

"You hiding youself in a shell like a hermit," Mohammed lectured, "and all you aiming at is working and making a pile of money. Take a care, Kaiser, tek a care. You know you could turn into a devil like Ram, and a stinking no-good carcass of a money-lender? O God you would hate youself then. What I believe is, you eating you heart out for an impossible woman. I seeing you in a way you don't suspect." Mohammed's red eyes had suddenly turned keen like a hawk diving on to the stream outside. He had these flashes of old-time command and discernment. "Ah been observing how you changing, Kaiser. Since that school-lady" – he spoke with contempt – "whom you did want for a wife (Ah always disbelieve in schooling girl-picnie, let them learn the hard way, I say), run away two year ago – bringing she daddy down into the grave, remember? – you start pining too. Is two year ago it happened nah?" Mohammed lost his commanding vision and the smoking fire returned: "O Christ, was 'bout the same time Muhra miscarry. Me brain and memory getting addled. Is a true curse fall upon we-all, Kaiser, since we half-brother. . . ."

"Stop," Kaiser spoke harshly. He was disgusted with Mohammed's repetitious logic. "Stop your rot. If you live to a hundred, Mohammed, I don't believe you can begin to see how some *body* like they born seeking for *mind*." He dwelt on his words a little. "Is the *place* is curse, if you want to know, and you got to keep on talking 'bout people curse. The *place* is curse and poison strangling you with a feeling you is no good."

"Strangling who?"

"She come to believe she was doomed to live with a pack of pure demon . . ." his voice was searching to mock Mohammed.

"You going off you head or what? Who you calling demon . . . ?"

". . . all she life . . ." Kaiser cried tauntingly.

"Is a curse I say falling upon every man jack of us since. . . ." Mohammed was solemn and vehement.

"Better to run away with a real dreadful beggar who can teach she what she never see . . ." Kaiser cried, and his tone rang ominously as if it declared the truth of the future.

"You really believe a starving man can teach anybody? . . . If one of me girl-picnie dare. . . ."

"Who is me to say no? Is not just a simple *school* she gone to. We half-brother teach we a thing or two that last till now, if you got to see this curse all the living way. . . ."

Mohammed protested violently and clumsily: "She ain't find a murderation of a death yet . . . but she looking for it. . . . If one of me girl-picnie dare to pick up a bastard and a vagabond. . . ."

"She *living*, whether you want to murder she or no," Kaiser cried in a voice unlike his own. "And you *dead*, even if you looking for she now to take she life and mine. Is too late. And I don't want to hear no ignorant threat and reminder from you. . . ." He had forgotten himself, living no longer in the loyal conspiratorial past but in the ubiquitous shoe and trespass of the future that had started to happen to him that day.

"You beside youself, Kaiser. Is me, Mohammed, you talking to. You know how I always trying for all-of-we-family-good? I sorry if I say anything I don't mean. . . ."

"Is an ignorant estate you can't learn to *see*, Mohammed," Kaiser had begun to recover himself. "You can only anchor youself and talk 'bout curse and responsibility, while other

175

body borning to learn to see how you really blocking them passport and free way. . . ." His uncanny spirit melted all of a sudden, and his heart grew lighter and clearer than he had ever dreamed. He laughed boisterously, relinquishing, in twinkling finality, the wild insane voices that came from without. He felt himself on the threshold of the darkest and clearest purgation and simplicity in the complicated bargain and reminder of death and love.

"Maybe Ah wrong to trouble you, Mohammed. You right to upbraid me. Ah destined to chase down me fine lady to the end of the earth or else I got to stay chain-up for good." He spoke to provoke and stir his brother again but with a curious return of the oldest affection. "I going bring she back for you to punish if you dare." His voice rang with the faintest foreboding and warning.

He had had only one drink so far, he reflected, but the effect had been to make him light-headed in a way that had not happened for a couple of years. It was an empty stomach, and the fact that he had not eaten for hours, he said.

The sun was blazing on the river, and a rice punt had just tied up alongside the crude stelling near the bridge. The name RAM painted on the bow drew Kaiser's attention. The letters shook in the heat of the glaring river, and he was about to point to the raft of coincidence when Mohammed said:

"Is what on earth you want *me* to give you, Kaiser, to stop you from throwing you life away?" His face was querulous and despotic and uneasy. "We been talking at cross purpose all the time. You is me only brother and you get so thin, so fading and scornful-like all of a sudden today, and still so pressing like a devil. Is money you really got in mind to squeeze from me? You want me to give you and the devil everything?"

Mohammed was growing drunk. Kaiser could not recollect that he had pressed him for anything. In fact he had not raised the question of an economic divorce and settlement yet. It was always this way, after a few drinks, he knew, feeling ashamed of himself too, for being as light-headed as Mohammed was. Mohammed wanted to surrender every-thing – without being asked – and bind himself in the bargain, in his intoxicated fear of a future judge and reflection of all, haunting him and pursuing him in every surreptitious demand. Kaiser's eyes started to close against his will, until he was unable to tell whether it was Mohammed who dreamed of the past and the future, or whether it was he, or whether it was Ram whose name swam within the river like torn idle scraps of waste paper.

IX

Kaiser woke; Mohammed was still sprawled, face-downwards, on the table. His black, greying hair was ruffled and his skull peeped through the thinning mass. All the fire was burning out of him, Kaiser thought, with momentary compassion, as he dwelt upon the dull sleeping figure. Their partnership and life together had ended. He rose stealthily, knowing he was abandoning not only a long-standing leader and brother, but an intimate history and shell.

He was more light-headed than ever, as if he had partaken of the rarest wine, and was walking on air. The world was in a state of late afternoon, time had stopped, and feeling was departing. The sun had passed behind a grey mass of ancient twilight and cloud, whose permanent sleep had long ago been broken and shattered, but whose anchor and spell still deceived even the dead.

In truth it was like an olden mystery to know the real hour and time. It might have been morning, and yet again evening: the morning after the most trying bargain of the night before, or the afternoon after the fever of the day was over.

The unearthly hour made one dwell upon the freedom of a soul, pacing heaven, and sketching the fine branches of a delicate tree against the leaden sky with inky feet.

One felt that one had relinquished everything for nothing, and in asking alms of no one and nothing had drawn everything upon the genius of space and within the muse of the mind. It was a floating thought that only the most light-headed beggar could entertain, and Kaiser dreamt himself light and fastidious as rarefied air, though an ignorant dark feather and beggarly groom of a man.

178

There were two other light reflective beggars waiting for him outside the swinging door. They knew each other at once and began making apologies for their old conspiracy and state. The fact was, they were still smarting and conscious of themselves in their pinching material shell an impossible hour ago, or perhaps a fluid single moment it was, between now and then, when Kaiser's head had fallen upon the table before him, snapping its thread of time and desire, and sealing its duplicate death. He was the second brother to go, as quickly and abruptly as the first, who had mounted an epitaph of fire. He drew his fabulous corollary and signature in branches and fingers of charcoal, and feet of cloud and ink.

One could not help being drawn to the beggars in this irresponsible state. An hour ago one would have passed them without a word as though ages lay between one's self and them; now one's self had miraculously become the same. Kaiser shrugged his shoulders at the alien absurd thought, laughing soundlessly when he saw his feet were all black with ink, and he had sketched two curious faces on the ground, whom he addressed like a child playing a foreign ethnological game.

The first of the two smoking beggars was a Hindu; he wore dirty flowing lines, and this attire, falling away from a vague, mooning, calf-like face, established a ghostly resemblance to Hassan. It was vague indeed, and remote, and yet psychological and unmistakable. The second beggarly man, a negro, also reminded one of a well-known acquaintance, such as one would stumble upon in a port of exile. It was the ghostly figure of Kaiser, transformed and finished beyond recognition, and yet not to be forgotten, the brow a heavy knob, and the eyes utterly dark. The cheeks were hollow as his, Kaiser felt, looking in a fantastic cloudy mirror and seeing himself burnt black by the mystery of the sun.

The Hindu spoke in a frantic impoverished dialect. The negro had a few words of formal English which he employed to suppress a terrible longing and need.

179

They leaned against the wall that appeared to float with them on their insubstantial back, wondering how they could still summon an obscure passer-by for the help they were too proud and too spiritualized to ask.

One felt it was criminal and wrong to let them feel one did not understand anything in their burning famished greeting and their sorrowful cry, that struck one to the heart. The Hindu beggar was clearly wrapped up in the smoking words he recited like a parrot, though he no longer truly required anything he asked for, to be translated, and said. It was too late, and one began to wonder whether in his youth he had been hungry to raise a passage from Demerara, that would take him back to Mother India, and this was now the voice of babbling ancient desire. He was fast approaching incommunicability.

The unearthly delicate writing on the sky acquired a new startling genius and hue in a spurt of unquenchable reflection that rose from the burning spirit and building. No one knew how the fire had started, whether it was a drunken brawl or a smoker's end and match. The fact was the wooden rum-shop was ablaze when Mohammed woke raving, choking like a madman, his eyes filling and smarting. A moment of horror passed before he saw that Kaiser had slipped and crumpled into a ball at his feet.

He tried to lift and catch him but a sudden explosion shook the walls and the floor. He was flung against the weak shell of the shop; an incredible section came loose, and sailed away like a burning raft in the wind.

He knew when it struck the river, and he felt himself submerge with it; he rose, clinging to a spar, like one incipient spectator and universal flame of identity.

Kaiser had been pinned and trapped beneath a wall of the burning building, and his charcoal death was the duplicate of Hassan's. He felt this in a puff of smoke like a cigarette-end burning his lips. He remembered rising before Mohammed

180

did, and stumbling to the door to shout to the barman for help, when a wave of smoke struck him as if it came from the mirror on the wall. It filled the room so that Kaiser thought his head was on fire. An uproar was reigning outside. He collapsed. And yet it seemed to him he had risen after all and was walking in blackening trousers and feet. He was light and floating in the sky of the mirror that had grown veined like a tree.

Someone was trying to address him and to lift him higher still, someone he knew. The voice raved and raged and Kaiser wondered what all the fuss was about. He knew he wanted nothing from anyone. He was not a beggar. He had slept a little too long, that was the truth. There was nothing in the wide world he wanted save his freedom, the freedom to die when and where he pleased, and to love whom and what he wished.

There was an explosion that threw him inwards and he recognized the man before him at last. It was Hassan: a changed, smoking Hassan, Kaiser saw. Hassan knew him too.

Hassan had just got the obstinate idea in his burning head that he wanted to return to India to circulate his ashes on mother-soil.

Kaiser protested. If he returned he would be looked upon as an outcast and an untouchable ghost. What language had he save the darkest and frailest outline of an ancient style and tongue? Not a blasted thing more. Remember too how much he had forgotten, Kaiser scolded him. The ceremonies and sacraments he fitfully observed were not a patch on the real thing. It was a dim hope, dimmer than their father's childhood and adolescence.

No, Kaiser said, I shall become a richer man than you. I am giving up rice and sugar for gold and diamonds. I can pass as a negro pork-knocker and I shall take a passage to the goldfields of Cuyuni and Mazaruni. I shall steal into Venezuela, and swim across oil.

Kaiser had heard Venezuela was rich. He had driven a German mining engineer from Berbice to Georgetown a year ago. He remembered asking ten dollars for the trip and the man requesting a receipt. It was a voucher to remind him to recover from his company. Kaiser had signed his name Kaiser, as usual. The man had smiled. I thought you were *Kayser*, he said, but I see you have written *Kiser*, K-a-i-s-e-r.

I am *Kayser*, Kaiser replied stubbornly.

You sign with the name of an emperor, the man said with a sweeping delighted smile.

Yes, Kaiser said proudly. I have heard of black emperors whose signature alone will rule the world.

The man looked startled and mystified, and a little distressed by the ignorant reply.

God forbid, the man said, that you should think of him in that light. Whatever may have happened since, in Germany, the Kaiser himself was a good man.

It was Kaiser's turn now to be heartily dumbfounded and confused.

The engineer lit a long American cigarette, offering the box absent-mindedly at the same time, and to Kaiser's astonishment began a long complicated lecture on economics, imperialism, fascism, communism, neutralism, and a great many other foreign concerns, as if these matters were vital business to an "untouchable" emperor.

"No, is foolish to think of that. Going back to India," Kaiser spoke to himself. "You have no language, you have no custom."

Hassan answered and declared he was a follower of Siva and Vishnu. He had read with glimmering enthusiasm of the avatars and descent of the god, but the ultimate intention of all was the ascetic Gautama.

Kaiser moistened his burning lips, searching for the ruling love and parable in the nature of words. A tree was a word, a river was a word, a man was a word: yet they were – all three – as imperishable and wordless as all substance, which is

182

compounded of fire and reflection, smoke and husk. He recalled the rare drop of precious liquor he had swallowed that day, making him light as a feather. It was the elixir of blood in the yoke of the egg and the sun. The warmth drew him to desire to counsel Hassan. There was an esoteric yearning for the mother's shell and womb, and there was a technical longing for the mined and subject earth. It was this secret and this technical understanding, whose marriage could make life new and desirable again.

There is a science, Kaiser said, which is in every true lover's thought, that can make a man crack his egg and fly. He had become a light-hearted, intoxicated soul.

Hassan looked contemptuous. He no longer wished to soil himself with self-destructive instruments and tools and machines like a Christian barbarian, he said. Bad enough to have had to make one's murderous living that way. But to accept it as an eternal paradisaical pastime was a foul business. Look at Ram. *There* was the dreadful plague of love and freedom and science on earth, the money-lending, acquisitive devil. One could never pass beyond that high flood of greed and obstruction one most feared and loved in all the world. It was too deeply ingrained to be overcome. Better to return to a sacred place and abstain from life altogether. Only the empty one, who no longer dreamt and sketched the vaguest desire, could kill the devil.

Time will teach us to undermine every obstacle, Kaiser said, like an obdurate child still playing in a kingdom he had a long way to go to begin to learn to build.

The fire died at last in the fable of Mohammed's drunken heart. It had burned long past sunset into midnight, scorching the trees and the ground. One fatal casualty alone had occurred. Mohammed was unable to look at it. He learnt, as he had dreaded, that it was his brother, to save whose life he would have given his own.

BOOK THREE

SECOND BIRTH

For the spent hurricane the air provides
As fierce a successor, the tide retreats
But to return out of its hiding-place
In the great deep; all things have second birth:
The earthquake is not satisfied at once.

William Blake

. . . the dayspring from on high hath visited us.

Luke 1 : 78

X

Rajah believed in nothing save filling his belly. Food was the beginning and the end of life. Whatever he had, he could never have enough to satisfy a gnawing anxiety and appetite. He suffered, as a child, he always remembered, from hookworm; and his empty devouring insides drove him to steal from his father to eat – in terror of being beaten if found out – though he knew that his parents would starve to provide him with a foul plate and scrap. He could not help stealing, however, as though in so doing he was destroying himself as a witness of their voluntary sacrifice. And he was also ensuring for himself the ability to live with a dark anxiety and terror. To steal was to murder all sentiment and vision in order to survive.

Rajah himself did not understand this condition so clearly, and this was responsible for a blind frustration and anguish, in which he appeared to be constantly milling himself, and thereafter reconstituting the unrecognizable features of his heart.

His father – the oldest brother – had always remained desperately poor, while Mohammed's father – the youngest brother – had managed to save and acquire a large estate. Whom he had robbed and killed in the process, God knows! Rajah was meditating, with the old milling sense of hate, over an enormous saucepan of rice, from which he ate spasmodically, and greedily, with his hand.

It was the middle of the day and he rested his oxen. All morning they had been mashing and separating paddy, by making a steady monotonous circuit, on the baking-hard ground, around a central guide and pole.

Rajah squinted at the sky with a dark look, where it shone clear like burning metal. He needed another fortnight in which to finish all the stages of harvesting. If only the sun would hold out. It was rain he dreaded at this time. At another time it was rain again – the same pitiless rain falling short of flood – he would desire most of all for his crops.

The savannahs were a white and blazing fire, circulating like a breathless sultry blast of unchanging wind across the dry earth and the brown cropped fields. One felt the sun burning on one's skin, uninterruptedly, relentlessly, as though it contained a violent storm and climax.

Rajah could have shortened his harvest and labour – as some of the neighbouring farmers had done – by using a machine, instead of the ancient steps with the feet of oxen. But the estate had only been able to afford, so far, a choice of machines. And Rajah had taken a tractor to plant seed and plough the ground. He had got it the very year Kaiser had died. It was an amazing bladed contrivance, looking like a spider and a butterfly rolled into one, or like an Indian fetish with many sprouting hands, and Rajah felt that here he had a greater labour-saving device than any other. Mohammed had said in five years he hoped to supply him with another emblematic cross to harvest and to reap, and then he would have complete ease the entire year round. There were many difficulties and expenses, he had said, and the returns had not been good of late, though he knew Rajah worked hard. The cost of irrigation had risen. They had had to rehabilitate the old drainage, and all these expenses had eaten into the new price their rice was now fetching, like a belated prize after the brutal years. At any rate they could afford to fill their paper bellies at last even if the profits written there had less material weight than they appeared to signify and carry.

Rajah was bitter. He felt he had been treated badly in not gaining all the machinery he needed. Mohammed was becoming notorious as a poor manager and accountant, and he (Rajah) had endured privation and hunger too long, and no promise could erase the brand and the scar of a flaming poverty. He was an extension of his own oxen, and that was all, while Mohammed had turned into an inconsiderate drunkard and a fiend and landowner. Blast him!

His grandchildren, perhaps, Rajah grumbled, might live in a different self, or his grandchildren's children. They would have little reckoning of the womb and the curse from which they had sprung to life, and of the vast relative dreaming canvas in which they found themselves, pinpointed and cocksure like stars, as though destiny had made the past and the future theirs all right. Rajah had finished the last handful of rice, and his eyes dozed a little, blind with the sun, as he crouched, hardly knowing himself and his dark alien figure and thought.

He forced his eyes open. Far away a frail ominous smoke and dust of cloud waved at him on the horizon. The ground was flat and one could see into the distance. Rajah was staring topside unseeingly where the fields, and the backs of scattered beasts and cattle stretched.

Behind him the view looked far again until one saw a black bush, almost indiscernible and one with the landscape, across the blazing land. It was only one's knowledge, and a frond, and a feather, sticking up awry into the low distant sky, that told *there* was the coconut depth leading to the public road far away, Rajah dreamed, where Mohammed's cottage was, and where he had started building his dark, mournful, blind mansion.

A man came upon Rajah, as he dozed in the noonday sun, and stood like a shadow over him. He knew someone was there but it was as if – to save his life – he could not open his eye. He recognized Ram. In the corner of his mind's eye he saw the hard grey toenails, and trousers rolled up to the shin. Rajah nodded. The shadow close to him was short and squat and like a ball. Rajah had been conscious of this visitor, and shadow, for some months now in his life, veiling and encircling the world. It was an obsession and fear he endeavoured to make short work of, and to slay quick and soon in his mind, like the childish conspirator and terror he had always been able to call upon, fearfully, on every occasion, and to banish afterwards. Now the unpalatable truth was, he no longer knew how to cast away his fault, as in his callow youth. It was learning to confront him and consume him. Rajah shook himself with mature scorn but his revelation and eye still remained bandaged and closed where the filthy head-band he had tied voluminously around his head had slipped and fallen.

Indeed Rajah was more deeply troubled than he understood by this helpless fantasy. It moved in a dimension he could never hope to discern in this life, and it served to complicate the ordinary response and dismissal he should have been able to serve Ram.

Ram was a man of about his own age; they had grown up as neighbours and there was no reason why he should feel subordinate and bound to him. It was true Ram was the devil. God knows how he had extended his grip far and wide. Many a strong, independent man had grown into his victim, losing lock, stock and barrel over the years. Why, this was the case with his cousin. No one in the wide world perceived how Mohammed – in spite of every advantage he had inherited and established – had fallen deep into Ram's clutches. Rajah doubted whether it would have happened to Hassan and Kaiser if they had lived. But then, there it was. Their removal had ideally stimulated Ram's ascendancy and Mohammed's decline. It was a remarkable inverse progression. Mohammed was a fool. Nevertheless Rajah had been affected by the foolishness, and he too had become conscious of Ram as a thief who was able to offer him – in robbing him – what he wanted.

Ram was turning into someone and something potent and gifted and strong, like the rotting grain and seed that springs in the planted shadow of the earth.

Rajah scorned himself for this sleeping helplessness and fear. He was a coward to crouch in this idleness and this subjection when there was work to be done. He should face the weakness and procrastination that kept him chained to his daily task, like a man idling and brooding on the millennium.

Ram had his eye on Beti (Rajah confessed this fact to himself at last). Was there anything in the world to stop him from arising and chasing the blackest seduction away, as well as the devil of comfort that had become the object of his life? Rajah dreamed he was chained to the fantastic ball at his feet, and that his desire now was to hold it and embrace it for ever.

He saw now that he had not succeeded in banishing the shadow of temptation, for good and all, the previous day and night, when he had stooped before it, like a slave upon an ubiquitous pot and stone. It had started around this self-same hour of noon and crisis, when Ram had sent a messenger to say he would give Rajah all the machines he wanted if he would let him have Beti, his daughter, a maiden of fifteen years, the very coming night, and afterwards he would marry her. If he took her now into his home Ram confided (speaking in the corner of Rajah's weary, defeated eye), he would be able to control her and discipline her in the proper style, something that every father must, in all conscience, desire for a daughter.

Rajah himself had taken Beti's mother to wife when she was Beti's age, remember? Rajah remembered, yes, he had been a young man of twenty-four then. But now both he and Ram were old crabbed rice-men, forty-odd years old (with the feeling they were eighty in them). Rajah could not help being troubled and upset by Ram's proposal, and when he dwelt upon all these circumstances, the rice turned in the grave of his stomach in revulsion and acid protest.

The man who had come – on behalf of Ram – to bargain with Rajah in the dark ball and womb of the sun plotted how to overcome these scruples and objections. He wore a goatee beard, one of those straggling dry tufts – looking like burnt grass on baked ground – old men sometimes cultivate like a mask for childhood, as they limp and hop with bent back. They adopt a third leg and horn and stick, to lean upon, and hop upon, and they wreathe themselves in a billowing, single, enormous napkin, tied around them expertly, in a coil

191

and twist, from neck to knee. It was the habit the old indentured Demerara Indians wore, limping their way, half-priest, half-beggar, across the savannahs and the land. No one knew where they were going, or where they had come from, and what their ambiguous mission was, whether it was death or whether it was a new symbolic birth and life. They had nothing to do except beg and hop and leap until in exhaustion they tumbled and fell to the ground, drawing their knee to their chin in a ball.

Rajah felt he had been swathed and overpowered in this fascinating womb and beggar who combined age and infancy and the holy prostitution of self. One lost the power to refuse anything to anyone so dedicated, who begged to be allowed to convert himself into a miraculous child in the midst of a world of misery and miscarriage and abortion.

The old messenger had at his fingertips the chart of Beti's history, and he was able to make Rajah see that on no account should he stand in his daughter's way to gain for herself a better and more comfortable fate, and chance for survival than her mother had had. This was a strong point that weighed heavily with Rajah. Beti's mother had died an old woman at thirty after the fifth and fatal miscarriage she had had.

Beti was born after three or four years of the marriage, a tiny infant, underweight and inscrutable-looking, and no one expected her to live. Her mother had had a desperate time, and Rajah had been told there was something wrong and she must never carry a child again. Rajah managed to avert the nightmare and fatal eventuality for a long time. Beti was eleven when her mother died. Rajah saw he had been stupid in not having a permanent outside woman, as this might have saved his wife's life.

Beti's mother had brought him a poor dowry, Rajah reminded himself sourly, and he too had little to offer that would attract young and handsome rice suitors to his daughter.

If he gave Beti to a hard-backed old man like Ram he would be doing the best thing after all. Ram would treasure a virgin of fifteen years like a rare prize. And after all, what great harm could he do her? In fact it might be well within his limits and capacity to leave her alone to a large extent, and save her from abortion and pain and cruel misadventure. The old crumpled messenger chuckled with a glee that made Rajah shudder with scorn and fear of himself as if a dark blowing wind had struck his spine, and set his teeth on edge.

He tried to rouse himself not to make any fateful promise – before it grew late – and to resist any further crafty overture but he was bound and helpless. Yes, he would see and talk with Ram at nightfall, he said to the old man.

Beti met him at the door, on his return home, telling him how a strange labourer had called in search of work, prophesying an early break in the dry weather, and willing to help Rajah complete his mashing and his harvest. Beti spoke in a puzzled haunted way, as if there was something odd resting on her mind. But Rajah brushed her seeming childishness aside. There was something, he said mildly, which he had to tell his daughter that self-same night, that would put her in a joyous adult mood and position where she would no longer have to dwell in fear of the rain and the sun and the labour of difficulty.

He told her not to worry, he would boil the evening rice. He expected a visitor. Beti had already put the pot on the fire where it blazed like a cooking stone and shadow, and Rajah took over from her, crouching and stooping on the ground in the age-old style.

The knuckles of Ram rapped the door at last. Beti opened. At first Rajah saw no one but the wind. His eyes were blind with the cooking fire and the shadow of the sun. And then he thought he distinguished the eyes of stars in the night.

"Come in," he said uncertainly. "Ah expecting you. Come in."

"Is the same man that been this afternoon me daddy," Beti cried curiously. "Look at he good. You know is who?" She spoke involuntarily recalling a childhood memory of a man walking and watering the dusty road early one morning when Mohammed's father had died, and her other "uncles" Kaiser and Hassan were alive, and they had conspired evilly together to bind someone whose ghostly name she had not plainly heard. The smoke and the dust of memory faded for good on hearing her father give a wild traumatic cry. It left her with a sense of blank pregnant freedom combined with dread.

Rajah's eyes had grown clearer at last. He remained stooping and still, unable to believe what he saw, until he was galvanized into action. The pot spoon flew from his hand, striking the forehead of the sky and burning a flashing place between two stars and eyes.

"Get out. Get out," he raved. "Ah don't want Ram no more. Get out. Ah don't want the devil no more. He want me to put the noose 'round me own daughter neck."

"Is not Mr Ram," Beti cried, in confusion. She was shocked by her father's terrible inhospitality, and the figure she had transposed into someone unborn she knew, fled into the night, and turned into a lightning companion and omen.

Rajah woke with a start to find the ball of noonday shadow had rolled away from beneath him. He had hardly slept for half an hour but a change had occurred from noon to night. A great black cow was swimming across the sun followed by a blacker flock still, and by a shepherd with his crook heralding the storm of a lifetime. Rajah groaned, realizing he stood in danger of losing a heavy part of his harvest. He had idled and dreamed too long over the past month until there had come the dramatic break in the weather. His oxen looked as wilted and weary and old as he was, and the dry grass appeared tired too, like the grey dusty earth. All individual shadow had disappeared save the flat reflection from the downcast sky between the sombre weathering movement and sculpture of cattle.

The heavens changed again, and grew lighter into a flowering incipient reflection that one sees sometimes on a very dark night in the direction of Georgetown, where the night-lights of Demerara lie, as one wanders over the savannahs, miles and miles away from nowhere. The distance had blossomed into a spectacle far greater than this, however, or any that one could dream of, a kind of crimson whiteness and spirit-fire and blush. This changed once again quickly, pursuing a secret rule, and turning into rolling features of molasses, and into faint shivering cracks and lightnings followed by thunder and a reverberating breathless clap. There was a moment's hush and stillness and one could hear a beetle walking on the ground. Then the far track of lightnings came closer, without warning, and flew into one's eye, forked and veined and vicious, flashing closer still, blindingly, again and again, and unrolling into a webbed hand and foot like a crumpled flying napkin and sheet, on which the sacred embryonic beasts of the sky crouched. The table of creation began to dislodge itself and to fall with the greatest crash.

Rajah was working in fury and helplessness. He was laying numerous bags over the paddy and upon the heaps that stood around, when his last devouring moment came. He looked up in dazed alarm, like a man in a crucial X-ray that exposed the contents he had consumed and stomached. The pole to which his oxen were tied had split as if pierced by a fork and an arrow. The pieces sprang apart, still hinged to their grain and base, and they snapped together again, half-askew, like lock-jaw in a wooden dreaming instant. There was no pain save this electrification and fracture; Rajah was dead in a flash. He stiffened and fell senseless to the ground.

The rain grew solemnly from the ground up, rather than falling from the clouds down, an enormous inverted theatre and curtain, upon which rose the webbed dreams of bird and beast the sky had unloaded on the lightning earth.

195

Beti had seen her father fall as she came running towards him. The rain grew all around her and when she parted the grey curtain of the sky to approach him, she was conscious only of the gift and feast of freedom from travail and pain he had entertained for her, and of the fracture of a cruel bond within him, so that the dripping cattle stood over their master and were still free to stand and go as they wished. She felt the rain and the sky sheltering him in a land that was nowhere, and yet where she herself wanted to go.

XI

A new rum-shop had been built where the burnt shell had stood. Mohammed met Ram on Friday noon, the vulgar market day of the week. This had been a testing and difficult season, this current year in the savannahs (it was two or three years after Rajah's death), and the crowd that used to come in search of an ambiguous sale or request or bargain had thinned to a trickle. People were saying the atom bomb trials had affected and altered the climate and weather in every continent, reducing a large psychic pool and crowd into a crumbling reflective stream.

Mohammed's hands shook a little after his first couple of drinks, and he could hardly steady his fingers to untie the package of papers he had with him.

At long last he gave Ram the document he had succeeded in finding.

"Yes, you transport in order," Ram said, scanning it carefully. "Ah got to tek this from you now, Mohammed, plus all them pro-note I already got. Is what really eating you, man, that you borrowing so much money? The whole estate going fall in pawn soon." Ram poured himself a drink as he taunted his companion, like a man who knew how to store and measure every trickle of the enormous ageless hate and contempt and fear he felt for everybody. It was just a question of time, he reasoned, before he would accumulate every little weak drop to serve his own ends.

"You got no sympathy," Mohammed said. "All the world know you." He spoke in the whining voice of a broken man, out of whom all the old commanding fire had leaked and gone, so that he retained now merely a savage touchiness and drunken spirit and hangover, that made him boil and grow dangerous on some occasions, though he was capable of little power and ruling strength.

"You got no sympathy," he said again. "Look at the bad luck and trouble me family had."

"What bad luck and trouble?" Ram asked, playing the innocent. "Ah don't know if is the estate you moaning about. But is who fault if the land fall in neglect? I did see that, and to help you Ah send you a good man in Oudin. He come like a blessing 'pon you, this long time, did he not?"

"Ah suppose so," Mohammed said evasively.

"Look it," Ram said. "Don't tell me you not grateful. You dry coconut fetching something in the copra market for the first time. You land looking heaps clearer. And is who else do it but Oudin? Oudin is a real good man. He doing all that for you in a couple of day every week, then he arriving topside after, to labour in *me* rice-land. A diamond of a man. . . ."

"Ah see all of that," Mohammed spoke irritably. "What you don't know, Ram, is since Oudin come, me wife turn invalid. She no good to she-self any more, and she dreaming she life away. Like me. Oudin bring a curse. You know what?" He stared at Ram, intent on unravelling a drunken fate and resemblance and mystery that haunted him wherever he went. "Is like if some kind of thing circulating me." He paused.

"What you mean?" Ram was involved and interested.

"I don't know exactly how to explain. But time itself change since he come. Is like if I starting to grow conscious after a long time, that time itself is a forerunner to something. But Ah learning me lesson so late, is like it is a curse, and things that could have gone smooth now cracking up in haste around me. I so bewilder I can't place nothing no more. What I used to value and what I used not to value overlapping. Two, three, four, face looking at me. Every face so different. I don't know which is private, which is public, which is past, which is future. And yet all is one, understand me?"

"I do," Ram said softly, and almost inaudibly.

"I suppose I is an ignorant man. Ah lose me grip long ago. I wish to God Ah could accept the fact that I changing. Ah feel that I, *me* then, is just a piece of moving furniture, and something else, bigger by far, pushing me about until I don't know whether I standing 'pon me head, me backside, or me foot."

"You drinking too much," Ram cried, wishing to banish the suggestion. "You crazy." He was more deeply troubled by the confession than he cared to admit, and he tried to pull himself away a little in superstitious fear of infection and conversion and paralysis and dread. After all Mohammed had become almost inseparably close to him in being his ideal victim, as Oudin had become another kind of cherished accomplice and cornerstone. There must be some way, he felt, of insuring for himself a foul immunity and a balanced tension, in the empire he wanted to build by exploiting every weak or submissive spirit, whether of apparent science or false belief he knew, and plastering all with a cheap sameness and inferior material façade. For the first time he sensed a potential nightmare in this essential weakness and this deceptive strength, though outwardly he remained as free of the slightest crumbling misgiving as ever.

"And me cattle," Mohammed scratched his chin. There was always this freakish inconsistency and break in his remarks, the inconsistency of an ill-educated, over-burdened psychic mechanism that wanted to disgorge itself of everything at once.

"Yes?" Ram was all ears. He drew close to Mohammed again.

"Ah don't seem to know how many blind head I got in the world."

"Is you fault," Ram stared at him, seeing Oudin in the background. Oudin had done a brilliant trick and work with Mohammed's cattle, not only rounding them up and branding the calves with Ram's mark, but attending to them, taking them to a good watering place, freeing them from the mud and the swamp of the foreshore where they often perished. And Ram, of course, had arranged their ultimate transportation and sale to the butcher at a fine price.

"Is you fault," Ram insisted in mocking solicitude. "You believe any one cowboy can manhandle that herd you got straying wild? They stray until they deading out like flies all around. Cattle need a bunch of cowboy. They want a lil special food and care. Oudin would got to be a god to do all of that and look after everything else too." He spoke craftily.

"Ah know," Mohammed said in a tired voice. "Ah just would like to know is how much blind head Ah got."

"I see a flood after this drought. You know how the weather stay?"

"Flood?"

"Yes, a flood. There ain't been a real high flood since we was boys. And when that come all-you must move all-you blind head to high, light position, plus sending a lot of heavy stock to the butcher. . . ."

"Ah don't want to hear 'bout *butcher*," Mohammed raged.

"You brain going soft or what man? Is you religion or what? This country so mix up, one never know who is Christian, Hindu, Moslem or what, black man, white man's fable or red. Sometimes is all the same it seem but it got a technical difference. Tek me word for it." He smiled his notorious, corrupt simple smile. "Look it. You got to treasure the worst of two worlds. You can pass striking well for Hindu or Mussulman, Mohammed, and them butcher man prepare to pay high price for religious cow and beef marked special with the devil brand. Turn over you stock to *me*." He laughed.

"You make me sick, Ram."

"Yes, Ah know that," Ram said with a glint. "I know too is either the hell of a butcher or the flood going carry you beef away. Them savannah ain't got protection man, unless you reckoning to tek all you got and move to heaven hill. And is a god you need to do that. Oudin slave hard enough for you already: he can't do anything else more than what he do." He spoke in his vein of mockery but in deadly unconscious seriousness as well.

"I never give me technical chances and rights a living chance," Mohammed confessed drunkenly, "and I ready now to give up all I thought I had. Tek all me beef Ram. Is too much of a curse and a slaving trouble." He spoke in mournful tones, divesting himself of everything. "But tek a care", he poked Ram on the chest, "you don't fall in a hole in screwing you head up too far and high above everybody. You sure you able to see and catch everyone and everything in this hell of a world?"

Ram was disconcerted by Mohammed's sudden unpredictable generosity and he could not help staring suspiciously.

"Look it," Mohammed cried. "I is an example of a man who dig he own grave. From that day I can't command time to run me higher estate. O God, Ram, you think the time I kill, killing me in return too fast? You ever drive a motor-car 'pon the dusty road?" He had suddenly raised his voice in asking this freakish inconsistent question.

He swept on again without waiting for a reply. "All me killing time I eating dust 'pon the road, I tell you. I never used to feel the dust so rotten and bad before me daddy dead. That was the beginning of all misfortune. A load of trouble face we family – Hassan, Kaiser, Rajah and me – and we come near to going in the alms-house."

"Alms-house?" Ram said mildly and innocently. "You daddy live long for he time and he dead outside the alms-house. Why must it be a strong man like you got cause to think of the alms-house? And at that time besides. You had no reason to feel poor like a church mouse. You didn't poor then man. He lef' you well off." Ram touched the transport near him. "He lef' you with a big estate." His eye glinted as he spoke.

"You don't understand," Mohammed said. "The next thing Hassan go and dead. . . ."

Ram chuckled. "The laws of nature," he said. "Every man

201

born to dead when he resign heself to die. These is a short-lived resigning people. You and me really strong to be still here." He laughed, and stopped short in the middle. A dark emotional desire, almost akin to the seductive death and resignation of control, had crossed his mind's eye. He was about to blurt out a fearful confession, in Mohammed's inconsistent, infectious way, when he narrowly swallowed and silenced his words. Instead he said: "Ah got something Ah want to discuss with you before Ah go back topside but not right now." He leaned earnestly towards Mohammed with a beating heart full of dread no one ever suspected.

"Yes," Mohammed said, wrapped up in his misery and his grave and his impotency, "Hassan is the law of nature you say. But Kaiser. He could have stood by me. He could have lived. He could have make all the difference. O God." There were tears in his eyes. A maudlin sentiment began to overcome him. "He could have fight all the slaving curse and condition. He could have make the best of two worlds, I know, I dream of he. But no. He burn to charcoal in this very place." Mohammed struck the table. "How you account for such endless misfortune?"

"O nothing," Ram said contemptuously, recovering himself. "Kaiser got power only to *dream* you. But rotten wood is no dream man, matchstick is no dream Ah tell you. This year is 1951. If I start to dream 'bout something borning and changing from next to nothing into something grand thirteen year from now is like if I start seeing everything miraculous and new in the scratch of a match. . . ." He was contemptuously laughing again.

"Why thirteen year?" Mohammed scowled.

"I pick an unlucky number to show you you own superstitious dreaming mind. Might be thirteen hundred year as well. You believe is simple to make this country anew? You can't make something from a dream man. Kaiser like he believe a beggar and a matchstick can change the world. Don't believe is so simple. I know is true, half of Georgetown store and office fill with European director, trained to commerce, did burn down some year ago, like this rum-shop, and it build stronger and better again. . . ."

"How you explain such a miracle happening?" Mohammed cried. "Is them Christian white man alone do it?"

"Ask Kaiser to dream you again," Ram replied with hate and fearful scorn. "The truth is you got to save money like a demon in the baddest, blackest way." His eye glinted.

"You mek to squeeze the last drop of technical blood from mankind, Ram." Mohammed was suddenly crying. It was a pathetic and terrible sight in a man who had once been so vigorous and strong. He had come close to being reduced to the feeling of a pawn, empty and valueless in himself, and yet the ground and source of all musing contending powers, and of every mystique and political and economic programme exercising the minds of others for centuries past.

Ram tapped the wall, sensing the pitiful resignation. "Is wood everywhere," he said, once again assuming his look of foul immunity and his invincible mask.

"What about Rajah?" Mohammed cried drunkenly and helplessly. "You mean is fair, he too got to leave me, and to die like how he die?"

"Look it," Ram said, wondering whether he had now completely succeeded in undermining Mohammed, "a strong man like you is leaning on ghosts. Every year, five, six, seven, eight man deading in the savannah like Rajah from lightning stroke. . . ."

"How you know?" Mohammed cried.

"You don't read the papers?" Ram said. "And further I know." He tapped Mohammed's transport. "I got several keeping like this after they dead."

"I see," Mohammed spoke as if he had been utterly crushed and emptied and silenced at last.

Ram saw the threshold of victory. Still he knew Mohammed was not to be taken entirely lightly. What Ram wished was of such a private and daring nature he felt he must use every precaution. He was not yet sure how Mohammed would react to *this* crude, economic bargain. After all Mohammed had once been a proud, over-mastering man. Ram had overcome him thus far, yes, but he must also learn to distract him from his gloomy preoccupations with the misery of defeat and the succession of death.

It was a new and difficult necessity that had fallen upon him, to dream of peacefully placating anyone, when it had always been so much easier to make an open threatening proposal and demand. Or was it that he had always been involved in an emotional crisis and cowardice he had always scorned? He felt himself drawn to set aside for a moment or two the old calculating, cruel nature by which he knew himself, and which he believed he had successfully divorced from any capacity for faith and sentiment.

"Don't worry yourself unduly, Mohammed. Everybody story always look bad when they start trotting out misfortune. You passing through a terrible lonely trial of strength and you mustn't feel bad if you don't know how to face the whole story." He was searching for compassionate words to soothe Mohammed. "The world is powder keg, man. Why the newspapers say communists penetrating this country from Russia and everybody is to be called 'comrade'." His eye glinted with satisfaction when he saw Mohammed had begun to show interest and to warm up.

"What you mean?"

"I mean you family is not the only one dying out, Mohammed. You is not the only man frighten of being lonely and disinherit in the future. The other day," Ram continued, "look what happen. We talking international story of 'comrades' so let we talk." He saw Mohammed was leaning towards him. "Korea – a country just like this I would say" – he waved his hand generously – "split in half, man. What a mix-up family story. God know who is killing who. You is not the only one in this new family trouble. And what happening to you is *private, plain* AND *ordinary* compared to that." He paused to study his reflective victim, whom he had tried to placate, but Mohammed had sunk once more into curious disinterest and confusion of faith, and it seemed to Ram that he saw Oudin suddenly in the background with a flaming revolutionary brand in his hand. The stupid ruse of gentleness would never work, Ram decided, and he must resort to his trusted accomplice and his secret tactic.

It was on the tip of his tongue to shout, scorning Mohammed and himself in one breath: "I going kidnap you niece, Beti. Forget all me sweet talk. I want a maiden like she." But he decided he would do the kidnapping first and declare his demand and intention afterwards. It astonished him that he could have dreamt of any placating method, or seen any ignorant necessity to bargain with a weakness and susceptibility in himself. There was nothing he need fear, or should ever fear, whatever his desires and crafty intentions were. He had a brilliant slave and trickster in Oudin, to enrich him, utterly obedient and loyal to the end. The misgivings he had experienced were shallow and incomprehensible and unworthy of himself. Oudin would do everything, and Mohammed would surrender everything, without asking anything of value in return. He dismissed a worthless trickle of thought, and the seed of reflection, that fear of the crippled Mohammed was responsible for his inability to make a potent proposal and demand in regard to Beti. Mohammed was known to cling to the last bastion of ruling frightful prestige where his womenfolk were concerned, but why should this discomfit the devil, Ram, venerated for being heartless and unscrupulous?

XII

The morning he abducted Beti, Oudin perceived there were barriers and difficulties ahead of him, through which he must pass as if they were nothing. These relative, ghostly encounters lay between himself and the consummation of his being, like hurdles and erections in the mind of a dying man, who possessed – without his yet seeing it, in his weak state – an undreamt-of corridor of success and achievement before him.

Oudin embarked on this fabulous dying journey, which was to comprise the series of his fateful encounters, three days after the meeting between Ram and Mohammed. And he lived and marched in fear of being killed and shot by the pursuers Mohammed had instantly put on his trail.

He felt in a stumbling intuition of self, that the pattern of a lifetime of migrating from province to province, was now being set, and the coming journey was a crucial rehearsal, a rehearsal that would be repeated once again over thirteen dreaming years of his marriage to Beti. He foresaw in the fire and smoke of fantasy, the running abduction, and the dim uncomprehending married years that would follow, ushering in – on the midnight morning that he died – the far journey outward, into the land that was nowhere. This dark, intuitive thought-sun was both an opportunity and a stumbling-block.

The motive in his abduction of Beti was neither simple obedience to Ram nor his own desire and lust. He had been drawn to Beti, since the first day he arrived on Mohammed's estate, because he was sorry for her, and had seen in her a curious dejection and misery. When Ram had been inspired to seek his help in winning Beti, Oudin felt the stirring spirit of an ancient compassion, and the call to obey a spiritual desire that cancelled out Ram's command. Later the lack of any real lust in taking Beti was clearer to him than ever. He was no longer impelled by the intimacy that drew them together when they were on the run. He was beyond Mohammed's reach. He had cancelled out and overcome Ram. He (Oudin), a slave, was her true husband since it was he who had accomplished all the ingredients of successful flight and romance. And now that this union and triumph were finished he was free to follow the ensuing years in their freedom from the enigma of childlike lust and loveliness alike, and in their sordid unenterprising character he shattered in the end on the dramatic morning of his death. That was the last match he lit of blinding enlightenment and discernment, turning the past into a cruel dream of nothingness, and into a time of ordeal that could have been averted if everyone had seen and foreseen it as Oudin had from the beginning.

It was this foresight and incipient universal compassion, lighting up the near future – as though each dark year ahead was alive with brilliant possibilities – that had fired Oudin into becoming the slave of Ram, and the labourer of Mohammed; and later the husband of Beti, and a father of one child and another still unborn. This combination of effects and ambivalent circumstances was no accident. It made Oudin conscious of the dreadful nature in every compassionate alliance one has to break gradually in order to emerge into one's ruling constructive self.

Oudin crossed the river with Beti and decided to seek guidance from a man who was fishing on the other bank. This was the morning of his death he foresaw and felt, looking back to see if there was any sign of Mohammed and the pursuers, and the morning of a new life, as well, that would convert everyone and everything into their responsible nature. It was a vision of freedom he entertained, and divine hospitality.

Rain had fallen the previous night, a light drizzle that gave an extra gleam to the grass. The sun rose like an enormous, grotesque spider, with the shortest imaginable flaming legs, climbing above the distant trees; the cattle were breathless, watching, and still dreaming, save for an occasional shuddering, flickering of body and tail and head. One wondered if the beasts ever slept and escaped from fly and insect.

The western bank from which Oudin and Beti had crossed was an open savannah – the smoke of the sky mingled with the green of the earth – towards which their long shadows fell and pointed.

The eastern bank, where they now stood, stretched also, but was interrupted by a dark, forested line of trees under the climbing spider of the sun.

The water in the river had been warm after the chilly air of dawn. Oudin left Beti squeezing and drying her torn slip and dress, and walked towards the fisherman on the bank, who stood with a large round basket near him like a live decapitated head, over which a fishing net trailed like fantastic ancient greying hair and twine.

The fish jumped in the basket that responded and jumped in turn. There were two compartments, Oudin observed, when the man lifted the lid from the basket-brain. One existed for fish that had just been hooked and the other for fish that had been salted and cleaned.

The fisherman looked up in a spirit of forewarning and foreboding when Oudin appeared. "I advise you to travel fast because I don't want no trouble," he said softly and abruptly. "I been passing slow along the cold riverbank since foreday morning, and I ready to march again just now." He gave his line an impatient dip and pull.

"If is a handful of fish you want," he continued, "tek them and go." He lifted the cover from his basket.

"Thank you," Oudin said, "salt *hassa* is a good breakfast."

"Ah got *houris* too," the man offered his fare a little shame-facedly. "Is a sweet fish bursting with bone. And Ah got *lukanani*. . . ."

"Thank you," Oudin said again.

"You better go," the man said now. "Tek all you want and

go. You got you hand full-full already running with *she*." He
pointed at Beti. "You risking you head for she. You must be
anxious, man, why you don't run and go? Tek everything."
The fisherman was agitated. He belonged to the tribe one sees
wandering along the foreshore and up the rivers, like
exhausted souls, still never tiring of their reflective baptism
and sepulchral fierce hope. They wore the same signature of
promise and expectation everywhere, whether in the hottest
desert fire and sun, or standing submerged to their shoulders,
decapitated by a line of water, a fluid and bulging sad
overcoat to withstand everything, under which had been
bundled up alarming snakes of rope and salvaged odds and
ends.

In this pregnant design their actual flesh and body no
longer mattered. "I hide me own bait from meself," the
fisherman cried, diving into a large forgetful knapsack.

"Tell me," Oudin was suddenly inspired. "Mohammed
pick on you to follow me?"

The man started, transfixed in Oudin's dream. "Mohammed believe I is a left-over stooge and a tramp. But I show you
plain that I desire nothing but that you escape with you life.
Go. I want to relinquish every part in murderation and death.
Go, I warning you. Godspeed to you and the woman with
you, or else she going bring you you death."

Oudin had not moved. "You face remind me of somebody I
know," he said. "But when and where I can't remember."
The resemblance had grown upon him and besieged him like
fiery pinpricks that were turning into a cramp. "I tired," he
said. "I can't go right now."

"You must be see me", the fisherman prompted, "cleaning
fish on the foreshore. I is one of the tribe of fisherman. Me
boat always tie up where the shadow of Hassan mound fall in
the water. You know is who is me now? You right to
challenge me because is Mohammed send me. And I telling
you – *go*. I want no part, no parcel in it. Tek all I got, all the
fish in me poor basket."

It was a round agitated face, Oudin observed, the duplicate pool of some spectacle of treachery and dissolution and disaster like when water outs fire, and then waits for the spirit-fire to return again and baptize every ripple.

"You believe fire and water ever mix?" the fisherman said slowly, absolving himself of all responsibility. "Is impossible. Ah warning you to run before Mohammed's crowd catch you with you fainting head in she lap." He pointed at Beti. "Don't say I not warning you. Tek all the sustenance in me basket 'cause if they catch you, you life worth less than that."

The words struck an intimate note in Oudin's heart, and he forgot where he was; the figure before him had become an image of transparency through whom he looked across the river and into the distance, as into a timeless womb and unconscious landscape. Or it might have been a soliloquy he had been conducting with the hunted reflection he had drawn in the river of himself and Beti.

The basket-head on the ground was his own decapitated one, he realized, that the first of his ghostly executioners and pursuers had fished from the sea where it had fallen under the shadow of Hassan's mound in the fluid duplicate of fiery baptism and death. It was the first shell and hurdle and offering of repentance and sacrifice he must accept in himself and must overcome, to be the forerunner of a new brilliancy and freedom.

Oudin and Beti made their way inland to the trees. The spider-sun had turned into a blazing ball and hedgehog with spikes of fire instead of flaming feet. The last Oudin saw of the cloak of the fisherman was the head of a man who had entered the stream, with his net, and appeared to have slipped down deeper than he had expected, so that his body was almost submerged and gone. Over the distance the growing reflection of the sun made the water turn rigid as a pavement until the land blurred into one; the black ball and

210

moonhead that now floated over the ground looked remote like the nostalgic image and reflection in the murder of a self.

Beti and he had had their first visionary breakfast from the basket-brain sailing on the ground. And it seemed to Oudin that his first superstitious fears of being followed had proven abortive and were all the reflective faces of ancestral hate and killing turning weak and insubstantial in himself. There was no shadow of disquiet he could not overcome once he accepted his immateriality and nothingness; this shattering vision was the sun, blinding the pursuing eye of every man, and creature of death like himself.

They had come near to the trees at last. The ground had declined and turned softer, and they were at the bottom of a trough and in an old tributary bed. The hoofmarks of horses and cattle appeared everywhere in indeterminate flight and pursuit; Oudin knew they must walk carefully not to collapse with a sprained phantom leg and ankle.

The ground hardened again as they cleared the depression and entered the first line of trees. Oudin took a winding trail he knew, passing through a clear, spiritual undergrowth, scattered with young, spreading trees, and with remote, proud, sad giants that resembled the ancient and bearded *sandkokers* where runaway slaves had been hanged little more than one hundred years ago.

The land had waved and risen from the scarred foot-marked basin to this flat empty height, and now it was sloping and falling gradually again.

The vegetation had begun to change and the first swamp signals appeared in manicole palm and stump.

The thoughtless trail vanished and they entered a *pegasse* belt. Oudin felt that if he could cross the new depression before him he would come to a ridge in the middle of the day that would lead him to a wood-cutting mission he knew, where he would be safe for the night.

The sun disappeared as they entered the manicole forest. It might have been the tropical dawn or the longest twilight in the world. Diffused curtains of light filtered down to remind Oudin of the covenant he carried with him, recording baptism and death, and the dreaming baptism and the shattering of death again. It was a pact that could never be hidden from his patron's curtained eye, however dark the stage and untutored the rehearsal.

The ground had turned soft and treacherous with the residue of enormously old stricken forests before the sea had stood on this very ground, and had retired again to leave it as it was. Or, if not that, it was some other bacterial and chemical body of waste, of relatively recent fall and origin, lying on the underground forest floor.

Oudin lived a slow, ritual walk in this *pegasse* lake and stream, the ritual of a grotesque funeral march and procession. There was a burial ground ahead, he knew, sinking to his knees, the place where they had always put down the troublesome one.

He lifted each foot with painful deliberation, like another man's foot, and he carried himself as if he were bearing a corpse, stranger and relation at one and the same time. In reality he bore the transparent memorable body of Beti, whom he had lifted from the ground to cover a very bad patch. In this region she became heavy as lead.

The *pegasse* shone and glistened everywhere between the roots of the trees, save where lighter openings and places emerged, covered by hands of ferns. These sickly pale plants sprang wherever the sun pooled and penetrated in the wake of fallen trees that had settled in the mould.

He stopped at last against a long *tacouba* barring the path. It was a fallen tree, stunted, startled giant that had been prematurely undermined in the shifting soil.

Oudin leaned against the wide spongy wood and put Beti to sit.

The trail along which he had come was black behind him; the light falling here, where they were, was pale as the cloud of fern on the ground.

The air had gone still, one of those incredible intervals well known to experienced bushmen and travellers, when the mosquitoes fly into nowhere and nothingness, and the long wings of palms, and the clustering leaves of creeper and tree hang still. One listens in vain, watching the phantom of the bush coming alive in its unearthly detachment, and in its muse of uttermost motionlessness. There is a sombre conspiracy in every line and twig, a power so droopingly conscious of itself, so alert to stand and drill itself into a deliberate threatening constancy, removed from the slightest whim and breath, that one knows it is never an accident when it happens. The concert is too perfect to be other than *consciousness*. But a consciousness clothed with gloom and impending horror and despair.

Oudin could not help the encroachment of alarm when the air darkened around him, and a clouding of space was the only movement of time, like the relentless opening and shutting of a dark silent window and door. All else was rigid and still. The light ecstatic sun of the morning had vanished, and he found it difficult to participate any longer in his intuition of a perfect One, whose creaturely nothingness he was. He was crazy to imagine that anything lay before him save hardship and oblivion. He had put his foot into it. It was death he dreamt everywhere, not the old sentimental glory. No wonder they all looked on him as an imbecile child, a kind of freakish, ageless ignoramus and saint, a menace to all. He was always acting out some extreme folly, and those who took him seriously were obviously crazy themselves, and unscrupulous, and unable to make mature judgments and distinctions. How could such a man win anyone's trust, and usurp anyone's place? And yet there was no saying. The world sometimes went mad to restore what had been amputated and stricken.

Oudin looked wildly and foolishly all around, as if he had been found out for the "double" he was, the "murdered heir", testing him now, mocking him now, as he held Beti close. The stillness of the bush was the same as ever but a new element had entered. He heard the whisper of feet on the ground, and the bubbles in the trail he had trodden sparking again, and alive. The ubiquitous sound spurted at him like muffled pistol shot. He was flattened. The buoyant sense he had had of sailing in a balloon that morning was pricked. It had been the devil's hallucination, the hallucination of a dying man over a dying landscape.

Oudin saw nothing now but insane bubbles of fear, still and watching, and yet exploding on every side. He wanted to run but he stood chained to his knees. His efforts were rewarded at last, bringing the most deafening pistol shot with the moving suction of his feet.

Beti and he climbed in terror across the *tacouba*, and started a frantic collapsing run and march. Everywhere they were accompanied by the breathless, watching stillness, and venomous confinement, and it was all Oudin could do not to strangle the fantasy of a woman with him. She seemed unable to understand anything he was experiencing. She knew they were in danger, but it was the kind of danger that eluded her grasp. She was with a hunted man, and that satisfied her for the time being. It was a blessing to be able to flounder with someone like that. It was a way of paying a debt and longing she owed herself. She had always secretly wanted to be able to redeem herself from being a kind of pawn, and the vicarious satisfaction she gained now, made her less suscepti-ble to physical distress than he was. Every time she gave a cry and wail for freedom it was more for his sake than for hers.

He could only learn to despise her for sheltering in so little comfort and understanding. There was no link between them, but rather a blind hurdle and barrier of insensibility. How could she deceive herself he wondered? His horror ran neck to neck with a growing pity.

Something had disappeared, something bright that was more important than life. How could she fail to see it? Something had ben snuffed out of his nostrils. How could she still call to him in a voice that no longer mattered? He wanted to hear the breath of dedication and power, rather than humiliation and helplessness. It had never been his object to run like a hunted man all the time. He wanted to be, once again, filled with omen, the omen of spiritual seduction and change and hope. But instead he was confined, boxed around, unable to assert himself, unable to play the role of an ambiguous beggar while conscious of being the heir and master of a world.

They had circled and come back to a *tacouba* that looked the same as the one before. She was young and vulnerable beneath the wet mould on her dress and skin. He made her shed everything, and she grew suddenly transparently beautiful and alive. He climbed on the *tacouba* and took her to him, as if in this way he would surmount the hurdle of deception. He felt he was betraying himself in doing this, since he dimly recalled he had made a pledge to leave her alone. But this was what he had to do, and not to do it would have been less than animal. They would claim they had overcome the grotesque earth, and the jungle would grow lighter afterwards and start to breathe when everything was finished.

The faint tinkling of bells came to their ears. Oudin arose. "Where are we, Beti?" he said in a clearer, wondering voice than he had long used. The clear mood passed quickly and he turned disjointed and heavy.

"Is where we get to?" he cried in another voice. "We run far eh? Is where we reach?" He was recalling something both agreeable and disagreeable in their journey.

Beti stared at Oudin, puzzled, but not really understanding in the ignorant strength and appetite of youth. She was satisfied, why should he feel distressed and lost? The tinkling bells came again in the distance, and as Beti listened it dawned on her that Oudin was unwell and that the initiative in continuing the journey rested with her

215

alone. She would turn into his hallucination and guide.

Though Oudin had possessed her with all the lust in the world, he had not been able to pierce the veil that divided him from the spiritual experience he wished to have, and the brightness he had seen before that had faded. It was as if he had suddenly been let down by a curious fantastic falsehood in every naked truth, and by an equally fantastic private truth in every process of crumbling discipline and falsehood. He rubbed his head and his neck, uncertain that he had a head to contain all. Surely nothing now stood on his shoulders. He felt nothing. He was mad. Someone had once told him he was an impostor who always pretended he was what he was not, and that this pretence and potent hypocrisy had enraged his brothers, who had struck him a concerted blow to show him of what little account he was.

He had been to many brutish places he knew, but he came from no brutish family he was aware of, who would have put themselves to so much trouble for nothing. It was such a painful relation and protest to unearth, after all, the black sheep of the flock, the proverbial, private, exotic member, shunned amongst his fair brothers and sisters, like one who had never been born. Surely if he had had a swinish and cunning family, they would have let him pass for an eternal ascetic, holy vessel in any election or collective representation in order to thwart and repress their brutish disposition. Why should they still goad him into becoming a heresy and the author of rape and revolution when they may have employed him otherwise in the past? It was a contradiction of states, future and present and past, he was unable to reconcile. He was at a loss to determine what their motive still was, and had been, and what they had actually ever accomplished, in the limbo of forgetfulness, whether it was discipline and repression that had been their object all the while, or whether it was the sifting of every truth from a lie. Oudin was stupid to imagine he had a constructive head to leap over their frustration and folly as well as his own. How could he hope to plant and invent a human brain and cosmopolis – of sublimation as well as of nerves – and to ingrain it into the fibre of a race whose darkest crime and brightest destiny had long since ceased to count as something one must clearly discharge and accept for the relative fantasy it was? Yet if he was unable to do this, how then was he to rise from the grave of a world?

The responsible pole of gravity had been buried deep everywhere. Nevertheless the need to resurrect it was equally at work everywhere in every blind partial relationship and superstition and clan, with a certain advertisement and signature and pigmentation, today, still another tomorrow, and the next day, who knows? Oudin had forgotten what he was doing and where he was going, in his fantastic blundering penetration and province. Perhaps he would end up somewhere like where he was, in the bottom of a swamp and a grave at the ends of the earth, and leave a remnant to figure out whether anybody had ever really lived and suffered fully in any place and time, and whether pain and pleasure were actually a phantom of intoxication and secret duty that had always been uncertain and taboo. He laughed in an embarrassed guilty way with an air bordering on foul sophistication and inhibited glory and sexual wisdom that Beti did not understand. It would have frightened her beyond her wits. The bells came tinkling again, and Beti realized Oudin was like a man a little drunk; she felt he was not to be entirely trusted. She tugged at him, and called to him, and he descended docilely enough. They resumed their difficult march. They took a new turning this time, and near them the bells tinkled very soon.

They had climbed out of the wide bed of *pegasse* and were standing now upon a sandy ridge amidst a cluster of young greenheart trees. Oudin looked dead with fatigue. Beti's heart beat faster than ever. She told herself it was not Oudin's expression that startled her. It was the thought of the grave out of which they had both come, a grave that left its vision of dead empires in him.

The change in Oudin was something she felt dimly she must learn to contain and to reduce to her own needs. She had become transparent to him but this should not lead her to fear what was incomprehensible and opaque in him when he looked at her out of the corner of his dead eye.

What she had to do was to make her kind of secret mark on him – the obvious mark an illiterate person must make in lieu of a signature and a name. With her toes she drew in the sand an incomprehensible fertile figure within a hollow cage at Oudin's feet.

It was a way of saying that she was equal to him after all. She had come as far as she had to go, and she wished to stop somewhere now, whatever the spiritual parting of their ways. It was a crystallization and acceptance as well of the dark logic of ultimate separation and division. This dark corridor of change and life she saw as her goal in place of the confinement of childhood, and the duties and loyalties she had abandoned. A simple cage of abandonment, however, was as far as she could venture to go in the present, whatever Oudin thought. Even if she were still, in part, a commodity to be bought and sold at his dead feet, at least she had scribbled a constructive desire in the sand, and escaped from the old brutal estate of her father and of Mohammed, in indulging herself in a game of wits with the devil of freedom reflected in Oudin's time and life.

Oudin was listless, like one empty of all thought and feeling as though he no longer wished to serve and to rule anybody. Beti drew him along, warmed by the mysterious fire he had lit, and the dreaming vicarious relationship in time. Perhaps, eventually, she would learn to go all the way to meet the last dreadful enemy, whatever imperial age it was, and to digest the nebulous fate, and the incompatibility, and the divorce from servitude, that were Oudin's. No one could corner such a spirit she knew.

Nevertheless Beti wanted to keep one foot in a corner of the ruling past, and to bear a child or two, whatever it cost her, even if it meant retracing the steps she had made. It was her nature to return and rebuild in the end the house and incarnation of all promise, however far she had run. And this practical distinction was the mixture of eternal compassion and equal despair Oudin had, half-wittingly, bequeathed her, that would rule the fantasy of the living world, and which no one could escape and cleave and finish.

The hardwood trees shot up and grew taller as they climbed the gradual sloping ridge towards occasional patches of the bluest sky where the ceiling of all enclosed space stood. When one's eyes strayed down from the blue sky-light at last, the forest was darker than before, and had become a massive dim section drawn from incredibly ancient fibrous stone. The impression of darkness and concreteness in looming phallus and tree and sky faded again, and turned into music and the rustling blind whisper of streaming leaves.

Beti felt a curious sensation of indestructible softness in her limbs, and a sense of relief in standing above the bottomless swamp. It was an essential uplift and bond in the midst of all figurative flight and chaos.

She drew Oudin along like the hallucination of freedom and power she knew he was.

They came out upon a wide path, running through the hardwood forest, that had been paved with occasional limbs of trees like round sleepers bedded in the ground. The tinkling bells suddenly drew upon them, and stopped all at once, and they stood face to face with a large mournful bull. The foaming black mouth had spattered the neck and the cheek with a saliva of snow. A ring was hanging from his nostrils with an exquisite, sensitive look of silvery scorn, human and rich and malevolent.

He suddenly broke the stillness, shaking his head like a crumbling ornament, in weariness and despondency, until a tiny group of bells began to sound on his horns. This was a signal for a new, lugubrious, comical expression of stability.

Each ring was a fresh consolation and a sad conceit that the end of the day of labour was at hand.

"Careful of that animal, lady," a man's voice sang out. Beti wondered whether she should retreat a little. She had started stroking the bull gently between his horns. The man who had called to her appeared on the path from nowhere. He had come from around a bend. A negro, heavily bearded, dressed in the rags of a woodcutter. They were incredibly tattered and dark as if they had been burnt and rescued from the ashes of a fire, and his bushy beard too, looked as if it still sprouted from magnificent glowing coal in which a fire of eyes had been ambushed and set.

"You really got a lucky touch, mistress," he cried, eyeing her. "Is a bad stone bull standing there. I always got to keep he in earsound and eyesight. You really got a gentle hand," he spoke admiringly.

Beti observed that the bull had been harnessed to a long trunk of greenheart it had drawn along the path.

Oudin had leaned against a tree, and appeared to have fallen into a dream and a sleep.

The woodcutter was startled to see him. "I never thought you had the flaming nerve to show you face today," he said softly and vindictively. "You hearing me?" he cried aloud, seeing that Oudin remained like one dead. "You hearing me and you playing sleep?"

"You know Oudin?" Beti was filled with dread and alarm.

"If I know Oudin," the black man shouted. "What you just ask me, lady? If I know Oudin? Well to me God, he got me strung up by me balls, and you asking me if I know Oudin?" The forest rang. The magnificent head of the bull stood just over Oudin where he had slipped to the ground with his back against a tree, and the chiming horns he had borrowed over his head replied faintly for him from what seemed a great distance. The woodcutter was furious enough to strike him where he half-sat, half-lay like an absent member on the ground.

220

Second Birth

"What you want with Oudin?" Beti trembled, stroking the bull's forehead. The woodcutter grinned unpleasantly. "You think I is just a presumptuous highwayman and beggarman, lady? Once I was a responsible teacher, let me tell you." He grew grotesque and formal. "I used to teach classes, young men and women of nearly your age. I used to wear a white collar and a white suit. O yes," he lapsed into a jagged cry again, "Ah wasn't always a beggar and a clown." He had forgotten Oudin for a moment in confronting Beti. "Politics was me downfall. The school management and the reverend brother and father say I invite a schoolgirl to my room. That was a shocking lie." He spoke fiercely. "I had a pure and simple heart for politics and the good of all," he said. "I genuinely wanted to improve everybody's lot. Teach them to be militant, bring the best out of all races, black, white and red, teach them to die if need be, and fight for a glorious wage, for a better way. . . ." He had begun to ramble a little like a man who had forgotten a great deal, but such fresh emotional colour glowed in his ancient eye that Beti almost shrank from him as if he mirrored two lives, at least, in one. She saw the bull's wild reflective eye, as well, and her fingers could not resist trembling in their stroking and wedding a new problematic forehead and fury. She too had forgotten Oudin and had been drawn to the unpredictable flight and burning pursuit of lust, which was all that truly mattered in the beginning.

"I lost me job," the woodman said. "I was a communist, they thought, a hot-headed fool who had been thwarted of the maidenhead of the school." He gave a little laugh, pulling himself together into a rhetorical figure. "Was a lie. I never dreamt of harming one of the kids. You believe me?" It was difficult to tell whether he was grimacing or laughing. Beti trembled, feeling the mysterious abandon and unity in the life of every man and age who still left all and followed literally nothing.

"Yes, Ah believe," she whispered.

221

"You want to know what politics and a trumped-up love story do for me?" he asked. "It turn me into a black beggar, you hear? Ah get scorch till Ah burn. That is the story of me brutish fall and evolution."

"What you mean?" Beti asked, not understanding, but still drawn as much as ever, admiring the way he had swung his axe like a violent romantic chip on his shoulder.

"Ah set out and Ah travel far to repair me fortune," he had lapsed into a kind of dogged marching speech. "Mazaruni. Rupununi. Cuyuni. Potaro. But as fast as Ah cut me way and mek a red cent, Ah spend it. If I did find a maid like you," he softened, "me luck wouldah turn, Ah sure, in the diamond field. There is something in this world", he confided, "that come before every rich diamond, and a man need it to make himself into a true millionaire and a king."

"What you meaning?" Beti said, not understanding clearly again.

"I mean the ink that running in every man's veins," he said passionately like a man who had drawn an image all his life when he had set out on the trail of a lost love. "I mean the ink of spirit. Is something you can't buy but if you can bleed it out of you life it can change you luck."

"Thought you say was all a trump-up love story," Beti said slyly. "Something that never happen."

"Life look like a trump-up love story for me at one time," his eyes blazed craftily in return, "and that's why Ah burn all me luck. There was absolutely nothing in anything for me. And still I went searching and following what I had lost. I use to lie in me bed in the bush and dream that the lie that send me out wandering was coming near and true."

"What you meaning?" Beti said again. But this time her eyes opened suddenly. An incestuous web of dreams had blown aside, and the bull's countenance brooded upon the timeless figure on the ground, and reflected every ancestor and ringed love and fable she had been taught to have. She recalled the resemblance between Mohammed and Kaiser, as she looked at the woodman's burnt face pressing down upon her. She felt the spirit of incurable pride and oppression and thwarted romance that counted and sold everyone, and even wished to pursue and enslave the world, with the best of mistaken intentions. It was as if she had not yet learnt to choose and reject a suitor because she was still part of a uniform lust and a "trumped-up love" and old estate, and this had dragged her back again to the beginning of her flight, and restored her to the unfreedom of her family. She shouted: "Oudin. Oudin. Oudin," like a woman who still leaned upon her chosen companion and protector in spite of everything and every ghostly one that sought to pull her back.

Beti found it impossible to tell how many days or nights or months or even years had passed since Oudin and she had set out together. The woodman had made them both his prisoners. He had been enraged by her clinging cry to Oudin, and had exaggerated the natural incident into a symptom of perversity. What hope was there, he asked, that he would recover the love he had once thought of, and lost? It was the question of adolescence and old age together, few would dare ask, out of shame that they would be thought mad and foolish.

Actually it was now two days since he had locked them into an insecure room in his cabin. There was a window that looked out on the leaves and trees that were a little bruised and tattered at the end of the clearing, in keeping it seemed with the woodman's apparel and disposition.

It seemed easy to hop from the window and run towards the shelter and inviting gloom of the forest. But the wild gaoler had two fierce dogs with snouts and teeth of swift intelligence. Beti dreamed they were alligators he had fished from the river to watch her and swallow her if she ventured forth.

Oudin was as indifferent as ever to the absurd and grotesque contrivances of creation and life. He had, however, shown one flicker of disturbance and interest and awareness. The woodman had confronted him with what he called the letter of treachery. Why had Oudin betrayed him, he demanded? Remember how they had first met on the public road at the rum-shop? He had spoken of his difficulties, and his desperate need for capital to make a go of his woodcutting grant. It was Oudin who had then offered to help him with money by speaking to the man Ram about the case.

Ram was a name, and that was all, to the woodman, whose interests were actually above the savannahs and outside of rice and cattle. The woodman's true principals were the big mill-owners and established lumbermen whose offices were in Georgetown, and they might shy from giving him a loan when they had inquired into his evil romance. Further, the woodman believed, they would scheme to snatch his grant from him by tangling him up in an impossible agreement. The woodman was at heart such a mixture, a simpleton in one breath and yet subject to every suspicion-and-persecution complex that belonged to the devil, a kind of inferior Christian fabulist who had abandoned the partial-system and the meaningless worship and placation of the old gods of appearance, out of an insane longing to possess the purest, highest intentions that could overcome everything and make him one day into a prime minister and ruler over men and nature. He had placed himself in this way, unwittingly, into the heart of appearances, whose superstitious power he had challenged, as though they were calculating demons, deliberately perverse, and conscious of *him* as their enemy.

Oudin assured him that this hostile encampment would not emerge to torment him once he (Oudin) had steered the business through Ram. Oudin had acquired some influence over Ram, and Ram, in his own way, had grown to love Oudin.

Oudin was confident that he would arrange for the woodman to have ten years before he started repaying on the capital, and in the interval he need not worry his head about anything save paying the interest. Every half-year, he, Oudin, would in person tender the old pro-note as a formality, collect the interest only, and renew the agreement for another half-year. They would beat the devil between them, he promised.

The first half-year had gone as Oudin said, but now at the end of one year, the world had come tumbling about the woodman's ears. He had been served a lawyer's letter demanding that he pay in full his debt to Ram, and stating that his not making even a small remittance on the capital loan, on the first occasion, was a violation of the agreement. Had Oudin lied . . . ?

Why had Ram, Oudin's principal, done such an unseasonal thing? the woodman demanded. Where would he get such a mature sum from at such short notice, when Oudin had given him his word he could safely afford to postpone such repayments for many years? Had Ram and Oudin fallen out over Beti? Had Oudin disobeyed his employer in any crucial way? Was he a mere boaster who had exaggerated his influence, and his control of Ram? The woodman asked these questions in his wild grandiloquent style as if a great deal was hanging on the reply to affect the fate of the world. It was his habit to make the simplest story into something of far-reaching, dramatic significance, like a kind of memorial excuse for his human failure, as if the grotesque lives huddled in a room and a cabin were deserving of universal attention and value that outweighed by far the mere character of open lust and simple treachery.

The woodman cried that unless Oudin could restore the tide that was rising to overwhelm him and to snatch from him all he possessed, he would surrender both of his prisoners to the sacrificial bull, where they belonged. The words were spoken like another vein of curious metaphysical perversion and conceit. Mohammed would crucify Beti's tail, the woodman added crudely, and drop a load of shot in Oudin's backside.

Beti had listened to the enormous tirade in half-comprehension, half-fear. It was a great fantastic jig-saw whose pieces she trembled to fit together in her longing for freedom and innocence. Sometimes it seemed that one cruel face emerged, sometimes another, sometimes one feeble illustration, she scorned, sometimes another, but containing all was a fascinating living house whose windows and walls crumbled and yet were able to erect themselves afresh in every corner, so that what dominated the phantasmagoria and cosmopolis of experimental life was a shattering and constructive mystery, rather than an ultimate and dreadful representation and end.

Beti played with the pieces in her child-like vision as she began to focus her mind on the premonition she had: the premonition of pregnancy. Oudin had made her pregnant. This was, for her, another flicker and signal of inner life superior to the police of the jungle. She saw the necessity to save herself and the unborn child, and to do something before Mohammed closed in on them, or Ram brought his empire of revenge toppling in ruins about her ears. It was the same grotesque kernel, in two shells, confronting her, that she must crack and consume to survive.

Beti woke in the raining morning staring at the sliced face of the forest. It was all she retained at the moment. The leaves were dripping and shining like bulbs, and the solid darkness almost protruded like a beam and support tunnelling the electric trees. Her eyes could not follow this shaft and corridor. They were held on the circuit of rain that wreathed itself into a transparent blowing mist on which the face of time evolved as though it had been forgotten, and was miraculously painted afresh. The cloud of canvas was the enduring unique substance, all else a crowding illusion and mesmerism that came and went.

The light rain began to slacken, the rolling spray came through the window, and Beti shivered, feeling the damp ancient touch on her new shrinking flesh. She got up to close the window and the rain ceased. The forest now was startlingly clear, the leaves even more shining than she had imagined, and the dim interior within the heavy ponderous trees appeared luminous too like the polished harmony of dusk.

Beti heard voices at the door, the bark of dogs and the restraining command of their master, a muffled consultation and word of farewell, and at last the sound of someone setting out into the silence.

She had seen no one, but a feeling of recognition entered her. It was Oudin. The room, she suddenly discovered, was deserted and empty, almost as if she herself were absent. She had begun to live in such closeness to the jagged uncertain cloudy picture of her world that she had become part of everything she hardly knew, and this was the stage where every form and parting footstep were charged with the hysterical imagination of grief, belonging to an illiterate woman who had lost every conventional art of self-expression to become an enigma to herself.

"Oudin. Oudin. Oudin," she shouted. The massive creaking trees replied. She called again listening to the trees once more until the thought of Oudin almost vanished. This time a man appeared around the corner of the house and came towards the window with his two dogs at his heels.

It was the mad woodman of her dream she recalled in a flash, but he looked unnaturally simple now, and modest in the dawn of a new day. His dogs too were no longer alligators, but thin, hungry beasts waiting to be fed a scrap or two. He spoke to her with an air of apology, like a man who could not help eternally doffing his cap to an image.

"Ah sorry mistress," he said. "You got to keep quiet here for a couple of day more. Oudin gone to patch up me business with Ram. Don't frighten." He smiled a little sheepishly.

He was a sorry person after her vision of him in the high forested gloom; she wanted to ask him if wild cats did not occasionally stray there from the distant foothills of the heartland, but she was too disappointed to say a word, a childish anger and scorn and disappointment.

The woodman scratched his head, wondering what he should say and do in the circumstances. "Don't misunderstand me, mistress. Ah not keeping you here because I mean to give you up to you Uncle. Ah was joking when Ah said that yesterday. Ah was a little angry, like a flash in the old pan. Ah wouldn't give you up at-all, at-all."

Beti was filled with an incongruous feeling of relief and sorrow. It was on the tip of her tongue to shout to Oudin again, and to touch every pointless memory and image with a potent magical word on her tongue that would bring all she had dreamed into the drab relationship of the moment.

"The truth is," the woodman said, matter-of-factly, "when a body decide to settle down and stop running and fighting, some of the colour does run out of life too. Every past mistake does pile up and look like raincloud. If you want to know Ah got a good mind for everybody, even if I does jump up full of incurable vexation sometimes. . . ."

"Yes," Beti said, staring at the dogs at his feet.

"Don't worry with them," the man said, following her glance. "They is a good protection. And *I* got to watch for them too. Deer tiger does walk in this bush. He carry away two other dog I had. . . ." He looked at Beti, until she felt the beating heart of ancient alarm and lust beneath his rags and flesh. She saw horns reflected on the tiger's head in the devil's searching eye. It was another piece of the unconventional jigsaw she had always adored; and she was indulging herself in her last flings now the parting of the ways had come for the bride of spiritual fantasy and the mother of actuality. It made her gasp a little with a sense of choking excitement, that almost outweighed everything, that she must, of her own free will, *choose* one, and leave the other for the time being.

"Is dangerous sometimes in the bush," the man said shrewdly, watching her. She was an adolescent and child after all, rather than a mature woman. And it was doubtful whether she could understand how precarious her relationship with Oudin was, in a region where women still passed

228

for grass. "As Ah was saying I got a good mind for everybody. I really want to do me best for the future." He looked at her in his deferential respectful way, but there was a shade of subtle accusation in his voice, challenging her to step out and assume a new role and destiny in life. He sighed, knowing it was a great deal to expect of a woman in the savannahs. "Is only that things got a stubborn nature, and God knows how careful a man got to be if he want to do something ambitious. Mistress," he pleaded, "there must be some way of sparking a new feeling, something more than just barely managing to keep body and soul together. At the moment I real hard-pressed. Ah can't afford to lose this lil grant. Ah got to hang on to it because if this lease and venture forfeit I is a done man. Oudin got to make Ram see that I is not a robber. . . . I intend to pay he all I owe in the end. . . ." He spoke a little grimly, half-envying, half-hating his benefactor.

"Where the bull?" Beti said suddenly, recalling an involuntary vision.

The man did not reply right away. The question had aroused something deeper than passing interest. He was staring at his dogs, who had begun growling under their breath. His ears too, like theirs, had turned to the ground and were listening.

"Close you window at once," he said sharply.

Beti obeyed, pulling the shutters close. The rain had just started drizzling again, and threatening to develop into a great fall and downpour. The room was enveloped in a greying gloom as she dwelt upon the frightened expression she had last witnessed outside. He was an insecure, fearful creature: she heard him moving away from her side of the house, counselling his dogs. A large gust of wind shook the forest, and several bullet drops of rain, stored in the trees, spattered the roof.

The atmosphere seemed to clear up after a while as her eye took in the familiar room, bare almost, plastered with old newspapers, from which many faces looked out, faces she did not know, though they appeared to her to be the vicarious

229

counsellors who attended their gaoler. The script on the newspaper made no sense to her, as usual. There was a greyness and confusion here she would never pierce as long as she lived, and for which she must supply her own half-free, half-reactionary, uncomprehending, primitive maternal shell and symbol. It was an unenterprising corner in the world of spirit, perhaps, but it was as far as she had been able to reach and migrate, for the time being, and for a long time to come.

There was an old mattress to lie on. There was an ancient Berbice chair, as well, with its outstretched rests for upraised feet, and its reclining sack, deeper than need be because of a ripping at the seams. It was the perfect room one would encounter in an ageing tattered museum to celebrate the ghost of glories to come, or long past.

There was a rap on the door, and the anxious face outside looked into the grey room to say: "Keep still and quiet, mistress. Ah believe somebody shouting and coming. Ah don't know if is Mohammed. Stay perfectly still. Even if he come in the house, I going keep he in the other room."

He disappeared without waiting for a reply. Beti fell into a trance of expectation, recalling the expression on the bull's face. She was choking with a terrible dread and she remembered with relief that her father Rajah had had a bull like that, and she had dared to stroke and fondle it.

All of a sudden a light shone for an instant, like an invisible match of sun, flaring in an invisible hand in the room. She had had the glittering pregnant flying premonition once again, that she had had before, that one faint day in the future all dreadful fear of life would vanish.

The rain had started coming down in sheets everywhere. Mohammed recalled how Ram had warned him of this coming flood. The rising chill in his bones sobered him a little and he began cursing bitterly. He gave a hoarse call, knowing he was somewhere near where the woodcutter lived, whose

name was Kaiser, he remembered. It was a nickname
someone had given him. Mohammed frowned with a drunk-
en, obsessive rage; such a name rightly belonged to one man
only, his blood-brother, he said to himself. No one knew
where this black, artificial beggar had got that relative name
from. Coming to think of it, Mohammed grumblingly reflected in disgust, it was becoming a common name, or nickname
as you wish, along the coast. Names were so funny and
contrary to all expectations. There was nothing in a name,
and there was everything, of all mankind, as well.

Mohammed called his brother again, without recrimination
and selfish bitterness this time, as though his mind had begun
to wander far in deed and in truth.

Why had he come on this insane journey after Oudin and
Beti, he asked blankly? Surely he was not courting his death
of cold. He dimly recalled arranging to meet the blasted
fisherman at a point on the bank of the river, as well as a
further select company. No one had responded and arrived.
They might have been dead men. Not a flicker and foot had
answered and appeared.

He had lost his conspiratorial command, Mohammed
reflected, draining the last drop of blood and rum, and
tossing the empty vessel away. It struck a jutting limb and
tree and rang close to his ear.

Mohammed peered, half-blind, half-drunk, into a corridor
of dismal trees, trying to hold the true sequence of thoughts
and impressions together, in spite of the sleeping eyes of his
mind. The branches were waving, he felt, and yet when he
tried to hold him they had never moved, and their shaking
stopped. The passage he stooped within baffled interpretation, all clotted with the miasma of veins and limbs and
webbed water. He saw himself like a fluid spider crawling
under every dense barrier and bush. Suddenly he sprang
back with a snort. He had misread the light and the horn of a
branch had ripped his shirt wide open. He heard the
repetitive tinkle of the rum bottle when a limb and hoof fell

from the still waving trees and ploughed the ground underfoot. The snort shook him again. Mohammed trembled like a wild bull.

The forest was dark. How could a grown man be weighed down by the childish immateriality of this eerie fantasy? It was not to be entertained. He had outgrown all of that. There was nothing to reckon with in this world save hard facts. No one fought today with idle nothings. Mohammed tried to toss away, like an ancient, rotten raft and branch, the subversive footfall that demanded a sacrifice. He had come a far way from childhood and this ghostly encounter with a spirit (that was after all an accumulation of petty roots and debts to discharge) had nothing to do with him he repeated to himself over and over again.

The rain fell on the forest with a steady endless drone and roar, like the rising surf and the sound of the sea. An occasional twittering of self-protection humbled Mohammed to seek a bird call of meaning in the foaming leaves above the deceptive ground. He tried to nest his eyes and his ears above, but he apprehended nothing. He searched the remarkable gloom everywhere, following threads and lines of sepulchral vision, pale and fluid, rising and falling. The leaves rustled like feathers and the tender illumination shifted and pooled and changed all the time. The forest was settling as a hen settles, or standing as a hen fluffs and stands to dry its raining feathers and circulate the light like a hatching cushion of eggs.

Mohammed grew impatient for the clear obstinate land, and he thrust everything away. The sharp beak of a branch scored him as if it would crack his shell in the premature light. He snorted and cursed again, calling Hassan and Kaiser drunkenly.

The twittering sought to warn him to remain still and not resist, but Mohammed did not want to listen. He was ringing with his own voices of drowning alarm. He stampeded. The wings of the forested hen shook its fluid feathers from him like a bird taking flight over his head.

232

Second Birth

The twittering ceased, and a silence, the silence of death, rather than the discernment of love and self-sacrifice, darkened the infested lanes of space on the ground.

He had cracked the premature egg of his dying time and he stood face to face now with the prospect of himself alone with terror and with nothingness. His spirit had flown earlier than he understood and wished and all that remained were the piercing horns of the nest and the tree. He tried to grapple with them, telling himself he was a strong man who could successfully father the brood of all terrors. Once before he had faced a mad, reflective bull on Rajah's ground. He had faced and shouted at it. For a moment the victory was his, and a well-deserved one too. But the animal had recovered and run and charged at his limbs and Mohammed knew then he was finished.

There was the crack of a shot. The bull stumbled to his knees and Mohammed awoke to retain the shell of near dying and to find Rajah had fired and hit the runaway animal. Rajah had had no alternative in the circumstances, though it had gone against his grain to kill the beast. It was a prize bull he had slain. That night Beti slept upon her father's deed. She was the bird of Mohammed's flying spirit that had returned to nest on its ancestral mystique and tree. The horns of a bull were nothing to fear, she said. Every man's death made him level nature and subdue it. Mohammed's father had been a brave man, Beti said, and his father's father as well, back and back into the past. Mohammed gave a drunken roar and shout. He expected the dead, self-same bull to charge, but it stood there tamed and helpless, Beti knew. Beti listened to Mohammed's breathless silence, sensing the fear he felt for himself.

It was not the plain forest that frightened him. It was another premature growth of ringing weakness. It was the dark labour and self-generation of horns he saw now as never before, it was the contest with the devil, and the collision of temples in nature, the egg falling and breaking on the hard unexpected ground, the sun and the moon meeting until the sparks burst and flew.

Mohammed recalled Ram telling him a grown man should never lean on ghosts. No brotherhood of prophecy or conspiracy could cope with the nature of universal terror. One must learn to accept this truth and to exploit it. There was only one staff of premature science and religion to lean upon, and that was the accumulation of other people's grotesque lives and insecurities and fears. Mohammed's peculiar growth was Ram's ideal terrain and commerce and ground.

The self-revelation came like a crash. It was more than Ram had actually ever admitted. Mohammed turned to see where the collision had occurred that split his skull. He stumbled and fell over the hoof of a falling tree, as over his own body of necessity and self-gratification. He had turned into an animal with a horned bullet in a blind eye, and the twittering childish voice in the air that had sought to instruct him rose from the fading ground and misconception of inheritance.

It had all started in the beginning of time with the dream of an heir in the heart of an old man like Ram, and in the unconscious womb of a child and a daughter like Beti.

Ram looked out across the sea of the savannahs. The rain fell in blinding sheets until the land seemed to sweep upward into a vertical wall, while it still stretched to the dim ancestral horizon. There was a spiritual zone of consciousness here that secreted itself in him, moving him and compelling him to become other than he was. Ram set his teeth to conceal this madness and to pretend nothing at all was happening to upset him.

The truth was, of course, that the death of Mohammed was a blow he did not think he had recovered from. What a blundering, stupid head of a man! He had driven himself to his death by alcohol and every kind of ruination. Ram tried to turn away from the fear and sorrow, that were so sharp and unexpected. He had lost his true victim; Mohammed was a kind of symbol of all his tenants rolled into one. Ram had teased the proud, religious bull, and the susceptibility to superstition, until he had fashioned the ideal victim and accomplice.

Ram knew he must learn to carry on as before, exerting all the terrible pressure he had adopted to become the ruling figure he was. He must do everything to recall Oudin, even if it meant issuing summonses right and left on every tenant and proprietor under his thumb. There was a chance that this might bring Oudin again. He would return to beg for them. Ram set his teeth, so that no one would suspect the insecurity and violence in his soul. He *needed* Oudin. He needed that kind of industrious beggar, willing to slave for any master, in a vein of incompatibility with servitude, that secretly opened a prospect of new levels and conversions on the oldest estates. Oudin was the symbolic fool Ram cherished, the managerial clown who always did every bidding.

Ram pulled himself up short. Beti had succeeded in parting Oudin from him. He must reckon with that in soliciting the return of Oudin with a prospective bride. He had erred in sending Oudin on the mission of abduction, as he had erred in goading Mohammed beyond a certain imaginary frontier and line. He had touched them both on the vital nerve centre of all, the nucleus and the tradition of their true inheritance and self-preservation, something far deeper than a piece of paper and an acre of land.

It was the question of the rightful heir, after all. The world wanted an heir and every one went to the most cruel, fantastic lengths to treasure, and even imprison, that intangible property and to seal it away from everyone else.

He, Ram, was an old greedy foul man who wanted a grafted indubitable inheritance more than anyone else. Oudin, the one he had grown to lean upon and depend upon most of all, had actually robbed him of this. Not entirely though. Why had he entrusted such a delicate mission to another man? If anyone had robbed him, Ram was the thief who had stolen from himself. Beti had been banished from him by none other than himself. All his attempts to ravish a woman had been so impossible to realize. He was such a fearful impotent man at heart. This was the truth he must circumvent and repair. He lacked the grace and the courage to plant a new seed himself in the womb of age and youth. Whether Beti was white or black, virgin or ancient, it was all the same. With the devil all things were possible, he knew, save the magic of potency and fertility and life.

The circumstances surrounding the death of Mohammed had somehow ripped from him his self-disguise, but he must repair it as if nothing had happened. To whom would he appear now to be what he was not, strong and brutal and subtle? He must recreate and convince the ghosts of the past. They had all found him out, the very ones he had scoffed at, and once threatened. They had become his real enemies when one would have said they always counted for nought. They were the realities of painful self-revelation and self-discovery, and of a fear in himself they had never generated in their actual lifetime. *Now* they knew him for what he was, and were forcing their self-knowledge and attention on him. He had deceived the living. How would he deceive the dead?

Ram felt he was finished, and yet he was far from reconciling himself to this. What further elaborate deception could he practise to conjure into life an heir to the devil? His hope rested on Oudin, he said to himself, as to the last straw of falling rain. The sky was growing a little clearer over the flooded ground. Once Oudin returned he would bargain with him, he said to himself, scanning the new bitter wastes of water over which a blue window in the clouds had opened. His object would be to create an unassailable appearance, and a certificate that Oudin's baptism and future order of survival were really his. Perhaps after all the end of Mohammed's time was but the beginning of things for him, Ram said to himself with a blind submerged glint.

Second Birth

The river was rising at his feet into the rain and fluid wedding with the technical window of the universe. He would bargain with Oudin for the perversion of all this in the hearts of men. This was the obsession and neurosis of an old, seemingly self-contained man, who would surrender everything, if need be, the administration of his business, securities, all the labour that had to be done and had been once done, if the one bargain for the future could be struck.

He wanted a son who would be the acknowledged child of his life to fill the widening blue crack in heaven like a picture. He was an old man, after all, who had hoarded everything until the need to extend himself beyond this piling had become crucial and phenomenal.

He had long seen how his need could be met by one of the illiterate, foolish and dim maidens of the time. She would not understand the monstrosity of her conception, another man's child that would be his. Ram did not dare to utter his thoughts aloud even now. He was determined to fool himself to the end, that it would not come to this, that a miracle would happen to heal him and make him an ordinary man. The miracle had obsessed him, until he had almost come to believe it would happen and he would not have to cope with a manufactory of the future. The crucial moment of blind adoption was not one he wished to face and invite until there was absolutely no alternative.

He would bargain with Oudin if the crucial time had indeed now arrived, he said to himself, and surrender everything. Would Oudin's child be his in return for scraps of paper, and the option they would bring to Oudin to free the land? It was the last card he would play, and even then the outcome was something he could not force. Would Oudin ever relinquish Beti to him? He dared not hope. His heart stopped beating for an instant. But there was still time, time to arrange something, time for a lease of living flesh to be transferred beyond anyone's knowledge.

Oudin could bring it about. There were other daughters

and widows who could be brought to bring him his ambiguous seed and his artifice of connection.

Ram could not help a scorn of himself. It would take him many superstitious unlucky years to utter aloud his thought of death and ultimate perversion and frustration in himself, even in the silence of his room. He must do everything before he actually admitted that, and bargained on that. Everything must step into gear as smoothly and dreadfully as possible. Beti was another name for "daughter", the daughter of a race that was being fashioned anew. He must do everything to repair the damage he had unwittingly set in motion that she was a free woman at last. If she believed this divine proposition, even in the limited way that called on her to make a true distinction and choice, it would be useless to put his horns on Oudin's spiritual head. They would pierce him in her childlike hand and annul his command and certificate of values in the end. Ram felt the sudden loss and tension of the visionary umbilical cord, the dreadful twine of shattering encirclement, stretching from far away out of a faint servant in the sun.

THE WHOLE ARMOUR

For Margaret, Alex and Margaret-Anne

Wherefore take unto you the whole armour of God.

Ephesians 6: 13

This Jack, joke, poor potsherd, patch, match-
wood, immortal diamond,
    Is immortal diamond.

Gerard Manley Hopkins

BOOK ONE

JIGSAW BAY

I am glad to have ideas without knowing it,
and to see them with my very eyes.

                                        Goethe

I

Abram dreamed he was crawling in a wood – on the high branches of a tree – and had reached the extremity of a curious twisted limb. The leaves of the tree turned into black swooping birds, obscene and terrifying. He surveyed what appeared to be a beach beneath him, on which lay an old rotted tree-trunk, or ancient *tacouba*, hard as iron. He knew he must jump but felt he would cripple himself in landing upon it. He sprang from his perch, meeting softer ground than he had expected, astonished to see the entire tree above him, its roots spreadeagled in the air, naturally and invisibly cradled and supported.

He awoke, not yet in command of his senses, wondering whether he would find himself in a land that was nowhere. His heart was racing and there was a cruel pain in his chest, the cruel demented pain of a dying and bewildered man who wanted to rediscover an innocence at all costs.

The bay swept around him – starting at the mouth of the Pomeroon River and going towards Moruca. He had built a parody of a hut on a spit of land that looked unyielding and hard amidst the trenches that had been torn and eroded on either side, until they were crowded with a gnarled husk and mask and a twisted alphabet of timber. Every private notice and fable and boundary against the sea stood in the turmoil of the foreshore as in a graveyard of sculptured history and misadventure.

He waited for the pain to subside and the rocking steamer to appear in the distance upon the bar of the river.

The tide rose and the steamer barely stood within a depth of water that hugged it like indispensable flesh crawling far out upon the horizon.

Abram's face was red and burned with the sun, his hair short and curling, his body hard and resistant like a tree. No one knew his true name – or from whence he had come – and it seemed fitting to call him Abram since he was considered barbarous in electing to live on the crumbling foreshore, at the extreme mouth of the river.

He was making ready to launch his small craft, grimacing a little with the memory of his cruel pain and involuntary fantasy and weakness.

II

The woman said – "You got to hide my son, Abram. They going hang him if they lay hands on him. You got to hide him. I begging you and I telling you, please." She was able to match Abram's curious appearance: a vigorous and a strong black skin of a woman, polished like mahogany, approaching forty. Chinese eyes, emotionless in expression and filled with the blackest unshed tears. Barefoot. The columns of her legs were sculptured to stand out from the loose formless miraculous stone of her dark body and dress, unadorned and plain.

"You got to save him, Abram. Hide him in the bay where you live. Nobody would look there. Is a heaven-sent chance."

Abram was startled. He stood in the woman's house, in the long coffin-like front gallery that was the fashion in this region of the world, looking out on the black water where the sun had vanished leaving a deep submerged hint. The trading-steamer – in whose distant foaming wake he had come – was tied against a stelling around a bend in the river.

"What has he done this time?" Abram demanded absentmindedly and still sternly like a man in a helpless rigid dream.

"Anybody see you coming to me, Abram?" she asked softly. "I glad you tie up you boat far from me landing."

"I always do. Whether is you I spending the night with, or another woman."

"The Baby Mills doll," the woman sneered.

"And what is it to you, Magda?" he said defiantly. "I have always paid you."

"Look, this is no time to quarrel. Don't worry about me. Is Cristo I begging you to help. Go and stay with Baby tonight. She always got a full house but she bound to make room for you. And the point is you going be seen. Early foreday

245

morning pass back here. I fetch Cristo. Hide him for a month, Abram, one hard bitter month, I begging you, and when his uncle Skipper Dutch sail in 'pon his schooner from Barbados we going smuggle him out of Pomeroon. . . ."

"Is it woman murder he done?" Abram spoke in a harsh crushed voice, agonizing and abrupt.

Magda nodded her head fiercely. Then growing gentle, she moaned in the same brutal theatrical tongue: "I know Cristo better than judge and jury roll in one. All he want is a man-sized chance to live. I want to put him in you hands, Abram."

"I sorry. I can't do this thing. Next time I going carry me trade into Moruca. Let Cristo find someone else."

"You can't go to Moruca," she cried vehemently. "You can't let Pomeroon people down like that. Listen," she pulled in the waist of her dress to show the power of her limbs, "every time you come and you want me, Abram, I be yours, *free*. You won't have to pay one red cent ever again."

Abram shook his head slowly and obstinately as if he had ceased to care.

"He could be your son." The woman shouted the fierce dinning responsible words in his ears. "You old enough to have a son twenty-one-year-old just like Cristo." She looked at him strangely. "Everybody say you got a heart of stone but I don't believe it. I don't believe you gone all the way out there to live because you really abandon the world in you mind. You are a man with feeling like all the rest, Abram. You are not a god."

Abram was angry. The muscles in his jaw stiffened in a kind of deadly rage and he was glad that the house had grown a little dark. Magda wanted to see his face and she turned and lit a lantern.

"Abram, I want you to help Cristo," she cried softly, holding her hands out to him and offering him everything she possessed.

A cool wind blew in and encircled them, stripping the heat from the skin of the day. "Not a mosquito biting yet," the man said distantly, in an attempt to ignore the woman's presence as he watched the last vivid streaks in the sky out of which a score of bats flew and vanished like a tumbling mad cascade of birds. He saw the watertop as well through the window black as musing ink. The banks all along the river were now glimmering, he knew, with fire-fly lanterns like a vague circulation of stars, and the forests of trees on either side had closed and extended their wings until a narrow chink of actual night sky was all that remained in the middle of the stream. A nervous throbbing came across the distance from a guitar, followed by the shrill complaint of a reveller – the coincidence of a skeleton of musical sound flying with the fading protesting senses and Abram could not help recalling the dying and newborn generations of the Pomeroon in his mind's eye.

"Look," the woman said at last, unable to endure any longer what seemed to her a stubborn silence, "I willing to sell everything I got and give you everything." She confronted him with a massive mourning black look. "Sometimes I feel we is a dying race, Abram." The words startled him.

"No," he protested, "I am not dying. *I am not dying.*"

She went on as if she had not heard him. "We're half-caste, is not so? It is as if an old race is bound to be always dying in the world."

Abram was startled again. "Don't parrot every fool you hear," he rebuked her with a feeling of acute discomfort.

"Then stop feeling eternal shame about me and you, Abram. I is you body-in-the-dark woman, you convenient sphinx of a woman," she laughed. "Is me Chinese blood. And you like to feel you standing far away upon some high spirit-branch like a bird falling every now and then to pick a blind red pepper. But I want you to see, whether you eye blind or not, that Cristo belong to you as well as me. He could be your real son. I want you to forget yourself and feel this power of belonging. Is there anything stronger than mating and borning in this world until you lose you dying self?" Her entire being glowed at him with the dark sombre question. "Cristo is you manchild by me. I make it so. I declare it so. Who in the world can say no to me? Am I not the best judge?"

"Don't be a fool," Abram protested harshly. "Cristo is half my age, and is only yesterday I start sleeping with you. . . ."

Magda suddenly burst into an electric laugh. "You is the biggest coward in the world, Abram," she said. "Even if you knew me and had me wrapped in you arms a hundred lightning year ago you still wouldn't *believe* Cristo is you flying seed and son; he too *black* and you too *white*." She pointed her finger in his face.

"Don't be a vulgar mad fool," Abram raged, brushing her arm away. He grimaced and his burnt expression turned old and violent like a model of introversion and involuntary distress and recurring stab after stab.

III

It was the end of the second interminable month since Abram had taken Cristo to the bay and the sail of Skipper Dutch still had not risen on the horizon. The season of hurricanes in the Caribbean had been a fierce one and rumour swept Jigsaw Bay – like the ghost of a storm – that the craft had run for shelter in the Orinoco River and had gone down for good.

Cristo felt the fixed landscape and perspective of the past had been broken for good. He hugged himself a little fearfully like a blade of grass growing in the wind. He was of medium height, slenderly built, poise of a dancer. High questioning cheek-bones, penetrating eyes, a restless way of shaking hands and wrists, the sensitive nervous shuddering joints and limbs of a sprinter at the start of a race.

The crumbling bay was a world outside of the world he had known and whenever he ventured along it he had to invent an eye in the back of his head for any passing fisherman and inquisitive trader.

The derelict premises Abraham ruled had no true geographic location Cristo felt, a region of absurd displacement and primitive boredom, the ground of dreams, long-dead ghosts and still-living sailors, ancient masters and mariners and new slaves, approaching the poor uncharted Guyana coast and beckoning the aboriginal mummy for whom all trespass beyond the sculpture of death was an act of brutal unimaginable faith.

Abram occasionally mumbled and cried out to these glimpses of the abnormality of heaven but Cristo declared, simply and violently and in the foulest way a young man could, that it was hell.

The man was mad, Cristo said to himself bitterly, mad to think of living here and mad to bring him here to live. Insane, Cristo repeated. Look how he communed with silence, an entire day smoking a pipe, staring into a corner, spitting into the sea. He would patch his patched fishing net endlessly and mind his small precarious farm and Cristo expected the bank to slip at any moment and the planted roots to protrude stripped of their grotesque soil and footing and earth.

What had he done, Cristo demanded of himself, to be chained to another man's compulsive image and thought?

He was paying for a crime he had not committed. It was as horrible and meaningless as that.

It was a frame-up, Cristo insisted, he had killed no one and had simply defended himself in a struggle.

"No," Cristo said aloud, "I refuse."

Abram looked up in half-comprehension, half-bewilderment.

"I shall stay here," Cristo said. "I can stand it the same as you."

"I promise to keep you. I know it," Abram said coldly and inhospitably.

"I am innocent so why must I give myself up?" Cristo insisted, goading Abram to unmask himself.

"Nobody innocent."

"I am, I tell you."

Abram cleared his throat, feeling a clumsy word on his tongue. "You ungrateful," he cried, "plain ungrateful. I bring you here. I hide you. I feed you. And now look you lie barefaced to me."

"It happened in a small village," Cristo shouted, "where I have many enemies."

"Liar," Abram said flatly, "liar."

"I could kill you with all the pleasure in the world," Cristo raged passionately. "I shall stay here as long as I like." He was weeping like a woman.

"I not forcing you to go," Abram spoke hoarsely, grimacing all of a sudden.

"I won't go back to be framed for nothing at all," Cristo wept grievously.

"You can stay as long as you like," Abram protested, unaccountably moved in an unfathomable and awkward way. To his immense astonishment he found that he meant his words of hospitality. They had been uprooted from an old vivid alarming dream. His heart was suddenly racing unto death in the furious ominous plunging way that happened to him time and time again when he saw himself on his curious twisted limb and tree: the ultimate moment to leap had come, he knew, and to abandon a grotesque imitation of life for the spirit of universal dust and the innocence of a phantasm of pollen. He reached out to tell Cristo he believed all was well and his expression wrinkled like an advocate, galvanized into frightful action, in the presence of a shocking devilish judge. It was his last image of himself he saw in the mirroring liquid eye of the accused boy, aghast and still weeping in a paroxysm of murderous rage, as he fell. He put his hand upon his chest, tottering in his chair and falling face forward upon the ground, twisting his head, wanting to say something ghostly and utterly reassuring but the confirmation of innocence froze on his lips in the self-reflection of ancient horror and reluctant fibre and dread of the unknown.

IV

Magda almost swooned. She caught herself just in time. After all she was a strong woman, she told herself. Her body and limbs looked like dark resolute stone (Abram had said so to her one day when he arrived to sleep with her). The involuntary smile of recollection felt like a grimace. Her brow and cheeks were a black fantastic mood of mahogany, her eyes narrow and unbelieving slits. She recalled the ancient glimmering look of reluctant resignation on her father's dead face. It swam before her – the crafty obdurate Hong Kong expatriate, the remote coffined brow of the man who had been her father. She remembered the violent news of how he had been killed in a devil of a brawl in a Georgetown gambling saloon. She was twelve years old then, and had just started going to high school. Her Negro mother was lucky to pick up a Pomeroon man and they left the city for good to seek their fortune in the Pomeroon river and bush. Magda had survived everything until she had matured into the toughest and best whore in the river district – from Jigsaw to Pickersgill. She swore *her* child would have the chances she had never had. She had scrimped, and saved, and had her men to send Cristo to college. And now look what had happened! She wanted to deny strenuously the true and enormous bizarre history passing before her mind's eye like the repetitive blows and stabs of a fabulous injustice. She put her hand in the region of her heart in the way Abram used to do when he was in pain. Her voice almost suffocated in her throat but she still succeeded in crying: "Cristo, Cristo, I want the living truth! How Abram really come by he dead? Is the same old ungodly fight all-you had? Boy, if is the first time in me whole life I want you to explain the living truth. *You*, my son, kill a man old enough to be your *father*? Is true?" Cristo had never heard such dark irrational vehement words on his mother's lips. He looked at her as at a new woman animated by revolutionary furies he had never seen or suspected. She was going out of her mind. Unless – could the troubling vision be his? He trembled. The months he had spent with Abram in Jigsaw Bay had unhinged him and he had begun to see a terrible and accusing mask in the place of flesh and blood.

"Abram died a natural death," he said slowly. "Not a blow passed between us. . . ." He became irresolute. He blurted out: "Not a blow passed from him to me or from me to him. He collapsed, I swear, without a blow being struck, his hand on his chest, and his face all screwed up like a devil. He was trying to say something but he couldn't. That's the God's innocent truth."

Cristo became restless under his mother's masked stare. He felt he had not told the whole story and had deliberately misrepresented something. It was a crazy notion. Why should he feel guilty? Abram had died a natural death and that was that.

Magda chuckled in a disbelieving mad way that made Cristo afraid: "You mean is simple heart-failure that kill Abram? He was the *only* man for me. He used to have some funny chest pain, yes, I remember. But I can't believe . . . Is better if he did dead with he boots on in bed with me. . . ." Cristo recoiled before something obscene and threatening in her manner. He was trembling with a sudden superstitious fear. Magda chuckled again. "Is *me, me,* you forget? get Abram to hide you in Jigsaw Bay. I swear to him how you innocent. I beg him to hide you the one place in the world I know the police would overlook. You don't know they hunting you everywhere else in the bush, every village, every road between here and Essequebo? You were safe with Abram for the time being, Boy. And believe me, everybody, *everybody.* . . ." Her eyes closed as if they had swooned for good; she caught herself in the same twinkling instant and continued: "Everybody saying is you kill

Sharon's sweetheart and sweetman." She rolled the words on her tongue in a sickening parody of affection. "All the bad blood in the world like it coming out in you, Son." She spoke brutally and darkly and self-pityingly in a tone of frightful maternal malice and groaning abandonment.

Cristo shook as if he had caught a fever. He felt that the white two o'clock sun burning the air had fallen on the black Pomeroon. The river heaved – full of glinting metallic bits – and he was drawn to the window to look out on the mesmerism of the water.

"Pull you head in from me window," Magda cried. "You want the world to see you?"

He pulled his head in quickly, dazzled by the white eyes of the sun drawn up on a dripping flashing paddle. An Indian-Arawak corial had darted past. "You can't take chances at the window. Somebody always passing. That remind me. Maybe *all* the damage done already. Somebody did bound to see you coming here." She made a gesture with her hands like someone pushing a crowd away. She approached the window and looked out, staring across the fainting water until the slits of her eyes almost closed in the blinding vigil of the sun. "You think anybody see you?" she demanded, turning and confronting him.

"I can't remember," Cristo said slowly. "I only know I couldn't remain a minute longer in Abram's cabin. I couldn't stay one minute longer in the accursed place. I had to run. . . ." His voice had risen.

"You had to run," Magda said coldly. There was a diabolic edge to her voice, challenging his, quivering with the curb she imposed on the cruel inward rebellion of every sense against every memory of life from the day she was born. "You run," she said brutally. "Why?" she demanded. "Look at me. I tell you before. I tell you again. I want the truth. If . . ." Cristo could see the stress and strain of her mind marshalling her thoughts upon her black brow: "If . . ." she was spitting at him. . . . "Abram died natural, why your common sense didn't assert itself and dictate to you that broad daylight was no time to show you

254

backside 'pon the river? You paddle down the river, uncon-
cerned-like, under the bright bright sun like an innocent man,"
she laughed as if she had invoked the greatest joker. "Like an
innocent man," she repeated, brandishing each word like a
foul jest. "No! Wasn't that. You want me to tell you was what?"
She spat her words at him. "The bad blood of two murder rise
up and blind you till you turn frighten of you violent self. You
lose all common sense. You *run*." Cristo thought she was about
to weep, her face had wrinkled so convulsively, but a dry
paroxysm was all that broke and expressed her throat and lips.
"Is you guilt that blind you to you own safety," she cried
sombrely. Cristo stared at her, feeling bound and gagged
before her theatrical and blinding performance – more real
than life itself. Save that even the flickering reflex of knowledge
of ultimate escape from a pure dramatic ordeal and dream was
absent in this case. Indeed everything was so *real* the truth
itself paled into a shattering insignificance. He felt that she
would never release him until he had utterly condemned and
surrendered himself.

"Cristo", Magda's countenance was distraught and rav-
ished, "I want the truth. Only the truth. Don't lie to me."

"If I told you the truth," Cristo said weakly and defensively, "what would you do?"

"I would help you to escape," Magda flashed triumphantly. "Who can tell what a young man like you may still *do*?
You still *young*. When you get seasoned and old like me . . ."
she drew her dress close around her terrible and powerful
limbs (in the way she used to show herself to Abram) strong
like the most ancient sculpture in the world . . . "when you get
ancient and old like me . . ." she laughed sardonically
". . . . perhaps you won't want to do anything any more.
Neither good nor bad."

"I want to escape at any price," Cristo confessed piteously,
turning away from her and feeling shamed to the core,
accepting the fabulous injustice of guilt. It was as if he had
killed her lover and could not give himself in return. "I shall

tell you whatever you want me to say," he cried. He saw his mother now as an unfathomable stranger in his mind's eye, whom he must placate and abandon at all costs.

"All right," he cried. "I killed him. I killed Abram."

BOOK TWO

THE EAGLES

For wheresoever the carcase is, there will
the eagles be gathered together.

Matthew 24: 28

V

Dawn sky had begun to clear a little and to whiten faintly around the flaming morning star. The mouth of the Pomeroon opened on the vague dark motion of the sea like an impalpable roller and breathless presence whose effect imparted an air of uncertainty to the motion of the boat rather than any quick change of gait or measure of freedom. They knew they had come to the brink of the sea but the surface seemed as steady as the river.

"This must be foreday morning calm," Magda said slowly. "But is half-tide now, Cristo, and water rising and it bound to blow rough soon. Thank God we nearly reach. How long it take us?"

."We left an hour before midnight," Cristo said.

"The last house-light must be vanish over two hours ago. Was when the tide turn strong, remember? Not a soul living around."

"Will be easier now," Cristo spoke apologetically. "We're paddling with the wave. . . ." He looked towards Jigsaw Bay, shivering slightly in the cold dewy atmosphere. They had turned away from the dark uncertain mouth of the Pomeroon. The sky of the bay appeared equally dark, a pale mist roofing the earth and mingling in dissolving placidity. The invisible motion of the waves became – all at once – mounting and evident. The small craft rose up, and then slid down, as if it had gained at last the anxious new ground and element of freedom.

The grey mist was lifting and the grey dawn was breaking. The spray broke and flew – full of an unexpected warmth when it touched their shrinking skin in the early relative tropical air that had made Cristo shiver. The tide had borne

259

them in, a mile away from Abram's hut, and the craft grounded all of a sudden. Two hundred yards of shallow listing water seemed to lie between them and the shore-line like an oblique tremulous uninviting floor. Behind their backs the waves had begun to quake and leap in all directions and the subdued subterranean roar of the vital repression of the surf began to invade their stranded senses. Jigsaw Bay always mounted this late sudden tidal reaction: the bay would grow violent and treacherous with the new erosive impact of the sullen seas where not long before had been seeming high ground.

Cristo flung his anchor overboard, and stepped gingerly into the water, Magda following. They set out inland in the knee-deep staggering flood, feeling and anticipating holes and trenches and restless uprooted trunks and trees.

"The boat should keep there," Cristo muttered. "In any case there's a spare dinghy at the house."

"Abram would have swim out on the high tide, Boy, bale it out and bring it in," Magda boasted. She had knotted a rope from the boat tightly around her waist, enabling her to hitch her skirt to the top of her thighs, and was looking down with a black disdainful smile into the water, like some fantastic washerwoman jeering at a foul mixture of universal foaming soap. The water hissed and swirled hungrily and evilly around her powerful limbs, Cristo thought, with shrinking fascination in the pit of his stomach. He felt the perverse buffeting spirit of change and distortion he dreaded in Jigsaw Bay, and the uncanny acquisition of guilt rose in waves around him. To all intents and purposes he had confessed to overwhelming and slaying Abram. What a nightmare that Magda despised him as an evident weakling and still credited him with an enormity of criminal execution, intention and folly. Magda settled into step behind him, driving him forward it seemed. He still saw her in the corner of his crowded and swimming eye. He struggled to tell himself that his violent confession and his impotent self-knowledge were infantile and insane in a grown man. He staggered ashore, clutching to himself a modicum of self-control. He must be crafty and clothe himself in every pretence that would help him to escape to a new life. He must shore up every shred of strength, and watch every changing spirit in Magda and himself. His mother had become the womb of terrifying contempt and meaningless execution and pride, a strong naked woman he had never suspected in his wildest adolescent dreams, someone he must consistently humour with a desperate pathetic lie. His heart beat with a curious maturing resolution as they set out to Abram's parody of a hut, buried it seemed from where they were, partly in a fiction of waste-land and partly in the rebellious drama of the sea.

The sun had just risen, balancing on the horizon like a flaming anxious ball, when they drew near. The smell of stumped roots and earth off the sour foreshore and in the tumbling tide blew strong in their nostrils; yet Cristo detected nothing actually foul and decaying in the atmosphere. The dead man had fallen an hour before the blazing noon, two days ago, and it was a long time to lie without burial in the impatient shadow of the sun, Cristo knew. He was struck all of a sudden by a horrible conviction and intuition more grievous than a disease of the lungs. It was nothing that had entered his nostrils; it was an unhinged sensitive gateway in his overlapping mind. They were close enough to see a sprawling space dark and staring wide to the land. Cristo vividly recalled bolting the opposite door that looked to the sea. In his haste he had run and overlooked the one that led to the land. He shuddered a little in spite of the sweat of exertion on his brow in the melting rays of the sun. He was shuddering out of sympathy for a ghostly complaint his ear could only dream to catch in the shaking noises of the sea. It was still too far for anyone to hear the harsh hinge on the swinging door.

They were coming very near now and Cristo tried to thrust his open inward sensation far from him. His consternation mounted with the sun in the sky. The door had been virtually ripped away – as if by a blast or a blow – and was barely holding to the sheltered wall on rusting nails that shrieked to the muffled wind. On this side of the house it was possible to hide a little from the direct aspect of the sea. Nevertheless Cristo was trembling like a living exposed feather and leaf.

Magda grasped the door to step on the low single treader. She flew back, falling abruptly on her back: the door had finally come loose in her hand and it lay on top of her. Cristo ran to help but she had already heaved herself to her feet.

She cried instantly and furiously: "You two must be had a bitch of a fight in there. You must be fall 'pon the door proper hard with all you double weight. It was waiting for *me* to finish it. . . ."

Cristo stopped her, all his grievous intuition mounting to a climax in the cry he gave. "The tiger. It's the *tiger*."

"*Tiger!*" Magda was startled and rooted to the ground. "*Tiger!*" The grotesque truth flashed on her face like a ruling fable of the land. She lumbered forward into the hut. It was deserted. The shirt had been ripped from the dead man's back and flung into a corner wrapped in the nervous stamp of blood. Of Abram, there was no sign.

Magda stared, full of the blackness of congealed thought, her brows nonplussed yet still wise. "Yes, Boy," she said, almost off-handedly, "you right. The god-dam' tiger fury been here." She continued as if she were reciting a lesson: "He kill a couple of oxen at Charity last month. He slaughter plenty-plenty goat and sheep. Then thing get tight with he. Them man been on the look-out. Everybody swear he turn away and gone back." Her voice had acquired the psychological ring and mimicry of fate and belief Cristo knew well since childhood. The visitation of the tiger was a feature that accompanied everyone's growing years, descending from the head-waters of the Venezuelan Cuyuni across the jungled Guyana watershed into the half-settled Pomeroon, prowling always on the frontier between changing fantasy and the growth of a new settlement. Once, he recalled, the tiger had taken a child, and the greatest animal hunt in the history of the new world had been organized. But the ancient tiger had vanished into thin air.

"I have never seen the beast," Cristo confessed miserably.

"You ever see you mother with a man?" Magda spoke viciously. She had suddenly vanquished and lost her fabulous air of credulity, acceptance and woeful surprise. "You never see the beast?" She was confronting him brutally and sceptically. "What I would like to know, Cristo, is how you know so sudden and uncanny and swift *tiger* been in here?" There was a savage wisdom and calculated suspension of unbelief in her manner. "I want to *believe* your inspiration was genuine, but I want you to tell *me* – how you happen to know so true?"

"Three days ago", Cristo spoke awkwardly and defensively – with an air of unreasoning fabrication – "Abram told me he met a huntsman who reported to him the presence of a Venezuelan tiger in Moruca. Said the beast had outwitted the Pomeroon farmers. Abram swore he would down him if he visited Jigsaw Bay." Cristo pointed to a gun in the corner of the hut, still standing innocent and unmolested as day. "You don't believe me?" he was suddenly shouting.

"Hush! Why shouldn't I believe you? I know many a man with tiger scratch on their skin." Cristo saw she was watching him. "I don't know what you mean," he cried, wondering whether he had lost his wits. "I was terrified to hear from Abram a tiger was so near to us. I have never seen the devil but I have grown up next door to him nevertheless. A couple of years could hardly pass without some frantic story. You know that as well as I do. The Pomeroon lies more than half in big ignorant Bush." He could no longer bear Magda's eyes. He turned away from their frightful calculation and accusing wisdom.

VI

Magda was standing in the door with her back to him. Cristo wondered what was passing through her mind. It seemed to him the most curious madness that she ignored him, treating him with such indifference, while at the same time she believed him to be a crazy killer. She now believed he had indeed killed the man who had been stabbed in an infamous jealous brawl – in spite of her first early acceptance of his protestations of innocence – and that he had followed this up by attacking Abram (who had successfully concealed him from the police over a long spell in Jigsaw Bay) and killing him in a blind moment of acute frenzy. She suspected him of every involuntary crime under the sun, he was certain. Unless, indeed, the whole image of suspicion sprang only from his distraught superstitious imagination! But no, she had made herself more than brutally clear to him from the moment she had driven him to lie upon himself and confess that he had run from Abram in fright at the act he had committed. He had read the judgement in her eye, in her every action, word and expression. "You don't believe me any more?" he cried suddenly and impulsively. Magda did not answer. "Look," he shouted. "Can't you see? Look. Here . . ." – he was pointing to the floor – "the nail-marks, the scratches on the floor. Look again where the devil dragged the dead man. *The traces are there*. Why don't you look, damn you," he cried. "He lifted him in his jaws, I tell you, and sprang with one leap outside." He was weeping passionately like an enormous violent frustrated child who had connived in the creation of his own scheme of punishment.

Magda turned at last and his childish paradoxical sobbing ceased. "I see everything," she said, with a studied casualness, in which, however, Cristo detected a cruel bitterness he resented. She was moving as if she had truly invoked the unpredictable style of a great cat – soft and feline and meticulous – that left neither trace nor scratch. She picked up the gun in a corner of the room, the haversack of cartridges, snapping open the chamber, loading expertly. There was a dream-like menace in her limbs and her glance, and Cristo began to tremble once again with a new fascination and fear.

"Is nothing," Magda reproved him. "Only in case we meet the tiger. Eh? Let's go." She pointed the muzzle of the gun to the door.

Outside the sun had climbed high, blazing in the sky.

"That way," Magda said, indicating the direction she wanted to take, pointing with the gun. Cristo looked up. He was startled. The bay swept, a glittering and waving sea; the bush bristled in the distance – mysteriously tricking the eye as if it were in the water. The picture framed itself – a reflex and ancient mirage in the mind. It was not this, however, that held him. The magnet that drew him was a lofty tree of black blossom. A couple of miles away in the direction of Moruca the sky was a column of crows, rising and falling like black leaves in the distance. "Carrion crow," he whispered. "Something dead out yonder." He spoke as a dramatic thoughtless child of the folk whose limbs were temporarily losing their power of movement and beginning to act in a dream.

"Let us go," Magda said, propelling him forward.

Cristo led the way like a sleep-walker, picking his path carefully between the sea on his right and the first straggling trees that mounted to a dense wall on his left. He kept the constant black signal before him, a distracted flying pillar that hovered and sometimes crumbled into pollinating ants upon the dark insubstantial bush and the light effervescent sea. The horizon was beginning to shake and quiver into bright refracted pieces that constantly returned vibrantly together again.

The crows straddled their curious victim and stumbled awkwardly on the ground, flapped their pinions in the low air, loomed with sudden startling grace up and still upward, began dropping again, rising and floating in an illuminating paradox of black wings. They withdrew – reluctant and disembodied creatures – on Cristo's and Magda's approach. Cristo saw them as trailing wings indeed, and nothing else, save that they truly belonged to a still-human shape and mangled shadow on the ground.

The odour of bright terrifying putrefaction smote the air and lapped the sea, waving upon the surface of the water and impregnating every rigid rooted trunk and branch.

"Go," Magda said.

"Go where?" Cristo demanded in suffocating confusion.

"Go there!" she was pointing unmistakably.

Cristo shrank, looking at her, thinking her mad.

"Tie something over your nose," Magda said determinedly. "See, he still wears his own ragged trousers, about your size now he's so reduced." She laughed grimly and murmured as though she wished to apologize for a bad joke – "Don't worry. His shoulders and his arms were always big. But his legs fine-fine like yours. Them trousers you wearing can fit easy-easy. . . ."

"What! Are you crazy?" Cristo gasped. He was suddenly convulsed and racked by a cough.

Magda was looking at him critically. She mused: "For all you slenderness, Boy, you got big bones. You going be a fat man one day. You and Abram skeleton match in heavenself." She gave a foul grimace. "That shirt you wearing bound to fit Abram after all. Don't worry with shoes. In fact he foot look naked and all chew-up bad from here. Take off all you garb, Boy, quick. Nobody want to spend their fucking life in this vicinity. Quick!" Her face had grown demoniac and black.

"No, no," Cristo whimpered. He was filled with a glaring sense of hallucination. "You devil! I'm going. Stay if you like."

"Stop!" She was aiming steadily at his breast. "One move in the wrong direction and I'll blow your guts out. Quick, off with everthing. Tie kerchief over you face. Quick, I say."

Cristo was fixed and wedged between the hellish face of natural corruption and the unnatural sensation of a living death. There was a click. Magda had cocked the gun. He began tying a grotesque mask over his face.

"Not so high, Boy. Leave you eyes clear to see what you doing. Drop you pants and hurry."

Cristo was naked at last, his clothing over his arm, his nose bandaged. He held his breath like a diver staring into the bowels of the monstrous deeps. The last crow saw him coming and flapped up with a vomiting rag in its mouth.

Cristo struggled to unloose the vestments he dreaded. His face turned swollen, mute and spectacular. He could bear it no longer. He turned and ran, falling on his knees by the sea, sobbing for breath.

He felt Magda's gun in his ribs. He stood up again and shudderingly went back. The black crow that had also returned, withdrew a few paces, its scarlet head cocked incredulously, its beady eyes full of devouring care and curiosity. It seemed to resent and yet to approve the transformation of the living into the dead and the compassionate alliance of the dead with the living.

Half a dozen ghastly excursions and Magda was satisfied. Everything had now been truly s ttled save the successful firing and burning of Abram's deathly rags. The crows would attend to the final rites of a captive disguise.

The last Cristo saw   as Magda shepherded him away – were the black wings falling from the bright sky to frame – it seemed to him in the delirium of the sun – his own features on the ground. He began to vomit like a gorged eagle. His eyes were wretched with the fumes of his arbitrary connection with death, and his lungs were bursting with the brimstone of the sea.

VII

Magda stood at the window looking down on the river. She turned, her expression sullen and full of mourning: "Abram isn't coming back." She spoke in an adamant way as she moved, sitting down and inviting her visitor to do likewise. The man acquiesced, staring with admiration at the sombre features before him.

He was dressed in the camouflage green khaki shirt and shorts of the jungle police, a thin wire of a man, brownish webbed skin, moustache the colour of rusting mould. It was he who had led the men to Jigsaw Bay following Magda's report.

"Cristo would have been living today," Magda said fiercely and majestically. Her voice seemed to brood upon and cry for the heresy of truth locked in her bosom. The police-sergeant had heard her story and complaint before but he was filled once again with curious awe. Every time it was as if the stage was being set for some revelation that would electrify the world. Magda's sculpture and breast heaved and melted before him and he was wrapped in a stimulating blanket that smothered the detection of a lie.

It was rare – amidst his frustrating duties in a poorly-manned, badly-equipped primitive outpost – that he enjoyed the performance of a task truly and well. Magda saw the hint of approval and vegetable lust in his eye. She challenged and proved him: "Is gospel-true, isn't it, Cristo slip through you fingers all along? Somebody actually report that they did see he plain as day paddling like he had sunstroke 'pon the river-top but they could only figure out was a hallucinated ghost at the time."

"Never smoke without fire," the sergeant said. He spoke

without reflecting on the import of his words. Magda had moved in her chair a little and her knees were touching his. He felt their magnetic ominous pull, her dark skin bursting and taut like a grape. She was mourning, he suddenly thought, mourning for the fever of grafted lust. He wanted to stroke her black thighs but restrained himself by thumping the sole of his military boot lightly on the floor. It was a way of recalling himself to his motive and mission, his engine-boat standing against the landing, and a constable sitting patiently in the broiling tent under the sun.

He cleared his throat to hide his embarrassment. Magda stabbed the air with her forefinger. Her dress was armless and the roots of her intimate hair gleamed to accentuate a wanton naked profession. She was a whore, the sergeant said to himself under his breath. But the conviction slid off his mind like melancholy spiritual water from a duck's back.

"Dog-tired Cristo was," Magda cried, the miraculous pupils of her eyes congealed tears, "he reach Abram's hut afternoon time like this," she pointed to the blazing western field of the sky and the white dropping sun, "and Abram *throw* him out. You hear me? All the boy ask for was a black night's rest." Her breath caught a momentary sob. "A night's rest, that's all. Abram would have been in no danger at all. Cristo was *safe* for the time being. Not a soul was following. He had given all-you the slip, pass clean through you open fingers. . . ." She appealed to her policeman of the jungle, drawing him into a conspiracy of senseless and sensible deception and woe. Her mourning was a double-edged sword of keenest theatrical pretension and of hopeless buried reality.

"Yes, yes, I know all this already, Magda." The pursuit-sergeant made a dutiful attempt to camouflage his feeling. "I don't want you to harass yourself by retracing the old painful steps of commission and omission. I would . . ." He was not allowed to finish. Magda faced him, exercising upon him a fateful compulsion to surrender all pretence and will. "Abram could have been my *real* man any time," she flashed, her eyes picking everything to fantastic shreds. "He used to come looking for me once in a couple of months with his sad sad face. Always pretending he in pain," she laughed at the comical image of self-pity. "Think of that," she exclaimed, "he prefer to stay all by himself storing a world of misery and sadness in Jigsaw Bay when he could have claimed *me*. The last-last time he came" – she paused dramatically – "he was more sorry and sad than he ever been before. Was too late. The damage was well and truly done by then. He confess to me how he refuse Cristo a night shelter. And Cristo was so fatigue when Abram put he out" – she was breathless with rage – "he walk two mile and fall dead asleep under the jaguar very hand. He couldn't stir a leg to run or defend himself." She paused again, gathering her rags of cruel fable together. "*Reaction* after all them months, killed Cristo, Sergeant. You ought to know" – she made a cynical hunted gesture with her fingers denoting a vicarious foul triumph – "what happens to a man hunted for his fucking life. His backside does turn into his frontside for the crows to feed. Is so many a proud man been devoured by double-nature to step into their two-faced dead. Christ alone can sew a man together when he *split*." She started weeping violently all of a sudden, convulsed in blinding self-knowledge and the death of love. A black ingenuity and brutal pride had saved Cristo, but he might as well be six foot underground where everyone thought he was, Magda felt passionately and compulsively. After all, there Abram was, though no one knew!

The sergeant half-sprang into galvanized attention and Magda's tears froze as suddenly as they had rained and commenced. She half-rose too and pushed him forcefully back.

"I am merely visiting you to check" – he reproved her, jolted into the recovery of his ritual appearance – "to check whether you had any further news of Abram since . . ." He despaired of anything he said. His words were straw in the gravity of the scales of imbalance. He searched for a redeeming topic. "I understand you are keeping a wake for your son tonight." But this too was useless. It elicited no comfort and response from her. There was only her riddling far-away glance. Whatever her true role and intention was, it was beyond his comprehension. He felt there was no alternative for him at the moment but submission to her mood.

"I chase Abram," she said, in a resolute frozen commanding voice, "when he *crawl* to me with his last sad story. He was the picture of misery. Chased him for ever and for good, you hear? Yes, he come *crawling* to me" – her words rang with the icy echo of loud contempt – "to tell me he never so sorry all his life about Cristo. Was too late to be sorry. The boy was already half-eaten up, chew-up, under Jigsaw bush. Abram declare if he could, he wouldah put himself in my son's place." She laughed abruptly and melodramatically as if to cover an emotional awareness in a generation caught in the grain and mixture of a struggle with incestuous images. "Tiger-meat," she insisted, "that was what Cristo was. Too late to be sorry. What I advise Abram to do – was to match his footsteps in jaguar print, to plant his toes in the jaguar's boots. I told him to *go. Go.* For good. Don't come back. *I never want to see him again.*"

"You're right, Magda." It was useless arguing. Nevertheless he wanted her – in spite of every fury – to make some concession to him. "Perhaps it will comfort you if I tell you – I didn't think it mattered before – I found a note in Abram's cabin. I don't know if this will now help you to feel easier towards him" – he spoke sententiously and hypocritically he knew – "I don't know if it will help you to feel a little better. Abram left a note confirming he had reported Cristo's death to you, and stating he had gone on the jaguar's trail. Moruca, he said. It was a badly written scrawl, obviously the devil was under great emotional strain . . . He wanted to make some sort of restitution to you . . . I could hardly make out his lines. . . ."

Magda remained frozen and unresponsive. She was waiting for something more. And the man was left in exasperation with himself and with her. He mopped his furious melting brow,

searching for the right way to bind a curious circumlocutory
bargain. She wanted him to drop Abram from his mind. Maybe
she had cut his stones out – when she had chased him from her
house – and had slit his gullet. Who could tell? Best to let a
sleeping devil lie. It was the only practical policy in a hazardous,
ungrateful profession involving constant and extravagant
deceptions and traps, sometimes to no purpose whatever.

"I want you to see my point of view," he blurted out. "Abram
is a damned outcast, a confirmed hermit, I know that. *You* will
never forgive him, as far as I can see. And *I* haven't the men to
look for him, I promise. It's his business if he wants to vanish in
Moruca for a month or two. Maybe he'll never come back. This is
the Bush after all. Maybe he'll find Cristo's tiger. I don't know."
He felt her rigid knees moving now against his; he saw her
features relaxing into approval and intimacy. "The point is, he's
under no compulsion to stay away for good. He may be a hell of a
stinking disappointment to you but he was doing what the law
asked in turning Cristo out. Cristo was running from the officers
of the law, remember that. True, he has paid a terrible price, I
know. But he brought it all upon his own head.

"I want you to realize – as far as Abram goes – it is my duty to
tell you that you must instruct him to report to me *when* he visits
you. If you agree that this is the simplest promise to make in the
world, it squares my books. I have too much to do to involve
myself in spending thousands of dollars boring Moruca bush. If
you never see Abram again", he let his hand come slowly to rest
on her thigh, "don't make it too obvious that you *knew*. No
further questions need be asked after a while. I'm a poor man,
Magda, and I like to keep the letter of the law. It's my job after all.
Once you promise . . ."

"I promise," Magda said. "No one will be able to say I
break my promise." They laughed together out of involuntary
conceit, sharing a web they had now spun. Her part –
exceeding his wildest imagination – was the hidden salvation
of Cristo's life out of hopeless loyalty and brutal maternal
instinct – his was the profound bargain and masquerade of

lust, dutiful to a grander design than it dreamed it understood.

The black mourning night of the wake (forty days had passed since the discovery of Cristo and the burial of the corpse) had fallen on the Pomeroon, burning with the ragged dust of stars and the acid of reflected fire biting into the depths of shadow. The boats sailed in to Magda's landing, their lighted torches and lanterns shedding flaring images everywhere in the dark bosom of the water.

Their voices rose, men and women, some dressed plainly, others attired in gay coloured shirts and ties. One could detect nothing of oppressive sadness in their laughter and appearance. It was as if they gave hardly a thought to the depth of meaning in the occasion. Birth and death were a time for curious wild celebration rather than care and forethought and a sense of gloom. The wake was a way of cementing a fissure in the ranks, repairing a seam that had opened, driving home a nail where one was missing. It was a collective roll-call, an amiable meeting, often the frantic smoothing of a grieving brow.

Everyone knew that their region and their home was an enormous half-world and half-shadow composed of empoldered plantations and a veneer of settlement against the encroachment of the sea and the river and – above all – the jungle reaching far and everywhere. A weak link in their armour (as on the occasion of a wild prohibited orgy inviting murder and death as well as the sneaking illegitimate birth of unwanted progeny) was tantamount to a surrender to the jungle they were called upon to face boisterously and to overcome in a spirit equal to the abandon of the enemy. It meant the rallying of all their forces into an incestuous *persona* and image and alliance – the very antithesis of their dark truth and history, written in the violent mixture of races that had bred them as though their true mother was a wanton on the face of the earth and their true father a vagrant and a rogue from every continent.

Magda's wake for her wayward son, Cristo, they felt, was a concession to outraged proprieties – foreshadowed for long years in whispered jealous secrets projected upon her, the compulsive mistress of men, by timid and cruel wives and women. It had seemed a foregone conclusion that Cristo – educated in a remarkable way out of *their* pockets – wearing airs *they* could not afford – should be involved in stabbing a man in a brawling feud over a woman. He was born wild. They wanted him to be caught and tried but in some curious way felt relieved now it had *not* come to that. No one wanted to be agent or witness of the arrest of Magda's son. There was something superstitiously holy about such an unholy woman. They were glad that nature and the tiger had done the trick. Magda had invited them to the wake. They would drink her rum and eat her food all night. They would laugh and curse and rebuild their self-confidence by admonishing her and embracing her with their very gaiety and presence. Her mourning wake was a debt they must exact for the sovereignty she had exercised upon them in their weakness, men and women alike dominated by a furtive desire for unrestricted union with the goddess of identity, superior to a divided unsettled world.

Magda studied her guests as they arrived. The dark bloom of her skin was adorned by a royal purple gown she had once purchased from Mattias Gomez, a Portuguese/Assyrian merchant of the Pomeroon. It enfolded her, making her look like a queen wishing to make a magnificent and enigmatic gift of herself to a hungry crowd, the more mysterious because gratuitous and barbaric; the column of her neck and her arms were bare, and her naked feet were planted squarely on the ground. She stood at a window surveying the river-landing that adjoined the hospitable laden ground under her house. A single lantern was hanging behind her, dim, accentuating a wave of shadows crowding the house, still abstracts, they appeared at times, cast up through the floor by the living souls that stopped and seethed again in the brilliant bottom-yard under her feet. The substance of the wake would enact its being there – on the earthen ground that met the approach from the river-bank.

The lights suspended from the floor, over everyone's head, were intense fuel lamps unlike Magda's ancient upstairs illumination; and the tall stilts and wooden posts upholding the house sent stalwart confirming shadows to the water. A long table, bursting with bottles of rum, soft drinks and meat, shone in the glittering tide. The crowd had begun helping themselves liberally.

"Miss Magda," a voice called, "you not ready to come down?"

"I waiting till Sharon come," Magda shouted in return. "All-you help yourself. The night is young."

Magda watched the landing and the river steadily and contemptuously, listening to the rising spirit in the voices, flooding steadily under her feet. This was a legitimate occasion for everyone to let off steam. They were arriving in small and large groups, each group representing a unit such as the father, the mother, a brother, a sister, a cousin, affianced sweethearts. Each group possessed this stamp, dogmatic kinship and approval, formal and narrow as every Presbyterian and Jesuit rigid ancestor had been, the strong-hold they maintained in spite of the turbulent adjustments they had made, superior landlord redeemed by inferior slave, proud indigenous folk married to the economic emancipation of tyrants. In spite of everything that continued to happen it was an archaic sanction that constantly sought to reassert itself and bless every flood of enormity in a present and past life.

As far as Magda knew, Sharon had not arrived. "Sharon come yet?" Magda leaned through the window and called out. There was a slight answering expectant lull in the voices; a throbbing guitar missed a mental beat. The pattern of sound resumed its sway almost immediately. Heavy boots clumped on the stairs and started to climb.

"Where Sharon?" Magda cried. "You leave your daughter at home a night like tonight, Peet?"

The man addressed as Peet had gained the top. He pulled off his farmer's boots as he entered the house. "Sharon coming in another hour with she new sweet-heart. They gone a little way top-side to fetch their cousins."

He looked a little sheepish and grotesque, Magda thought. A ragged moustache and beard ringed his lips in a careless ageing loathsome growth. He appeared to have come straight from his coconut farm; his hair and beard and dress may have been made from a foul kind of straw, and from smoky unnatural copra, half-singed and rotting in an imperfect day's sun.

"Sharon coming soon," Peet said again, searching in his mind for a way to express his lust. Magda nodded, turning away from him, regarding once again the river and the boat-landing painted in a gleaming wash of light like a permanent meteor established amidst the milky stars in the water.

Peet approached her, twirling his hands like a conjurer playing with the invisible brim of a hat he carried between his fingers. It was a nervous trembling habit that had become second nature to him after years of hard labour against the Bush.

"Magda," he said awkwardly and foolishly, "Ah sorry 'bout Cristo. Sharon didn't really *want* her old sweetheart that met his dead at Cristo's hand. In point of fact she really *grieve* for Cristo, and nobody else. I is a hard-working man. All me life I grow up and I never understand the ways of love. *Nobody* ever understand. . . ." He was pleading with her.

Magda turned. There was something in his voice, the inflection and sentimentality of a drunkard, that revealed his thoughts to her. She smelt the strong coarse liquor on his breath. Her detestation of him mounted and then changed in a flash into the most acute self-revelation. Why, after all, should it horrify her that he wanted her? His trembling uncouth manner was something she knew by heart. He was still a strong man, despite his labouring temper and mood, his lack of grace, his burden of guilt. She had entertained Abram in other shapes for long years in the half-shadow and the half-world. He always looked rusty with fatigue when he was driven to come, and still violent with desire for untiring strength. He wanted to be, in that rare moment, a beloved outlaw coming to his mistress with a reckless spirit to match the envelope of appearance. It was this he desired most of all – an outlaw's natural dignity. She had always been this enduring need in him. It was all so stark and true she nearly sobbed the news aloud. If she had known it before she could have endured no other man. It was too late, impossible to sleep with a dead man's image however promiscuous his bed. She felt Abram's foul breath almost with terror in her nostrils. It was an obscene breath (no sum of money could erase from her lungs) blowing from the distant hallucinated foreshore. She had never bargained with *this* before. She recoiled, barring out with her arms the memory and the odour, the corruption that belched in the stomach of Peet's derivative love. She could no longer endure herself as a vicarious scavenger and vulture of men, describing in the wilderness their witness and dream of purification, and providing them with wings for the commonest womb wherein they died and flew above all erosive strife and invalid ambition.

"O God what wrong, Magda?" Peet gasped. "You staring at me like I is your ghost. Like I is you dead body's carcass – no living man at all."

VIII

Peet clumped his way downstairs with a stricken expression he instantly tried to mend when the vision and gaiety of the lights struck full within his eye. The guitar twanged a cacaphonic chord and raw voices saluted him. He was drunk, he knew, and yet he felt more cruelly sober than ever before, the cruel soberness of a shocking sense of extreme rejection, hallucination and destitution. Despite this he still wanted everyone to believe he was on top of the world, a potent guardian and whimsical conspirator, whose joust with the queen of fate marked him as a seasoned campaigner.

His friends and relatives would applaud him and honour him all the more for certain insinuations of sexual craft and conquest on a night like this. They knew he was normally gentle as a lamb. But still waters always ran deep! And that was the missionary highlight of good old Peet.

Peet knew they were expecting him to be both mysterious and mischievous so that they could find in him their own vicarious uplift. This was the vital intention of the wake. Peet reached for rum and swallowed it quick. It was a fiery brand and he was glad to screw up his face, trusting no one saw him for what he was behind his straw and his mask.

The new shot of rum revived the misty fumes in his head but the effect was as eerie as a lightless foreign bulb, with broken filaments, that no longer had the receptive power to glow in an electric current. One might as well crush it under one's heel and light oneself afire like a living primitive torch. But this was equally impossible without the active co-operation of painful sensibility. He swallowed one – two – three – four rums, trying to laugh with the victorious spirit everyone desired. The current of thwarted hope began to

278

abandon him. The wake had sensed in an ageless vigilant way that he had become a "corpse". He had become a curious liability, a victim. He was *not* the medium everybody wanted. In the "communique" of the initiated he had gone over to the enemy. It was something instinctively grasped and recognized. He had ceased to live as the spearhead of attack and the wake must look elsewhere for a vessel of rehabilitation and defiance.

Peet knew that they knew he was "dead". He was so passively sober and bottomlessly drunk that he could not believe they did not *know* everything that had happened. Magda had overwhelmed him with an invocation of revulsion and scorn that shattered him to the core. Peet saw every loud face and gesture in his dazed eyes as an echo and reiteration of calamity. He had left his farm that afternoon half-blinded with sun, stopped home long enough to consume a big bottle of rum, and stuff twenty dollars in his pocket. He knew what was expected of him tonight. He had qualified to put himself forward as the profane and equally sacred receptacle of the wake. He must pour good fortune upon all. He and Magda must make up to each other and something must happen, something must transpire between them so that the wake would find that "East and West had met", the opposite camps of order and chaos had been bound in a truce. Peet's daughter had lost her first affianced man at the hand of Magda's son. There was the problematic fable of history in a nutshell. It was a murder and breach the whole community alone could repair by sponsoring a rough protagonist out of the heart of the innocent party. The wounded sheep must clothe himself in the garb of the ravening wolf; tomorrow's sun must shine everywhere on a victorious respite, shine on the blind privilege that overcame the old gulf and separation.

When Magda had called for Sharon, Peet had perceived his drunken cue. He had marched heavily and loudly upstairs. He had blundered into the mesmerism of shadow and flickering illumination. He gulped in the spell of seduction with his befuddled senses. His foolish apologetic confession concerning his daughter's grief for Cristo was unripe and premature. Magda had not been touched in any way save that she grew curiously aware of him. Her dark slanting eyes appeared to draw all the light in the room and to spill their own blinding solder and silver. He felt his advances repelled with a force of reality residing paradoxically in his own senses like those of a man whose embroiled arms had always been their own gaoler and their knotted chain. It was a most grotesque overpowering instinct. He was turning insanely foolish and helpless and he began to babble pitiful things, the intoxicated darkness of dead wit. Magda denounced him and her rage split the roof of his skull, letting in the biting acid stars. The floor opened too and the raw surf and voice of the wake clamoured and vomited. Someone was beating a trembling waving drum in time to a nervous plodding guitar. He caught himself lying on the floor in a foul spittle and mess. The room started to remind him of what had happened. Magda had pushed him violently away from her and he had fallen, striking his head hard on the wall. The sound of his fall was so loud it could have startled the tiger of death but the wake had mounted into a burst of raucous applause cushioning him upon the wild earth. He may have been six foot underground for all they cared.

He began to pull himself up from the floor, rage seizing his mind. The palm of his hand slipped on a scrap of greasy paper. He could not help looking around to see. It was a torn dollar bill pasted with the contents of his stomach. Yes, he had offered her his desperate money. She had torn it out of his hands with her fiendish claws. He had grimaced, thinking *now! The true picture was coming back to him, the true circumstances of his struggle with the woman.* She had backed away, he remembered it clearly now, and to his astonishment, torn the handful of bills into shreds. She flung them on the floor. He lunged at her. She eluded him. He followed. She ran to the door. He made for her, swearing viciously. It was all over in a few seconds of naked cat-like feet. She caught his heavy boot off the threshold of the door and crashed it on his forehead before he could wink. He fell into a void out of which he was rising now with a sickening compelling memory of urgency to make her pay for *everything*.

But even as he began raising himself from the floor he was filled at once with the helpless sensation of being manacled to the ground. His limbs refused to act and the whole room underwent another change in his skull. The light in the roof was still shining he knew but it had turned into faint moonlight crossed by branches of cloud through which shadows of black birds flew across the sky. He tried to dismiss these notions and images, straining his attention to follow the well-known voice of the wake. The sound, however, came from an alien body of experience – a breaking sea on a jagged coast at Abram's doorstep. It assailed him, full of pounding threatening sibilance, a striding breath of grandeur, whispering and overlapping and rising notes in a hushed vagrant roar that suddenly grew and became so deafening he was transported to see the flecks of tigerish foam on a dark fluid body, striped by the animal light of the moon, flying across the room towards him. The glistening dim fangs sank into the bellying sail of his chest, breaking the manacles that still held him, and flinging him in a heap near the door.

Peet caught himself in the nature of his true surroundings in a lightning instant. The truth was, he remembered and saw clearly, he had half-risen tremblingly and insecurely, to spring at Magda. She had scrambled at him before he could stir, tearing his coat into rags, dragging him towards the door. He felt an unexpected blow. The room spun around him again and the void held him now in its frightful jaws, blotting out the serial property of recollection. The sound of the sea raced in the chattering teeth of the wind with cruel delight. The ground was criss-crossed by dead memory – the floor of an ancient jigsaw, stylized furrows and mats belonging to a temple, naked roots on a fantastic farm, ditches of alabaster in the jungle. The shadows were frozen and white as Abram's blood on tropical moonlight-snow. They ran between a dim wave of crested sea and a dark forest of cultivated night, the sensational corpse of the medium of man borne swiftly by the living tiger of death.

Peet returned out of the jaws of Abram's tiger to Magda's house and the living wake. It was an intolerable strain to assess the horror of what he had dreamt. Magda was watching him from the opposite wall in the dim light. He recalled in his manner of split recollection how she had grabbed him and ripped the shirt almost off his back.

He sat up, holding his shattered head, searching his body and limbs all over in a dazed and curious way, wondering whether he was still *there*. All at once his hands, which were running over himself, stopped being his and became someone else's. The spirit of alienation was terrifying; he tried to groan. His lips refused to utter a sound though they opened and shut, turning into a helpless gaping thread hanging from a sharp button and tooth. The slightest pull would dislodge a stitched mouth and cave in a fixity of gum.

The busy hands began loosening a foul skin and vest, peeling away the rotting shell from spirit and seed and bone.

Peet stared at the nervous terror of spidery fingers. Were they his? No! They belonged to another person. This gradually became clear. *There* were the other man's wrists. One could make out the forearms. A purplish light was shining on the elbows; the film rose into shoulders, chest, abdomen. It was a blue anatomy and presence Peet saw bending over him, floating above him with an incandescent flame and eye. The perspiring dilated pupil shone and wept as a candle's melting grease.

Peet began to perceive the dark features. The high bone structure resembled his but the fleshy shape of the mouth was individual and new, the eyebrows were inclined to be thick, the lobe of the ear was fragile, the colour of the skin was blue as one of the shadows on the moon.

Peet's mind was sweating with torture to discern every tiny strand and particular like a mother seeing her newborn child for the first time. These distinctions stood between him and the shadowy person over him. But at last he *knew*. It was Cristo. The weeping eye had flared brighter than ever into a scheming match, flame to eye, flesh to spirit, bone to mind. It was Cristo's sulphuric face in truth, burnt by the fumes of hell and reality. The skin had been cut to the bone, and a long wound stood under the left eye running down the cheek to join the lips in a convulsive triumphant grimace.

This vision of Cristo instantly fled on Peet's recognition and awareness. Only Magda remained, swaying lantern in her hand. She had unhooked it from the roof and was critically regarding him.

"Is time you get up and go down, Peet," she said. "The folk waiting for you and they going be wondering if you stay long-long with me. Don't give no more foolish trouble. You should have known better. A woman got she refusing days. Now you sober I hope you know." She spoke in a deliberate and commonplace tone.

"Is what really happen?" the man groaned. "You put bad spirit-jumbi or what on me?"

Magda grimaced. "Ah had to bash you head with you own big boot. *That* is the bad jumbi. It belong to your naked foot! You were too drunk to understand anything and drunk man always dead to the claim of responsibility. Don't shame if you feel bad. Remember not a soul downstairs see what happen. If they *hear* you fall they believe me and you been having fun. Fool them and satisfy them. I don't care two dam'." She laughed crudely. "Is up to you to stitch your mouth shut and thank your stars you really in one piece. Because, believe me, I was never so *mad*. I see me own hell wake up in you face tonight. I couldah tear you limb from limb." She began to probe him: "Come on, get going, man. Stand up on you foot for Godsake. I want a chance to clean up this *den*, you hear me?" She pointed to the state of the floor. "Look, I just been and get a good shirt for you. Your own did tear in me hand like rotten rag. Take it. Put it on. Used to belong to Cristo. Bound to fit you with a pinch."

Peet was struggling to his feet at last. He took the shirt absent-mindedly. "Where Cristo gone?" he asked, still a little bemused.

Magda stared closely at him. "Where you think he gone? Up to heaven or down to hell? Maybe he familiar with all sides now. Quick, put on the boy's shirt. Don't tell me you frighten of you own skin." She gave her sombre crude laugh, turning away to restore the lamp to the roof. The man was changing his tattered shirt and turning away slowly as well to descend into the blinding eye of the wake that had become as empty to him as a dry thirsty receptacle under the dominion and menacing departure of every fickle cloud. The vacillating spirit and soul of all his life had fled from him to overshadow him with the consciousness of being a broken vessel. However much he tried to mend a carnival conceit and glory it remained a basket and a sieve – crippled by the compulsive perception of the bizarre womb of Abram – out of which Cristo had been reborn and spilt.

BOOK THREE

TIME OF THE TIGER

Tiger, tiger, burning bright
In the forests of the night . . .

William Blake

In the track of thy footprint The young girls
run along by the way.
At the touch of a spark, at the spiced wine . . .

St John of The Cross

IX

The night had changed over a long interval of waiting, the frozen stars had become crystals of dew immured in the alchemical waiting shadow of a mirror. All nature was waiting with a passionate longing for the thaw of love buried as deep as everyone wished to dream. The tide and fusion of chaos stood almost at its highest expectant peak, too still and grave and dark to be discerned moving and dislodging the tiniest planted seed of a star.

Magda felt the faintest hopeful shiver – as if she were able to sense the vaguest growing ripple in the water. She was repelled by the violent memory of the night and drawn into acute self-reflection and self-preparation for what was yet to come. The river remained vacant and untroubled as ever but Magda still sensed – as a hunter keeps an aroused ear to the ground – everything was moving with great subtlety and Sharon was coming now. The bed of stars was splitting into the faintest almost imperceptible swell and swirl of roots ripening into branches in the sky.

The night knew how to clothe the growing tree, the heavens rustled, a new leaf, minute swooping echoes of a flight of birds fell to settle above Abram's cushioned head. Magda felt the tension of their beating wings in her mind. The shadowy wing and intuition of the new arrivals suddenly heaved to a climax. Sharon and her escort had appeared on the river and were sailing in to land.

"Sharon," Magda called imperiously. Sharon, knowing she could not evade the summons and command – made her way slowly up the long flight of stairs. Mattias Gomez, her new-found fiancé, looked at her with an intuitive sad stare.

"Don't make it too long," he said with the ominous spirit he always carried to conceal a profound boredom, "or I'll have to come and fetch you." Sharon answered him with a slightly nervous smile slung over a delicate shoulder. Her dress caught a complex shaft from the lights of the wake, blew and settled a little in a breath of wind – an instantaneous naked perception, fragile as the X-ray of a shell. Mattias seemed to catch indeed the seductive compliance of a ghost. He gave an absent smile in response. Sharon admired him because he brought to her a matching slenderness and charm as evasive and yearning as the glowing blossom of a cigarette far out in the night-black forested river. No one knew whether the spark was the unsleeping eye of hermit or beast.

Mattias was a thin-faced man in his late twenties, Portuguese/Assyrian descent, skin bloodless and pale under the yellow paint of the sun, black funereal hair, meticulously brushed and dressed. He worked in a large shop owned by his father – *Mattias Gomez, Snr* – a name that spelt prosperity and success. It dangled over the entrance to the merchandise store in which Magda had procured her purple gown, as well as above the hardware division and the big grocery counter. The business had long ceased to have any serious competition.

Young Mattias, the only son and heir, superintended the accounts. One could see him, day after day, on his high stilted bench, presiding over books and bills of tax, papers and requisitions, staring through a window upon the dark Pomeroon. It was an unhappy musing ironic face, unconscious, one knew, of the painstaking figure that upheld it: brooding with an accent of sardonic distrust, that needled brow and eye together (Mattias seldom dreamt he looked like this) upon mercenary calculations and provisions. The thin mocking face did not appear to belong to the scrupulous accounting hands and fingers. One wondered whether Mattias would ever awaken fully to the riddle of himself as he twisted his shoulders and stooped and shaped on his high lofty stool a loyal figure yet question-mark.

Now he approached Peet, whom he was beginning to accept as his future father-in-law. "Has Magda stayed upstairs all night?" he asked curiously. "It's nearly midnight." He glanced at his wrist-watch.

"She been downstairs half-hour ago then she go back up." He was watching Mattias with a hollow suspicious glare like a silver penny stuck over the eye. He forced a haggard smile and welcome on his lips. "You-all stay really late to come. I already give up hope of seeing you. Help you-self to a drink, Boy."

Mattias poured himself a rum and swallowed it. Hot distaste appeared to rise and leave a mark on his countenance. Nevertheless he poured himself another and endured the same process of acceptance and the same record of displeasure. "We were on the point of changing our mind," he explained. "When we got to your cousins' place the house was in one hell of an uproar. The blasted jaguar again! *I* have never seen the beast though everybody else has."

"You spent too many years away taking education at school. Like Magda's son," Peet was fingering the collar of his shirt in afterthought. "He get anybody?" He leaned forward with an air of groping drunken alarm. "*The Tiger*," he cried all of a sudden again. "He *eat* nobody?" The full stroke of the news had now struck home through a cloak of illogical awareness and stupor.

"No, everything is all right. Nothing happened really." Mattias spoke a little wearily and carelessly, pouring himself another drink, and casting a disgusted eye upon the crowd: it was a sorry and indifferent glance indeed, full of dreary calculation about the value of the wake. Everybody rubbed everybody's shoulder, talking vociferously and yet remaining totally blind to each other. They were beginning to lose each other in the midst of their chronic density and identity that had become an archaic and meaningless rubber stamp. The furious grant of exuberance the occasion warranted had begun to spend itself and leak away, as if the violent cleavage

they imagined they had come to mend defied their traditional
yoke and narrow intention. And yet he could not be sure. . .

"Funny thing," Mattias spoke as he looked around contemptuously, "a couple of sheep were standing there all nice
and handy. Standing in the abandoned field at the back. They
were still there safe and sound as before."

"Who *see* such a harmless tiger?" Peet was demanding. All
at once he had grown crafty and suspicious.

"One of the women. She said she heard someone moving
outside. The dog was all chained up as usual. It barked
anyway. She shone a torch out of the window. There he was,
standing on his hind legs." Mattias wondered whether he
was creating an effect. He was feeling empty and bored as he
always did, out of place, incapacitated almost. He never
confessed it to anyone but the truth was, there was nothing
worth while he ever seemed to have to *do*. He had had
nothing to *do* over the past couple of years since he had
returned to his home in the Pomeroon. Once or twice he had
known there was something of self-denunciation and frustration in his distracted expression that intrigued and alarmed
people. It was too fleeting a figure for him to grasp in himself
save as the most marginal of riddling reflections. He knew it
was there because he saw it in other inquisitive hopeless faces
(though they did not dream he did) as they grew aware of it in
his. It was the birth of a universal discontent and the shadow
of the death of the past, the presentiment of an apparition
combining the serial features of archaeological and racial
mystery. The figure of speech dawned on him like the
infectious misery and involuntary dreadful conceit of the
wake. He had never conceived anything so alien and curious
before.

"Standing up on his hind legs?" Peet's vomiting laugh
drew him out of the compulsive reverie. "Ah, Mattias,
you and me is a good one for seeing things tonight. I *see*
fuck all upstairs, you hear me? Magda split my head open
and Cristo jump out." He pointed a crooked intoxicated

finger to the house above their heads. "Before that happen I was so bewitched a tiger been running with me like a corpse in his jaws. I dreamt I was Abram-self." Peet laughed as if he had coined a pitiful joke. He did not know what he was actually saying. "Now you tell me you see that same tiger walking 'pon foot like a man. Is *who* really *drunk*, you or me?"

"*I'm* not drunk." Mattias was scornful. "*You* are." The same rubbish over and over again one imbibes with one's mother's waking milk. "The truth is all of you" – his glance swept all around in a disparaging way – "like to pretend too much. Or is it that you understand so little you cannot really begin to pretend about anything? I wonder." The rum had wakened a shameful bitter flush on Mattias' cheek, a bitter flush indeed aroused by the involuntary dark sense of exile in his native home. "I'm telling you simply what I was told. Understand? The girl said she shone her light. Unfortunately the battery was poor and the ray was dim. . . ."

"Dim as Cristo's backside on the moon," Peet groaned and interrupted him.

"She saw the tiger's front paws lifted straight like hands. . . ."

"Hee, hee, hee! Maybe the beast getting ready to jump on the little maiden after all, eh, Mattias? What you think of *that* now, eh, Mattias?"

"The light was poor but she made out the markings, the stripes, you know. . . ." Mattias had needled brow and eye.

"What happen after? Cristo scratch the maiden pretty breast?"

Mattias was growing more exasperated than ever, and yet at the same time a strange and blundering excitement and participation grew in his breast, a new beating heart of possession and antagonism. He felt himself summoned – as if he had been challenged by the wake – to discern a deep, ancient, irrational logic on the most troubling question of all mankind – the meaning of individual innocence and guilt.

291

"Nothing happened I tell you." He was speaking half aggressively and half-shamefacedly. "The night was dark. He sprang off in the moment she turned on the light and screamed. You know women! The farm lad had been having a wash at the landing. He came running, naked in the night. . . ."

"Naked in the night! I hearing you, Boy. Drunk man *drunk* but he not always pure stupid. . . ."

"The other women came running too," Mattias went on quickly, "from the kitchen and wherever they were. You're staring at me as if you don't believe a word I'm saying. You're drunk I can see. To make my long story short," he declared, "they took the gun and the brightest lamp they could find and looked all around. There was nothing. Made off. Clean away."

"No tracks? You didn't add up, subtract, multiply all them tracks – a bright educated son of a gun like you? You mean to say you beginning to lose all you good sense, Mattias? You turning into a stuffed dummy, a shell of a man? As empty-headed and dead as me?" Peet laughed and stared lugubriously.

Mattias felt the most curious anger – in addition to excitement – welling up within him. The sap of this mingled bitterness grew steadily like a new film and bark – replacing an old insensible skin – shaking the conscious spirit of forgotten limbs. Words formed upon his lips with an import and utterance he had never felt and believed mere sounds to possess. "A mere shell of a man?" he was crying to himself. Something had disturbed and moved him, galvanizing him into disproportionate response as a cue would stir a tensed overwound actor. He recalled the scarecrows he had seen farmers put up in the fields, as well as a group of radio-active robots – spying through telescopes – he had scanned in a recent photograph of a bombed desert. "You old fool," he cried, "what in hell do you mean? I'm no stuffed dummy" – the new spirit in his voice gripped him – "whatever you are. I

292

wasn't *there*. And in any case don't you know the ground is hard? Not a drop has fallen for six weeks now. What trace could anyone find?" He was glaring at Peet, with an unnatural vision of hate, a blind and still seeing look, something he understood now he had always possessed – without perceiving it – a reflection of violent instinct that wanted to smash the mirror of false accusation containing Peet's "dead" lips. He had been caught by the corpse of the wake – like one betrothed to a contagious shadow – and he resented it with all the normal indifferent habits of former command. Peet wanted to pin all the blame for the night's débâcle on a future son-in-law and Mattias wanted to free himself from this "dead" legacy and this wedding to fearful responsibility. It should have been the simplest thing in the world to shake off the parody of involvement – featuring Cristo and Abram of Jigsaw Bay – before it grew again into a theatre of vindication established and rooted in Peet and himself. Mattias wondered whether he had spoken his fantastic half-dreaming vision aloud. He did not know where the idea came from, the incongruous linking of branches and names and identities in his mind in an involuntary serial way that made no sense to him whatever save as an inversion of prophecy (bringing difficult news from the past) and the reflex of an all-encompassing future in the curious bonds of the present. *He was dreaming*, Mattias tried to warn himself, dreaming with the most wide-awake eyes in the world – bulging seed in a growing head.

Why not turn away, walk away, shrug off the haunted tree on his shoulder? Dummy indeed! Such helplessness, such featureless idiocy! Nothing whatsoever held him bound in reality to anyone and anything. It was the fabulous injustice of universal nightmare that made him feel himself saddled like this.

He was still Mattias Gomez, was he not? a rich man's heir, free to come and go, free of the past as of every beggarly origin. His grandfather had been a beggar (but what of it?) on the streets of old Georgetown, whining and peddling scraps of merchandise from one end of the Guyana coast to the other. It didn't matter in the slightest what kind of commercial witchcraft had done the trick in the end. The comfortable fact was the old man had succeeded in amassing a minor fortune and in winding together the roots of enterprise for Mattias Gomez, Snr, young Mattias's father. Mattias, the grandson, could afford to despise everyone in a way the grandfather had never known possible. Why he even secretly despised the grandfather for leaving him so little to do save carry on a humdrum business and scan the daily sums the business drew. Did he really want to change anything? He had never asked himself this question so directly before. It came to him now with such violent inner force that one would have thought it had been the conscience-stricken ambiguity of a lifetime. He had always been able to shelter behind a fault of nature and history that lay outside of his intention and will since it had happened long before he was born. Had he indeed sought to conceal and thrust away from himself the major opportunity and question of his life? Surely he was not such a fool to try and answer the riddle of himself. Might as well seek to overcome the sphinx! In such ambition lay the seed of self-aggrandizement and self-delusion. So childish to have to remind himself again and again – in different ways and forms – of the folly of *doing* anything at all. Did it mean that to find that one had nothing to do was synonymous with not wanting to do anything at all save wear one's mask like a proud hopeless fault? He could not hold himself responsible for the silly mess everybody was making of life, contemptible murder, petty jealousy, pretensive orgies of corruption and secretive theft. It was all too far beneath him to catch him. Until *now* –Mattias gasped as if he stood on the threshold of profound participation – it had never loomed large and had never seemed to affect him at all in the strict disdainful ordering of himself.

Compulsive eternity stood while every disjointed upturned

picture and impression revolved in his mind – a series of revelations, engagements and disengagements, each pattern appearing the very unstable antithesis of another and undermining even itself as it dawned. Mattias was held by this spirit of dissociation and hypersensitivity, a boiling scalding mask he had never truly suspected one ever wore. His new consciousness and blood of dreadful fire in the melting nature of himself was a burning curiosity about the walking tree and family of mankind. Time had stopped, he thought with a premonition of the future, looking into Peet's extinguished eyes; it started again with a gasp as if the mask of Abram had returned to play once again an evolving and still accusing part. *It was Abram who stood before him.* Mattias closed his eyes. When he opened them again Peet was replying to the remark about the drought in the Pomeroon as though there had been no interval whatever of monstrous identity, and the bridge that stretched across limbo – from the "dead" to the "living" – had always been there, conjoint with time and eternity.

"Not since Cristo bury. Not a drop fall since then. I feel parch. What 'bout you?" Peet was pouring himself a large rum. Mattias picked up the bottle. "Go ahead," Peet cried, tilting Mattias's elbow so that the liquor splashed and filled half a glass, "help yourself big-big, me Boy, now you here. *Now you really here.*" His eyes were absent, staring at Mattias but seeing someone else in the distance. Mattias tossed back the fiery spirit recklessly.

"Everybody been waiting for you," Peet cried in a savage mood mingled with uncanny gaiety, "you don't know? Look, you don't see how drunk and friendly they beginning to gather round the two of we? They smell the rat in the air. They know *you*." Mattias could not help shuddering a little. His spine tingled and flushed as when a cat crosses one's grave. "We all know you been spawning and matching some good old wives' tale to bring to we, and it was *that* keeping you back, naw Boy?" Peet was transported by a venomous laughing cunning. "Draw close," he was waving to the ecstatic crowd, "all of you think I died upstairs in Magda's house but look – look, I doing better still – look *who* I got here. This is the one who earn all the blame. Not me. All you going get you bellyful and satisfaction tonight. Look at he face good. All it need is a long-long scratch I tell you" – he passed his fingers along his cheek, indenting the loose skin from eye to lip – "to demonstrate to all and sundry he really did meet with a tiger of excuse. Then perhaps he wouldah fool we all to perfection." Peet laughed, bottomlessly, sententiously drunk.

"I told you plainly I didn't meet the tiger. . . . Can't you understand?" Mattias was protesting to the crowd that had formed a ring all around. "Why," he could not help laughing too at the ridiculous injustice of his position, "your cousins can vouch for my story. . . . Why if they hadn't been so upset they would have been here tonight to tell you it all themselves. . . ."

Peet snapped his fingers in a conjuring derisive way under Mattias's fascinated stare – "Mattias," he exclaimed in the frenzy of possession, "who you trying to fool? You money can bribe any of me hole-in-the-corner cousin night and day. Who in heaven name you think you can fool, big Boy? Next time they let you fill their head with lie they must advise you to dig you face deep with a long nail."

"Are you telling me I'm mad?" Mattias was almost beside himself.

"I'm telling you – tiger me backside! No tiger been *here* and no tiger been *there*. Is all a good excuse. Why you can't come with the living truth?"

"I have told you the truth, you old fool."

"Why you can't ever bring the living truth?" Peet was implacable and furious. "No, you must always wrap yourself in a lie. I know you. I know what been pleasuring you all the time and making you arrive so goddam late. I telling you now and I want the whole world to hear what been keeping

296

you" – he was waving blindly – "you catch me daughter Sharon and you lay she down like if you in heaven."

Mattias was unable to speak and defend himself.

"Soon as me old venerable back turn you tek me prize and maidenhead. You give she a deep sinister stroke good and proper. I know. The tiger is none other but you. *You*. Sneaking behind every helpless maiden in the dark. You can't wait until you marry in a lawful form."

The crowd burst into furious aggrieved drunken acclamation. Peet's head suddenly began to hang, as a dog's tongue protrudes, running close to the ground of all endurance to overtake and overcome the most elusive game. It had long ceased to be a question of conscious volition that kept him moving and alive. It was a blind incredible extension of all living unfathomable resources by a spent soul in the throbbing heart of the wake. Someone was pounding a drum, a curious muffled sound that incessantly died to beat again, suffering no interruption even when the voice of the crowd roared in Mattias' ear as if the ancient tiger had truly entered the wake out of chaos and eternal nightmare.

The curtain was being torn from Mattias' eye by every waking fateful circumstance of drunken inheritance and frustration, engagement and exile. He felt the desolating uprush of panic and rape and death reflected in every snarling face. One side of him longed to return to the counting house and the state of being a stranger to himself. The other waking open eye – in a marble resolution of countenance – saw beyond every former shadow of forgetfulness into the scope and nature of the devil's illusion and drama. Mattias beheld the terrifying mystery of being accused by one's demented spiritual father (whose garment of cruel longing and grotesque responsibility had to be converted and to fall on a despised and hated pretender and son) of misdemeanours and crimes that would have been an intolerable injustice to anyone, committed to a relationship involving anything less than perfect insight and loyalty. It was the most fabulous

297

unity and terrible honour to be chosen by the shattered medium of the wake to redeem the relics of crippled perspective, and vanquish the devil of a broken spirit by an acceptance of guilt in the seduction of the "virgin" of Cristo's choice on the very night of the dead man's wake.

The crowd began to close in upon him. Peet's hand was uplifted to crown and strike. Mattias gave a loud imploring heartrending cry. He could no longer endure such a frightful resolve and sovereign complicity – crushed and buried alive in all innocence in a fantastic and insensible body of men.

Sharon climbed the stairs with a strange paradoxical sensation at heart. Her last glimpse of Mattias, looking up at her, and warning her not to be long, filled her with a hint of a consummation to love she had never actually experienced, a ghostly annunciation and nuptial, insubstantial and mysterious as an interlocking shadow under a full moon in the dead of night.

It was a feeling of need and perturbation and sadness she could not account for – an acute spirit of meeting and parting and of eternal distance that was still nearness. It was as if she was saying an inexplicable goodbye.

Magda opened the door for her and Mattias was lost to her view. She stared into the dim room, hesitating for a moment when she saw Magda's countenance, for all the world like a dark flickering terrible mirror reflecting every dim consciousness in the house. Sharon wondered if the face she saw was her own bemused vision.

The house bore a slightly wild perfume. Sweet and sour, stimulating and degrading, a breath that participated the half-groaning, half-laughing, miserable, inspired voice of the wake. The voice and the breath filled every corner, coming from a great distance one imagined (though in reality close at hand) like a built-in, invisible radio that had been tuned to catch and render a particular tonal impression and roar an inspirited demented value and sound.

298

There was a wild-beast spirit and smell everywhere, Sharon suddenly thought with emotional memory. She could not help recalling how she and Mattias had arrived at her cousins' place to find the family in an uproar.

The beast lived everywhere at once, in every breast, on every breath. Mankind itself was the tiger. Sharon could not imagine why in heaven's name she felt this. As if the strongest, most vivid desire rose in her to slay the tiger with her "snow-maiden's" hands. It was an erotic fable, one of the white fables of the wake and the mixed ancestral legendary land. No one believed in such extreme nonsense though every now and then everyone paid curious lip-service to the host of intervention and communion in the cruel breast of the wake.

No harm ever came to anyone at a true and legitimate wake though sometimes a little blood had been known to spill. Everyone knew – when this happened – they would feel all the better the morning after.

The wake for Cristo! – the strangest wake everyone had known, for reasons no one could absolutely express. Whatever the obscure reason was, therein perhaps lay the seed of a subtle and yet enormously overpowering branch of difference. Maybe that was why Magda was standing in the house, in the curious way she confronted Sharon, inhaling the sweet stifling odour of a young woman's blossoming desire mixed with the envy of a brutal older woman for a softness she had never been able to possess. Sharon found her mind straying beneath the scent of a youthful perfume to the trail of old human vomit.

It was an involuntary hideous notion and it made her feel she must leave Magda at once. She did not know why she had come after all.

"Shut the door, Sharon," Magda was saying peremptorily, yet stealthily. "Come close, I have something for you."

The girl felt the fantasy of a presence before her like some enormous jungle-cat. She suddenly saw a flash in the dark mirror and countenance, an anxious reason and conviction that bound them together like fate. It was dark and still utterly clear to her now why she had climbed the flight of forbidden stairs. She was startled: it was more than she wished to know, however much she *knew* it already long ago.

"Cristo said I can trust you," Magda whispered, so close Sharon felt the touch of scornful lips. "You think you really know what is this trust?" Sharon shrank before a shrewd coarse tongue and disdain.

"I been waiting patient for you all night, Sharon. . . ." She lifted her hand to smother every excuse. "Yes, I know all you going say, girl, don't worry youself. I know full well you been on the rivertop with your new sweet man Mattias. . . ."

"We couldn't help being delayed because. . . ."

"I know," Magda brushed the explanation aside, "I know all the foul and the fond excuse in this world. I been down 'pon this earth a long enough time now. You is Pomeroon milk, my dove. The fairest in the land even if you granddaddy been black like me and sin put together." She was laughing soundlessly. "The cream of the joke is – one man catch his dead for you already in a brawl we all remember," she mocked, "and God know who else twisting 'pon a fool's rack tonight but your pretty soul still staying *white* as Christmas card with snow, while everybody else own turning black with hate, black-hearted as the devil of a rape. Is so Pomeroon people stay, my love. Naw, I wronging them. I being unjust. Is so the whole world stay, child. Not we alone in this bush. You don't agree?" Her voice was contemptuous. Then her lips froze. "Cristo believe in you too and that is God's truth. The boy so weak." The hard breath cracked and whistled. All at once the violent expression underwent another theatrical flickering reflection and change. Something bloomed like a tender smile, beguiling, flattering. Magda was wooing Sharon as a mother flatters a daughter by inciting her to share a common vulgar predilection. "You know how it is when a man gets to want a woman like he own mad flesh." She spoke ingratiatingly with an air that said in effect "let bygones be bygones", and with a brittle desire to fabricate a relationship in spite of all the previous misgivings she had entertained.

Sharon was unable to respond. She was repelled and filled with intimate horror. She had a crushing sensation of being seduced, refracted and distorted in Cristo's ancient serial mirror. The face and image were surely *not* of herself and Cristo but of Cristo and Cristo's mother, feline, devouring, incestuous, implacable, the lust of the hermaphrodite of the species she had been summoned to participate in the wake.

"What do you want of me?" she cried, goaded into cradling her arms in an act of rocking submission and woe. "What do you want me to *do?*" she cried again, *"You're Cristo's mother. I'm not. Do you think I can bring him back alive!"* She flung her arms out defiantly, repudiating every robot and parody and maternal fixation. She felt in some inexplicable way the mantle had fallen on her to struggle for a paradox of faith Magda had succoured and lost. She must preserve an independent role – if she wanted to succeed – even if it meant turning into the very witch of ingenuousness, heartless and barren as stone.

Magda's expression had grown cold and retiring too before Sharon's singular obstinacy. "What *I* want you to do? Not me. *I* want you to do nothing. Is Cristo. Look – read this. It's all there in black and white. He think he can trust you." Her voice was bitter.

"What in God's name is this?" Sharon said slowly, taking the letter and commencing to open it. She could not say how, but she knew what it was before she had read a line in the difficult trembling light in the way one knows a thing in one's dreams long before it happens, a straw in the wind, a curious message on the unknowing lips of a stranger, the jigsaw of nature and the dialogue of reality, the compulsive oblique mirror of Magda's countenance shining in the strangely-lit house.

"I warn him to forget you and every other little bitch," Magda whispered hoarsely. "The consequence be on his own head. I do me best. Is I manœuvre the whole deception to save he skin. The coast was lef' clear – police, everybody gone home, believing their nasty work was done – and he couldah mek a run for it. He wouldah pass Venezuela border by now. Forty day he been in the bush malingering. When I done believe he make a dash for good, he sneak up 'pon me one dark night in this house. Scare the daylight out of me 'cause was the last body I expect to see in Pomeroon. The boy couldah reach far. Naw, he want *you* instead. He beg me to break the news to you at the time of the wake when all body turn into spirit and I turn into their queen of fate. He say I must trust you. . . ." She could not help laughing at herself.

"Cristo's alive! O God!"

"Sh . . . sh. . . ." Magda rasped.

The two women grew stock-still, listening to the deafening voice of the wake. "You want the blind wake to know?" Magda spoke hoarsely. "For Cristo's sake don't shout the news 'pon the housetop."

"I'm sorry," Sharon was babbling softly, "I didn't realize I spoke aloud. It's all like a dream as if I always *knew* Cristo was coming back. Innocent."

"Innocent?" Magda almost spat. She was furious. "Because he's alive he's innocent? I suppose everybody else innocent too. You know where to find them pure sweetman fast and simple enough. . . ."

Sharon bowed her head.

"I suppose you is still a virgin too after all of them," Magda laughed. "Pomeroon want you to make youself into a jinx of a daughter with all the men. Well, is Cristo's fault and request, last will and testament, if you bring he down into his grave. I done do all *I* can for him." Her jealous lips were snarling and Sharon fought to resist an image of ferocity hiding in the darkest corner and pool of the jungle. It was not *true* that Cristo was on the frantic run like this. She wanted to maintain the coolest self-possession and stillness and judgment before the hopeless counsels of self-preservation and lust. "I shall tell Mattias," she protested, thinking this would unsettle Magda's all-consuming vision. "I shall show Mattias Cristo's letter. Mattias will help and he will know better what to do than me." She lifted her hands, pushing away all tigerish responsibility and flight and acceptance of guilt, the fable and wilderness of inhumanity.

Magda quickly snatched the letter from the outstretched fingers, and began to tear it into scraps. "Show Mattias, eh?" she gasped. "I warn Cristo you were a fickle treacherous bitch. . . ."

"Cristo's innocent. He mustn't go on running for ever in the bush. He must come back." Sharon clapped her hands softly in her agitation.

"O, I see," Magda exclaimed. "It isn't Mattias you want now, is it? You want Cristo to come back, divine trumpets blowing, all happy and nice. You want Pomeroon fairy tale to come true. All my born sweat, from the time of the cradle, to make and save the manchild that come out of me, and all his guilty bad blood that I hide, mean not a dam' to you. Listen to me – I vexed, vexed bad, you hear? Is time you start to see what you be. Look," she was convulsed with resolution. "Keep it after all. Here – the letter, stitch the pieces together. Give Mattias. Give Mattias I say. Give the police sergeant too if you must. I wash me hand for good. I warned Cristo. But one thing – when you give these, there's something else I want you to give . . ." she had kneeled and was fumbling in a corner of the room. "Look, these too. Take them I say. Is tear-up dollar bill, you still can't see? You know who they belong to? Ask Mattias to mend them and count them accurate and to hand them back to your fine father. Cause is too black a job for you to do. Would bruise your tender virginal flesh. Show him me son's private letter as you please but show him too you whoring father nasty dollar bill. Take the lid off this medium of hell by all means, but make a real Judas conversion and portrait of everybody while you going about it. Is time to begin to see your own true roots and self when you put Cristo to hang on the gallows-tree."

Sharon could not repress a startled violent cry. The mirror of seduction she had pushed away from her had now embraced her for good. No trace of self-possession was left. All had been confirmed to be evil, the rape of living nature. She felt she was suffocating and dying on a scaffold – crushed in the arms of a wild beast. A loud piercing cry – issuing it seemed out of Mattias' dying heart – upheld and fused her as it entered her crumbling body and feet.

X

It was all very confusing and strange, Sharon mused in the curious hollow bed of moonlight where she lay under the fantastic wild pressure of Cristo's body and arms. She could not stop herself from seeing Magda's room at the wake – even as she felt Cristo now, lying upon her, in the jungle bush – and once again she lived the terrifying process of enveloping seduction as Cristo made love to her. It was difficult to conceive of the climax of the wake as other than the dreaded preliminary stage of one total mounting embrace and abandon. Weeks (millions of years they seemed) had gone by, she knew, but still all time remained in one serial fused moment like an inescapable waking rendezvous with death and life.

Once again she saw the perverse countenance in the dim room as Cristo held her, the incestuous tiger of the jungle, the hiding mother in the son, once again she heard Mattias's dying murdered cry in her own virgin open throat, until in the instant of annihilating perception and lust, when all appeared painfully lost, the gross burden flowered and moved and one knew in one's bed of shadows that one lay in the arms of the universal bridegroom of love, pierced by all the ecstasy of constructive innocence.

The moon stood high overhead. Its full radiance had been intercepted by the forest so that the light which still fell and painted stripes and bars under the trees was purplish and vague and blue.

A branch in the air suddenly cracked like a pistol-shot, broke and descended, ripping open a shaft and a window, along which the thwarted flower of the moon now bloomed in a mysterious bulb of fulfilment in a dark confused room

305

and roof. Sharon stared along the tunnel of the moon to the womb of the sky cradling Cristo's shoulder.

It was as if she suddenly saw her father in the moon's blue effulgent eye. Her heart perceived him in a way it had not done over the past years and weeks. She no longer felt that Magda's treacherous portrait and burden weighed upon her and upon him. Every torn dollar bill fluttered in the bright tunnel of the night like a foul garment and a moulding leaf he could afford to discard.

Her father had not been in his right mind for years, everyone whispered, wishing to explain to themselves the tragic medium of the wake. That was why no woman had married him since his wife had died, and one woman only had lived with him – the jinx of a virgin daughter (with the blood of three men now at her feet – Cristo, Mattias, and the jealous one who had died first from Cristo's alleged stab).

The forest was sighing a little along the moon-stained paths bringing all the sad blue distant rumours and superstitions of time and place. Better to leave such a pair alone! the leaves said. Not that one was truly afraid of a shadowy figure like Peet or a wraith of a girl like Sharon. Might as well believe Cristo had come back to life at his own dead wake to take Sharon in his arms, and that one's true clock of fate ticked in the breast of the tiger as it beat in one's own heart. Something was wrong with everyone, everyone knew, and it was no use pretending one could cure all the ills. Might as well accept defeat and leave the devil alone. It was the first time a wake had brought the world to such a sad painful pass.

Sharon no longer believed a word the rumorous leaves sighed and shook around her. She felt herself divested of the taint of ugliness and fear (of which her father had struggled to divest himself in Magda's house). So light she became she was sailing to the top of the open tunnel of the moon. She could see the naked river in the distance, the shining roof of her father's house, the dense waving curtain of coconut palms stitched together with silk and silvered thread. She stood on a

306

sheet of crumpled forest kissing the bare breast of the Moon.
The dam shone like flowing milk between the legs of the trees
in the plantation. She had left Peet, heavy and sound asleep in
the mooning house, to flit like a ghost into the bed of the forest
where Cristo waited for her in the shadow of a tall mora tree
whose roots alone were wide as a giant's thighs.

Sharon saw the spirit of her father for the first true organic
time rising within the fable of his sleeping land and home; *this*
was what he might have been. It made her feel someone
should have known how to climb into him with the beauty of
all compassion.

In the past all healing intimacy as well as proper distance had
been equally unreal, as fanciful and removed as the roots of the
moon which lay within the earth.

She remembered how she had returned – after many years –
from the Roman Catholic boarding-school in Port of Spain to
which he had sent her. She came back to the Pomeroon, intent
on perfecting a curious image of herself, an image compounded half of scorn for the earthy disgusting creature Peet
was, half-admiration for the plantation and the home he had
built with his naked hands. She quickly crushed any notion he
might have had, that his proud daughter would be a little
"mother" and a little "wife", by holding him at a kind of
evasive picturesque distance all the time, treating him as if he
were a strange privileged labourer and odd relation who slept
within the same walls and under the same roof. She boasted to
her friends about her father's self-sufficiency and independ-
ence in order to impress everyone that she was a born creature
of sterling pioneer folk. On the other hand when the young
men fought over her (it was a brutish tradition in the river) she
would keep them at arm's length so that they would learn she
was of a different quality to any crude battling misconception
they might take into their head from their fathers' way of life.

It was a moonstruck world, Sharon knew. Woman grew into
an unattainable idol that stood on the highest blossom in the
world or into a compulsive fantastic whore with black roots in

the wilderness. Sharon could not help shrinking a little in her skin at the memory of her every limb and bond of extremity, as when the serial dreadful vision of Magda and herself fused into one. It had all melted with tenderness and she had gained the reins of freedom. She could see beneath her and around her for a great distance with a sanity she had never before possessed. If Peet had been mad, and Magda was mad, she too had been mad, and the sleeping population all around her were as mad to find the soul they had given to the bush. Hundreds and thousands of years they had been labouring against the sun and the river, betraying each other and stabbing each other, hounding their free spirit deeper into all of themselves and searching for the man and the maid who lived in the desert of the moon. Sharon let her hand slide tenderly along the vibrant backbone of the land. It had all come home to her, Cristo's innocence and Abram's dream of love (which she had always curiously dreaded) and their flight.

The feeling in her stroking fingers made her see far away across the moonlit river – as if she rode in the beam of light-sliding hollows and rising features, growing into stones and foothills. It was along this very mysterious backbone and watershed – between ancient terror and new-born love – that the frightful jaguar of death had roamed, leaping across emotional tumbling rivers from crag to crag, across Devil's Hole Rapids and the Nameless Falls, greenheart ravines steaming with mist, blue mountains frowning in cloud, coming from as far as the heart of Brazil into Venezuela's Orinoco and Guyana's Potaro, Mazaruni, Cuyuni and Pomeroon. Her fingers travelled across the map of Cristo's skin, stroking the veins in every ancestor's body. It sought to establish the encounter with the lost soul of all generations, the tiger roaming through the trackless paths, rapping at every jungle door, calling to the sweet meat belonging to the dead sleeping flesh of the night, pausing by every pool of meditation.

It was here that Cristo had found himself reflected, the floating backbone and watershed of hope, striped with all the mystery of the female touch of night. He had followed and tricked the beast, inviting her with all his heart to meet him, and coming upon her in a dark blinding moment of pure reflex, daring impulse and instantaneous perception. It was a close gun and narrow escape Sharon mused. Her nail had ripped one cheek from eye to mouth. Cristo bore the mark of all the tiger's sinister intent and had inflicted the consummation of all nature's vital lust. Fear died within him as it died within her. She had been the most frightened terrified animal of all the species up to the very moment she had been prostrated and slain.

From Sharon's tower of perception the landscape had come alive with Cristo's fabulous adventure and the treasure of victory he had won. One day it would become the legend of the new schools of the heartland – how Cristo had killed Abram's tiger and the lovely striped feminine skin of the devil was the coat he now wore wherever he went. He had shot the lurking brute above the headwaters of a tributary, had dried and treated the beautiful skin until it was perfect, and had donned his new colours on the very night of the wake. Magda had delivered his summons and letter to a crushed Sharon, half-bemused and pierced utterly by the full burden of events. She – musing now on every passionate coincidence she had conceived in her rising senses and flesh – could not help seeing Peet in her imagination in pursuit of every striped jungle moonbeam. He was sprawled on his bed, dead asleep, covered by bars of light that streamed into the house through the blue skylight in the roof. He dreamed his daughter stood in the moon looking at him with Cristo's eyes. They both knew he wanted to kill them though he had always been afraid to take anyone's life.

The nightmare hunt to kill had actually started in a losing devilish chase, many years before. Sharon had just gained her eighth birthday, and a jaguar had run off with a neighbour's child who was seven. The region was electrified by the news. Why it might have been anyone's child! Only a month ago someone had shot an enormous male tiger in the headwaters of the Akawini tributary, and everyone wondered superstitiously – on hearing of the violent theft – whether this was a reprisal inflicted by a female devil and mate.

In a couple of hours human fantasy and unhuman reality had become the intertwined roots of history. A phantasmagoric obsession grew to follow the beast to its lair. Was it indeed a woman-tiger? Might it not be a man-tiger? The demon's sex and gender was as confusing as the origin of the chase. Was it half-man, half-woman they pursued? Could any creature truly change its sex at will and take on a different subtlety and cruel intention? The stolen child was almost forgotten in the mystery of the chase. Something had wakened in everyone's mind akin to the glory of destroying a soulless beast.

Peet was chosen leader of the expedition. They started up the Akawini river, they interrogated every suspicious settler who had made a secretive clearing on the banks. They camped in every branch and channel, watched the sun climbing down the trees, a blazing web and a red spider. They rose with the dripping sponge of dawn, scoured every trail. They fanned the brow of the sun at noon, climbing every tall tree, sweating themselves into running frenzy to see to the top of every stream. They left their boats and took to the field, dividing themselves into two parties, one on the left bank and the other on the right. Peet and his party encountered a swamp after following a firm trail and ridge through massive bush, all eyes peeled for every cavernous womb and recess in which grew strange shapes like dead monkeys. It was as far as they could go without incurring fresh economic expense. The swamp ahead opened a rotting extension and mouth leading to an old clotted stream and impenetrable jungle. Old roots and trunks stood above every stagnant tongue of water like evil teeth protruding from a monster's head, whose staring eyes were festooned with mud. It was a vision of buried fertility, its head under Peet's feet, while its feet lay far away from Peet's own, far across the continent in the mists of buried time. Peet shrank from exploring the navel of the world where the mate of all generations of fantasy was devouring the umbilical chord of a stolen life. The search came to an abrupt halt in this sensation of severance from the child they sought in the heart of their gloom. Another day perhaps, and another time someone else might follow the tiger into the darkest bosom of lost life.

Peet knew he had failed in some profound inexplicable way and he returned with his mind full of the gnawing spirit of disaster. The entire expedition took their cue from him and turned back. He came home to learn that while he was away, his wife (whom he jealously loved and adored) had slipped and fallen heavily upon the landing by the river. She was a delicate woman, six to seven months gone in pregnancy. She had been rushed to the Government Hospital at Suddie on the Arabian Coast. At first it had seemed she would be all right, then a variety of complications developed and like a whiff of one's breath the spirit of mother and child had gone. The baby (it was a boy) would have been coming into manhood today, Peet said sixteen years after the event, staring across the land into the navel of misadventure.

It had been a stunning incredible blow from which he had never recovered, however much he had plastered his abysmal wound with hypocrisy and stoicism. Everyone pointed to him with the sympathy everyone has for a medium who provides an opportunity for the region to commiserate over its failure and sin. He was a sly, deceitful dog, they said, dressed often in near-rags, though with a big bank balance he hardly touched. He had hundreds of dollars in a hollow tree-trunk he had axed into a dreaming treasury under the bed where he slept. He drank heavily on many an occasion and cursed and talked wild. But he could also be a model of discretion, turning away from the really evil rootless temptation that ruined many another man. O yes, Peet seemed to know every time how to save his bark and his skin and everyone could not help admiring him. He was a hearty old-school pioneer, they said, and his mad moments were human after all. Why should they feel otherwise? He had never leaped anywhere beyond what they knew, and had often proved the abortive soul of many a soulless party.

Sometimes they experienced a wooden alarm they could not easily express, the alarm of a phantom limb they had sacrificed. Why did he insist on dragging his left foot, when he was drunk, as if it was a paralysed trunk he drew after him? Why did his arm appear to turn to wood, and his body twitch a little like a falling tree? Why did he take a wooden finger and indent his skin, advertising a faint mark a whore had scratched on him? She had robbed him and wounded him as he tried to jump on her, when she spotted the drag of halting indecision.

These gestures and confessions occurred in his most ambivalent moods which fortunately rarely lasted long. Peet would quickly go to sleep stretched to his full length on the ground. When the critical fall and exhibition was over, everyone was grateful. The sleeping log had pulled and shifted their chains of hardship, summoning them to come to the very edge of themselves and to fall into an unnatural relief which was godlike repose. They never actually fell, as he did, thank God! But they let off a lot of steam from their roots, growing a little better for it, after all. Next time perhaps something more would happen. But *now* it was better that everything should remain as it was. They had poked their wooden finger of fun into someone's open mouth and that made up for many empty things.

The night of the wake he descended from Magda's room, dragging his left foot worse than ever, and indenting the loose skin of his cheek with a wooden finger that had been crushed like a spoon. Magda had beaten him. It had been grand fun, of course, for Peet. The wake was getting into its swing. The tiger had bitten him, he said, not a woman-tiger, a *man-tiger* it was. He laughed loud and long. He had followed it to its lair, he said, and it was *not* the bloody mother he feared. It was the blue man, her son, the man in the moon.

My son, he shouted crudely – in way of parenthesis – killed his fucking mother long ago by the riverside, killed the last spark and hope of love in her. It was not *she* who had taken him down, but he who had consumed her. Peet was too drunk to know what he meant. Cristo, Mattias, they were all one tigerish conspiracy to subvert the womb of a man's woman. *They would eat their own mother alive for a chance to survive.* Look, Mattias was getting as drunk as he, drunk with the tallest story of how he had raped Sharon, Peet cried, by pretending he was gentle and soft. Time had come for everybody to discard their foul vest of hypocrisy! Let us see ourselves for what we are. The grave was the subversion of the womb and the womb carried a deception into the grave, and that was all there was to sing of paradoxical love. But by God! he would save Sharon from any prowling resurrected trickster like Cristo and Mattias. *It must not happen again to his daughter. To be eaten alive by the blue man in the moon.* Peet half-vomited, half-laughed, hearing himself utter many things in his mind he had no words to whisper aloud. He was growing into the greatest monster of hallucination. Not again. No man must be allowed to plant the devil of his seed in the image of a woman's heart, and *he* – their own fond Peet – was the most guilty one of all since he had led them on a wild-goose chase long ago.

"You," he cried, his eyes seeming to look inward on himself, "you devil – you beast – I shall kill you." His voice rose in the tumult of the wake, and Mattias suddenly understood in the way someone swiftly reads between the lines of a letter or hears unspoken words in the midst of loud foolish dialogue. It is not what one is saying in superficial reality one recalls and hears. It is what one really knows one has been saying deeply all along from the moment one finds one has crawled out of the ancient egg of the sea into a new brutish shell and hatching family tree and camouflage. All hunted and hunting sensation was draining from Peet's creaturely face so that it turned half-woman, half-man, turning instantly again on itself in order to bite itself. He grabbed a knife and lifted it high in the air to strike the nearest visionary one. Mattias caught the raised arm just in time, twisting the wrist and extracting the knife. The crowd went mad. A little harmless blood must spill in the foreday morning, they began to chant. Mattias tried to push his way back. Someone pushed him forward. He fell upon Peet who pushed him from him as a ball jumps from foot to hand and hand to foot.

Mattias bounced forward again and tripped on the leg of a chair. He was in a state of curious intoxication. He thought he was falling on the iron trunk of Abram's tree and he stretched his hands out to save himself from being terribly bruised, losing sight of the knife, he still grasped. A scream burst from his lips, so clear and discerning, there was a dead silence all around. No one trusted their eye as it beheld the dripping treasury of blood.

Peet slipped to the ground beside Mattias the very moment he screamed. He was totally exhausted. He could not stir hand or foot to make one step from the scene. If he had run compulsively they would have accused him and because he was equally unable to move there was the same facile shout: "Peet killed him. Peet stabbed Mattias. Look how they both lying now."

Mattias understood the garbled menacing outcry. He stirred and opened his eye, seeing Magda and Sharon a great distance off, weighing down on him in the heart of the crowd. Everyone had started to move far away however near they had come. He cried before it grew late – "Peet didn't do it." He went on involuntarily and urgently. "Peet didn't do it – I'm all right – Look!" He put his hand to his chest, grasping the handle of the knife and demonstrating what had actually occurred. There was an eager piercing look in his eye – a lover in the arms of the universal beloved. He lifted himself into a grotesque position. The blade sliced the pulse of life as he moved and Peet's hand slid across his chest pulling him gratefully down. Before anyone could think again he was dead.

He lay almost in the identical position (save for Peet's unconscious arm across him) in which Sharon's first suitor had fallen. It was an accident in truth and indeed now as then. Everyone saw it afresh now with a stricken serial stupefaction as if they had fallen upon the vantage ground and log book of the future. Three men were alleged to have died like brutes – the man Cristo had been accused of stabbing to death, though everyone now intuitively saw he had fallen on his own blind knife – Cristo himself (whom the tiger had not truly devoured, as they were able to perceive in this moment of truth) – and Mattias, bearing the thorn of all dramatic reconstruction that was able to pierce their sleeping vision.

A startled awareness emerged, the undeniable spirit of truth that had entered one mind – in order to free the others – even in the midst of seeming death.

Peet's hand lay across his illusory tiger of the wake in the pale blue light of dawn. He had reached the head-waters of all timeless adventure and he heard the last dying beat of the devil's heart, his own monster of deception.

BOOK FOUR

ALL THE AEONS

In the habitation of dragons, where each lay,
shall be grass with reeds and rushes.

Isaiah 35 : 7

. . . the penetration of Heaven into Earth . . . the *One*
. . . circulation of the Light . . . when all the aeons are
like a moment.

The Secret of the Golden Flower
(translated by Richard Wilhelm)

XI

The spider of dawn had appeared and the moon had far descended. The morning star spun its long frail threads to touch scattered islands of cloud in a delicate wheel whose radii and circumference rolled on every high peak, foothill and valley.

Cristo and Sharon were making their way slowly through the plantation to the sleeping farmhouse at the riverside. They had helped one another to come to an important decision about the future.

The ground of night smelt fresh in their nostrils, the almost stifling freshness of the earth, the smell of a mingling of roots and leaves and branches all turning into a web of cognition that entered their blood. They walked with their new-found arms twined together, making a light almost aerial touch and step.

The falling moon and the rising star illumined their shadow with the spirit of leaves as if spikes glanced out of every shoulder, a tree of raindrop and dew. In the past three weeks, Sharon suddenly recalled, the drought had been beaten and had started to retire from the face of the earth. The change was unassuming and unspectacular and many may have missed the drops of miracle, the first spreading trickle that would swell into a rising cohesive flood.

Why, she remembered, the very morning after the wake the first gentle shower had fallen. There had been other quiet mounting showers too over the days and the weeks everyone seemed to forget an hour after they fell. The river had begun to swell also in a secret way since (hardly anyone fully realized it) the rains had started falling in earnest on the distant Cuyuni watershed and a volume of fresh water was

319

pouring gradually into the Pomeroon basin, a continuum of flow that overcame the salt desert of the sea and chased it downriver away from the sluice-gates of every besieged plantation.

The inhabitants of the region had not properly wakened to the slaying of the dragon of drought by the spidery feet of the rain which left their trail in every thread and green shoot on the land. The stern winter of hardship had yielded to the spring of fertility but the roots and branches of transformation descended and arose only in the starred eye of love. For all who were blind to this miraculous dawning frailty, the new time appeared only when it manifested an iron shell and proportion, rigid as the grave season that was past, inexplicable as all time before, and unhuman as the rhythms of the tides on the earth. The trunk of triumphant prosperity became – in this context – a recurring fate and epitaph rather than the ascension of everlasting thanksgiving.

Thank God! the times were changing, they declared in the spirit of universal cliché, though the devil alone knew how. Trouble was bound to come again, they shrugged wisely, as they planted their seed and their grain. Watch out!

Cristo's wake was the last one they would see for a hell of a long time, they grumbled, bemoaning what seemed like bad luck. Why the District Commissioner himself had said the practice must cease until every passion had cooled. He would not tolerate unexpurgated violence. The region had gained a name for irresponsibility, subversion and feud, and it was time to learn the need for a new restraint. He made no bones in declaring his rank impatience. The police had grown obviously slack. They were slowly being overcome by the harsh camouflage of the climate. Something was always cooking but hell alone knew what.

Peet had narrowly escaped being charged with murder, and had it not been for the strange confession of the dying man, Mattias, things would have gone hard with him. It was clear he was a lunatic though no one had seen him in his true

demented colours before. The spirit of the place had always
hatched up excuses for him, no one knew why.

Time alone would determine, in the long bitter run, what
would become of him and that daughter of his! Tongues were
talking wild. She was a bewitched one, they swore, a witch,
yes, the evil kind of woman who drew all her menfolk into the
shadow of the gallows – even those who loved her and
wanted to protect her. Magda was a saint beside this little jinx
of a virgin, they cackled. Imagine that! The devilish man who
would claim her and bind her to himself *must be* the very
prince of hell. Cristo, Magda's hopeless son, was he coming
back from the grave, they said and laughed? Would he be the
impossible one to bend her and make her?

The wake had blown all mocking perversity and paradoxical rumour to a curious speculative head, and some had even
sworn in their agonizing moment of truth (truth! my eye,
there was no such thing the people declared) that they had
misjudged Cristo. He was innocent of the crime with which
he had been charged.

It was tragic how old and confused the world was
becoming. Maybe the District Commissioner was damned
right to stamp upon their fertile irresponsible fetishes and
imaginings. He must have heard how cursed silly they were
the morning after the wake when the police had arrived. Each
one had a different version to give of the night's affair, and
they had all stood like whipped puppies with their tails
between their legs and their legs wrapped around their tails,
questioners and questioned alike. Who could tell the real
difference between the lust of the interrogators and the
submission of the interrogated? All were exposed as puppets
of fear and the victims of a system of self-deprecation and
self-parody, and no one dared – neither commander nor
commanded – to accept a total perceptive responsibility. Such
a burden – free of hopelessness and self-righteous denigration
– belonged only to the shadow of atonement in the Saviour of
Mankind. It was a far cry and flitting assumption that barely

moistened their lips like the first drop of rain-water falling from the sky after the long drought when it passed from their mind as if it had never happened, and it became impossible to admit further their total incapacity – save in the most grotesque involuntary postures of attack and self-defence – and this rankled and exacerbated their inmost pride and superstition.

They were clearly in perverse religious dread of accusing Peet after Mattias' dying phenomenal outburst (it was as though a dead man rose up and spoke) and they hated themselves for their spiritual helplessness. They dreaded everything they had seen in their shattering moment of truth. Truth, hell. The wake had started up every ancient supposition of folly. Must they look next for Cristo and Sharon inside the face of the moon? Watch out, everybody.

The river-police – in their turn – had long ceased to fathom the ground of all impotent authority. Was it that they had tied their own hands in the consenting spirit or in the lust of the law? They were like a band of mercenary soldiers in a foreign mythical land. Peet was one offender, they felt, it should have been easy to catch this time. Troublesome old enemy and instigator! It was high time to make a living example of *him* for everybody else to see. No witness, however, they found to their chagrin, would consent to level a cheap accusing hand at the father of the witch who had spoken through Mattias' dead mouth. That accusing finger would rot afterward, every one knew, and drop like a moonstruck coconut in the face of the dragon of drought. Every reprobate old farmer was mortally and unseasonably afraid of the malice and the miracle in the humus he cultivated. Why, every time the weather changed, every man whispered in his skull, it brought the fall of the old blind dead with the ascent of the newest spider of the living, and one wanted to make sure one would never be bewitched in strange times like these. It was best to leave such a crazy couple severely alone, they said. The father was a dry old lopsided nut (they had learnt in the wake of horror) and the daughter could take on any shape she wished.

This swelling tide of helpless rumour grew in the whisper of dew in the grass, as it equally fell from every swaying rustling watermark in the sky. The days began to mount into showers – starting out of cloudy fables and origins that moved like the heraldry of threatening armour across the breaking dry spell of the land.

Sharon could not fathom her own stupor – drawn out of almost meaningless fragility – and creeping things – the brooding voices of the past mingling with apprehensions of the future. She was being uprooted from all the fixed assumptions she had shared with everyone and everything into an order so tenuous and fleeting it aroused a terrible insubstantial uneasiness.

It was the web of blind tropical spring that sometimes arouses the human spirit into a banner of excess, especially when one has been enduring privation and the fabulous air of fertility which starts to enmesh one is sown with an hysterical current that drives one nearly mad. A fine distance appears between oneself and everyone until the prosaic living one had always taken for granted – turns into one's own model of uncertainty, and the prosaic dead one has always ignored begin to hang their features of necromancy in the rising clouds.

One charges their countenance with past and future intuition, memory and revulsion, choking disdain, unnatural in the wild breast of a young girl who begins to exaggerate and multiply and stitch her witch's straw and shawl in the wind. *This* was her destiny and everyone was forcing it upon her and Sharon felt herself turning wild, as wild as everyone wished her to be. She wanted to turn into the secret creature they said she was, running from and yet containing the beetling fibrous faces she pictured and the insinuating tongues which coated every ditch.

She wanted to be free of her father for ever, to conceal herself on a leaf in the grass, when he came dragging himself after her in nightmare pursuit. She barely endured his presence, hating him since the night of Magda's over-powering revelation. He had slept all through the day following the crisis, into the next day and afternoon when he had woken stricken by partial paralysis. The river-police had questioned him, endless day after day since then, asking innumerable questions to get to the root of Mattias' death. Sharon wanted to scream that they were doing no good like this. Couldn't they see – what was plain to everyone else – her father had lost his mind? Look how he was shaking his head of a robe of cobweb in his eyes. Look how he pointed to the river, trying to say something about the witch, his daughter (surely they *knew*), pointing too to the skylight in the roof where stood the reflection of flowing water. All one could see, when one followed his eye, was a tiny fluid spider, scuttling as fast as its feet would run.

He was a spasmodic homunculus in her imagination she dreamt at night, growing rebelliously large to follow her and drink the sprinkles of her blood. Sometimes he caught her in a lump of mud, squeezing a bead of moisture into a crooked hand, lapping it up with an eager tongue. Sharon was swallowed and reduced once more to nothingness as it had seemed at the very beginning of her life.

The climax of terrifying conversion came when she awoke one night, exactly three weeks after the wake (she had been counting the rosary of days in her heart) by an abrupt nervous incessant thumping upon the wall. She was filled with unreasoning pounding panic and she ran out of the house into the yard. Her upturned face under the moon was wild. It was nothing she said over and over again. Nothing. Her father was sound asleep, she prodded herself. Hours and hours ago. How could he come after her? For all she tried to reason she still grew mortally and inexplicably afraid.

It was the kind of night when one begins to feel how one was conceived long before one was born. As if it might have started with a dreadful conception and desire to escape at all costs. Escape from whom and from what? From the father of nothingness into the mother of dreadful somethingness? Or was it that one ran and escaped to make a father of something out of the mother of nothing? On such a night one was reduced to the genes of being nothing again, in the wildest mad embrace, one's ghostly seed and ghostly parents and all.

O yes, tonight was the total female night of initiation and self-surrender before time ran into a vitally changed tomorrow. Cristo had predicted the all-embracing change in his letter, Sharon recalled with the last twinge of self-mockery as she wondered fleetingly whether she was coining a most gratuitous excuse to keep a rendezvous she both hated and cherished. She started out along the dam in the plantation, towards the bush, no longer seeing anything save one blind spirit.

The air was close and warm and wild as a bitch in heat; the wind accompanied her like a spasmodic shivering and breathing. An invisible sharp stone suddenly tripped her and she panted for another breath and another hysterical lung within her to endure and outrun everything. An involuntary form began to crystallize in the womb of her mind. She held it against her until the wounding edge turned into the terror of another's flesh. She grew faint with incredulous surprise on finding one was making oneself into what one had forgotten to be. Cristo's new breath became her triumphant living soul at last, and a ruby of blood revived her. It was all she needed to transfuse into the new-born world she was envisioning and creating around her, now that the sinister volume and community of herself had changed with the opening of a conception of origins in the orders of lust.

The sun rose over the horizon as six o'clock struck in the farmhouse. There had been a shower of rain twenty minutes before. Cristo and Sharon sat in the front gallery, a quiet almost empty look on their faces, drinking coffee, as black as if they had dipped it from the Pomeroon.

"I want you to think of my mother as a changed woman now," Cristo stirred reflectively. "I feel you will understand this in the light of everything. As though three weeks ago everyone was a dream, and the *one* who dreamt us was not present at all." He paused, startled by the inadequacy of words. He continued seriously: "We were all there, of course, but now surely we have an entirely different conception of ourselves." He was suddenly regarding her with an absolute intentness. "It's like when a man and a woman lie down together and make a myth, Sharon, without even knowing it. Who is the parent of what in the long run? It starts by being as brutal and as fanciful as my grabbing you close last night, remember? A lot of mysterious things always happen to bring two people together, to bring us *here* this morning, you and me, and we're deeply together in *this*, though it has often seemed like the last thing one cares about." He was waving to the river and to the vague broad spirit of place and sky.

"You mustn't worry too much," Sharon said gently. "When last did you meet Magda, tell me?"

"A couple of times since the night of my celebrated wake." He was smiling sardonically. "I was astonished to see her. Always crept in after dark, you know, and there she was like a frightened child, frightened that her hopes were all going up in smoke. Kept peering out of the window, praying no one had seen me come. Nothing I could say really comforted her. Kept begging me all the time to run far for my good." Cristo could not help laughing a little.

"She wanted to save you," Sharon said impulsively. "You were the ghost that remained of everything."

"Yes, I know." Cristo was half-frowning, half-laughing. "Save me from all disgrace, all failure . . . from everything. Even from you. She agreed to give you my letter only when I swore I'd give myself up right away – must have been a week or two before the wake when I first visited her – if she didn't do as I said. Ah Sharon, my mother is not the same woman though you would hardly believe it. She's a child. Yes, I would never have thought it possible. She's a child after all. Why *you*, frail as you are" – he held her delicate wrists in his hand – "could contain her now. It takes a hell of a long time before one comes to know anybody and anything, if one ever really does." He stopped, waiting for her to say something, but she remained still, her thin face bent on the river. A man was paddling a boat along the opposite bank.

"There's something I would very much like you to do." He released her wrists.

"What?"

"Let my mother come and live with you, Sharon. She'll give you no trouble at all, you'll see. She's really completely changed, I swear. And I would feel lots better, knowing this. The truth is I don't know when I'll come back."

Sharon listened. For one moment all the clocks in the world appeared to have stopped. Even the ticking of the grandfather clock in the house was plunged in silence. She rattled the spoon in her cup and time started again. "It's true," she said with a smile of strangest resolution. "They're going to lock you up this very afternoon when they come. Then there may be a long trial. Then. . ."

He interrupted her: "Don't worry to think beyond that. . . ."

"But I must." She could not help growing excited. "Why, you're innocent. Everybody knows that. They all confessed it the morning after the wake."

"Now, Sharon, you know yourself the police never did." He knew he had to shake all her prepossessions to the ground. "They're still looking for somebody, anybody, upon whom they can properly and legally pin the blame for everything. I don't want us to fool ourselves what the odds are we have to overcome. We must know clearly what we're going about. I haven't a shadow of doubt they'll unearth the bundle of statements they collected the night I ran away.

Thank God! one is no longer living in *that* wild fear and so one can come out and face them, whatever they do. They'll jump out of their skin, I tell you, when they see me. The records of the chase are still breathing the spirit of fire and revenge, and never before have they caught a dead tiger alive." He was chiding her gently, pointing to his striped bizarre coat.

"Yes, you're so utterly different," Sharon confessed. "I don't think they'll remember you. You've grown this beard for one thing. And then there's this long nail and scratch. . ." – she drew her finger gently along the sinister trace of a wound. "You look older, ten years, maybe twenty years older, as if you really went out somewhere and changed places with someone." She could not resist a curious smile. "I know I'm crazy, but anyone can see you're not the same man they were chasing ages ago. And there's nothing anybody can really do to you now." Her voice had grown vehement. "Last night I *know* I couldn't have faced such a parting, any parting, short or long. I couldn't have borne to lose you as I had you then. I would have run clean out of the house, clean out of my mind."

"You promise never to forget last night?" His face had grown sad.

"I could have killed you up to the very moment you stopped me. I held you and it was only then I knew what I had always wanted to be. I wanted to make myself *new*."

"Neither will I forget you," Cristo musingly said. He changed his tone and expression quickly. "Everybody will now say you're really mad, Sharon," he smiled half-bantering ly, half-seriously. "Before, when they said it they were pretending. They needed to have a witch in the neighbour-hood. They could shake it out with the cork when they opened a bottle of rum. But when the witch shakes her bones to bring *me* clear out of Abram's black bosom, the fable becomes a little too damned entertaining and serious. They begin to ponder on their own miserable life which they know is so blasted unhappy and unjust and monotonous. And out of the most perverse stubborn humour they'll accuse you of every crime under the sun as well as God knows what." He pointed to the door of Peet's room. "They'll accuse you of *that* for example. Why did your poor devil of a father choose such a dreadful guilty way? They'll declare every man you touch is ever after hopelessly accursed." He was weighing his words, carefully, making them brutal and theatrical, searching for the shadow of a chink in Sharon's armour. "God knows what drove him to put the skylight-rope around his neck. . . ."

"They'll all say they always knew he'd do it," Sharon interrupted bitterly and sharply. "They'll say they knew it was bound to be, but that won't be the end. After a while something else is going to happen." Her eyes were a little strange. "I'll tell you, Cristo. *Now* that they've reduced him to nothing, they'll begin to see how wrong they have been about everything. *Wrong!* They were wrong. Just like me. I was wrong too." She paused for an instant. "One far fine day they'll rise up and come to look for him (they'll want to see him in the pure unadulterated way I can see him now). They'll dig him up from his grave as gently as you and I cut him down from his roof. He became somebody for me and you then because we *knew* no man is born to die in this way. He wasn't real hanging there at all. It was all our burden of misconception. . . ." The tiniest nervous hysterical spider was running across her lips. Cristo detected it. His eye had grown keen and sharp, sharp as the devil's chameleon, after forty days and forty mysterious nights in the camouflage of the bush.

"Are you sure you're not making all this up, Sharon? How do you know it's going to be like that some day?" His glance flicked along her face. "Are you sure they will come to care so deeply about a living soul anywhere at all" – he was waving all over the world – "as much as you make out? Believe me if they know that this is what you conceive of them they'll be surer than ever that you've gone stark staring mad." He was watching her lips for the slightest crumble of fabrication.

"Look," he cried all at once, "get up, now, come along. I want you to see him once again. It's high time you did now you've begun to chatter about digging him up after he's gone. It isn't so easy to face, I can tell you. I want you to size him up well and properly. After all you had only the ghost of a chance before. Dark foreday morning, remember? A smoky lamp and both of us *drunk*, full of excitement." He put his arm gravely around her: "It's easy to make light-headed talk sometimes, isn't it? But I want you to be dead sure of everything you say you'll do." He was leading her resolutely to Peet's door.

Sharon was sobbing her heart out. Cristo sat beside her at the coffee table; the sunlight poured unsteadily upon the streaming river, dark and light all the time, drifting in a valley of cloud and burning shadow.

"It was best that you should see", Cristo was helplessly saying, "how ugly it really is." His spirit was mortally sad. "You can't begin to hope to treasure *that*." He was pointing to the room out of which they had just come. "No use digging up anything like that, you hear me? Because it's only worth a damn when it shelters one's free spirit. Free, understand? That's what we've come to believe, isn't it? And when one knows one's free, *one's free*, and nobody can begin to bitch oneself up, because one's flying and one's free. Like the wind blowing, see? The only time a shell like that can make a shred of sense" – he was trying to pull her close to him – "is when it becomes a kind of pregnant fortress. I want you to remember this when your terrible testing time comes. You've got to be able to see *this* clearly." He had put his hand upon his own breast. His body began to shake uncontrollably as he spoke, tense, overwound, fraught with emotional heredity and destiny, though he was trying desperately still to utter a stubborn miracle of protest, but the words stood too deep as yet to be shaped by a material tongue. They were words one must struggle to bring to birth in one's lived life, like offspring of being. *Death can never be a perfect fortress.* Just a trick he wanted to cry, an eternal dumb trick whereby one could gain a little time to fight the appearance of hell. Gain time, yes, but not eternity. One's spirit had to meet the sun in the long run, absolutely free. Make its declaration to all the other spirits of light.

He was sobbing now as wildly as she, because of the difficulty of making everything absolutely understood. He felt he had to warn her to be careful all the time of the grave truth he thought they now shared and knew, in life, as it were, the conception of life, and death, as it were, the illusion of statuesque resurrection and love. They could not help clinging to each other like children whose lot it was to learn that their education had been paid for by the economics of regional instability, however far they may have appeared to have journeyed out of their fathers' land. "I want to tell you everything that happened when I was away," Cristo managed to say at last. "It's a great story." He was wiping his tears and hers with the fist of his beautiful tiger. "There, there," he said. "Don't you want me to tell you my story?"

She nodded her head. The sun burst forth from behind a cloud and a mountain peak, the first true absolutely fiery blazing shaft. The grandfather clock struck half past seven. "They'll be here soon," Sharon said, "you'll have to hurry. I'm so sorry I couldn't stop myself just now. But it's over now, I promise." She drew her finger gently along his sinister mark as though along the folded pages of a Holy Bible.

"I'm just as bad as you," he half-laughed. "That's why we can help each other." The uncontrollable spasm of their weeping seemed to die away as if they had indeed helped each other by shedding an identical access of woe. His body stiffened suddenly into acute attention. A boat had come in line with the window where they were. Someone was looking up. "Did you see?" Cristo asked. "Mattias' father!" The boat passed. One man had been steering and paddling adroitly. Mattias' father, the other one, had been sitting in the middle, listlessly pulling a paddle too. The tide was in their favour. He had looked up for a long instant into the gallery of the house, a big hunched sorrowful man, staring stonily at the nervous conjunction of a white and a black face.

"He's selling out everything," Sharon said, after a while. "He's taking his money to Canada and will settle there for good." She sighed, finding herself unable to repress a sense of deep sadness about the fate of Cristo, the decision they had forged together, that he must give himself up.

"Do you think he saw me?"

"He saw *me*," Sharon tried to smile. "He hates the sight of me. He always advised his son to have nothing to do with me, and *not* to marry anyone in the Pomeroon, no matter who. Looking back it all looks so dreadful, so silly, the picture of inferiority. Now, of course, it doesn't matter. . . ." She hesitated a little. "I'm sorry for him and I do feel in some ways I was equally stupid. It's so clear to me now", her voice raced a little, "that I never cared for Mattias at all. I always wanted *you*. But I had to be vain and dreadful and silly as everyone else was, and that was how it was. I only wish I could have seen it all then as I do now." She had grown wistful.

"You did like him a little though, didn't you?"

"O, I liked him a lot. He never seemed to know what he wanted of me. We would sit for hours talking. His face would turn all cunning and refined. I can't explain it. He talked about plays. It was always *Waiting for Godot*."

"His father hadn't a clue, I suppose," Cristo said thoughtfully. "For him Mattias was the biggest disappointment in the world. Cambridge and all that and yet nothing to show except . . . well . . . nothing . . . don't you think? If I had had Mattias' money, when I had finished my confounded time at college, I would have painted Pomeroon red. I suppose it would have all ended the same way, anyway, with the police like bush ticks clinging to my backside." He began to laugh tastelessly at his crude joke.

"Mattias' father worshipped him," Sharon said unsmilingly. "And Magda worshipped *you*. One was father's boy and the other was mother's boy. Something magnetic and psychological in that."

"The unstable twins, eh? Ah well the old folk are saying it. A poor showing we've both put up. All of us are failures, you too, don't forget it. Why did we go to school? Why in heaven's name?" He could not resist exploring the vein of self-mockery. He stopped a moment and listened, but it was a breeze blowing in the trees. No one was coming yet. TIME. There was still time to breathe, to be free. "Yes, I was saying, or rather they are saying we never know our own minds about anything, we're fickle, full of idleness and conceit and God knows what. Yes, my girl, that's what they're saying, but tell me, who cares, anyway?" He had grown a little rough and impatient in his manner, and he waved the question away.

Then suddenly he jumped up like one who had been burnt by an electric spark. "I wish with all my life", he cried passionately, "one could show them they're *our* problem child after all, that we're *hundreds of years* older than they dream to be. And why? Because we have begun to see ourselves in the earliest grass-roots, in the first tiny seed of spring" – he paused a fraction of an instant and then proceeded fiercely – "the ancestral tide and spring of Jigsaw Bay, I swear, and that's why we're so different. We're reborn into the oldest native and into our oldest nature, while they're still Guyana's first aliens and arrivals." He shook his fist at the window with a challenging expression. A world of furious tension was forming within him, aching muscles, aching to spring, to fly from his would-be captors. He glanced across the river and knew, whatever he suffered, *he would remain at all costs*. He had returned and he would not fly again.

"Why, think," he exclaimed, fighting to hold the reins of responsibility and freedom, "Pomeroon is the best place to be born to know this whole country, the whole of Guyana, British, Dutch, French, everything." He waved his hands. "First, to know we're all mixed up, East, West, North, South, every race under the sun. Second, to know what we possess

333

comes from the ground up – coconut, copra, plantain, banana, wood-grant, sawmill (don't forget Pomeroon is a nursery of boat-builders, think of the lively schooners as well as the sturdy seamen). Wait, don't interrupt. I'm not through. There's cattle, goat, sheep. I know you *know* all this already, but the point is – it's all ours. Can't you see now what it all means? Nobody *need* carry a self-righteous political chip when the only slave-driver we've ever had is ourselves. And that's why the Pomeroon is a bloody anachronism. Where's the sugar-bed and sugar-cane monopoly, for example? I ask you. You'll find the grand sugar estate and mark of the absentee proprietor on every coast of Guyana, except here. Which means we have never had *here* the Dutch, English, French hidebound imperialist." She made a slight movement. "I'm not finished," he cried. "I was pulling your sweet leg about that. We've had our imperialist, the same pattern of blue blood and true mixed with yellow and black. Our own parents and our blind scraping grandparents, *there* you are. As ignorant as every new overseer who arrived from the U.K. in Demerara yesterday. Poor chap! he becomes part of our native violence and neurosis, unique frustration in all the world, the ancestral scraping together of every penny a man can find without the ghost of a conception of what it means to belong to the grass-roots. And for that reason, Sharon, our *black* parents and capitalists (sometimes they're as white as snow) don't know the instability of their own earth and soil, I tell you, which *we* are now beginning to sense and find out. All the restless wayward spirits of all the aeons (who it was thought had been embalmed for good) are returning to roost in our blood. And we have to start all over again where they began to explore. We've got to pick up the seeds again where they left off. It's no use worshipping the rottenest *tacouba* and tree-trunk in the historic topsoil. There's a whole world of branches and sensation we've missed, and we've got to start again from the roots up even if they look like nothing. Blood, sap, flesh, veins, arteries, lungs, heart, the heartland, Sharon.

We're the first potential parents who can contain the ancestral house.
Too young? I don't know. Too much responsibility? Time will
tell. We've got to face it. Or else it will be too late to stop
everything and everyone from running away and tumbling
down. And then all the King's Horses and all the King's Men
won't be able to put us together again. Like all the bananas
and the plantains and the coffee trees near Charity. Not far
from here, you know. A small wind comes and everything
comes out of the ground. Because the soil is unstable. Just
pegasse. Looks rich on top but that's about all. What do you
think they say when it happens, when the crops run away?
They shrug and say they're expendable crops. They can't
begin to see that it's *us*, our blood, running away all the time,
in the river and in the sea, everywhere, staining the bush.
Now is the time to make a new-born stand, Sharon; you and
me; it's up to us, even if we fall on our knees and *creep* to
anchor ourselves before we get up." He had forgotten
himself, waving his hands, gesticulating. He stopped all of a
sudden, his heart racing wild. The window shook. A wind
blew suddenly, rippling the river, like a flight of darting fish
that skimmed the air. No one was coming as yet, and he
groaned in the nervous expectancy of spirit.

Sharon addressed him, thinking it best to get him to speak
about anything. "Tell me what happened in the bush, Cristo.
You were about to say something and then old Mattias came
along. . . ." She stopped abruptly and put her hands convulsively upon his, not daring to scan the river for fear the time
of parting had come; there was the sound of a roaring
outboard engine drawing closer every minute. They both
waited, their heads bowed, eyes bent on the floor. The brutal
moment had come, and Sharon's eyes were filling with tears
almost against her will. The fear that shackled them in this
shameful instant rose in her mind and body against all
wishful intention; it was as incomprehensible as the force of
spiritual resolution that also bound them together in the
crumbling heart of the community. Sharon could not prevent

herself from trembling as she grasped Cristo, and it flashed upon her that he too – whatever his proven boasts and sentiments – was as weak as she. Their invulnerable resolution was as ironic and paradoxical as the fantastical sensation of a nail being driven into disintegrating wood that splinters farther and farther apart, a determination of unfathomable mystery, unhuman and unnatural almost. Why? Why should he come to her only to give himself up? she wanted to shout. Wasn't it rank folly to wait like this? What had been the point then in Magda's brilliant forceful ruse which had closed everyone's eyes? Why should he want to stay, be locked up, put on trial for his life? Why, why, when no one was hindering him from escaping? The jungle was wide; there was a continent before him. Everyone knew that, she wanted to shout louder than ever, and she raised her trembling hand to her mouth to stifle an hysterical scream as the roaring engine drew level, and *passed*; the sound gradually lost itself in the distance until in the stillness they heard themselves start to breathe again.

"Did you meet any Arawak Indians?" she asked, trying to smile in a way that would conceal the panic of irresolution and fear. Then she saw that his hands shook too and had gone cold like hers. He had thrust them into the nest of her thighs and lap.

"I wish I did not have to leave you, Sharon," he cried. "I love you. I love you." He was ashamed of his childish outburst and he gave a forced abrupt laugh. "Arawaks?" he asked quickly. "You little witch, who told you? I wonder whether I should tell you what I saw."

Her curiosity was aroused. "What do you mean?" she begged. "Tell me."

The grandfather clock began to strike the hour, eight o'clock. The rain suddenly began to drizzle. The river acquired a pale drifting film, thin and strong as steel – lying upon a dark underworld of water – wrought by a seizure of elements containing wind and stream and trespassing sunlight out of a rift of cloud. This closed, the phenomenal texture settled, the rain pelted down in earnest, a multitude of granite rivets and stars bouncing on the river.

"The truth is, I couldn't believe it," said Cristo whimsically. "Not in this day and age, anyway."

"I don't follow."

"The Arawaks I saw belonged to two or three centuries ago. As far back as that, I would swear."

Sharon began to laugh and Cristo began to stare at her uncomfortably. "You asked me," he protested, "and I. . . ."

"O, it's not that. I do want to hear your story. But I believe I know why you were fooled. At least I think I can explain. The Catholic Mission in the river has been staging a carnival."

"Carnival?"

"The Indians were in mock battle. . . ."

"What do you mean?"

"Well, you know, don't you? that it was around here – Pomeroon to Moruca – that the Arawaks and the Caribs last clashed. A ferocious war it was. It is said the Arawaks won because their healing medicine-men knew how to restore the dead. Their fighting strength therefore never diminished. . . ."

It was Cristo's turn to laugh. "You love all the fables, don't you, my little one? You were born like that.' His lips brushed the roots of her hair, murmuring against the shell of her forehead. "I'm sorry but I don't believe the Indians I met were your carnival creatures. . . ." He was teasing her. "They were too real to be pretenders and ghosts. . . ."

"What do you mean?" She was startled beyond the memory of crisis.

Cristo kissed her again, sat back. His eyes turned full of curious nostalgia, piercing the magical river, the rain and the sun.

"Who knows", he grew a little uneasy, surrendering himself all at once to the helplessness of all recollection, "what is and what is not? One can only repeat what happens to oneself. Coming to think of it now I suppose your explanation is reasonable." He spoke absent-mindedly, tapping his forehead. "The truth is, I was mad, I was running in the bush, God knows what was going on in here." He was tapping his forehead still, thoughtlessly as ever. "I was looking for a factory . . ." he paused.

"A factory? What do you mean?" Sharon cried, thinking it incongruous and absurd.

"I had Abram's gun, haversack and cartridges and I set out first for Moruca. Seemed to me I would get game there easily. Even if it meant living on the hard-boiled flesh of parrot. I had heard that topside Moruca an American company was exploring for oil. Firing seismograph soundings and so on. I understood too there was a factory beyond Moruca in process of making glass from Moruca sand, and paper out of wallaba pulp. I thought – as I was no longer on the run in the same way after all" – he could not help expressing his conceit – "that I would be free to take a job with one of these companies, raise enough to pay my passage to north-west perhaps, and then I would slip over the border into Venezuela. : . ."

"Cristo," Sharon could not help interrupting childishly (in reality she was starving to be convinced) "there is no such factory around here . . . in this . . ." – she waved – "wilderness . . . it's a mirage. . . ." She was sorry the moment she had spoken and could have bitten her tongue.

"At the time I swore there was." He stopped foolishly. The falling rain cloaked the river, obscuring everything. He groaned, baffled and unhappy, unsure of anything now. Sharon stared at him, willing to be hypnotized by the suspension of every conventional basis of belief, even by the relative goals and industries he had made in his mind, the magnetic targets he had inspired in himself.

"I see now", she confessed, "what you mean." She was aware of a stupendous emptiness, the hoax of a spirit, the sensation that one had to be born perfectly true not to need to discover oneself, and that one's parents had never conceived the glowing suspension of miraculous seed in the dark geometry of the womb. She looked into Cristo's eyes demanding of him the uncanny penetration of all her nature. Anything to make him forget the prison-house closing in on him all the time. Everything began to fade save the prospect of facing each other, drifting into each other's curious acknowledgment of emptiness as into the purest embrace and fiction of life.

"Tell me", she said, "what happened." She drew him into herself and restored the triumph within themselves over every present and past phenomenal condition.

"I was saying," Cristo said, as if he had regained the impulsive recollection of all adventure, "I thought of picking up a job in the glass-making factory."

"I see," she said matter-of-factly.

"Seemed a good idea. I thought I would cut across Jigsaw Bay quickly and reach Moruca. Ran into a soft bog. The sea had buried a long spit of giant forest, deep tobacco-ish sort of stuff lay on the ground. A beastly rubbish heap, the ashes of many civilizations. Every branched chimney in the world had gone up in smoke. I decided to cut in, and come around on harder creation and ground. Was late afternoon as far as I remember" – they sat close together, immersed in each other's eyes – "afternoon like this." He looked around all of a sudden, waking up a little to the rain that was still falling, and to the hands of morning on the grandfather clock, pointing to a quarter past eight. He brushed the appearance of time aside: "Afternoon. Light. . . ." He gazed into her mind as into the clearest crystal of participation and recollection, and he forgot the falling rain: "Light . . . as the memory of you will always be light. . . ." He kissed her, long and sweet and hard. His lips were perfectly bemused: "Sort of falling through the trees, the lovely dying smoke and light of the sun, filtering down, like every dying breath," he whispered almost to himself. "The forest I was entering was cloudy and high and

339

thick, dark as you wish to imagine, and then my eyes grew
accustomed and were able to catch every vestige of light. I
saw the first member of a band. A degenerate profile and
crew. They were Caribs, I knew. God knows where they were
coming from. Their skins were dyed, I tell you. Almost
naked. Tattooed. They wore a yellowish muddy dye as if they
had been rolling on the ground. Parrot feathers – bright
macaw too – framed their heads. Some, no head-dress at all.
They had spears, long pointed flying spears. Some, no
weapon at all. Moody and savage as the devil looks when he's
in love. I swore they'd do me in. Couldn't understand where
in God's name they'd come from. *And then I realized they took
me for one of themselves*. Would you believe it?"

Sharon gave a tiny move. Her lips consented but she said
nothing.

"Yes, I was one of them. My hands and my chest were
caked in a dye too. Just like them. The filthy bog! Do you
remember? I had fallen in the muck, you see. I looked
hopelessly yellow and black, in fact the blackest of all the
degenerate Caribs. In the flying rush they assumed I was one
of them" – his lips bore a sly, almost humorous triumphant
look, then they quivered and came to themselves – "one of
this" – he glared into his crystal – "shattered tribe. A terrible
broken family. *On the run!* They were running, running, I tell
you. Full retreat. Full flight. God knows who started it. You
would think the blasted tiger of hell was chasing them."

"What did you do?"

"I was glad I had not been molested and I kept going with
them. I calculated they were heading for Moruca, probably
intending to come down to the sea. I kept along as best I
could, gradually slipping back though, dropping back to the
rear. They didn't worry themselves in the slightest what I did.
In fact I began to wonder whether they were seeing me at all.
They were just running, Sharon, and I suppose they
bargained that God would save the hindmost." He chuckled.
"In any case I don't think I could have kept along because

eventually when I had succeeded in slipping behind I was done for. No one knows how flesh and blood could keep going. I was ripped to tatters. Why, it's a hell of a thing forcing one's way through that bush. Just torn to shivers I tell you. That's when I got this . . ." he pointed to the long bitter scar on his face.

"No," Sharon protested involuntarily, "that's the tiger and me."

"I suppose so," Cristo said, without perceiving his inconsistency, "a long vicious blade of razor grass, sharp as a bloody Carib's knife. My chest was all incision, criss-crossed, my arms, legs tattooed for good. I was beaten, beaten, I tell you. Decapitated. God knows how in hell's name those Carib devils could do it. I had seen the last of them, running, running. Running for their lives, through mora walls, I saw them jumping every *tacouba* like a feather, slashing razor blades to grass, everything. Wild, I tell you. The last one passed as I fell on the ground. He left me lying alone in the dark. It was black-dark. Then the rain!" He pointed at the river without seeing a thing. "The rain started to slash the stump of my neck. I couldn't lift my head to brush off a drop. The sound of my own gurgling throat made me jump. It was a little stream running to Moruca or to Akawini perhaps, I don't remember. Didn't know where the hell I was. Stretched out, gore and self and stump. Blood. I pushed my tongue in the pool. The water tasted like hell, a trace of grit or something. A runaway slave was standing over me. I couldn't believe my dead blind eyes. God, it was only myself, the close image of myself in the water." He stopped and looked a little self-conscious and comical. "I'm a black man, I said at last, coming to myself a little, from Africa. I'm no confounded Carib. What the hell am I doing here? I should be safe at home across the sea." He gave a little glancing laugh.

"You're my man," Sharon said softly.

"Night was closing in, bringing me no answer. I couldn't see a thing. Mosquitoes," Cristo said, stricken by the

341

inadequacy of every blind image. "I don't know if you have ever felt them coming down in a cloud." He was reminiscing to himself. "The biting moon arose, bringing another cloud of demons. But soon the black pestering sky lifted. O God, what a relief! Beautiful, clear. The stream had turned to a pool of blood now the night was no longer so dark. A coagulated mirror in which to ponder on myself. The mysterious man on the moon. I could not help grinning." He looked at Sharon, wanting to convey to her every paradoxical whimsy and itch of laughter. "When a man is lost you never know what he'll do. Sometimes he'll weep, sometimes he'll dance. I heard the voice of the roaring baboon all of a sudden. Too frightened to run, I could only remain where I was. It's not me, I said. I have done nothing. No one's chasing me. Maybe they're moaning for rain because of coming dry weather. Maybe they know a real drought is coming along. Or maybe they're afraid of the man in the moon after all. ME. Afraid of me." Cristo laughed. His manner was acquiring a curious resignation and relief. Almost (one wondered) he might have been making an unpretentious ironical joke on himself, searching in all unwitting burgeoning fearful desire for a way of redeeming the curse of nature's self-parody. "What a roaring voice in such a small ghostly animal."

He stopped as if – while he was earnestly trying to stretch his human length along – he still wanted to see himself in an alien body, uncaring and unsentimental as an animal could be. The thought laid hold of him with a flitting hand that belonged to the carnival as well as the tragical spirit of place, ancient and modern masquerade, Christian and pagan disguise, the fluctuating grimacing sorrows of all mankind.

"Bloodsuckers," he cried to himself at last, "I felt one on my cheek. Bats. You meet them in the depth of the bush. Dark and light, light and dark, all stripes, the filtering light of the moon like every conceivable wraith in my mind. They are all passing again. . . ."

"Whom do you mean?" Sharon asked.

All the Aeons

Cristo roused himself. "It wasn't Pomeroon. I was in a far forest. The earth looked like Cuyuni . . . really heartland ground. . . ."

"The heartland, I see."

"I don't know. Must have been Pomeroon after all. But far above and inside. They were running again, I tell you. All the shapes you can ever see in your mind's eye. Every black ancestor and bloodless ghost. What had they done to be running like that, Sharon?" he demanded of her, speaking to no one in particular. "What were they guilty of? I was one of them, a morose witness shadow, one of a crowd of fictions. I was dreaming. No, God knows, I was never so wideawake. I tried to box my brains but all I could remember was Noah's ark. I couldn't remember the afternoon or the evening before. I tried to think. I tried to think I was talking to *you*, you and me swinging like two precocious monkeys in the trees, the huntsman peppering us with mosquito bullets. Then I said – look stranger, suppose this is South America where you belong? Don't forget history is a fable, baboon man. You read it in school like a monkey, little girl. The mountains turned valleys and the valleys turned mountains and everybody was running from cataclysmic disaster. Glad to hide in the trees and look down on the lost Incas and the dead kings of Spain. Stupid. Why worry? I wasn't in South America. I was sleeping in bed at home. All this crystal-gazing historical nonsense, Sharon, you started it the day you were born."

"Me?" Sharon said helplessly. She couldn't make up her mind whether Cristo's stand was half-improvisation, half-truth.

"All mixed up in my head," Cristo said, making an excuse, "on all sides like a grotesque tumbled pack of cards." He hesitated, smoothing his thoughts, wanting to soften his deadly blow. "And then something really happened that woke me up. I was lying by the pool, the only straggler who remained. The others had fled far away. And I was sure my neck was broken. I was afraid to move to find out. It was too risky. Out of the corner of my eye I saw a pale patch of sky, an open trap-door. Dawn on the moon, God knows. A trap-door. I remembered everything perfectly now. The gallows, the trap-door, the execution . . . I was dead. . . ."

"What in God's name are you imagining?"

Cristo leaned forward, half-serious, half-mocking. "Do you know the last thing I thought about was your father, Sharon, and how he had been drunk and rude to me the first day I came to see you? He executed me that day he forbade me to come and see you. I ran away with my tail between my legs and I felt I would have to do something grand to make up for my cowardice. Paint a famous picture or sculpt a bloody hero. I was as furious as Peet was drunk and we didn't realize we were both being stupidly sorry for ourselves. The whole scene filled my mind – to the exclusion of everything else – as I stood on the gallows. I was involved with Peet when I should have been thinking my last thoughts of you. He was waving his fist at me under your grandfather clock. *There's* one's grotesque fallible human nature. Before I could erase the impression from my mind – BANG – dead as a stone. BANG. There it was again the erect explosion in the bone of folly and repentance."

"You're playing the fool," Sharon cried. "Fool!"

"A kind of bang in the shoulders and neck brought them along," Cristo said half-defiantly. "Can't you play the fool too and see me as someone who was young and grand and bold?"

"Brought whom?"

"The victorious scouts of carnival, your carnival, Sharon, not mine. They were absolutely real for me." His voice was instantly free of all bemusement and self-mockery. "However" – he appeared to correct himself – "you must remember me in whatever way you wish, once it makes you happy. Don't come digging me up though, whatever you do! I won't be there." The boastful words were hardly past his lips when he felt a little ridiculous at their grandiloquent assumption.

"Brought whom?" Sharon insisted.

"For me they were as real as the sun," Cristo was glad to return and rush on. "I was the last member, remaining behind, of the flying band. Every guilty body rolled in one. Vanquished as well as slave, rapist, Carib, monster, anything you want to think. Names give out," he explained in a spate of flying thoughtless images and words. "I really couldn't distinguish myself, who I was. I was lost. That was all. I didn't know what I was doing so far from home surrounded by white priests and magicians." He stopped wondering whether he had let his eager impressions run too far.

Sharon lost herself for a moment and clapped her hands: "The medicine-men."

Cristo smiled with spontaneous relief: "I thought you would see it. Their skins were yellow and white with dye. Chinese ink. Like my grandfather's ancient race. Older than parchment. Lifted me up. I heard them talking in a strange tongue. . . ."

"What happened then?"

"They looked after me." His voice flagged a little but he kept his head up. "The truth was – I was dead tired. Fitted me together again. Chest and stump. Broken neck and skull. Gave me *this*." He held up his tiger's coat helplessly, almost shamefacedly. "Said the last thing I had done was to shoot the beast. I didn't believe them, of course. I told them it wasn't me but they who had killed the ancient jaguar of death. Older than any conquistador. They said: 'No, I was the one who deserved the greatest victory of all.' Imagine that! Doesn't it make you happy?" Cristo was laughing a little at himself, nevertheless he was proud all the same.

"You must wrap him in *this*," he said impulsively, pointing to the door where Peet lay, and giving her the tiger's coat. "I still see him as the last of a desperate flying band waving at me and hounding me on. . . ." His lips suddenly broke – against his will – into a self-pitying smile and he grew ashamed of expressing and deceiving himself any longer,

The Whole Armour

words, ambitions, love; he slumped, remembering nothing now of any hideous weakness and encounter save the purest victory and self-conquest of ancient youth.

"Cristo, Cristo," Sharon called – in an involuntary recollection of all intimacy. "I shall keep it and wear it next to me all the time."

He had fallen on his knees and she stroked the weathered stone of his neck with a childish immature fabulous hand. Her fingers had lost all mutilated presence and sensation.

XII

The child was crowing to the clock at five minutes to ten on the morning of the execution, saluting with all gusto the anniversary of Cristo's arrest. Twelve hallucinated months had passed, nine to be born, three months more to begin to stare at a wall.

Cristo was dreaming as he lay with his head in Sharon's lap.

Only five minutes more your father has! Sharon was crying. Magda whispered a helpless prayer and muttered an empty word to herself. But time and sentiment signified as little to a ghost as to a child, pointing its fists to the clock. Time was everything, a ghost was nothing, nothing always contained everything, and this was his first and last dissolving sense of the value of himself as if Cristo foresaw the twelve months of his dying when he put his head on Sharon's lap.

He wanted to lift his eyes for a moment to meditate on grandfather's anniversary clock, thinking how it would startle the world if a little buried angel popped out of grandfather's dead breast, singing the strokes of the senseless hour, with the clearest involuntary conception of birth, and the clearest involuntary intuition of death. It was all a dream, a dream of the execution of time. For all Cristo knew he had died with Peet, the angel's grandfather, but his ear was still alive, listening at the door of the womb for Sharon's musing child to begin and crow. Cristo was waiting with this singular attention and indifference for the sleeping clock to strike; his mind was so empty it had become a frame for the future, almost as though he had stopped existing already, in fact no one existed, a hundred serial years had passed, and they were all dead fused portraits on the wall for anyone to recognize and learn whatever they wished they understood.

The rain had stopped and Cristo was studying the shining picture of the river drawn by the childlike spirit of place. He admired the lucid design which demolished all dimensions, the black midnight water and the nervous ridges of sunlight, the interior landscape of Rimbaud painted by the subjective hand of Van Gogh. He was lost in this revolution of time, which turned around the little fiend in the clock – his own son after all. He saw the hour of execution approaching, superintended by the child's sceptical song. For at the instant of death he felt he would know that far back in its infancy the universe had been pointing to all he had visualized and loved. One would begin all over to perceive particulars of draughtsmanship as never before – in the way one secretly observes (whether one knows it or not) a reflection in a mirror or a material portrait – by standing hypothetically outside of the dead time, with a capacity to make oneself perfectly aware and free.

Cristo's legacy to his son was the legacy of every ancestral ghost – the appraisal as well as the execution of the last fictions in time.

His head lay still on Sharon's lap when Magda burst into the house: he was still half-dreaming of the painted surfaces of life, the spirit of nature that always escapes from the canvas even as it invokes the budding schools of idolatry and thought. No one could really be sure of anything that had been done, life's infinite motive and intention. No one could intervene and trap the essential spirit, not even the crowing child, pointing his rigmarole fists at the clock. The spirit of place still grew beyond its offspring, whether it was Magda or Cristo or Sharon, past, present and future, Peet or his unborn grandson. Cristo was thinking he might as well be dead now he could see time as a curious shell one constantly evolved and surpassed since it belonged to several modes of dying and living, peoples and places, all immaterial and elusive. Magda was crying and this woke him up. "Wake him up! Wake him up! He believe he done dead already! All you two playing mad or what? You son of a bitch! Look how he sleeping with he head on you lap. And you crying you eye out. Is who all you two think you be at all? Mother and son for Chris' sake?" She spoke helplessly and still violently.

"What? . . . doing what?" Cristo was shocked into forget-fulness as he lifted himself up. "I was dead tired," he confessed at last. "Fell down like a log. Didn't dream a thing. Why, it's five minutes to ten." He looked surprised, his face all crushed and sad.

"I didn't want to disturb you," Sharon said softly.

"O God," Cristo said, groaning a little and looking across the river. "I suppose they'll be here at any minute."

"Who?" Sharon cried absent-mindedly.

"Who?" Magda repeated incredulously. "You mean to say you don't know who? You crazy? Is the jungle-police, I telling you." Words failed her. She gasped: "Look, you been so lost in youself, you didn't even hear me coming along the river-dam. You didn't even hear me come up the step." She rushed forward compulsively and began to shake Cristo in order to make sure he was absolutely awake. "I try me best for you, Son, but like is all to no good. I come to tell you, you got a last chance." She was breathing hard after her long run along the dam and her dress was spattered with mud where she had slipped several times to the ground.

"A last chance?" said Cristo in a wondering voice. He was staring sombrely and attentively at his mother and at Sharon too. Magda had aged indescribably, not in a way to do with her features at all. These were the same, he knew. Still it was as if she had been artificially transplanted in time and one knew she was not what she appeared to be. The mask that stood had long since fallen.

All her violent mood had become a transparent conceit like the black Pomeroon water in the palm of one's hand. Something had drained out of him, blood or sap, and in passing out of him it had also served to reduce all her fantastic compelling ardour and frustration into powerlessness and petulance. He knew naturally enough that the face before him belonged to his mother but it did not seem as if this was the truest likeness in the long run. Why, they might be perfect strangers after all, whose resemblance to each other merely established curiosity about themselves in the past and the future, and that was all. The magical identity and heredity had departed, and it was she who would retain a traditional resemblance to him, her alleged son, as she turned into the child in truth who survived the father, innocently beginning to accuse him of all sorts of ancient fabulous things. Who could say what history would do? It was an odd strand of recollection, but before he could properly encompass it, Magda had begun indeed childishly pointing at the clock.

"Look," she cried, "two minutes to ten. Is you last chance, Cristo. Let me tell you quick, I so agitated. The river-police suppose to get here at ten, see?"

"It's usually noon when they come to question my father . . ." Sharon interrupted. She put her hand to her mouth and looked apprehensively at Peet's door.

"Not today," Magda said imperatively. "They get word from old Mattias. He mek a dash to he motor-boat. But I get a tip," she nodded cunningly. "Don't worry to probe me too deep. I'll tell you after all – me and the sergeant mek a deal long ago." She pulled her dress hard and tight around her heavy sculptured limbs. "He wanted me bad – understand? And I get the tip now; after all is only old Mattias word against nobody." She spoke irrationally. "He could have made a stupid mistake, anything like that. Is you last chance, Boy, to cut out for the bush. You know you way now. Nothing going frighten you. I done procure you twenty minutes' grace, understand? Twenty eternal minute, understand?" She was repeating herself lamentably and breathing hard.

She rushed on awkwardly: "Cristo, you ain't got a ghost of a chance if they catch you. The law funny and it bound to make an example of you. A lot of crime been occurring. Not only in Pomeroon, all the world over, bad hot-tempered crime all mixed up with a study of violence. Is so the papers say. I not stupid. And the evidence pointing at you, Son. You know is how many statement they got? How many bodies' hands raise? Lots-lots. Then you lead them 'pon a long wild goose chase, you know. . . . Shake youself up, Cristo, you face look really dead. And look is ten o'clock, you deaf or what?'' The grandfather clock was now striking in the house – one – two – three – four – five – six – seven – eight – nine – ten. Implacable strokes. Everyone remained absolutely still for a reason no one could divine.

Magda was the first to catch herself and move to the door. ''Quick, quick,'' she whispered, afraid to lift her voice, speaking musingly to herself like one surveying the past from the future. ''Quick! Go. Don't fear. I going stay with she.'' She twittered like a bird, her voice turning to a whispering feather in a window-frame and jalousie. ''If is any pregnancy and Sharon in the family way'' – she waved aside interruption – ''I going stand with she, closer than she own child. All you two young and all you bound to have had you good time, I know. Why, any child mekking in she, is me blood. Good blood, Cristo! It come from far and wide. Don't give youself up, I telling you. You ain't got a ghost of a chance. Don't you understand? Don't stand there so stupid. You is not such weak trash as you look. You is my son.''

Sharon cried suddenly: ''Look!''

Magda had opened the door wide in addressing Cristo. Sharon's exclamation shook her into gazing swiftly outside with eyes that appeared to be turning inward on herself. Suddenly she realized what it was. The house was surrounded and armed men were approaching in the walks of the plantation, their uniform almost one with the bush.

''Is a trick they play on me,'' she screamed in an access of frantic despair, slamming the door, and glancing wildly all around. ''A bloody whoring trick.'' She dashed to Peet's door, shouting: ''Peet, Peet, I want you help. Anything I willing to give you in the world you want. Tek me. Mek me you plaything. I going be better to you than if you were Abramself. All I ask is hide Cristo for me." She flung open the door. "O God," she cried. Peet's dead eyes were staring at her. She rushed forward blindly and grasped his hand, letting it fall at once. The hand descended slowly and gravely, signalling the naked impetus of flight from self-reproach and insensibility. Cristo would be free in the end, it seemed to state, in an armour superior to the elements of self-division and coercion.

Magda fell on her knees and prayed. There was nothing else to do.

THE SECRET LADDER

**For Margaret
and to the memory of my mother**

With our vegetable eyes we view . . . visions.

William Blake

There is in nature, a specific dimension of immaterial constitution which preserves its value in all changes, whereas its form of appearance alters in the most manifold ways.

Mayer

It is indeed an integration of the movements of the agent with the movements of the Other, so that in action the self and the Other form a unity.

John Macmurray

BOOK ONE

THE DAY READERS

Where He stands, the Arch Fear, in a
visible form. . . .

Robert Browning

I

It was the month of September, noon on the Canje River. The gauge against the stelling exposed the greater part of its slender height. The black solid line of the river divided the painted scale, needing seven feet more to rise to brim the deck of the stelling; the river-gauge shot three feet still above this. Fenwick, the government surveyor, was looking up and it seemed an interminable way for the water to mount over his head. Still it could happen in seven days, he decided, adopting for no clear reason whatever the number that stood in his mind. The sky might suddenly declare to rain and fall. Who could tell what phenomenon and change would occur? He remained staring up curiously as if he saw an introspective ladder of climbing numbers rather than actual feet and decimals placed on a strip of vulgar wood. He wanted to curse the glaring cunning of the receding heavens, the oppression of the everlasting bowl of sun in the dense white sky. Instead he closed his eyes and his figure drooped a little in his narrow corial and shell of a boat. He opened his eyes and looked around him once again. The river was dead-still save where his own paddle had broken the mirror and surface. All at once he leaned down and splashed the liquid extravagantly on his face to clear away all doubt of a concrete existence.

Staccato voices rang out in explosions of menace from the bush in the neighbourhood of the stelling. Fenwick listened, wide awake now on the swooning river, wanting to shout an entreating command but unable to move his lips. The water on his forehead began to dry and to drip like large unnatural tears falling into a basin and exploding into mental punctures and shot, muffled and inscrutable, yet clear and loud with the parody of self-abuse and violent reflection and fateful recrimi-

357

nation. He felt crushed by the overwhelming spirit of mockery and place and by his curious responsibilities. It was becoming increasingly difficult to control his discontented body of men. . . .

He pulled his boat against the bank at last and stepped upon the ground. It had been easy to clear this side of the stelling, where he now stood, of long-john trees, razor grass and moca-moca. On the other side – twenty paces away – the ground was low and swampy, and the jungle kept crawling and returning, stretching its ancient wiry knuckles and long grassy sleeves high up as well as across the black face of the river.

He had hardly stirred when he saw the crew coming to meet him. They occupied a resthouse on stilts, set back a little way from the river, and flanked on one side by the clearing where he now stood, and on the other by the encroaching image of the forest reaching into the riverside.

The floor of the stelling jutting over the water seemed from his new vantage ground to resemble the men's rest-house save that the planks were open to the sky, supported by their own tall stilts and piles, planted naked on the dry land and up to their middle further out in the water. Both the finished house on one hand and the open stage on the other appeared to cling to a haphazard billowing wave of land, changing and declining into swamp.

The snarling voices of the men turned to a low mutter and then hushed and died away. They stopped irresolutely in the middle of the clearing, looking down as if each had grown strangely aware of his springing shadow reduced almost to nothing under noonday feet. The sun stood directly overhead, the sun of equatorial Guyana, of the inchoate Amazon basin, dissolving at this hour into a latitude of spendthrift furies and intensities. One could hardly bear to look up into the sky or down upon the earth. All shadow had ceased save within veined grassroots, and along lines of transparency the light made in a couple of leaves clinging to an arm and branch, belonging to a solitary plant in the clearing. The sun shone through dark flesh to illuminated skeleton, the greenest garment to the whitest bone.

It was this sensation of exposure and defeat, amounting to confusion, one experienced standing in the clearing until one almost forgot that within a hundred yards of where one stood – under a shade in the swamp – or within rising undergrowth and overgrowth – the jungle turned blind as a shuttered place and the eye learnt to relinquish the neighbouring sun for a tenebrous, almost electrical gloom.

Fenwick did not know whether to be glad or sorry that the men had stifled their abusive complaint. It was not the first time he had seen this strange impotency, and while in the beginning he had been a little flattered (thinking they were somewhat in awe of the authority he carried as a government officer) and glad, too, to be able to escape being called upon to pass judgement on any of them, *now* he was not so sure he did not want somebody to speak out. Surely an open duel would be better than the threat of all succumbing to a mute spirit of naked isolation, uncertainty as well as frustration. Nevertheless he found himself pretending, as he approached them, that nothing had happened, he had heard nothing, seen nothing, suspected nothing.

"Whose turn is it at the gauge?" he asked matter-of-factly.

"Weng, sir."

"Where is Weng?"

"Gone hunting, sir. Over Kaboyary way."

There was a short silence.

"As soon as he returns, send him to me." Fenwick could not stop himself from speaking sharply. However much he tried to pretend that nothing had happened, he knew there was *something* which his helpless manner and the blistered manner of the crew betrayed, something disturbing and possibly even terrifying in their air of curbed violence. Perhaps it was only this self-created spirit, he reasoned, catching a vague, spasmodic breath of relief. . . . There was a trespassing movement far away over the sheltered jungle and the parching savannahs. The leaves and the grass were stirring in the stealthy air. Weng had absented himself when his spell had come at the gauge. It was a simple matter after all they had made such a fuss about, as simple as the last quivering leaf and blazing straw that cracks the world's back. Fenwick pulled himself up. Sometimes he felt he had no logical freedom of his own. Even the thought of relief and disaster had ceased to possess room for distinction and had turned into the mirage of a desert and a jungle rolled into one. He forced his mind to return to the clearing and the immediate job in hand. Someone would have to take over Weng's shift, the boredom of it, the monotony of watching the river and being watched in turn by one's reflection. Fraction after fraction of an hour, another stumpy pencilled figure appeared in a notebook, day and night, night and day, it did not matter. No rest days came, the river's cycle was ordered by a succession of devils, galvanic crooked leaden fingers, the shattered spokes in a wheel. It was an endless drama and obsession and Fenwick turned aghast at himself. What had started as the slightest pointer and current of duty was assuming enormous unwieldy proportions.

Perhaps he was not the man for the place or the job. He would apply for a transfer. "Chiung!" he addressed one of the crew without seeing him, "take over the gauge until Weng comes in."

"Yes, sir." Chiung replied in a rusty chopped voice. Fenwick now became aware of the man he had chosen. He waited, sensing the burden of something on the tip of Chiung's heavy tongue. But the teeth shut fast like a black rotting cage, the muscles in the jaw gave a rhythmic corresponding action. Fenwick stared at the yellow face. It was difficult to tell the man's age. He may have been forty-five, fifty-five, or even sixty-five. The skin was unwrinkled and yet harsh, the eyes were narrow, ancestral as a Chinese god, the hair on his head was close-cropped and bristling like a porcupine.

"Poker. All night and day they playing poker." It was Dominic Perez who spoke slyly; thickset, expressionless, obvious Portuguese descent. "I belong to day-shift; the noise last night nearly send me mad. Not a wink of sleep then or now." He yawned unceremoniously. "Excuse me, sir, but please speak to the crew to be more quiet." Perez glanced at his companions for approval as though it did not much matter what he actually said, once someone succeeded in voicing and camouflaging their precipitate appearance and suppressed brutal complaint.

A murmur rose on every side and it seemed as if they were all with Perez rather than against him. Who then was the mysterious culprit? Was it Weng? Weng had left for Kaboyary before sunrise. Fenwick decided to question him closely when he came in. It was not the first time he had escaped the trouble of reprimanding anyone. He had always been glad not to have to do so but now he began to suspect a depth of conflict and exacerbation he could not sound. It was a humiliating bottomless extremity to find oneself in. Indeed it was as if their design was a technical and theatrical parody of the hellish nature of their work and existence. Fenwick wondered whether he had begun to credit a crew of ignorant men with the most sinister enduring talent.

There was Bryant, a thin-boned African with sharp razor cheek-bones. There was Van Brock, big, black and sleepy-looking. There was Stoll, a gangling pale-skinned mulatto youth, tall like an unnatural overstretched spider.

"Where's Jordan?" Fenwick asked abruptly. He had had a sudden fresh intuition. "Has he been playing poker too?" Jordan was his cook, a close-fisted crafty man, not liked by the crew. Perhaps *he* was the one. Jordan had cheated and they had come to denounce him though at the last moment they had felt that Fenwick would be annoyed if his trusted camp attendant were accused openly and violently. Fenwick knew by this time he would be more relieved than annoyed. He would much prefer to be called upon to speak to Jordan than endure a psychological mystery and the drought of all reason. Jordan was a good man though mean and cautious in the extreme. He kept a careful watch over all camp stores like a child guarding a crude necessary plaything. He never parted with an extra biscuit if he could help it. No wonder the crew disliked him. It was easy to dislike an exacting store-keeper and banker. Here then stood the whole naked conspiracy. All directed against Jordan. They could not help making a mountain out of a molehill. Like savages and children living within a violent creation and world they had to expend all their spite and malice somehow.

"Look, is Jordan the culprit?" Fenwick demanded.

"Not Jordan." Stoll brushed aside Fenwick's speculations with one of his gangling facile movements. (He spoke in a curiously contradictory voice as much as to say – "Jordan! he's no gambler, but he's always at liberty to cheat us through you. How could you *dream* of asking such a thing, Russell Fenwick, man? You're responsible" – Stoll always carried the spirit of accuser or trickster with him and Fenwick could almost hear the jibing unspoken words.)

"Would you like me to call Jordan, Mr Fenwick?" Stoll asked. "I believe he's lying in his hammock under the tarpaulin."

"No." The surveyor spoke sharply.

Fenwick passed under the men's resthouse and picked up a narrow track which ran parallel to the river for nearly a hundred yards or two through the bush. This brought him to another and smaller clearing in the centre of which stood his own camp. A tarpaulin of medium size (large enough to shelter two or three persons) had been tied over a rude skeleton chopped from long-john trees and young hardwood.

Fenwick had to bend to enter the camp at the side facing the trail. The frame had been laid out inconveniently in this respect, at right angles to the river, in order to utilize the only stable piece of ground. One open triangular face therefore looked straight upon the river – rather than upon the trail – while the other confronted a wall of bush.

Fenwick had been exasperated by the cramping exigencies of the Canje bank, brittle in places, scored and ravaged by itinerant streams that sparked their way into every crevice, basin and cranny every rainy season. He looked up a little anxiously at the ridge pole shooting forward to the river, along which the canvas had been laid, divided equally and pulled both ways into a sloping roof coming close to the ground against the trail. He did not trust the wood the men had used for this purpose especially as the canvas was inclined to belly a little and to sag along the ribs and frame beneath it like a hollow, half-bloated, half-emaciated cow.

"If the rain suddenly falls, we may be in trouble," Fenwick said to Jordan. "This dam' tarpaulin looks full enough of the most likely pools."

"Don't worry, skipper." Jordan spoke confidently. "The water will run off faster than you think." He gave the tarpaulin a hearty slap. He had risen from the ground where he had been squatting, peeling potatoes.

"I've lived in a camp where the ridge-pole came down one night almost plumb on my hammock – out in the open *Oudin* savannahs – nearly split my skull in two." Fenwick was still troubled.

"Why you like to worry you head off, skipper?" Jordan wore a huge half-grin, half-frown. "I know Oudin's Demerara/Abary savannah. All wide open and exposed to the rain. The breeze that can blow there, and the lightning, O God. *This* is another place, a different world, this Canje. In this stifled bush mankind could do well with a breath of wind, I telling you. Jesus, *this* is hell. You not thinking of changing this skeleton we raise up so good all over again, sir? Where you think we going find better wood?"

"Well, I suppose not," Fenwick grumbled, "you're such a lazy fucking bastard."

Jordan laughed. He was fanning himself with a piece of cardboard; a large baby-faced man, exuding a curious self-importance mingled with pride in the easy footing he had established with the brilliant young land surveyor, Russell Fenwick. Fenwick took him for granted and even trusted him in the way one trusts a well-known effigy and target in whom one ploughs home shaft after shaft and bullet after bullet, knowing how painless and useful an exercise it all was.

Fenwick suddenly gave a responsive smile to Jordan's beaming countenance. "I wouldn't put anything beyond you, Jordan, you crafty devil. Are *you* the cheat? Have you been cheating at poker? That's the game they play, isn't it?"

"Me, sir?" Jordan was taken aback. "Me, sir?" he repeated. "I have never played poker all my life. Is this a joke or what, skipper?"

"It's no joke," Fenwick said. He stretched his long legs out before him and leaned back in a camp chair. "The usual frustrating business is going on over there." He pointed towards the trail leading to the men's resthouse. "Never can get to the bottom of it. Maybe it's *my* head they want. It's a stupid game anyway – whatever it is they're up to, and I wish somebody would speak out straight. Tell me something, Jordan, what do you make of Stoll? He's a new man. In fact they're all new. The only team I could pick up this blasted year. It's a long time to be together."

"Stoll's a bright one in his own way," Jordan said quietly, in such a soft-spoken voice Fenwick had to listen attentively. "He been to Berbice High School and he say he want to become a surveyor-apprentice. . . ."

"I know all that," Fenwick interrupted impatiently. "He has told me this himself, and I told him what to do. I am not the Colonial Secretariat, thank God. . . ."

"Stoll's a little edgy, a chip on the shoulder, skipper.

364

Believes if he had social influence you would bring him into your camp *now*. . . ." Jordan's voice had grown phlegmatic. "Make a kind of unofficial apprentice out of him. It would ease him with his cooking and washing – *me* being your camp attendant and therefore having to do for him too."

Fenwick could not help laughing. "Has he offered to bribe you to arrange this, Jordan?"

"Well, to me God, Mr Fenwick, sir."

"Do you really believe it would help indeed if I promoted Stoll into my lousy mess? Would everybody grow so overjoyed (including you, of course, Jordan) that I could live in peace, perfect peace with every son-of-a-gun of you?"

Jordan could not help laughing in turn, a hearty greedy sound that whistled between his teeth. "Whatever you decide to do is OK with me, skipper." He decided to drop the subject of Stoll. "Weng is the man you got to watch steady, not Stoll." His voice was softer than ever, so soft Fenwick did not catch the last fleeting remark – "But I don't suppose you would want to bring *him* in your camp as mess-mate?"

"Weng?" Fenwick was lost in thought. "Why Weng?"

"He got the men under his thumb," Jordan declared. "He stealing their time (forcing them to do part of his shift at the gauge) and he stealing their ration. They frighten to tell you."

"Christ, Jordan. Why, man, can't they tell me? I'm going back over there right now."

"Steady, skipper, steady," Jordan cried. He almost thrust Fenwick back into the camp chair. "Is no use, you would only stir up bigger trouble."

"What the hell do you mean? Are you *sure* of what you're saying? About Weng, I mean."

Jordan hesitated. "You can't be sure of anything in the bush, Mr Fenwick. Nobody ever see Weng red-handed. Fire him – and a load of question going drop 'pon you head from the Labour Department. And if you can't prove anything, you in trouble." He shrugged. "Who knows? Maybe you can't do no better. The next thing is, when Weng gone, Chiung bound to take over and he may start riding them men worse than Weng. Chiung may be worse than Weng, skipper. If one body stop taking advantage of everybody, some other body going to do it. Is so bush work stay. . . ." Jordan suddenly found himself compelled to step out of the tent in order to sneeze wildly and blow his nose on the ground. He returned with watering eyes. "A black fly waltz up my nostril, excuse me. As I was saying – is so bush work stay. Especially on a job like this. Don't make a move, skipper, until you get a positive complaint. Just bide you time. Another couple morning, the survey done, you pack you bag and *home*, Canje cobweb left behind."

"Your dam' couple morning may be another six months, Jordan." Fenwick nevertheless could not help being strangely charmed by the man's cunning words. They made a curious sense. "Who knows how long this dry spell will last?" He waved uncertainly at the river.

"Just wait and see, sir. You can't do nothing to rectify nothing, believe me. Get rid of one body and another going plague you. . . . The truth is you poring over them chart and tide-map and God knows what too hard. Another thing. Weng (with all his faults) is still the born leader of the bunch. You still need him to hold them down. Wait!" He lifted a finger. "Somebody coming!"

Fenwick listened. In the far distance the baboons were roaring for rain and their voice struck the black sunlit river like subterranean lightning and thunder.

Jordan was bustling industriously. He had thrown a cloth over the dining-table. "Is already late for lunch. I got a lovely fish cake."

A dry branch snapped close at hand. Bryant was coming along the trail. He turned and went to the riverside – towards Fenwick's dinghy and outboard engine. He touched his cap to the surveyor.

"I'd almost forgotten, Bryant," Fenwick exclaimed. "We're going up river this afternoon, aren't we?"

"Yes, sir," Bryant replied, "I come over now to mix the fuel supply." He turned to Jordan. "Where you hiding the Mobiloil cook man? This engine can't run on gasolene alone!"

Jordan pointed to a new case covered carefully in a corner of the tent. Bryant whistled and began to unscrew the cap of the engine.

Fenwick had named his dinghy *Palace of the Peacock* after the city of God, the city of gold set somewhere in the heart of Brazil and Guyana. He liked to think of all the rivers of Guyana as the curious rungs in a ladder on which one sets one's musing foot again and again, to climb into both the past and the future of the continent of mystery.

It was a waking dream that would overcome his senses, especially when sitting in his speeding boat, the high drone of the outboard engine in his ears, and the bow of his vessel uplifted to the blue empty shell of the sky, while the black Canje foamed and bristled and encircled a revolving purpose and propeller somewhere in the vague regions under his feet.

It was one of those inward flowering truths that kept him spiritually alive, making him able, as it were, to create an image out of hardship. He had known men who pretended they were attacking an enormous worth-while devil as they chopped and cut their lines through the thickest marabunta jungle. It nerved them to go on, it steeled them to stand on their feet and to burn and stay alive. How quixotic one was! Fenwick could not help smiling as if he had confessed to a strange weakness and eternal bolster and root of embarrassment in the face of some secret mocking enemy within himself.

The Canje was one of the lowest rungs in the ladder of ascending purgatorial rivers, the blackest river one could imagine. Every tributary had buried its grassy head in a grave of wilderness, green as diabolic flame, with a high waving colour of fresh seeming youth belonging nevertheless to the darkest fluid of the river's age. No one lived upon, or cultivated, the Canje swamps and savannahs. On higher land where the water still appeared to possess the actual banks and definition of a river, the inhabitants wrestled with themselves to make a living within their uncertain ground which was continuously threatened by an erosive design eating slowly across the river's catchment.

The Canje stretched before him, the smoothness of a mirror laid upon its sleeping endless back. Wreaths of grass that had escaped from the corners, and joined the reflecting shadow of the stream, constantly sought to close the path. He occasionally lifted his hand sharply to warn Bryant of a difficult patch ahead.

They were approaching a particularly difficult area. The waterway before them was more confined than ever. The grass growing on either hand came far out nearly to the middle, appearing submerged in a lake of greenest fathoms under a secretive pitch of mingled transparency and gloom. Large open leaves looking cracked and strained as a man's stretched footprints stood here and there on the water. At the best of times this was a narrow passage to be manœuvred with care to avoid fouling the engine's propeller. Now it was almost blocked by an immense hurdle of grass. Fenwick signalled and Bryant shut off the engine, pulling it forward with the same movement until the propeller was drawn clear of the water. The nose of the vessel dropped with momentum and Fenwick grabbed a paddle and switched the boat to the bank where it ran snugly within a great subsiding globule of water which had stranded itself on an enormous leaf. Bryant held a slender stem growing out from the land and wound it into a scarecrow's noose – leaf and grass knotted swiftly together.

"Old man Poseidon occupying here, Mr Fenwick," Bryant

volunteered. He moved his jaw involuntarily as if the sharp
spirit in his voice had sliced each word in half so that only
the mutilated shadow of humour appeared on his lips.

"Here?" Fenwick was startled. He had occasionally glimpsed an ancient presence passing on the river before his camp
but had never properly seen it or actually addressed it.
Rumour had created a tortuous and labyrinthine genealogy
for Poseidon, the oldest inhabitant of the Canje. His grandfather had been a runaway African slave who had succeeded
in evading capture and had turned into a wild cannibal man
in the swamps, devouring melting white cocerite flesh
wherever he spied the mirage of high baking land; feasting
on the quivering meat of sensitive turtle (until he turned to
human jellyfish himself) as well as the soft underbelly of
fearsome alligator.

Some people said Poseidon was now a hundred years old,
and that his grandfather's half-crazed, hounded spirit possessed him. They dreamed he had been in the Canje when
the first wave of freed slaves arrived there. Now everyone
saw him as the black king of history whose sovereignty over
the past was a fluid crown of possession and dispossession.

Fenwick sometimes succumbed to this order of inner
rhapsody and grotesque meditation from which, however,
he always instantly recoiled (whenever he caught himself)
like an endless spider of reflection upon the unstable ground
of time. He would excuse himself, of course, by telling
himself that the habit of aerial contemplation had been
planted everywhere around him in the unearthly stunted
forest, and within the uneven horizon the trees made as they
enclosed and beckoned him at the same time to look through
windows upon the empty savannahs.

"Perez arrange to bring his wife up-river. She going stay
in the old man's house. The old man too old to do
anything." Bryant spoke almost to himself. "Poor old devil! I
wonder if is true."

"What? Perez? Bringing his wife here?"

369

"O yes, sir. Portuguese girl – Catalena Perez. Is nobody's business I suppose. She won't be in anybody's way here. Perez can come out often enough. She'll be three or so miles outside the actual survey camp. Perez is a uxorious man, that's plain. So is nearly all of us, I suppose." Bryant shifted the shadow of his hands reverently, almost ironically on the ring of bush to which the boat was tied. He seemed to be exorcizing and entertaining – at the same moment – a groping suspension and contractual judgement on the nature of every possession as he moved his hands and spoke a little absentmindedly and illogically to himself. "Primitive mankind is. Pure primitive." His voice was lost in the sudden rash sighing of the trees where the wind blew, so that his words may not have been what Fenwick heard at all.

"But where's Poseidon's house?" Fenwick demanded loudly. He was exasperated by his own ignorance.

"In there." Bryant pointed to a cunning path leading from the river. He lifted the sharp critical bones of his face and listened. "Somebody coming, Mr Fenwick! Is the old man, I sure. He hear the loud noise the engine-motor make when it stop and he coming to see is who."

At first Fenwick saw nothing. But as he peered closely into the barely perceptible door of vegetation he discerned Poseidon's small upturned boat or corial buried in the grass. It could have been the black startling back of a boa constrictor, many of which often lay like this in the swamps and then vanished. There was the faint hoarse sound of an approaching body swimming in the undergrowth. Fenwick adjusted his eyes. He could no longer evade a reality that had always escaped him. The strangest figure he had ever seen had appeared in the opening of the bush, dressed in a flannel vest, flapping ragged fins of trousers on his legs. Fenwick could not help fastening his eyes greedily upon him as if he saw down a bottomless gauge and river of reflection. He wanted to laugh at the weird sensation but was unable to do so. The old man's hair was white as wool and his cheeks –

covered with wild curling rings – looked like an unkempt sheep's back. The black wooden snake of skin peeping through its animal blanket was wrinkled and stitched together incredibly.

"Poseidon!" Fenwick asked, feeling himself turning to stone. He did not trust his own eyes like a curious fisherman, playing for time, unable to accept his own catch, trying to strip from the creature who stood before him – the spirit with which he himself had involuntarily invested it. This was no god of the swamps, no leviathan of the depths, he protested. This was an old bent artifice of a man, clothed in the changing witness of age and lamb's snow, shading his buried eyes from the glare of the sun – after the clotted memory of darkness – in order to see clearer the two men sitting on the water before him.

Poseidon addressed Fenwick at last. His mouth moved and made frames which did not correspond to the words he actually uttered. It was like the tragic lips of an actor, moving but soundless as a picture, galvanized into comical association with a foreign dubbing and tongue which uttered a mechanical version and translation out of accord with the visible features of original expression.

This bewildering dichotomy – which the old man now expressed – placed Fenwick at a greater disadvantage than ever though it seemed to find a ready natural ear in Bryant. Fenwick's outrage began to turn to guilt. He listened, no longer with a sense of contempt, to the agitated crooked voice of the creature he had caught, trying at the same time to follow the silent accents of an ageless dumb spirit. It was as if he (Fenwick) however much he protested within himself at the ceaseless ruse of cruel nature and sentimentality, could never, any more, rid himself of the daemon of freedom and imagination and responsibility. Poseidon had been hooked and nailed to a secret ladder of conscience however crumbling and extreme the image was.

On their way back to camp Fenwick and Bryant were caught in a storm – branches of lightning appeared in the sky on which grew a sudden bursting pod of rain. First stinging wayward seed – broadcast by the rising wind – pelted their face and hands. Then a forest of rain sprouted and enveloped them thicker than the grass in the water. Fenwick recalled (standing now under his tent) the instant jungle of night which had settled and vanished again in the heart of the day. . . . He had just wriggled and stepped out of the wet skin of trousers and shirt. The river was smooth and naked for the rain had ceased as quickly as it had begun when they were a mile away from home, and the trees had settled once again into their dual place, reflected in the water at their ancient tug-of-war with the ribbons of the sky. He tried to stand still on the edge of the river, to match the restoration of tension and immobility in the atmosphere which held the earth, but his image trembled a little against his will. *Palace of the Peacock* had been tied within the transparent gloom of the landing, and the boat's propeller stood agile and clear of the dark mirror and stream, a frozen summons to action. Fenwick retired and seized a couple of garments beside his hammock and began dressing quickly. Jordan would be back shortly from the men's resthouse and Bryant, too, who had gone to change his sopping things. . . . He began turning over in his mind a number of questions. The afternoon's outing had been strangely rewarding but equally unsatisfying. He had planned to inspect the Kaboyary Creek, one of the tributaries of the Canje, but half-way there had run into the grass. There had been a considerable delay and when they left Poseidon's landing it was already four o'clock. His inspection would be too hurried to prove useful so late. Yet he was unhappy when he gave the order to turn back. . . . There was the question of Weng, too. He had hoped to meet the man possibly in the Kaboyary line, a rough path into the savannahs Fenwick had cut along one bank. . . . Bryant and Jordan were now approaching. They had stopped on the trail. Their voices escaped the silent dripping walls of bush and lingered upon the suddenly loud surface of the river. It seemed they were taking an interminable quarrelsome moment to arrive. . . .

Jordan did not wait for Fenwick to address him. "Bryant been talking about old man Poseidon, skipper," he cried the instant he appeared at the open riverside of the tent. "Don't trust a word of complaint that come out of the old black devil's mouth." His large womanish face was creased all over jealous and furious at the same time. His eye caught Fenwick's clothing lying in a heap on the groundsheet. "You get soaking wet, skipper," he cried in a tone of solicitous warning, clutching the garments and squeezing them rapidly, flinging them on top of the overhead tarpaulin. A wet pool remained on the groundsheet which he feverishly swept away, waving Bryant brusquely aside.

Fenwick found himself at a nightmare loss for words. He was often repelled and fascinated by his camp attendant's calculating and yet spontaneous industry. It evoked in him a sensation of curious and abnormal helplessness as if a great distance stood between himself now and the faithful amenities of every past and truly harmonious domestic world, whatever loyal contrivances he had managed to establish. The jungle remained an eternal primitive condition. Everything and everyone could become threatening, even strangely privileged and demanding.

Furthermore – on this occasion – he did not want to confess how he had been moved and disturbed to the greatest depth by the apparition of Poseidon, and how little he had made of the old man's complaint, the voice and expression were so alien and painful and extreme. He was ashamed of his ignorance especially as he had sensed that Bryant understood all that the old man was saying. There were reasons for his failure of comprehension, of course, simple ones perhaps to do with a refined upbringing (as his ageing mother in Georgetown would put it) he must learn to face and assess. The psychological nature of his thought remained like spiritual introspection in the air. . . . Jordan was speaking again – "Bryant declare Poseidon complain, skipper, that I don't pay the right price for the fish I buy. But I pay him what he deserve to get, every time. After all, is whose interest I must protect? Is you – your interest, sir, that comes first. . . . You musn't pay serious attention to these outlandish Canje body, skipper. I warning you they bound to lead you astray and into deep trouble." Jordan spoke with a great air of injured fellowship and authority.

"He say you paying him less than half the market price he would get in New Amsterdam," Bryant declared. "The old man too old to carry his catch down to the mouth of the Canje River. . . . Poor devil. . . ."

"Half the market price?" Jordan raged. "The old black beast can't count, let me tell you. And be careful how *you* accuse me, Bryant. Five shillings is the price for his fish in any town. I give the old man three and six." He turned and faced Fenwick – "The amount is there large as life in the mess book, sir."

Fenwick was taken aback by the bitter feud of emotional earnestness. It seemed such a small matter to raise a grave fuss about. (Yet wars had been fought for dubious reasons, and dynasties had crumbled under a straw of provocation which supported the groundless apparatus and endless constitution of conflict.)

"I pay him a good price," Jordan insisted, "taking into account how far in the bush we be. Is common sense." He pointed to the river which scarcely appeared to flow in the late afternoon light like a snake whose motion had been reined into graver stillness than ever and embalmed for good.

"The old man say you would give him just two shillings", Bryant rasped, "for the last drop of his blood." The sharpest glint rose in his eye – disdain and hatred.

Jordan's expression turned bitter. Then he exploded: "Well to me God, skipper, Bryant really forgetting himself. He accusing me of pocketing one and six and paying the old man two. Everybody in this place seem to feel because I am a strict storekeeper and camp attendant I am a bloodthirsty thief. Three shillings and sixpence for a creature so big. . . ." Jordan was measuring the length on his arm.

"Poseidon say *two*," Bryant interrupted ungraciously. "Two shillings was all you give." Nevertheless he was ill at ease and turning uncertain of the depth of his accusation.

"Ask Weng," Jordan cried triumphantly. "The last time I walk to Poseidon's land and pay him three shillings and six dam' pennies apiece – I tell you – for his catch, Weng was with me."

"Weng!" Bryant remonstrated, recovering his suspicions. "A fine one. Weng would have drown his own mother in the cradle, given half a chance. Excuse me, skipper. Poor old Poseidon! Everything he say going fall on deaf ears in the end. Deaf ears." He had turned from Jordan and was staring accusingly now, mournfully too, at Fenwick.

"I am not deaf, Bryant," Fenwick could not help himself crying out. "I understood Poseidon perfectly today." He knew that he lied, but his vanity and self-possession had been strangely shaken. "I shall investigate all the complaints he made against the members of the crew. And until I have cleared the matter up, it will remain my burden and responsibility. The facts, however, are far from being clear. Time and history seem to have made us all equally ignorant about who really exploits whom." Fenwick realized he was becoming sententious and even foolish. But it was the only way at the moment to uphold the spirit of his authority. "You do understand me, Bryant, don't you?" he pleaded.

"Yes, I do, sir," Bryant said almost apologetically. "The old man look like my grandfather, too, and that is as far back in history as I could go. He would never accuse *me*."

"Nor me," Fenwick agreed impulsively, half-smiling, half-serious as in the yearning nature of a solemn and enduring pact which repudiates an ignorant necessity and desperate treachery in the heart of things.

"The day I go with Weng he accuse *you*, Bryant," Jordan interrupted malevolently.

"Me?"

"Yes, you. He say he know how to bribe you every time."

"It's a lie."

"Then the food in your guts is a lie."

"What you mean, Jordan?"

"I repeat that the food in you guts is the born conception of a lie. Like the food in every squeamish body's guts," he added, looking significantly in every direction and declaring pointedly: "Is not you carry Perez there? Did you not bargain with the old man to take Catalena in when the time come for she to arrive, and is not you arrange how much rent Perez must pay for his wife to have a room? And you! What benefit come to you? You alone know best, but let me name the common-or-garden fruit you get: the old man scrape together (and give you) off his land, plantain to make you strong, dry coconut to give you fibre, all free, gratis and for nothing. . . ."

"It's not true. Poseidon's house is the only house of Canje's black caves of houses, you know that, within ten miles from here which empty of a large half-starving family. . . . The old man is the only one who can offer a room. . . ."

"Why you didn't share out all the fruit Poseidon give you, up and down river then, if everybody else suffocating and hungry? Why you keep every scrap for yourself, as you aiming still to do now and in the future?"

"I didn't drive any kind of hard bargain," Bryant cried. "I seem to remember the old man long before I come to work in the Canje,and he too seem to remember me like a grandson. He invite me around to ask my opinion about Perez. I give him my views, that's all. Perez was there too. He agree. I try to help how I can. Perez is a designing man, he want his wife to come. Don't ask me why. And the old man really in need and hard up for cash." Bryant shrugged. "Is their mutual affair. Poseidon give me a bunch of plantains, yes," he went on. "If I had suspected anybody would turn it so hard against me I would have refuse it. . . . Why up to today he give me a small heap of dry coconut again. It signify nothing. . . ."

"In front of the skipper," Jordan declared. "You see, sir?" He turned to Fenwick: "Poseidon believe he got to make energy to bribe everybody. The most innocent body guilty, too, none exempt, when all living hand to mouth, bartering their soul away for a couple of shilling even when they don't know it." He suddenly gave Bryant a stab. "The old man bribing you to plead with the skipper (if you can find a familiar cunning tongue in you head) to save his land. Is not so? You tell Mr Fenwick yet? How Poseidon afraid he going lose all his land which fast threatening to go down under the Canje flood-top?"

"I still don't believe the old man accuse *me*." Bryant's thin bones were slicing his face – the image now of conflicting interest and emotion. "Not me," he repeated. "Not me. He would be mad."

"Yes, *you*. And let me tell you," he looked all around him, "he accusing everybody. Even Mr Fenwick as well as dam' scamp like you and me, Bryant. I know the truth if nobody else do." His large creased sphinx-like face was heartless and calculating as stone.

II

Fenwick woke suddenly with the dream fresh in his mind. It was seven o'clock (the morning after the first memorable day of his encounter with Poseidon) and voices outside his cocoon of a hammock with its long opaque net, designed to withstand even the minute sandfly, wound their way into his consciousness. His watch was hanging from the roof of his net ominously ticking like a gigantic disciplined mosquito which had been made prisoner overnight. He realized with an absurd start that he had overslept, and was about to spring up wildly but recovered himself, listening to the monotonous current of sound beyond his envelope. The members of the crew were collecting their weekly supplies. He could hear the familiar baleful tinkle of the scales as Jordan measured the rations in strict conformity with printed Government Regulations. Salt beef, split peas, condensed milk, rice, etc. . . . not a grain or drop too little or too much, Jordan declared. Everyone grunted, cursed foully and indistinctly, and departed.

He had worked late the previous night, analysing the network of tidal readings, oppressed and moved by the vision of Poseidon and the trapped faces of Bryant and Jordan. Jordan had been victorious in the argument in the end. Perhaps Fenwick wanted it that way since whether he chose to admit it or not, Jordan was his shield against importunity, an agent of governance to exercise over the men in lieu of a genuine and profoundly human natural understanding he would have given all he possessed to possess. The crew both feared and despised Jordan, sometimes they sought favours of him, sometimes they tried to discredit him, they were an enigma to themselves, an enigma to Fenwick as Fenwick was an enigma to them. It was always Jordan's head – Medusa-like – that inspired in them a certain cynical helplessness, the helplessness of men who could be contained by forces of greed or self-interest or guile. It was a strange fellowship and barren condition. The binding ancestral apparition of Poseidon contained a new divine promise, born of an underworld of half-forgotten sympathies. And yet who could tell whether it was not the old monster of deception everyone secretly feared in themselves?

Here was the ambivalent *lapis* of all their hopes of ultimate freedom and archetypal authority as well as the viable symbol of inexhaustible self-oppression.

Fenwick could not help this flood of half-waking fantastic thought breaking through the sluice-gates of every ordinary sceptical grain and self-imposed precaution. He had had the strangest dream and this was responsible for his present mood of self-surrender. He remembered blowing out his lantern and scrambling into his hammock soon after midnight. The darkness was full of ubiquitous tongues, croaking and alien, stiff like the ancient *crapaud*, subtle and whispering as the vague breath of a leaf in the forest. The last thing he remembered was his breath on the flame of the lantern. Then he was standing on the edge of the savannahs, the stars dying into dawn. In the distance a couple of trees spread their naked still arms into the air in such a manner as to create a moving design – a tall nameless person mounted on horseback, armed with a sword or a spear. Fenwick set out towards him and became aware at the same time of a lively body of horses the rider seemed to be conducting around him. As he drew near the obscure horseman vanished and there remained a white decapitated mare, prancing on the ground vibrantly amidst her companions. He could clearly see the fleshy, headless trunk of her neck, her smooth white powerful body and her strong dancing hooves. But her rider was nowhere in sight. . . .

It was becoming close and hot and Fenwick abandoned his hammock. He emerged to find the river black and sparkling where the early morning sun broke through the trees out of the eastern savannahs. Each tiny aperture in the bush had been

The Secret Ladder

spreadeagled into a star. Jordan had now dismissed the last member of the crew. His hands resembled a dusty parody of the writhing horseflesh in his dream, Fenwick thought in a flash of revulsion, with a crude coating of flour, and there were a few involuntary musing streaks on his face where he had put his fingers on his perspiring cheeks and brow.

"You look filthy, Jordan," Fenwick cried. "Have you been up to your old tricks, robbing the men?" He began to dress quickly.

Jordan brushed his hands. "If it wasn't for me, all the ration would have gone long ago," he grumbled. "Weng arrive late last night, sir. He bring worries, skipper. Bad news. Poseidon stirring up a head of trouble in the river." He tapped his forehead significantly. "But you can outwit him, skipper."

"Bad news?"

Jordan was thinking deeply. "Bad news, sir. But nothing you can't handle, I insist." He paused for a moment. "You breakfast done ready, Mr Fenwick. Let me wash my hands and fix you up. The crew really stupid. I often got to put their ration in all sorts of old paper-bag they bring. Sometimes it breaks and spills all on the ground – when I take it off the scales – upon my hand and my foot. They get vexed and they want to butcher me for more. But no. They must learn. Not a thing. This is no philanthropic society."

"What's this about Weng and Poseidon?" Fenwick accepted a steaming cup of coffee and a plate of ham and eggs. He suddenly realized he was ravenous. He had had no dinner the night before, just a cup of soup. Jordan watched him as he ate, wondering how deep was the new-found sympathy for Poseidon. He had witnessed the spark which had united Bryant and Fenwick in an instant and he felt it was a threat to his own sovereign ideas and petty interests.

"Weng will tell you himself, sir," he declared. "But the fact is, the river people – all the black people from topside and bottomside the river – flocking around Poseidon. They ready to make trouble." Jordan laughed contemptuously: "As if they can really make trouble! One good look at them and they scared stiff.

380

A pack of crude children." He added softly, under his breath: "Savages, too! You wasting your time believing they up to any good."

Fenwick was amazed. "But I don't understand," he said. "What do you mean by flocking around Poseidon? Are they staging a rebellion or something?"

"It's the land they want," Jordan said darkly. "The land that they going lose, Mr Fenwick."

"Now, what in hell's name is all this?" Fenwick demanded. "What damned trickery is going on, tell me, Jordan?"

"The news leak out, sir, that you surveying the river preparatory to the government making a flood reservoir and drowning the whole catchment. Everybody's land will duck for good. . . ."

"Oh, *this* is what you were insinuating yesterday, I see. . . ."

"I insinuating nothing, sir," Jordan declared, a little aggrieved. "The news get around about the Canje flood project. . . ."

"You're all a pack of fools," Fenwick burst out. "I'm doing a plain job here. That's all. I haven't the ghost of an idea what use will ultimately be made of it all." He pointed to his tidal graphs and notebooks. "Old Poseidon may be buried six feet or even sixty fathoms down before anything does happen for all I know. And in any case – if the government finds the vast sums of money they would need for all this – these poor farmers will be compensated. A jolly good thing too! The land isn't all that rich up here – in fact it's a mess – and they wouldn't want to keep it in face of a scheme that would do untold benefit to the sugar estates and rice-lands of the Courantyne and Berbice coasts" – he found himself speaking as if he were recounting an obsession and a lesson – "which draw their irrigation supplies catch-as-catch-can mostly from an unaided river now. Fortunately the Canje drains very slowly to the sea because the main and subsidiary watersheds are broken and every tributary – as a consequence – is retarded and slow and ill-defined."

"You asking too much," Jordan said stolidly and unimaginatively. "They can't see it. They may be living hand-to-mouth but *this* wasteland," he tapped the ground, "everybody long since abandon except them, is all they've got. . . . And to make it worse they believe because they *black* you want to punish them, and the crafty East Indian man on the Courantyne savannah going get what they lose. . . ."

"I shall explain everything. . . ."

"Don't explain anything," Jordan said rudely. "Just put the fear of God in them, Mr Fenwick."

If Fenwick had not felt conscience-stricken, he would have laughed. A wave of sadness rose within him. "Your ideas are as barren as those of a witch, Jordan." He spoke, however, gently and without a trace of anger. "I would like to see Weng. He brought the news so he might as well come and tell me himself what's going on."

"He'll be along soon, sir," Jordan said reassuringly. His face had grown child-smooth and sad as though to reflect Fenwick's mood cunningly. "He worked Chiung's shift – midnight to six this morning. . . ."

"Oh yes, I remember. Chiung read for him yesterday. I suppose he's sleeping now, is he?"

"He'll be along soon, skipper."

Fenwick began to busy himself with a number of papers and Jordan retired to his own duties. The mail-boat was expected this evening or tomorrow at latest. Fenwick had no official correspondence to catch up with this week, but he owed his mother a letter. He began to turn over in his mind what he would say to her, brooding a little on the quixotic absurdity and sadness of things. He was her only child. This had established an exceptional bond between them. He had never known his father who had been in his middle fifties (his mother being at the time in her late thirties) when he was born. Soon after, his father died suddenly. His mother possessed a very good snapshot: it had acquired a sub-aqueous background look over the years but still revealed a dark big man of vivid African

382

descent. His mother - on the other hand - was a delicate, almost aerial figure of a woman, half French, half English. Her skin was like a fair East Indian's shadowed by night-black wings of hair. It was rumoured that along with her European stock she possessed a fraction of Amerindian blood, as well, and that her grandmother was as Arawak as her husband's grandfather had been uncompromisingly African.

Fenwick smiled. He had grown to discern a curious narcissistic humour and evasive reality in the family myth. He was not ashamed of the unique vagaries and fictions of the ancestral past. Far from it, he was proud. Nevertheless it made him profoundly uneasy at times. There was something guilty and concrete he had to learn to face, after all. Possibly it was all coming to a head and he would have no way of escaping in the end. Still he longed for an easy way out. For the past two years he had been constrained to save every penny he could, and had therefore accepted long spells of tiring survey work in the bush. It was easy to save something from his salary when he was away from his headquarters in the capital city of Georgetown. He had been steeling himself to carry on in this excessive way in order to pay off the mortgage on his mother's home. She was an elderly and ailing woman now and she had eaten up her economic reserves in extravagant, even foolish ways. Her beauty was the ruin of what it once was and she had suffered also an acute nervous breakdown three years ago. Thank God, she was better now and she would feel even safer and freer when he had lifted the debt she had contrived to build over her roof.

In many ways she was a sensitive and imaginative woman. Her weakness was that she devoured detective stories, gruesome murders and ancient legends. She had wanted her son to be a distinguished advocate at the bar or even a minister of religion – least of all a land surveyor. Nevertheless she had not actively tried to stop him from studying for and taking the territorial examination. Furthermore she had financed his going abroad – a year in Canada – a year in Britain – where he had done special studies in air photographs and hydrographic surveys. He sighed. He was glad to be in a position to repay her at this stage of her life.

He began writing almost mechanically, blindly, and yet with a warm sensation she was there, out of focus perhaps, but still large as life in his mind's eye. It was as if he was sorry for her in an obscure – even totally incomprehensible way – which had to do with his father's death – her late marriage and sudden bereavement. The strange thing was she had never married again – out of some inexplicable emotional seizure of embarrassment she, herself, had been unable to define – and had lavished all her affection on him. "Whatever pleasure there is – there is greater pain when one dwells in the past." It was a remark of hers she often used to him, and he started his letter to her with her own rhetorical sadness. He went on: "I have been giving a lot of thought to several things lately, and am hoping whenever I can to take a long break. At the moment, however, I am convinced I must remain, though in distress, in the greatest distress, by the way everything seems to be going.

"I feel I have stumbled here in the Canje on an abortive movement, the emotional and political germ of which has been abused in two centuries of history. This is a little grandiloquent, but I know how you adore grandiloquence, Mother. What will you say when I tell you I have come across the Grand Old Man of our history, my father's history in particular? (I doubt very much whether you would care for him now. He has fallen into strange ways.) He has a Greek name – Poseidon. Lord knows who gave him this! But then, after all, let us remember he's the privileged son or grandson of a slave. Don't be offended. I wish I could truly grasp the importance of this meeting. If I do not – if my generation do not – leviathan will swallow us all. It isn't a question of fear – it's a question of going in unashamed to come out of the womb again." Fenwick paused. He was annoyed with himself and he deliberately blotted out the last sentence. He occasionally found himself making black thick marks across lines he hated the instant he had written them. Not simply crossing them out. For then it was possible still to decipher what was underneath. But annihilating them. He went on: "The practical situation, as I see it, is that East Indian workers and rice farmers will win a majority of seats in the next General Election against a large number of Africans. Indeed they may come into their own in a striking way. Do you think they will be able to reconcile their emergence with what I would like to call the liberal germs of the past? I am not being political. Far from it. The issue for me is fundamental and psychological. It is the real issue of genuine and worthwhile authority. To *misconceive* the African, I believe, if I may use such an expression as *misconceive*, at this stage, is to misunderstand and exploit him mercilessly and oneself as well. For *there*, in this creature Poseidon, the black man with the European name, drawn out of the depths of time, is the emotional dynamic of liberation that happened a century and a quarter ago – to put a rough date on it. Something went tragically wrong then. Something was misunderstood and frustrated, God alone knows why and how. Like an affair between a man and a woman gone wrong. Maybe it was all too emotional, too blinding, this freedom that has turned cruel, abortive, evasive, woolly and wild everywhere almost. And yet the affair is still fresh in our mind, and so it is not really finished. Maybe it has only now begun. What nonsense! I admit I'm confused. It weighs on me because of my own difficulties. I confess I have a longing for wisdom. You will forgive me for going on in this way, I know. After all, a letter can be like a private conversation. Full of inconsistencies. And in any case I know you will enjoy my news when I have finished – it is like the plot of one of your beloved mystery stories. By the way, please do not send me any more books which are so full of tragedies. My dreams are beginning to be coloured by the vision of the nameless horseman (Perseus?) slaying the cruel muse, to arm himself with the head of a Gorgon. (A touch of the sun do I hear you say?)

"This reminds me of Jordan. I know you will smile at the ridiculous pun. Nevertheless he would make a fine head for a prime minister and a governor rolled into one, believe me! He knows how to tax everyone and draw blood from stone with dignified irrefutable supporting entries in the mess book. It all looks very neat and tidy on the surface. Actually I can't explain. Even if he's a thief, he's eminently sensible and as economic as anyone can desire. As for the crew – without his advice – I would be lost. They would destroy me with senseless worry.

"Now for the *pièce de résistance*. A rebellion seems to be cooking in the river. No wonder – it's a strange brooding murderous place as I've told you several times before. If this threat of uprising can remain bloodless and still be truly successful it may clear the air for good and restore something we have all lost – the authority and the psyche of freedom. What impossible irresponsible words. Needless to say I shall be on my guard against the holy rebels. So don't take me too seriously. Don't worry. I'll be careful. Look after yourself well, Mother, and don't sit up till 3 a.m. every morning devouring thrillers. – Love, Russell."

Fenwick folded the letter and sealed it without reading it. He would have torn it to shreds, if he had. It was the kind of gothic self-confession he liked to write, but never dared to read. After such a letter he found himself sweating as if he had been wrestling with another indigenous skeleton in the cupboard (quite unlike the black bones of Father Poseidon), the mental image his mother evoked, the racial figment of her over-wrought imagination. A feeling of nameless self-pity welled within him. He reproached himself for the habit of self dramatization which demanded of him, if he were to overcome it, the most thorough-going reformation of character.

The sun boiled up into a day of stupor along the river. It was nearly impossible to think within such a landscape of burning farce. There was not a breath of wind anywhere. Though the heat was intense and the sky had turned into an extraordinary state of brilliance (as though a score of suns were waving in the atmosphere) an enormous shadow still appeared to lurk everywhere even where it seemed to dwindle into the roots of grass. It was a landscape of comic deception, perhaps, but also of terror. The original unity had been broken and time had become the needle and fabric knitting the catchment of the past as well as preparing a gulf in the heart of the present and future.

Fenwick was reluctant to return to his inspection of the Kaboyary Creek. He decided to put it off until tomorrow. Nevertheless he surveyed the creek in his mind's eye and began slowly unrolling his maps. He was in a mood to resist all study of the ground: yet he was drawn as to a powerful magnet. His reconnaissance surveys – conducted with chain and compass – had disclosed glaring inconsistencies between his plot and the maps compiled from air photographs. The headwaters of the Kaboyary were a case in point. They had been shown as starting out of flooded savannahs when, in reality, the creek existed in the very savannahs (coming steadily across and commencing entirely beyond the savannahs, in higher wooded land). Because of the misconception – based on an interpretation of a set of photographs – the head of the Kaboyary had been joined (in the current maps) on to a foreign tributary body, called the Potwaya.

The nature of the error grew plain when one traversed the flooded savannahs (out of which the headwaters of the creek were supposed to start) and found instead the continuous, strict bed of the creek, its subtle current wreathed around one's chest. . . . Air photographs pick up defined features easily, Fenwick knew. In the savannahs, he had discovered, the Kaboyary had lost its original banks, and its watershed, too, had been swamped and eroded. . . . No wonder an empirical hiatus or gulf existed, to a bird's-eye view, severing the river's head from its trunk and feet. . . . The mysterious foundation of intelligence, the unity of head and heart had become for him, Fenwick knew, an inescapable obsession, and perhaps a

387

foolish myth and a dubious vocation in science. All he could ever grasp was the relic and travesty of groping uncomfortable existence . . . He rolled his maps together, in despair, and then slowly, forcing a strong discipline on himself, flattened them out on the camp table again.

He perused (for the hundredth time it seemed) the economic features he knew by heart, the grants of land, leases, etc., along the banks of the Canje. Many of these had been abandoned over the years, but a great many were still being farmed by Africans. They were not rice-bearing lands (the only rice Fenwick had seen growing there turned into inedible glue in the pot); for this reason, possibly, the East Indians on the Courantyne and Berbice coastland (twenty to thirty miles away as the crow flew) had never penetrated up the Canje. Nevertheless the ageing Canje River was invaluable to the absent East Indian rice farmer and the European sugar planter. It provided their rice and sugar-cane plantations with a store-house of irrigation water in time of drought, and supplies were pumped along theodolite-lined canals linking the primitive snake of the river to the wavering disposition of the coast.

It was touch-and-go, however, and though the Canje withstood the critical salt tides of the main Berbice River and Atlantic coast, preserving into every drought its fresh head of supply, the danger remained that a longer still, unseasonable spell might upset its miraculous poise and balance. Especially when a greater and greater call, every year, was being made upon its resources.

Taking all the circumstances into account, Fenwick saw that the extinction of the remaining grants and leases along the Canje, and the logical construction of a flood reservoir to meet the increasing demand, along the coast, for irrigation water in the dry season, was perhaps the best thing that could happen to the country. On paper it all looked praiseworthy and straightforward. But in concrete terms it called for an astronomical sum to pay for elaborate surveys and works. And, equally problematic, it signified the resurrection of

Poseidon, the digging up and exposure of the buried community he represented whose flight from slavery had ended right here, in the ground, under one's feet.

Fenwick looked up from his maps. Someone had arrived, soundlessly, and was standing framed with his back to the river in the wide open doorway of the tent. Weng – the hunter. It was not so much the sudden appearance of the man, but the unexpected violent impression which had seized Fenwick's mind – the grotesque sensation that the frame of the tent and the placid river mirrored his own uneasy shadowy reflection. It had seemed for a moment that he was regarding himself, not Weng, and he was glad no one would ever know how crazy he had been – dreaming and overcome (in broad daylight) by the involuntary twin of *angst*. The thought occurred to him, as if to console him for being such a clown, that the startling illusion had to do with a trick of the light, the light reflected in Weng's eye which had been exposed to him in a deep flash. The thinnest thread of anxious lightning had then encircled his brain, galvanizing him and electrocuting him in an instant of self-recognition. In that flash (which had passed the split-second it had occurred) Fenwick had seen Weng focused in the reflection of himself, and being drawn out again from within his own (Fenwick's) eye like a rubber twin turning into substantial alien being – Weng, quite distinctly, after all.

"Skipper, this tarpaulin fiery hot. You must be baking under here," Weng exclaimed. A bunch of coal-black half-Amerindian hair fell down his forehead. The brooding naked alarming spirit in his eye had vanished. . . .

"What the hell have you been up to?" Fenwick was curt, wanting to banish from his mind what he had felt and seen. The truth was, he disliked Weng, possibly even feared him a little. It was something he rarely confessed to himself, something irrational, in the nature of a curious prejudice.

"Take it easy, skipper," Weng said placatingly. "I ran Chiung's shift midnight to this morning to make up for my

389

absence yesterday, and I fix up with Perez that I would turn on at one o'clock this afternoon."

"Your shift starts at twelve, not one, Weng."

"Is about five past twelve now, sir, and I wanted to come over and see you before I start," Weng protested. "Perez and I agree that tomorrow I'll take over from him at eleven so that he could get back the extra hour he now going lose. Don't worry your head, skipper, everything going okay at the gauge."

"What worries me, Weng, is the thought that you might be taking advantage of your position over there. You're foreman. You're the only one who can make changes in the times without consulting me. . . ."

"And without troubling you, sir . . ."

"Without troubling me, you say, but I'm a damned sight troubled. I want you to understand me clearly, Weng. I have nothing in the world against you. You're a first-class man. A fine tide-reader, chainman, a surveyor's compass is no mystery to you, last but not least, you're the best shot and huntsman of us all. . . ."

"You showering praise on me, skipper." Weng laughed – a high-pitched grating sound. (Selfish bastard, Fenwick thought.) Weng tried to fling his hair off his forehead, but it fell once more like a strange black mane thick across his brow.

"Indeed, I have the highest regard for you," Fenwick spoke glibly. He knew he was lying, and this left a bitter, almost bilious taste in his mouth. (It was Weng who was exercising judgement over him, not he over Weng.) "The highest regard," he repeated, swallowing his lie and reflection. "I want to be fair to you in every respect," he went on, "to see you in the best light because the fact is, Weng, I can't help feeling the men don't trust you. And this could be bad for the job. It puts me in a dilemma. They all feel you're abusing your power, Weng. . . ."

"Anyone complain to you of me, skipper?" Weng spoke sharply.

Fenwick paused. "No one," he confessed at last. "Perhaps I shouldn't have brought the matter up at all. I don't know. Not a soul has actually complained of you. But something is wrong. They're jumpy in the camp over there. And I think they resent your fiddling around with the set times. They may not openly say so but I believe they're unhappy when the times are changed at every whim and fancy of yours, Weng. . . ."

"Let anybody come forward and complain like a man, skipper, and I'll answer him straight. You yourself say nobody at all complain. The fact is, Mr Fenwick, they would like me to be less strict. . . ."

"Less strict?" Fenwick was startled. "What do you mean?"

Weng laughed again. "You don't know how careful I am, skipper. In fact the men say I resemble you in this – I don't make fun about certain responsibilities – I can be *hard*, hard as stone. . . ."

Fenwick was amazed at this version of himself. "You're talking in riddles, Weng."

"Not riddles, Mr Fenwick. Hard facts. The men want me to side with them. Give them their head at the gauge. Let them play poker for time while I turn a blind eye to everything. I tell them it don't matter two hoots to me if they gamble their soul away. But I won't give in about the job. Not for fair or foul play. In the long run they're bound to cheat. And they'll probably start by cheating me and you. The same way they want to cheat Jordan, if he would let them. You know these fellows, skipper. I don't have to tell you. I always make it clear to them you *hard*, hard as hell on me. So I got to be just as hard, hard as hell on them. The only excuse I normally allow myself for changing around the times at the gauge, Mr Fenwick, is when I out hunting. Hunting for *them*, too, as well as for me and you! After all fresh meat is no crime and we all like it. That is the only reason that cause me to force a switch of turns at the gauge (barring of course anybody falling sick when a change is justify). Yesterday I was out hunting. The

391

best herd I ever see in my life, sir. Tapir running frisky like horse-race. I outflank them and force them into the savannah. . . ."

"You must be crazy, Weng."

"Crazy, skipper? No! The water level drop two feet and more in the back country over the past week. The drought turning low as gravy. All the creek-hands showing up a little better now. I was able to follow the herd after hitting a big one, a big wounded one. . . ."

"Did you get it?" Fenwick was interested in spite of himself.

"I hit she square," Weng said. "And I was able to follow she into the savannah to the spot where she drop down at last. I finish her off there. Night catch me but I still bring her in. What I could manage to bring in! I had to damn well treat the meat, too, so it wouldn't start to spoil. I left Jordan at the riverside by the resthouse scraping a prime piece for you dinner, skipper. He say he going make choice head-of-tapir soup. Didn't he tell you I struggle fierce and bring him his head of meat last night?"

"No, he didn't. I can't remember his saying a word about it. He told me this morning that you brought bad news – about Poseidon and the rebels."

"Rebels? You really impressed, skipper? A couple of balata bleeders tell me the story. Jordan take it serious."

"Who are these balata bleeders?"

"They bleeding a little rubber in the bush, Mr Fenwick. Is their trail I come with last night. . . . I hand them a whacking big piece of meat and it loosen their tongue. . . ."

"Frankly, I don't know how the hell you manage to walk any trail so bloody late at night. . . ."

Weng gave his brutal, self-centred laugh. "Trust me, skipper. Like you, when I got a job to do, I aim to do it, come high water or low. I taking a page out of your book."

Fenwick was embarrassed. "I don't think I'm such a hard task-master, dam' it all."

"I taking a page out of your book, Mr Fenwick," Weng insisted, lifting his voice a little. "Is the only way of responsibility." A hard, almost hysterical, grin appeared on his lips. (Sarcastic bastard, Fenwick thought. And then he was not so sure. Weng might be in deadly humourless earnestness, after all.) A curse trembled on Fenwick's mouth. Instead he demanded: "Tell me about the balata bleeders, Weng, I want all the facts."

"They come from topside. They milking and bleeding a few trees on the high reefs. And they tell me the Africans in the river going rally around Poseidon and sabotage all this survey work. Maybe there's nothing in it. But you got to be careful. Don't trust that black old man, skipper. Jordan would tell you so himself. And Jordan can see a thing or two steady and better than most body can."

The same afternoon Fenwick changed his mind and visited the Kaboyary. The water level in the savannahs had indeed fallen as Weng had reported, and the catchment now stood at the lowest it had been this year. He looked at the glaring sky and wondered when the rains would begin to pour. It was a record drought from all accounts, eclipsing the last one of seven years ago. The time was ripe, he decided, to install a gauge at the mouth of the Kaboyary (where it united with the Canje) five miles above the Skeldon stelling where his crew were. A bench mark had already been planted on the bank of the creek; and this would ensure his setting the temporary pole on the same datum as the Skeldon gauge. (Readings at both places would give some useful indication of the river's mean slope at this phenomenally low stage, he mused, sketching in his notebook the rough dispositions of tide pole, bench mark and creek-mouth.)

He had come fully prepared, and Bryant nailed the pole they had brought with them to the overhanging limb of a tree. Fenwick set up his spirit-level midway between the new gauge and the permanent bench mark.

393

"I wonder whether it'll be safe to leave this gauge here until tomorrow?" he thought, his eye glued to the inverting telescope of his level as he checked his reading on the bench mark. The staff suddenly pitched and vanished, and Fenwick's astonished sight beheld instead the accusing image of Poseidon, eyes inverted, brow pointing down. Fenwick shot up, and the old man straightened his bent back (upon which the sky revolved). He lifted a load of firewood from his shoulders and deposited it on the ground not far from Fenwick's feet.

"What the hell is this, Bryant?" Fenwick demanded. "Did he push you from the bench mark?"

"I slip, sir," Bryant gasped. "The old man come upon me so sudden, he give me a terrible start. I trip in a basket of vine when I went to move my foot a little – look!" He was pointing to several dangling pieces of bush rope. "Sorry, skipper."

Poseidon said nothing save that his eyes reflected anger and confusion as before. He appeared somehow a more shrunken figure than Fenwick had realized when he first saw him. He was as dry as a gnarled stump which had lost its ruling submersion and element in the drought of the river. His ancient feet – webbed with grass and muck – were bare (he had not worn his flapping fins today) and his hands were wreathed in a fisherman's writhing net of cord (all twined veins and knuckles with which he moved his fingers in a constant wrestling movement). . . . The living cords seemed to grow along his arms and body until they turned matted as thick hairy straw upon his chest – and on the black nipple over his heart – where his shirt was half-open from throat to waist. . . .

Fenwick suddenly began to plead: "For your own good," he said persuasively, "and everybody else who lives in the river." He pointed to the ladder of numbers inscribed on the gauge. "For the general good," he repeated. "Tell the people so. It's put there for their good."

Poseidon moved his head blindly as if he were deaf and dumb. He had nothing to say on this occasion. He kept his veiled eye fixed on Fenwick, implying he had already said all he wanted to say at their first meeting, turning away at last and staring solemnly and thoughtfully at the gauge; then at the Dumpy level and tripod beside which Fenwick stood. He distrusted these, seeing in them the heartless instruments of science which were aimed like sentient forces at him (and whose monstrous profession would turn the tables on him, and rob him of the last freedom he possessed).

Fenwick sensed this. "Yours is no freedom," he burst out at last. (He was unable any longer to master the current and atmosphere of self-deception, alien sympathy or feeling which had assailed him the moment he knew Poseidon had arrived.) "It is still slavery, don't you understand? I wish I could explain. I wish I could make you see."

"The old man is no slave." Bryant, too, had been affected by Poseidon. "He freer than you and me. . . ." He spoke softly but Fenwick still heard him.

"Freer than you and me?" Fenwick retorted. "Look at him, man, he's like a fish in a net. Where's his freedom, tell me?"

"When the time come he going return across the sea where his primitive freedom lie," Bryant spoke sombrely. A couple of sharp razor-bones jutted against the skin of his face, and the malice of intimate agony he had long learnt to endure, as one bears the misery of toothache, suddenly flared and made him aggressive. "Even if he in a net now, I tell you he freer by far than complacent body like you and me."

Fenwick was startled. "You forget yourself, Bryant. . . ."

"I sorry, sir. I didn't mean to say what I say. . . ." Bryant knew he had gone too far and could have bitten his tongue out. The bond Poseidon had first forged between himself and Fenwick was turning into involuntary bitter recrimination.

"You were damned impertinent, but perhaps you're overwrought. I am too. It's this hellish place!" Fenwick was growing excited. He felt he had been challenged in the heart of his life. "What you say is utter nonsense," he cried. "You shout of freedom but with every word you ignore the inescapable problem of authority. And without understanding the depth of authority you can't begin to understand the depth of freedom. I want to tell you again – as I tried to tell you yesterday – that I *know*, as well as you do, we've all been punishing and exploiting him," he pointed to Poseidon, "exploiting him, robbing him." He stopped all at once, feeling the inadequacy of words, the sententious politics, the conceit, the cliché. (Might as well talk of robbing God. All these extravagant deceptions one loved to coin. Did they help anyone to understand anything at all? Just as well he had surrendered his voice. His lips were moving soundlessly, and Bryant gazed at him, equally silent and startled by the riddling confession. "I confess I am appalled at his condition," Fenwick spoke inwardly to himself. The sound of his voice had been buried in the spirit of his avowal, so abstract and far-fetched it seemed, it vanquished the pride of speech. "Yes, I confess I owe allegiance to him because of his condition, allegiance of an important kind, that of conscience, of the rebirth of humanity. And this is the highest form of allegiance of all. It is the kind a man gives to a god. But surely this does not mean I must reduce myself to his trapped condition, become even less human than he, a mere symbol and nothing more, in order to worship him! I would be mad.") He smiled woodenly at last – like someone who had been humouring a hidden intractable child – and began to speak openly again:

"Plain wholesome understanding of history and facts and possibilities is important, Bryant. Take the unadorned facts of science, the plain economic structure of society shorn of worshipful emotion, shorn of this fiction of freedom you claim Poseidon alone possesses. I am glad we can see him as he is so that we can know what *this* life is, the hard business of this life, here and now (do you follow me?) and indeed we can *see* – beyond a shadow of doubt – the necessity for human freedom." Fenwick stopped abruptly, trying to dam the flood of expression. He was filled with mounting uncertainty and an excess of misgiving.

("Maybe that is why Poseidon is a god, after all." He was instantly glad he had not spoken this aloud. In his mind, however, he continued to cry – "He teaches us the terrifying depth of our human allegiance, our guilt in the face of humanity, our subservience to the human condition. But he cannot force us, surely, to make an idol of *this* present degrading form – crawl on our bellies in order to make ourselves less than he is, tie ourselves into knots in order to enslave ourselves deeper than he is. . . ." The words of protest almost mounted to his lips. "Oh God", he wanted to shout.)

Instead he turned and confessed to Poseidon: "I can see in your eyes you don't care about anything I have said. Why don't you?" He involuntarily lifted a hand imploringly, feeling like a spent fool. He was disappointed and exhausted (as if he had not truly succeeded in emptying himself of everything) and he was both glad and sorry to see Poseidon recover the bundle of firewood lying on the ground, and turn to go. Bryant whispered something to him as he left.

"What did you tell him?" Fenwick asked.

"Only told him to wait until he hears from you." Bryant spoke guardedly. "He not going to trouble the gauge, skipper, I swear. He been warned to watch you and your work. Rumour say it going bring him bad luck. Poor old devil! He don't really understand what you stand for at all." There was the faintest endorsement of misery – amounting to accusation – in Bryant's voice.

"I know. I know." Fenwick wanted to brush it all aside. "And what about you, Bryant?" he found himself asking pointlessly after a while, knowing he could have spared his breath. He was growing to distrust Bryant, in the same way he had distrusted his own blind emotional tide of excess a short while ago. Bryant stood now in a totally new, unswerving intimate light, related to catastrophe and fate, hesitating over his reply, chafing under a rising sense of humiliation and difficulty for which he, too, had no living tongue. "The old man is like an old grandfather older than all I come to know since," he began haltingly. "Since I can remember. I been wanting to meet him for a long time, Mr Fenwick." He paused, then continued defiantly: "I want him to accept me like a lost son. Don't mind what Jordan or anybody say. He not bribing me. *I* would pay him all the price he want." He stopped, thinking he had said far too much. "Don't worry with me, skipper. Is just a figure of speech I was using. I apologize for anything I say before."

"*Is* it a figure of speech?" Fenwick smiled wryly to conceal both his sympathy and increasing distrust. "You'll make him suffer, Bryant, if you're not careful, in a worse way than he's suffered before. You will even kill him in the end. I know you don't believe me." He was suddenly startled by the unequivocal gravity in the sentence he had passed (almost as if he had been bullying both Bryant and himself into confronting the spectre of their unreason). The truth was he could not shake off the conviction of a dual net of ancient spirit and helplessness – divine pride and human fallibility – Poseidon had found in the air and on the earth they walked upon.

III

Catalena Perez had arrived on the mail-boat *Andromeda* the afternoon of the installation of the Kaboyary gauge. Fenwick had not seen her though he understood she had disembarked at Poseidon's landing, and that Dominic Perez had joined her and spent the night with her, returning by paddle to his spell at the gauge early this morning. . . . It was now noon, the third day in a crowded week, Fenwick mused. He was waiting for Perez and Stoll whom he had just summoned to his tent. He knew now – in the light of a morning of inspection – that Poseidon and his following had delivered their first blow. Bryant had been proven wrong. In reality, of course, he could still say it could be somebody else, a person or persons unknown. There was no way of indicting anyone. . . . The gauge at the creek-mouth had been wrecked and burnt to cinders. This was a fact, whoever was not, Fenwick swore. He had never felt so angry. . . .

The three men took their seats around the camp table. Fenwick came to the point at once: "I am going to station you further upriver, Perez. The old man's house. You slept there with your wife last night, didn't you?"

Perez was genuinely surprised. His thick-set expressionless face – with its small watchful eyes – compressed itself into curious wrinkles of dough. "Me, sir?" It was an inane remark. One could never tell whether Perez was being crafty or stupid or both.

"Who else? Aren't you the best man to send?" Fenwick was quietly furious.

"I been thinking of finding other quarters for me wife sir," Perez began. "Bryant put me on to Poseidon in the first place. But I don't feel too happy now. Not after what you discover at Kaboyary today. . . ."

Fenwick ignored the last remark. "Look here, Perez, don't you like the room your wife has? Have you had any complaint from her?"

"I like the room all right, sir." Perez had never seen Fenwick in his present mood before. A few days ago he (Fenwick) had been losing his command, as though the very instruments of power he possessed were draining and confounding him. But now it was as if he had tasted blood. "I like the room all right, sir," Perez repeated. He saw Fenwick was impatient. "No complaint either. Last night was the first time Catalena sleep there. What could *she* complain about? But a bad rumour now start up about the old man. And that worrying *me* . . ." Perez was insisting. Fenwick lifted his hand: "Rumour, rumour, all of you are full of rumour. It's getting me down, day after day. The time has come to put a stop to *rumour*. What I want is plain facts," Fenwick's eyes were flashing. "Look here. I intend to track this business down. No more grumbling from anybody. We can't prove a thing. But it's time we tried. I feel we can nip this whole trouble in the bud. The whole trouble, you hear me? That's why I've called you two here. You've both got to play your part like everybody else. Now, Perez, wake up! I'm being frank with you. I can't afford to build a watchman's camp at Kaboyary. We haven't the money for that. What I can do is to install a temporary gauge at Poseidon's landing. It's two miles below Kaboyary and the best we can do. Instead of sending someone every day to Kaboyary to pick up a set of readings, *you* will move in with your wife under Poseidon's roof. The advantage is enormous. At night you'll be sleeping practically on the spot. Once somebody is there, no one will dare to touch a thing . . . and you, Stoll . . ." he turned a little to face the other man . . . "will take over Perez's morning to noon shift. I will take over your meter and floats . . . Understand?"

Stoll nodded. He too was a little taken aback. He had often felt – over the past weeks – that Fenwick wanted to shelter behind a convenient mask of stone, and was growing incapable of issuing a direct command. His thin fingers (which were usually harping with scorn) lay now passive and dumb as the skeletons of spiders. They appeared to confess their startled reflection on the unpredictable web of being. Perez was still uncomfortably digesting the strategic news. Fenwick could not help laughing all at once. His access of fire was turning into rare humour and confidence. "Lord, Perez, it's *your* wife, man. Not mine, not Stoll's, not Weng's, not Jordan's, not anybody else's."

Perez grimaced a little (as if confronting a veiled threat) on hearing the names of Weng and Jordan, and Stoll moved his hands and shrugged. Fenwick went on quickly to make his point: "You chaps have got to become responsible. I don't want to *drive* you. The way you look, Perez, one would think I were sending you to your death. In actual fact I'm sending you where I imagine you would want to be. It's a good thing after all your wife is here. I had misgivings when I heard of it but now it provides us with an accomplished base. You won't be bored every day now. And it's boredom that drives so many of us mad." Fenwick lifted his hand again as Perez was about to speak. "I may sound as if I'm joking but I'm serious, Perez. Listen to me. There's nowhere else in the river to send your wife. Poseidon's house – as far as I have been told – is the only place with spare room. All I want you to do is to move in there, take a set of readings on the gauge every day (I'll explain what I need) and keep your eyes and ears peeled, understand?"

Perez blinked and listened. He was rather a heavy man, made of despondent but strong limbs. There was a suggestion of dormant (even treacherous) cunning and power in the way he moved.

"You'll be glad to have your wife near you, won't you?" Fenwick was exasperated.

Stoll decided to put in a word. "Perez beats his wife, Mr Fenwick. Let's hope he won't murder her in the bush."

Perez snorted but he did not appear offended. "Catalena beg to come. I didn't want to send for she. The fact is she family does give she hell when I away from home. . . ."

"She's always jumping from the frying-pan into the fire," Stoll laughed. "Witness her arrival here." He gave the characteristic facile movement of his fingers on a harp of air.

"Mr Stoll joking, skipper, but I serious."

"Why can't she get on with her family when you're away from home, Perez?" Fenwick was curious.

Perez hesitated, and Stoll leaned forward and gave him a little jab with a crooked finger: "You leave her without cash, Perez. Tell Mr Fenwick. A beautiful girl cannot feast on air. . . ."

This time Perez was annoyed. "You got a stupid habit of carrying you joke too far, Stoll. . . ."

"Too far?" Stoll appealed to him. "Isn't it the true picture, Dominic? Poor Catalena, you let her come here where it's cheaper for you in every respect. . . ."

Fenwick broke in. "I understood you genuinely wanted your wife here, Perez. . . ."

"I do, sir," Perez protested. "Mr Stoll think he still playing jealous pranks at school. Big man and little boy can never see eye to eye over a woman."

"You got me there, partner," Stoll laughed to cover a shade of emotional embarrassment. "You win."

Perez gave an expressionless grin, half forgetful now of Fenwick's presence. "Woman and poker is a big man's game, young Stoll."

Stoll turned red, resenting the gloating crudeness. . . .

"If your wife is such a centre of attraction, all the more you should want to go to her. . . ." Fenwick tried to regain a sanguine humour. But his expectancy was half ebbing away. He felt he was flattering the illusion of responsibility. "I can't send anyone else except you, Perez," he said with a note of finality. "Pack your things together and get ready to leave in an hour's time. You hang on for a moment, Stoll. I want to have a word with you."

Stoll had half-risen but he resumed his seat, and Fenwick clasped his hands thoughtfully before him, listening to Perez's departing footsteps. Jordan had not yet returned to camp. He had gone a little way topside to buy a parcel of sweet potatoes. (Nobody knew how Jordan managed to ferret out things in this wilderness.) Stoll, who wore spectacles, began to fidget with them.

"I don't feel we've hit if off very well, Stoll," Fenwick said at last.

"I've never complained, sir."

"True. No one ever complains. Rumour, the lying jade, is the only one who has anything to say."

Stoll appeared to collect himself, grasping the air. "I can't tell you anything, Mr Fenwick," he spoke quietly. "I have no doubt there are men who bring you stories. But I have nothing to say."

"You had a lot to say when Perez was here."

"That's different. He *was* here. And maybe I went too far. . . ." (It was on the tip of Fenwick's tongue to ask about the mystery of Catalena but he restrained himself.)

"Don't you think you should assist me to keep things going straight?"

"You have a foreman, sir," Stoll replied. "He's paid to do that job. And you have Jordan, your camp attendant. He's your right-hand man. . . . I try to do my own job as well as I can."

"I know. I know." Fenwick spoke testily. "I suffered my own apprenticeship too. (Sometimes I wonder if it's over yet. Some days, frankly, I don't know.) I do know what a treacherous time it can be. I didn't carry quite the kind of chip you bear, though. . . ."

"Chip? What do you mean, sir?"

"You feel you've been ill-done by, Stoll. You feel you should have been an official apprentice rather than one of the general crew. You feel this strongly and you have brought the men around to thinking this way too. This gives you a certain power over them. It's like a game of poker. Sometimes you overplay your hand in emotional ardour. Only natural after all in a young man. Tell me, you don't always succeed in pulling the strings you want to pull by being *funny*, do you?"

"I won't profess to follow everything, sir."

"Actually I believe you do. Be careful, Stoll. You may think that all men are malleable. You may even manage to acquire a hold over them, psychological and natural, after all. You may even succeed in playing on a great depth of sympathy and resentment. You may also pander successfully to their corruption – with a great show of dispensing *largesse*. But sooner or later it is all going to become serious. It ceases then to be a game. You may think, at the moment, you're getting your own back on me, demonstrating a genius for insight and native superiority. But . . ." he lifted his hand to continue . . . "one day you'll realize the game has become deadly serious. Even a matter of life or death for you. . . ."

"I still can't profess to understand, sir."

"I'm not asking you to tell tales on your camp-mates. I am merely pointing out to you that if anything is going on in the camp which I – as the titular head, the officer-in-charge – should know, it is your duty (as an educated man) to tell me about it."

"There's nothing I am aware of, sir." Stoll had turned into a hump of resistance. He adjusted the frame of his glasses as if he wanted to trick the light out of his eyes.

"Do you know, Stoll, I have found this the most stubborn lot of men. Only yesterday I couldn't convince Bryant of something though it was as plain as a tide pole. Now *you* could be the last straw. I can see you have no intention of saying anything. I'll tell you something that may surprise you. Up to a few days ago, I had decided to leave this job. I felt I was cracking up and not far from a collapse. I made up my mind to get a transfer. There's a friend of mine who's working on top of the Kaieteur. Another world compared to this place. I decided to ask him to let me go there and he come here for a while. But I changed my mind. I'm going to remain and see this thing through."

Stoll was curious. "May I ask what caused you to change your mind, sir?"

"I met someone in the river. The meeting disturbed me in a way I had never been troubled before."

"I don't understand."

"I realized at the time – in a way I had never seen it before – that we'll all sink or swim together."

"Sounds like Greek to me, Mr Fenwick."

"Possibly it is," Fenwick smiled. "Maybe even further back than that, the mystery of a lost continent. . . ."

"I thought you were a solid Christian, sir." Stoll could not resist the jibe. "But I see you're partial to *all* the fables." He slid his hand along a number of titles on a bookshelf beside him.

"Fables?" Fenwick smarted. "What do you know of fables?"

Stoll shrugged and sneered.

(Solid Christian! Fenwick reflected. He felt a ripple of shame, insecurity almost, and loss of face. It was involuntary the way one instantly shrank before derision, acknowledging uncomfortably in oneself how weak was the threshold of consciousness leading into a new age which might prove both solid and Christian, after all. A threshold which was also the ground of self-contempt and idolatry. Dead easy to join in pointing a facile finger at the mocking portentous letters of an age and to acquiesce in misreading its true meaning and spirit.)

"Nothing more for now, Stoll," Fenwick spoke abruptly. He felt suddenly (as was the way always with him) that he had said too much. It would be greater folly, however, to retract anything. "Think over carefully what I have said. And, by the way, land surveying is a hard life and it's better to come up the hard way. Believe me, it would be no sinecure if I brought you in to mess with me."

"Jordan's a beastly liar," Stoll cried. The shaft had struck home and the sneer was fast fading from his lips.

"Is he?"

Stoll tried but was unable to speak. Fenwick had succeeded at the last moment in arresting his pride.

IV

Bryant arrived to drive the outboard the morning of the fourth day in this memorable week of his life, but Fenwick decided to walk to Poseidon's place in order to approach as quietly as possible. (He had installed the temporary gauge there late the previous afternoon when he had taken Perez in his boat to the landing. He had not seen Catalena then. She had been in the house – which was rather farther inside than he had realized and therefore completely hidden from view.) He chose Jordan to accompany him – instructing Bryant to come for them at noon – and the two men set out together around eight o'clock. There had been a heavy fall of dew, the ground was damp and a cloud of overnight mosquitoes appeared to bar their way. They kept slapping their necks and brushing their faces. Their path snaked across the first grassy trail they met which wound into homestead or grant; next they were in the middle of a clearing which came down wide to the river. Two mournful horses (standing beside the black cave of a hut) appeared still as waiting stone save for the indefatigable sighing brush of their wooden tails and the quiver of their leathern hides.

"I always see three horses grazing in this clearing. Wonder what happen to the third." Jordan half-questioned Fenwick a little uneasily. He wanted to break the other man's reserve. But Fenwick did not reply. He was staring broodingly and self-forgetfully at the black hut which looked deserted now though ashes from last night stood in the clearing beside it. The morning fire of the sun was now clear risen: a large patch of blue had been stitched between the trees. An air of enormous artifice rested everywhere, the gnarled shadow of cloaked branches, naked leaves pinned fortuitously to the sky, these worn materials of earth stretched almost to the limits of enduring apprehension. Fenwick wanted to brush his thoughts aside. They were needling him into supplication, making him conscious of the immaterial thread of awareness he possessed of the nature of himself, and other creatures and men. All was an artifice of mystery to which one addressed oneself often with idle and pretentious words. The shape of mystery was always invisibly there, each representation the endless source of both humility and parody. Nothing lasted that did not show how soon it would crumble again. . . .

They had come to the end of the first wood of trees, and they heard the horses they had left behind suddenly neighing and whinnying. The sound was borne to them along the watertop as if the beasts had been pursuing them and were at their heels. The path led out into the eaten ground of savannah, a hole and a mound everywhere, a large general basin, nevertheless, tipped to empty itself into the river. Two hundred yards across thick bush faced them, and Fenwick's eye (with the alarm from the horses still ringing in his ear) was startled by a taller tree he had overlooked before. It was one of those infrequent tropical skeletons of growth (in the past it had been clothed with leaves but was now bare to the sky) which shed everything before blossoming again. He recalled instantly something he had almost forgotten – the moving naked design and the nameless horseman in his dream.

The view altered as he approached across the savannahs. The neighing spirit of a horse addressed him (this time from right ahead under the rider's arms in the tree). He thought he saw her bare flanks vanishing into the roots of a deeper winding trail in the bush.

"There she goes," Jordan spoke in a burst of recognition.

"Are you sure?" Fenwick cried, excited in spite of himself.

"Sure, skipper? Yes, I dead sure. The mosquitoes must be drive she out from she two sisters we pass in the clearing. They biting bad this morning, skipper, like a plague following us."

"Enough to drive one mad." Fenwick was brushing himself furiously. They found the path they wanted running beside the river, and began to hasten along the way. The trees became dark suddenly in the unexpected way storms cloud the atmosphere.

"The rain's coming," Jordan cried. "The drought going start to break."

"I wonder," Fenwick mused. "I'm not so sure. There was that hell of a shower a few days ago but it didn't make much difference." He confessed: "Hope the dry spell will hold out at least half a week more to give us the final figures we need. . . ." He stumbled as he spoke and nearly fell. The bush (in addition to growing dark) had begun to breathe forth a new suffocating odour, the curious scent of rain before it begins to pour. One could smell the dry quivering hoof of the earth beginning almost to lift like mist in the flaring nostrils of the wind. The growing spirit of charging oppression scarcely moved the arm of a branch though it inflated each leaf in the forest until a gasp rose through every sensitive pore of skin. The startled almost audible perspiration began to run down their limbs under the hot still blast penetrating everywhere. And still the trees hardly moved save in the unison of a still gallop ceaselessly barring the way. A dark root reined them in. They dodged and hastened as fast as they could, coming at last to the bank of a creek.

"Somebody burn down the bridge, skipper," Jordan cried, pointing to the ground before him. "Who in hell playing such tricks? I pass here three or four day ago and it was lying sound as ever. They must be all *mad*."

The air of the bush had lightened over the creek, and Fenwick saw how densely overgrown it was with moca-moca, razor grass and bunduri thorns. The bridge Jordan lamented, Weng had felled by axeing a convenient tree in the neighbourhood. It had come to rest just over the creek-level. Now all that remained was a sullen smoking shell. A slow, cunning fire had caved in everything, turned the connection the felled tree had established into a trail of viscous charcoal like a dark hideous ribbon laid upon a repulsive mat.

"Benim Creek is an ugly one. Look at it. Is how we going cross now, skipper?"

Fenwick too was at a loss. The creek stood before him like the course of all irresolution. It would be folly to step into the black cave and connection before him, and the thorns on either side knew how to bite and cut. He cried with a resolution he was far from feeling: "We must find a way across, Jordan."

Jordan was suddenly inspired. He remembered Weng had spoken of a higher connection he had abandoned after providing this one. He began scouting along the bank peering through every wild dress of bush into every related form along the creek. He came upon an ancient fallen tree at last (brandishing its head close to his own) wreathed by creepers and snakes of vine. Its image and forehead summoned him and they were able to mount on the brutal cast-iron countenance (cured by long decades of rain and sun), to slide perilously along the mortal slime of its neck into the reach of the water, and by exploring each footstep cautiously to balance on a submerged spine, waist-deep, until they had scrambled on to the other shore.

"God, that was a nasty bit of work." Fenwick looked back almost with dread. A baleful eye of water shone for a moment with livid undying flame. The air instantly turned metallic, the forest groaned and heaved, shook its breast and burst a rain of contents. A massive crystal torrent (milky with darkness) began to pour. With each step they made, however, the storm lightened, beginning to sweep across the land, towards the Courantyne, and away from their plodding backs.

They had only come half the way in an hour when usually they would have covered the entire journey easily by now. The sun appeared once more at every spare skylight, hinged to the trees, to greet the consenting spirit of place which had changed, turning lighter it seemed, almost of its own volition and jewelled with rich floating illusions, each leaf now offering its shield. A drop of water like a glittering diamond. The earth appeared to rise a little and sail under their feet, no longer in a suffocating trampled breath of expectancy but full of the moist uplift of dying and living roots.

Fenwick had almost forgotten (with the surrender of the atmosphere to him) everything that had happened, but Jordan's senses spied for every possible flying trick. He was vigilant for the latest ruse of rebellion (whatever form and witness it took, whether fire and catastrophe or natural beauty and seduction). They descended into another basin of savannah, rose again and entered the thick bush upon Poseidon's land.

The house came into view and they paused on the edge of the clearing. It was one of the most solid (though disintegrating) houses in the Canje, blackened and weather-beaten and religiously old, roofed by rust like blood on aluminium. One of the decaying sheets belonging to the roof-top had been dismantled and blown down by the storm. The sacred comedy of materials had been transplanted from Baracara, a Roman Catholic Mission higher up the Canje, when the Mission had been rebuilding ten years ago. There were front steps and back ones, too, in comfortable style. The former led straight up to a veranda, jutting out on either side of the body of the building like the arms of a cross, and intended, as was the custom to accommodate visiting hammocks; the rooms in the rear of this were long and narrow, a little wider than the front veranda, unbroken all the way save for gaping windows and resting upon the other axis of the cross. The stairs at the foot of the cross led down from a kitchen which had been hooked (almost like a commanding afterthought) to the body of the house. The entire structure had been uplifted, above the reach of a flood, on crooked elbows and stilted arms. A dramatic rooster, looking as archaic as coincidental life, lifted his scarlet head and crowed in the bottom-yard; a couple of grey chickens were pecking on the ground. The clearing extended inland, encompassing a grove of coconut trees amongst which could be seen the green skulking stalks of bananas.

One's eyes were drawn back compulsively to the exotic mission house, created equally by destiny and accident, and Fenwick experienced a peculiar thrill as if he were witnessing a curious historic question of fact. To what and whose spirit did the house belong? Had it been grafted from above (unconscious of itself) on to the land, or did it possess a self-conscious kinship and identity beneath? It had an air both foreign and native, ideal and primitive, at one and the same time; and yet it seemed so precariously and absolutely right, belonging so truly in this natural or unnatural context of landscape, that the thought of an imposition, of pretentiousness or absurdity in the life of the crumbling building, seemed equally ridiculous and impossible. In fact – if it had been the gift of an imposing high divinity – it bore a certain generous conception, economic and still humane. There were no marks of exclusiveness – rather a spirit of all-inclusive privacy, the most welcome artifice of humanity. What was at stake here was not the inevitable ruin of an old house, but a perception of depth more lasting than time, the moral privilege and right of place. This was Poseidon's asylum and home. It had acquired a special seal and privilege, the stamp of a multiple tradition or heritage. If *he* did not want to abandon the place, who and what could compel him to leave at this stage save brute force? Had he not the right to defy all the sciences of the earth in the blessed name of his humanity?

Fenwick caught himself day-dreaming in this incongruous way. Thank God he would never confess these thoughts aloud to anyone. They would say he was mad. He was about to step out of his hiding-place when Catalena Perez appeared on the veranda and began to descend to the ground, looking towards him almost as if she had seen a ghost from the heart of the forest.

Fenwick emerged to meet her, Jordan following close on his heels. She saw them and stopped at the bottom of the steps, full of agitation, and looking as if about to fly in an instant. Instead she raised her hands as if to push everyone and everything away from her: "Stay away from me," she cried.

"Mrs Perez?" Fenwick asked. He spoke in astonishment mingled with a certain uneasy admiration. She shrank away more desperately than ever, pressing herself against the rail of the steps, half-crouching with anguish until she exposed the deep cleft between her breasts which were white as chalk in contrast to her bare arms and sun-burnt skin. Fenwick stopped, wondering whether the marks he bore of his passage through the Benim Creek and the storm in the bush had made him an object of terror to her. His outstretched hand could have touched her though he hardly believed it. Her appearance seemed almost unreal as if it might even be unintelligible in such a place and circumstance; her eyes were startling blue-black set in a livid distracted face which seemed to flicker with the shadow of long intense dark eyelashes. Indeed so black and so sweeping they accentuated everything she did with mechanical regularity like the frightened manifest of a living doll. Fenwick's long stare had both held and unsettled her, and he gained the impression that the woman before him was in a strangely wild and confused state. Something almost hysterical lived in her eyes like a pure accident and whim of nature. And yet something desperate and on the threshold of a clear consciousness, too, which she wanted to bring out and did not know how to express save by shrinking into the dumb ladder against her back.

"You'll hurt yourself," Fenwick remonstrated abruptly. She said nothing, stubbornly persisting in riveting herself upon the ladder of the house.

"Where's your husband, Mrs Perez?"

She turned over his question slowly and then pointed abruptly to the trail of grass which led two hundred yards or so through the bush to the riverside landing where the gauge was. (Poseidon's house was equally concealed from the river's view.)

"I want very much to see him. Do you mind calling him, please?" He half-smiled. "Perhaps you'll feel safer when he's here."

"No, no safer. I *know* why you want to see him." She looked mortally distressed. Fenwick almost expected her to turn and fly up the steps. But she stood chained to where she was. (He was trying hard to place her in order to know how to reason with her. She was immature or unstable or both. He was not yet sure. He recalled other young women of her race (Portuguese?), growing up in the same poverty of existence, she, probably, had experienced, barely literate, able to write their names, if nothing else, on some greasy shop counter along the sweating Guyana coast where they sold groceries and rum: possessed nevertheless of a bloom which was almost unnatural it was so perfect while it lasted. He had seen them running barefoot on the public road, half their breasts exposed, inexplicable as a wild flower or a blade of grass, archaic as a cripple, as innocent as corrupt. Nature was arbitrary and mysterious – it seemed – in dispensing beauty as in furnishing models of imperfection. Fenwick could not suppress a fit of impatience with himself.)

"Stay away from me, I tell you," she spoke again wildly. He had moved – without thinking – towards her.

"Look, I'm not here to do you any harm," he protested. ("How helpless we all are, all of us, really," he reflected. The words remained unspoken on his tongue, and his lips became the involuntary frame of curious remorse. Probably he was grossly uncharitable and condescending in trying to fix her in his mind. What did he truly know of her, after all? She might prove in the end an insoluble mystery.)

She suddenly glared at them accusingly: "You and *he* . . ." she pointed at Jordan accusingly: "What is it that bring you two? It's me, isn't it?"

"*You?*"

"Yes, me. He say you would come. You win me a couple of nights ago at the gambling table, ain't it?" Her voice had turned muffled and soft.

413

Fenwick wondered whether she was a little crazy. "Gambling table?" he cried, amazed. And then started at the spectre of unreason and revelation. "You mean Perez has been staking *you* in his poker games? No, it's impossible. I don't believe it. Where the hell is he?"

Catalena began to sob. "All beasts," she whimpered. "Beasts. I won't let you touch me. Who you trying to fool that you don't know about *me*? You know but you don't want to admit you come for you short time." Her eyes grew unexpectedly dry and flashed, and then she began to laugh. The shift of mood struck them with lightning surprise. (Perhaps she was contemplating some hideous vulgar reprisal, something which would challenge the unfeeling heresy in the sceptical weight of existence. She appeared in an instant to be the most designing theatrical figure of a prostitute, nerveless in the midst of being nerve-wracked.)

"Good God, Jordan," Fenwick gasped. "What in hell is going on, here?"

"Ask Dominic, sir," Jordan said brutally. "He's her husband. He know what kind of a woman she be, after all."

"You," Catalena pointed at him, beside herself with rage. "Never you for me. Nothing with a face like you."

Fenwick felt a little sick at her expression but Jordan continued staring at her fixedly and adamantly. "Dominic may be coming at any moment," he said coldly. He did not want to confess that he, too, had been practically overwhelmed by her appearance. "You want him to find you behaving like this before the skipper?" The timely rebuke scattered her loaded senses. The childish tears sprang up and poured down her face; she lifted her dress and began wiping her streaming eyes. A shock of surprise ran through Fenwick and Jordan. There was a long red mark (the colour of brutal lipstick) running across both legs as if she had been whipped and bitten. The two men could not help staring, fascinated and repelled, by the brand of punishment. "The skipper," she gasped at last, letting her dress fall back upon her thighs. Fenwick's identity

414

had now dawned on her. "Dominic didn't breathe a word *he* was coming from that way. . . ." She pointed into the heart of the bush and addressed Jordan.

"Is a surprise visit," Jordan said slowly, trying to dispel the compulsive command of atmosphere the woman now exercised. "We got our duty to do. The outboard motor coming at midday from the camp to take us back. Be careful mistress, I don't think you realize the implications of all you been saying to Mr Fenwick. . . ." He felt he was protecting Fenwick and himself by being officious.

"I didn't know was Mr Fenwick I was addressing. He's the last one I would have spoken to like that. . . ."

"Be careful," Jordan insisted. "Careful you not speaking too fast even now. Careful the complaint you already gone and make is not in your own fevered imagination. Maybe you're *sick* and hungry for sympathy and so you're stirring up useless trouble 'pon everybody's head. You talk about gambling but maybe you're gambling worse than all. Is mankind bread-and-butter you playing with. You want your husband to get fired? Plus other body? If anything bad is happening, isn't it you and Dominic private affair? Suppose you make your life *worse* than it ever been before by always rebelling?" His voice and manner were insidiously threatening like an offensive shield over his own discomfiture and over Fenwick's astonishment and crude revelation of surprise. Fenwick broke in: "Look here, you tell me anything you want to say," he addressed the woman. "I don't need this man's advice."

"I . . . I . . . I don't know," Catalena was staring at Jordan's wrinkled brow, barren and ominous as stone. She seemed to see great trouble reflected there for her. The nerves of horror appeared to grip her – fright at the jungle of implications in what she had said and done. "Is impossible to explain a threat, Mr Fenwick," she pleaded. "Maybe Dominic was drunk. When he drunk he always swear he sell me to the devil. . . . Sometimes I stupid enough to believe. . . ."

Fenwick was stricken and confused by her childish night-mare inconsistency or helplessness; he turned and looked up at the fractured house, wondering whether it was, after all, the joints of a trap into which she had fallen.

"Where's Poseidon?" He was filled by the blackest splinter of suspicion.

"He left and went into the bush early this morning." Her voice was so flat and apathetic, it made him pity her with an abandonment he was unable to restrain.

"Call Perez," he cried abruptly, "I'll hear what he has to say. He or somebody" – he spoke impulsively and illogically – "is driving this girl out of her wits. Call him at once, Jordan. Go on, man."

Jordan started almost unwillingly and took the path that led to Poseidon's landing and Fenwick wondered whether Catalena would snatch the opportunity to tell him anything. Instead she only stared at him and it seemed to him she feared and loathed him, too, in a way, however, that had to do with a new (because well-nigh forgotten) establishment of trust. Something she had once distantly hoped for but never found. If anything, hope had only been the cheap source of profitless adventure allied to the beginnings of terror. He realized it was useless to force her to confess anything before she was ready to do so and the silence turned almost into relief as he grew increasingly self-absorbed, too. He discovered he was shock-ingly tired (he had worked late in camp the previous night on a new stage-discharge curve), drained to the bone in wrestling with the accursed science of love, something that outraged him (it was so cruelly misleading and intractable) and yet drew him with fantastic energy and strength. It eased him a little to indulge in an ejaculation and portrait of fancy. His curious exhaustion and tension awoke in him every contrary sense he possessed and the past four days (he already saw today as if it were spent) assumed in his mind the clearest embrace of relief.

Maybe they were the spiritual climax of months – even years – of boredom, strain and intense self-preoccupation.

Four days had seen the task begun and far advanced of dismantling a prison of appearance. Seven days it had taken to finish the original veil of creation that shaped and ordered all things to be solid in the beginning. So the oldest fable ran. Perhaps seven, too, were needed to strip and subtilize everything. Seven days which would run in logical succession in time but nevertheless would be appointed or chosen from the manuscript of all the spiritual seasons that had ever been. Each choice – drawn from its claustrophobic epoch – would be a sovereign representative of its age, and all would be strung together like a new immaterial genesis and condition.

The seven beads of the original creation had been material days of efflorescence and bloom to distinguish their truly material character. But now the very opposite realities of freedom were being chosen (not phenomena of efflorescence but shells and skeletons) to distinguish an immaterial constitution (which after all was the essential legitimacy of all creation).

First, the black bones of Poseidon had unsettled oppression and turned the members of the crew in upon themselves.

Second, he (Fenwick) had been driven to confess his rhetoric and sterility in the face of duty mortgaged to a maternal shell.

Third, the gauge at the Kaboyary had been discovered burnt to cinders like the measure of all contemplation and action.

Fourth, he had climbed upon an old Gorgon's head – over the Benim Creek – to reach where he now stood, confronting the woeful constellation of borrowed beauty. . . .

Catalena Perez suddenly clung to him fiercely and Fenwick wanted to believe – half-sleeping still in his exhausted mind – she had been transfigured by a sensation which bred the end of her terror. Actually he was deceived and carried away as he often was. Dominic, her husband, and Jordan had arrived. That was all that had moved her.

"Is what this mad girl been telling you, skipper?" Perez could hardly contain his anger. Jordan, too, was furious. He had been made to feel he was a helpless servant whose privileged back could easily be broken. His eye was distracted by a flight of brilliant butterflies sailing out of the bush. They hovered overhead and one enormous distended creature – wings breathing like fans – settled on Catalena's shoulder. She brushed it off, releasing Fenwick's arm which she had grabbed in frenzy a moment or two ago. It flew straight at Jordan and he struck out savagely, venting his spleen on a mad wraith. The fantastic wings were shattered save for the spirit of their design which persisted on the ground like stars of gold painted on the blue skeleton of crumpled heaven.

BOOK TWO

THE NIGHT READERS

No surrender
To sleep . . .
Eternity's hostage,
Captive to time.

Boris Pasternak

V

It was the evening of the fifth day (Fenwick made a cross on the calendar). All day the rain had appeared to threaten. Very little, however, had fallen and the sunset stood clear in the end. The river was beginning to shine with the first reflection of stars between deep shadows starting out from both banks.

Fenwick leaned back from his camp table. He had just finished dinner. His eyes turned to the bright lantern which had been lit in the tent, then glanced away slowly and meditatively. In a moment the falling darkness outside grew black.

"A word with you, sir," Jordan said, coming up from the other end of the tarpaulin where the kitchen was. Fenwick turned. "Hope you don't mind. I know you been in worries all today."

Fenwick nodded. Jordan sat down. "I got to warn you, skipper," he began slowly. "I got to warn you."

"What is it, Jordan?"

"You make a big mistake to fire Perez. The whole crew gone against you for deciding to send him down on the mail-boat next week. I know you feel sorry for the woman. But she's the picture of a whore, skipper. And she crazy, too, in the bargain. She know how to play on a man's sympathy. Perez never stake she at no gambling table, I swear, except he do it in fun. When mankind living in Canje bush they got a way of making stupid fun. . . ."

"It's no good, Jordan. I've made up my mind about this. I don't want Perez here, and I don't want his wife either. I've decided they must go."

"It's not like you to lose your head over a little bitch like that, skipper. After all, however bad Perez treat his wife, the remedy lie in her hands not yours. If she really off she head –

421

as I have no doubt – who in heaven's name responsible for that?"

"I tell you my mind's made up. They'll both go with the next mail-boat. . . ."

"I talking to you frankly, skipper. You not seeing this matter straight. You allowing false sentiment to colour you and rule you. . . ."

"Look here, Jordan, I know you mean well. I know you want to help. But this time you can't. I've often listened to you in the past. I confess many a time I've been hopelessly at sea about things. But I've got an intuition now – the kind I can't withstand. I believe Perez is up to no good with that woman. And, frankly, I don't trust the crew. They're liable to do almost anything. . . ."

"The crew is a good one, skipper. You got to keep a firm grip on them, yes, but they're not a bad lot. They must have a little recreation. All over the world people stay so. . . ."

"I can't take chances with that girl. . . ."

"No truth in it," Jordan insisted. "Perez is a bad man, yes. So is every man. But most of the bad things he plan to do, is in the nature of a joke. Is a way of giving spice to life. It don't mean a thing. Is true he beats Catalena. Beats she bad. But the girl wild, skipper. That's why her family marry her off quick-quick to Perez. She's not right in her wits. . . . The fact is, skipper, I see you beginning to lose trust in me, so I'll be honest with you." He paused. "You got a hell of an unscrupulous bunch of men in your crew. Is so the world stay today. Many thing that happen in the camp (I still insist half of it is a joke) can turn dead serious, too. The point is – you got to trip them up like if the net you tangle them in is the biggest joke of all. You got to hide you desperate seriousness, and shelter behind something or somebody not half as good as you. They may hate you for it but it's all they really and truly understand. Take it from me, skipper, I know. The moment you come out in the open and start seriously condemning them you putting youself in a position for more than hate, you putting youself in for mutiny.

Let them hate you. Let them hate *me* (I is the storekeeper, I expect hate). Let them hate Weng (Weng is the foreman, he, too, got to expect hate). Let them talk behind your back about you. Let them say you is a scheming devil riding the hell out of me. All that means no harm in the end. It's the sort of game they understand. They can turn it into a bawdy joke. But the moment you step out, the moment you get so serious that they feel you really *care*, that you really and truly more involved with them than they knew, that you not so superior to them any more, *the moment* you make that slip, you gone and done the worst thing you can ever do . . . and whenever that happen is always some goddam woman in it. . . ."

Fenwick could not help smiling wryly, but shook his head: "I've made up my mind, Jordan. . . ."

"Listen, skipper, even if Perez has been staking his wife for some man to have a short-sleeping-time with in lieu of cash," Jordan insisted, "even if it's true – *you can't prove it*. Remember that. Then – bear in mind, sir, I begging you – if he doing such a thing *here*, he doing it out yonder – *there* . . ." he pointed vaguely in the direction of the Atlantic coast, ". . . if he doing it *here*, I tell you he doing it *there* in the city or in the village, wherever he happen to be. And everybody must be know the kind of woman she is, and the kind of man he be. And if all the world (save you) know, who in God's name got the right to intervene? You touching the kind of serious spot you got no right to touch, skipper. These men you condemn by sending Perez away got their own morality. . . ."

"Morality?" Fenwick started.

"Who is you, skipper, forgive me talking plain so, to declare what going on here is not the same rule of prostitution like what I read of taking place in Paris and New York? It may be bad policy to interfere with a rule people grow to accept all their life. Why in New York . . ."

"Blast New York. I'm not responsible for New York. This isn't New York. And you're forgetting something, Jordan. This girl has not grown to accept any such rule. I grew up in this country, man."

"Not grown to accept? Did the Chinese women grow to accept?"

"To hell with what Chinese women accept. We're not in China."

"Give me a chance to explain, skipper. All I was hinting . . ." he lowered his voice for no conscious reason, "I used to hear when I was a boy that a parcel of immigrants to this Guyana country where we belong, those who come from the bowels of China and all about like that, used to gamble behind locked doors, staking everything and everyone they possess. And yet who more respectable than them same yellow man? Some of them rich like mud now and the kindest people you could meet under any shape of the sun's countenance. Everybody got two natures, skipper. The only way to overcome it (Confucius say) is to overlook it like a joke." Jordan stopped. Fenwick grunted: "A joke, is it?" He spoke humourlessly and a little viciously: "I've decided about these jokers, and if the men don't like it, they can lump it. Perez and his wife will leave from Poseidon's landing next mail-boat day. And that's the end of it. What they do outside is their bloody business. You say I shouldn't care what happens but dam' it all it's more than I can put up with at the moment. . . ."

"The other thing, skipper," Jordan said slowly and unrepentantly, "that put the men's back up today is when you send Bryant to warn Poseidon. . . . You showing too much real sympathy all around, skipper . . . I telling you, you can't govern this crew like that. . . ."

"Now, why in heaven's name should they be put out over my sending Bryant to Poseidon?"

"I telling you before and I telling you again, sir, you showing youself to be deeply involved. . . ."

"Deeply involved? But I am! I *am* involved."

"You mustn't be. You never used to be before."

"If I never used to be, I was crazy."

"Excuse me, skipper, but you now showing the true sign of going mad."

Fenwick laughed.

"Don't laugh, skipper. I'll explain. The crew would have understand it if you had send Weng. He's a bad man and a born foreman 'pon top of all his good qualities. They would have see (if you had send Weng) that you mean business, just business. The business of running this survey job how it should be run. Nothing more. Who can blame you for that? Grumble, quarrel, talk, yes, but that's all they would say to that. Is so human nature stay! *The moment*, however, they see you send Bryant – rather than Weng – they suspect you got other personal sympathetic experimental motive. They see naked sentiment on you brow and they get afraid at once you might be exposing them. . . ."

"Exposing them? Good Lord! Now this is absurd. In the first place, can't they see Poseidon wouldn't place a shred of reliance on Weng? He wouldn't listen to Weng. This morning – as you damned well know – Weng came along and reported to me he'd been hunting around Benim Creek, and he ran into a party of black men. They told him – this is the story, isn't it? – that they had seen a newspaper from Georgetown which stated that the government intended taking away all their land very soon. They believed further that my survey was the thin edge of the wedge; I was here to iron out the final difficulties and put the seal on their doom. Oh! what the hell? You know the facts as well as I do. The point I really want to make is this. Weng behaved badly this morning when he ran into the party of men. It's my turn to be frank now, Jordan. Weng threatened the men, didn't he? He himself admitted it. You can't deny it. Told them he would shoot every mother's son who trespassed anywhere near where we're working. Told them I, too, wouldn't hesitate to blow their brains out. . . ."

"He did the right thing, skipper. I know these people."

"To hell with your idea of the right thing. What he did was to make it impossible for himself or for me to speak reasonably to those men on any other occasion. He destroyed my chances as well as his own. . . ."

"May be so, Mr Fenwick. If Weng wasn't eligible to go, then . . ."

"Nobody should, I suppose. . . ."

"Not nobody," Jordan hesitated. "The crew know somebody must go, O yes. . . ."

"Who then? Bryant loves Poseidon, don't you understand?"

"No, not Bryant," Jordan broke in. "The police," he spat, "the police."

"Police?"

"If Weng couldn't go, if *he* would have no effect, fair enough – you can't send him, then you need to inform the police."

There was a deep silence. Far away the baboons began howling for rain like the fiercest parody of roaring tigers. Jordan smacked his brow, smearing his hand with a trace of sticky blood. He had crushed a greedy mosquito.

"I don't think the occasion warrants my calling in the police," Fenwick said at last, slowly. "It would mean sending down-river to New Amsterdam. The situation isn't as extreme as all that. Once the police arrive on the scene, the lips and hearts of the Canje people would be shattered for good. . . ."

"You exaggerating, skipper. You becoming dramatic. . . ."

"I tell you such action would smash all hope of explanation. . . ."

"Smash obstreperous conduct too. . . ."

"If I send for the police I would kill the last ghost of a chance, don't you understand?"

"You don't really know, skipper. You can't tell. You might save somebody property or life. . . ."

"Poseidon and his men are not violent–"

"Who burn down the gauge at Kaboyary, skipper? And the bridge Weng fell across the Benim? Who burn this but them men?"

"I know. I was bloody angry about that. But it doesn't

constitute violence as I understand it. It's more a witness of
protest, the spirit of protest. It should make us stop and think
rather than fall on them and smash. Another thing. They
haven't troubled the gauge at Poseidon's landing. It would
have been simple as shaking hands to knock that one down.
Perez is much farther inside – when night comes – than I had
thought. The truth is he's not likely to hear a damned thing.
No. They're not really violent in the way you want *me* to be.
They're just incapable – up to now – of understanding what's
going on. Once they follow precisely the nature of what's
happening they'll turn reasonable . . . And Bryant is my only
chance. I'm putting my trust in the true affection he bears for
the old man. I know he won't want his 'grandfather' – as he
calls him – to suffer. . . ."

"You becoming involved I tell you, skipper. I warning you
solemn again . . ." he stopped all of a sudden. "Listen!
Somebody coming." He shouted harshly: "Who's that? Who's
there?"

"Is only me, partner. Don't be nervous." The sighing
footsteps Jordan had heard gained the tent. A face appeared.
"Good evening, sir. Is me." It was Chiung, the night reader.

"Oh, Chiung! Come in!" Fenwick said. Chiung advanced
squarely out of the night, pulling off an old shapeless torn cap.
His head was clean-shaven save for a tuft of sharp points
sticking up in the middle of his skull like an instinctual
protection and obsession. "Sorry to bother you, skipper." His
features, though unprepossessing in their naked, almost
hairless purity, shone under the light with a curious frighten-
ing dignity, the dignity of a shell – age and agelessness
together. No one knew how old Chiung was, Fenwick
reflected.

"It's no bother, Chiung. What can I do for you?"

"I want to ask a favour, skipper. Hope you don't mind."

"Go ahead."

"I don't know if you could lend me one of your raincoat."

"Raincoat?"

427

"Yes, sir. I doing nearly a double shift at the gauge tonight."

"Why, what's happened to Van Brock?"

"Van Brock not well, sir. He reading at the gauge now. He start manfully – full of fever – at six. And ordinarily he would go on until midnight when I take over. But he start shivering and shaking worse than ever the last ten minutes. A bad touch of malaria. It only half past eight now but I intend to take over soon as I leave you and carry the balance of Brock's shift then do my own regular spell until morning. . . ."

"I'm sorry about this, Chiung. Sure you can manage?"

"Sure, sure, skipper." Chiung rattled the rusty hinges in his throat. "That's why I come about the coat," he grinned. His teeth were black as muddy tobacco. "The river getting up an unhealthy mist, skipper. Worries me old bones. I believe the drought getting ready to turn, I don't know. I know you got a lot of extra raincoat in camp. If I could borrow one?" He paused. "All I got to wear this shivering night is me cotton shirt and trousers. Me blood never run so close to water before." Chiung grinned again and placed his finger upon his lips like an accommodating feature of eloquent silence.

"Bring out the thick brown coat hanging there, Jordan."

Jordan obeyed Fenwick's command reluctantly.

"Thank you, thank you, skipper. Why, I know this coat. Is the one I always see hanging in front the tent. . . ."

"Mildew," Jordan volunteered sourly. "I put it out to brush every day to stop mildew developing. Mr Fenwick don't seem to value his things. Give him a chance and he would throw away everything. . . ."

"Never mind Jordan, Chiung," Fenwick interrupted. "He would martyr me in the name of discipline." He laughed and smothered his words. "This will keep you good and warm," he continued. "I know how beastly cold the river can get. By the way," he pointed to Chiung's cap, "your head-gear is bursting with holes. Take that old helmet of mine in the corner. It's not much good but it's better than yours. I intend chucking it out any day now."

"Thank you, skipper. Is a godsend. . . ."

"You better try it on," Jordan said sourly again. "It doesn't look big enough for your head, if you ask me."

Chiung accepted the helmet gratefully. He put it on judiciously and pulled it down. "Perfect!" he announced.

"Big enough to console me ugly cranium. It feel close and good."

"You haven't try the coat," Jordan persisted pessimistically. "Mr Fenwick thinner than you. It won't fit."

"As a matter of fact it's a little big for me around the shoulders," Fenwick waved at Jordan, deprecating. "Put it on, man. Don't worry with Jordan."

Chiung unslung the coat from his arm, reached one hand in, then the other. "Is like me own skin, skipper." He was jubilant. 'Thank you, Mr Fenwick, sir. The river look so nasty, I need reinforcement." He bent his head and the shadow on his cheeks gave him the expression of grinning from ear to ear.

Fenwick tried to smile back. "Jordan," he explained, "give Chiung a shot of rum. I can see he needs it."

"You shouldn't encourage these men to drink on duty, skipper. It befuddles their wits." Jordan was grumbling.

"Me wits strong," Chiung declared, looking up. He swallowed the stiff rum at a gulp. "Thanks, skipper. You done save me life tonight. I hearty now to relieve Brock. Good night." He buttoned Fenwick's coat and adjusted the helmet.

As soon as his footsteps died away, Jordan declared: "Chiung would never have approach you like this last week. You got to watch you don't fall captive to this crew from now on, Mr Fenwick. Before now they look on all familiarity you show as a condescending joke – it didn't matter what you do, they knew you had a hard counsellor beneath – but *now* you really showing you care too much. And they know this is the beginning of the end. They smell your weakness and your trouble so they going grab all they can from you while the going good. . . ."

"You're mad, Jordan." Fenwick was angry. "Absolute rubbish!"

Jordan tapped his brow sorrowfully. "All brains look like rubbish because it tells you, you mustn't trust your heart, Mr Fenwick. I tell you – mad or no, you got to be guided by your head. Is the only way to keep the world in check. Chiung come tonight like a sure sign. He thinks he can open his breast of worries to you now. Never before, mind you. He used to shut up like a clamp. (In fact, the whole crew, the moment you challenge them, used to turn to stone.) But now soon he going invite himself to dinner like if is nothing when he hungry. He feels you's not the same man you used to be and he losing respect, skipper." Jordan was almost pleading. He looked so incongruous, Fenwick half laughed. He felt a sharp cruel sensation of revolt, confronting the anachronistic features of morbid self-protection. Maybe it lay within his power to relinquish such an image or shield for good. His voice turned calculating and bitter: "Chiung did a perfectly sensible thing. Don't you know it's the government's job to provide these men with raincoats? You've got to bow to the wisdom of the Regulations, Jordan."

"Never heard of such a high and loose regulation," Jordan said stubbornly. "But even if is true, Chiung should approach Weng or me. After all I is storekeeper."

"It's a regulation that has practically gone out of use," Fenwick explained. "You may know nothing of it. I know it's practised on hydrographic missions out at sea – standing off the coast. If the night readers had come directly to me before I would have ordered a couple of coats. . . ."

"What about the day readers?" Jordan demanded.

"The day readers, too, of course. Though I don't see they suffer from the night's mists and the river's cold. . . ."

"Whenever the rain fall they get soak to their superstitious skin," Jordan cried. "Don't you know that? There's no end to everybody's excuse, I swear. You will need to revive and correct in you own magnanimous self a nest of high forgotten regulations before long. Is no end to what them men going entitle to demand once they know you hang up and done lose the last ultimatum of fear you used to present to them." Jordan spoke with the fervour of grotesque inspiration, spreading like a shadow over his features which turned wrinkled as a woman's barren countenance in a dead pool. "The point is," he declared with rigid abandon, "nobody ever come to you so open before. Only *now*. Nobody dream of playing Chiung's direct hand before. They prefer to keep their complaint to themselves and approach you roundabout. Their tongue was never so far loose in their head before. . . ."

Fenwick could remain silent no longer. "Well, it's a damned good thing Chiung found the humble decorum and guts to come to me. I've always wanted them to speak out about things, man to man. I don't want to hide behind anything or anyone any more, Jordan. I hope it means they're all turning over a new leaf. . . ."

"A new leaf, skipper?" Jordan spoke slowly, his face more wrinkled and deepset than ever. "The tree that bear such a leaf is a tree of grave open disrespect. Watch they don't string you up on it."

VI

Around midnight Fenwick left his tent to see how Chiung was coping at the gauge. He shone his torch on the ground and made his way along the trail from his camp-ground to the clearing around the men's resthouse. He emerged at last out of the tunnel of the bush of night and stopped, startled by the spectacle of the open sky – the vast proliferate illumined jungle of the Milky Way. The stars had been sown like dense brilliant seed within the supporting shadow of the earth. He remained looking up until the crowded illusion expanded and turned diffuse and remote – no longer a painted fall or view, but an everlasting frail bombardment out of the greatest unimaginable distances: each needle of light took its rooted stand as if to prick his eyes where it had been aimed with the timeless precision of the ages at him, alone, of all creatures in the world.

He shivered with the visionary tattoo of every branch and constellation, conscious of the threads which bound him to their enormous loom. He was filled with an almost mathematical ecstasy, the poetic frenzy and delirium of a god. The fever of emotion almost overwhelmed him – it was so unexpected and brutal and vivid – the dream of belonging to space, his suspension, in space, his possession of, and conquest of space – the most enduring fiction of the human brain and heart, old as the first astronomical crab alighting from the wall of a cave upon the roof of the sky. The heavens had been thronged in the beginning with all the planted creatures on earth (not excepting man), Fenwick mused. They were all glowing in proud perennial creation up there as if their material being had grown into the loftiest tradition.

432

He caught himself at last. A faint light was burning in the crew's resthouse, he noticed, though not a sound came from within. Everyone was asleep. He began making his way towards the stelling where the gauge was.

This appeared deserted, at first; a slow exhalation was rising from the water like a vacillating blanket over the river. The trees on the opposite bank reared themselves into an unearthly hump under the stars, dressed by the confusing clarity and mist of the night. . . .

Fenwick almost fell over the figure lying at the end of the stelling. . . . He tried to flash his torch but the switch jammed and stuck to his thumb.

"Blast it! Chiung!" he addressed the man, vaguely discerning his own helmet and coat. "Chiung," he cried again, stooping and shaking the figure on the ground. But the man did not respond; he appeared as lifeless as the wooden planks and frame on which he lay. Fenwick was filled by a dark wave of uncontrollable panic which rose out of the black river under his feet. He gave a great nervous shout: "Weng, Weng, somebody up there, come quick!" There was no immediate reply so he raised his voice to the heavens again and again. At last there was the answer of waking commotion.

The temperamental switch under his thumb slid forward at the same moment and a pencil of light darted upon a wounded helmet. The familiar coat was outflung, half-wing, half-shroud. And Chiung's hands were grasping at someone or something in all helplessness. Fenwick sprang upright like an automaton. He had lost all coherent principle and action. One wild irresponsible thought galvanized and upheld him – Chiung was dead. He stared with compulsive fascination at the single brush stroke of blood leaking from the man's head until the trickle magnified itself into a great canvas in his mind – wide as the firmament over his head. The pencil of light drew the constellated wrinkling outline of the unconscious coat, dwelling upon the shade of every well-known particular as if for the first time. "It could be me lying here," Fenwick thought.

"What an escape. It could be *me*." His mind had turned into a sieve out of which everything fled save the mystique of selfish relief. The sensation of involuntary freedom was as automatic as the reflexes of panic and the springs which had moved his feet.

But now the overwhelming wave of blind obsession with himself began to retire and he felt sick with horror and self-contempt. He was giddy or he would have turned and fled away from everything. But his feet (which a short moment ago had been full of the impulses of flight) grew cold as stone. He could not remove himself from the deck of the stelling (like a commander on a stationary bridge in space), his eyes were riveted to every relic on the ground which had been flung down into the lowest trough of brutal self-consciousness from the highest crest of spiritual pride and hope. He wanted to turn and run but was unable to move a single step in any direction. He wanted to dissociate himself from every vestige and ordination of self-parody, divine and human resemblances and conceits, every reminder of his own image, the investiture of his dreams in heaven, the habiliments of conduct and mystery. He wanted to fly from all, in shame and bestial humiliation, from the most wretched shape of all, the delusion of material vision and survival, the most wretched narcissistic solution of man and dreaming god. . . .

He held the cowardly torch in his hand (with the rigidity of a signal draughtsman or a trembling statue) as Weng and Stoll rolled Chiung on his back. "He's dead," he cried, wanting to be self-condemned and justified in some deep irrational way. He wanted to flee from the image of himself (from his errors of practical mis-judgement) and yet was drawn all the more into the basest theoretical salvation of himself.

No one replied. And then Weng burst out in triumphant repudiation: "No, skipper. Chiung not dead. He OK He get a knock-out blow plumb and hard as hell on his skull. Whoever the bitch that do it," his voice rasped fiercely, "whoever do it, do it clever. Just hard and hellish enough to banish a man's

wits long enough to make him mortal afraid when he recover."
Weng looked up under the wild shock of his hair: "I got a mind,
skipper," he spoke slowly, dwelling upon the self-evident
discovery, "that it's you somebody been aiming at. Not
Chiung at all. *YOU*. Look, this is you hat and coat. . . ."

Chiung groaned now and stirred, silencing Weng for a
moment. Fenwick, too, could not speak. He was dumb with
incredible unbelief, breathless expediency mingling with the
normal senses of organic sympathy. After all, he was
genuinely glad to hear Chiung was alive! And yet curiously
and inexplicably startled (even crestfallen) that it was so! He
found his lips moving as though across a great anti-stage or
divide of climax like an actor reciting a trivial lesson after the
primitive paradoxical instant (wrapped in self-centred misconception) that cries for the sublimation of death. "It couldn't
have happened long before I arrived on the scene. . . ."

"Not too long," Weng cried. "Look, the blood fresh and
Chiung head just swell into this unholy bump like a twin head
'pon top. A clever beast and a devil make it so. I going for my
gun, skipper. I going hunt for his trail this very night. I warn
them not to trespass and I glad now for living excuse to shoot
somebody down. . . ."

"NO!" Fenwick shouted with the greatest harshness as if
delivering a rebuke at the same repressed need in himself for
violent self-expression. He moved a little at last and lifted his
torch until the pencil of light disfigured Weng's eye: "No guns.
Do you understand me? I expressly forbid it."

"You must be dreaming, Mr Fenwick," Weng gasped,
enraged. "You know is what you doing now? You inviting
everybody to stay passive until they find they dead. Maybe
you want it so. But not me. Ask Chiung what he think! Is he get
the first knock-out blow just now. Not you or me. Ask him. He
recovering good enough to speak for himself."

A fiery retort quivered on Fenwick's lips and died into frozen
astonishment. He was aware of the members of the crew like
hallucinated ghosts strung out against him. They had taken

their challenging stations along the deck jutting out from the bank – between himself and the clearing of land. He was, therefore, in a vulnerable position, standing over the water a mere step or two from the last plank in the stelling. He brushed his glaring torch quickly and painfully along the half-stalwart, half-crouching pillars erected against him. So they looked to him in a flash: they had come on the scene so rapidly, when he had raised his outcry, that they had had no time to disguise their appearance or to change their miscellaneous sleeping garments of bodiless blanket material, the stilted memory of walking hammocks, drawn against the misty charcoal of night.

Fenwick directed a disordered nervous beam towards his own faceless feet. Chiung's startling features emerged: the man was beginning to sit up. Maybe Weng had been perfectly sound in his diagnosis, after all. Nothing really serious had happened. Still, Fenwick felt, everyone's eye was now riveted in all dreadful earnestness upon the magnetic clown on the ground whose skeletal solidarity was the focus which drew them into a treacherous rehearsal of possibilities. Would they provoke a false recapitulation of the past or summon an untrustworthy guide into the future? The truth was, Fenwick himself was uncertain in his inmost theatre of mind what to think or do. He saw himself in a critical, unstable corner of time. (He could not destroy this dramatic inflation of consciousness.) Stoll was stooping and assisting Chiung who sat up, groaned, rested the palm of one hand on the ground while with the other he drew his fingers incredulously over a wet handkerchief plastered to his skull. The flow of blood had ceased. He began investigating the air around him, desperately intent on locating a hidden particle he could not find: it was the gymnastic display of a dazed man who dreamt he stood on his feet while in reality he was barely able to sit straight up. He would have fallen back (flat on either side) if Stoll had not remained close to support him, and to draw support from him (Fenwick mused wryly) as well. Fenwick began to wonder, too, in curious sympathy whether he himself was not as dazed and famished as Chiung was of both perception and recollection. His mind felt strangely clear, nevertheless, in spite of its burden of fascination which invoked only terror and confusion – clear in its power to specialize and brood on minute particulars, but confused at the same time by a chasm of unwelcome uncertainty. He bent down – grateful for the words of distraction Chiung provided: "Where he gone, eh? Where he gone?" Chiung was hoarse.

"Who?" Stoll demanded. "Who, man?"

"I tell you he been near me just now. He rise up and crack me skull."

"We were near you just now." Stoll could not help jesting. "But we didn't rise up and crack your skull."

"Eh! eh! Stoll man is you? Boy, me head!"

"Who hit you?"

"A crab, boy, that's who hit me. I never see so many blasted stars in me blasted head. A fucking crab." The remark was so instantaneous and ludicrous, everyone laughed, save Weng who began to curse Chiung's idiocy under his breath.

"What sort of crab?" Stoll resigned himself to humouring Chiung.

"Crab, did I say? I wrong. Was a bloody big turtle." Chiung groaned. "I remember now. One of them large bush turtle everybody like to eat. Delicate!" His mouth watered and he spat.

"I smell that dam' turtle," Weng exclaimed viciously, sniffing the air of the river. "You is one big dam' shit of a fool, Chiung."

Chiung tried to abuse Weng: "You filthy Buck man – you. . . ." His head stabbed him excruciatingly and he stopped. He remembered something and pointed to a spot on the stelling. Fenwick flashed his torch. Nothing was there. "It gone," Chiung said at last, after straining his eyes. He pointed to the stars reflected in the river. "It gone," he said again, "*there*." He recalled something else: "And it carry me bright torchlight with it plus the box I used to sit on near the gauge, me notebook, everything."

437

"Carry it where?" Stoll demanded with mocking patience.

"Overboard!" Chiung declared clumsily. "The last thing I know was a splash."

"Aw hell, just a splash!" Weng was disgusted. "I might as well ask the box you been sitting on. It ain't overboard as you think. It safe and sound. I move it off the stelling. Maybe it got more brains than you if it could talk. . . ."

Chiung formed his hands into an affected stupid crown which encircled his brow.

"All you explaining so far is pure balls," Weng rasped. "Stop playing the dummy and speak up. A few accusing words is all I ask. Even if you see nobody, just say you hate the body that strike you down. Say you hate some creeping Canje man! Is better," Weng shook his head bitterly, "if you head been really crack in two so you tongue could loll out and tell a crazy story. Once people could understand! Why! I would see with you if you say" – he spoke contemptuously – "that Mr Fenwick himself crawl up secretly and knock you down. After all you sitting 'pon he empty hat and coat . . . It would make better madman common sense to declare so than all the rubbish you see so far. . . ."

"It makes not the damnedst sense to me," Fenwick exclaimed.

Weng laughed brutally. He had begun to throw all discretion to the wind in his desire to implicate the crew in Fenwick's capacity for grave indirection and speculative weakness. He almost spat: "I just showing the ridiculousness of it, sir. Nobody longing to remember anything. Nobody seem angry to do anything. All of we brains going soon be addled like this fool on the ground. Poseidon can come and cut our very stones out and all we'll say is 'thank you'."

Chiung burst out: "Me brains addled, eh? I got a good mind to knock in your lying teeth."

"Knock in your own. Next thing you going to say is one of these planks rise up all of itself and strike you down. . . ."

"What I going to say going take all of my sense to explain," Chiung confessed. His face was a naked plea. He stopped, afraid to go on. Someone had deposited a lantern near to him and his bald forehead and countenance gleamed in the sorrowful light.

"Why don't you open or shut you mouth for good?" Weng cried furiously. "If you had been *killed* tonight everybody would have made up their mind by now what we got to do without waiting to hear you speak. You should be *dead*. . . ."

"You must tell us everything, Chiung," Fenwick urged. "If you can't give a proper explanation, I would have to assume the worst kind of business is afoot. . . ." He spoke glibly, even foolishly, he knew in his heart, hoping to distract or conciliate Weng a little. The truth was (and Weng knew, Fenwick confessed to himself) he was in the grip of currents that were fast reducing him into a mere weathercock, paralysing his ability to frame or assume any explanation whatsoever, however sensible, however absurd. He was turning into the greatest coward he had ever known. *He realized now how frightful and strange was the role of consciousness he played.* Only a short while ago he had been unable to conceive of Chiung as being other than dead; this was a psychological and crippling fact; it made him distrust his own consistent policy of a living rational truth. Why, it was Weng who had goaded Chiung to speak and live. Now the tables were inexplicably turned – Weng desired Chiung's death. The idiotic invention and instigation of life might yield an unpalatable truth. Unpalatable to whom? It was impossible to say. What a deplorable state of helpless conviction. The fact was (and Fenwick wanted above all to believe this in spite of every material contradiction) he would not yield to the threats or counsels of force. He would hang on blindly to every sacrifice of time, the most inessential fabric of everything, an inmost abandonment of everything, an indestructible frailty which bowed down to and yet confessed its freedom from the hideous reflexes of brute survival. . . . He knew Weng had succeeded in lining up the crew against him and the threat of disorder – if not mutiny – was in the air. And yet who could tell whether the immaterial sacrifice of time was not wearing them out? And whether every word Weng thrust at them did not cut into the very fibre of their resolution, with the knowledge that he lied in the identical helpless and violent way Fenwick spelt out the selfsame almost corrosive lie that coated everybody's tongue?

"I going to tell you the truth, skipper." Chiung spoke with the strength of malice and determination. "Even if I lose me job after . . ." His forehead wrinkled helplessly. "I mean to speak out plain because if is anybody I hate now – this very moment – it's Weng. I refuse to be ruled by him," he paused. "Why must Weng try to push words in me mouth? Why must anybody who do somebody a favour feel they got the right to push that body around?" He turned and glared at Fenwick. The complaint had bubbled up, grotesquely, even childishly, on his lips as if he were under the effect of an intoxicant or drug. If the occasion were not so serious it would have been easy to see it as extraordinarily ludicrous, Fenwick thought, but he felt now that the strongest prejudice of his nature (the faculty of straight vision) was impoverished and lost.

"I refuse to be pushed around," Chiung maintained, "to suit Weng or anybody. Scorn me if you like but don't push me into your design any more. . . ."

"Well, to me God," Weng declared. "Must *I* take the blame for who ever knock you out and leave you like a half-wit so that you can point a dam' finger at me?"

"I not pointing a dam' finger at you or anybody save to warn you to stop pushing me around." He bent his head and listened to the stricken companion noises of the night: the bent croaking of frogs like the death-rattle of breaking metal, the loud free splash of a fish jumping out of its flickering net, the crackling explosions of insects like invisible fire everywhere. The sky rustled. The men looked up where it congealed and flashed like a flying fist of rock.

"Come on, Chiung man, for God's sake tell us what happened," Fenwick broke in impatiently.

Chiung looked down, contemplating the means at his disposal to release the almost unintelligible picture of his soul. "A corial-boat was passing with like two men fighting for all their breath to paddle quick," he began.

"What time was this?" Fenwick could not resist asking as if it really mattered.

"Coming to quarter past eleven, I think." He fumbled involuntarily with the muse of his watch.

"I see. Go on."

"One of the men in the boat flash a light that play all over me. I flash me own light and then I knew was really two men for sure. I couldn't be real certain of a shadow before. The corial decide to pull up and come right under the gauge and stop. One body call out softly, calling *you*, your name clear, Mr Fenwick. They did mistake me for you. . . ." He murmured indignantly as if this confusion of identity had encapsulated his world.

"Ah! My helmet and coat. Did you recognize them?"

"No! they look like every other native Canje man to me. I couldn't make them out from Adam. I realize they only come to me because they think me was you. I address them and tell them plain who I be. When they catch on to their mistake I ask them what I can do. All the time I watching them cautious and careful. I don't like the looks of them. They say they been down the river to sell some firewood but all the business they do was such a poor bargain they made no money at all . . . Then one body come to the point and ask me outright if I want to buy his turtle. . . ."

"Turtle?"

"They repeat how they desperate short of even the ghost of cash. They tell me a real stupid tall story. They take me for a prize fool. I laugh and say is a wonder they not offering the skin on their back. They get offended and say they got honest uses for everything they own. They not whoring gamblers like me.

The land was their soul which they would never sell. Big talk! While on the other hand, they say I would gamble my mother to win a penny . . . They were turning to paddle away, but I get suddenly, like never before, stark staring angry (who the hell was they to accuse *me*? I hate them then worse than Weng or Jordan or a cunt like Perez). I muffle my mouth and I ask them to wait a few minutes more and let me see what kind of trick they got to sell." Chiung grew despairingly crafty, the vaguest hint of a parable in his flat insensible voice. "You never know who make who or what make what in this tangle-up creation of a world. I reason I would squeeze that bloody neck of meat. It might be a villainous thing for all I know. Turtle meat is rich and everybody tries to fashion it for himself so beware any time it come to you on a cheap platter. I try hard to sew up me lip tight but the strings start bursting out and inverting me life like if I talking to an image of meself at the other end of a telescope. . . ." He could not restrain himself from throwing off the steady disguise of uncreative memory. His was a long dumb festering seal registering the balancing notions of faith and duty. But now the plaster of hypocrisy he had accepted was overturned for good. Fenwick's handkerchief, poulticed to his skull, fell and exposed the angry bump of dreadful cupidity. "I not apologizing for anything I do," Chiung went on emphatically as if he wanted to disengage himself from everyone he knew. "Maybe you think I wrong but I not apologizing, see! The truth is I decide to strip and rob them two Canje men there and then. I grin at them and invite them to show me the big crab they got under the sugar-bag in the body of their boat. They pull out a monster of a turtle – the best kind I ever meet. One man pass it up to me. It was worth a good pound or two." Chiung paused and then ran on: "I grab. I make up my mind to rob them. I stretch the neck like if is something I myself manufacture. I refuse to pay them one blind cent. Then I tell them two men, speaking low and like all the wise surveying devil they ever meet rolled in one, to dive to hell where they belong. . . ."

"But why in God's name, Chiung?" Fenwick was absolutely stricken and startled.

"Maybe was because they accuse me of gambling me mother for a penny . . . I don't know what it was, but I couldn't stand looking down and seeing them villain and beast looking up at me as if they would never peddle a loaf unless it was hard as the devil's seed. I tell them to capsize themselves and go." Chiung paused, almost as if he had once more forgotten the perverse things he experienced and made. He reflected and continued: "After a while" – he was fumbling for the upright face of time – "when they take flight and gone – digging a solemn grave with their paddle – I bend down to read the level of the river. Is then suddenly I feel me hair stand on end. Something fall on the bright page of my notebook when I straighten me back to write the time and reading in. I look up, the darkness all red in me eye. All I see was the monster of a shell turning over in the air – I don't know who was lifting it up. Then the sky itself turn straight round and crash from another quarter like wood." Chiung groaned. "Maybe I was speaking to the paddle of death this night, I don't know, because me mouth forget every seal and me breath start to blow." His voice was now both stammering and raucous. His lips moved with the agonizing dispersal of every threadbare principle. He sounded as if he had changed places with his listeners and could see the shadow of himself (born with death) created in the dark pool of their eyes and striving to be understood.

BOOK THREE

THE READING

We are born with the dead:
See, they return, and bring us with them.
The moment of the rose and the moment of the yew-tree
Are of equal duration. A people without history
Is not redeemed from time, for history is a pattern
Of timeless moments.

T. S. Eliot

VII

He must have slept for three or four hours (it was already morning when he had lain down in his hammock). When he awoke it was just nine o'clock. The rain was drizzling and the light looked even earlier than the time was. Fenwick went down to the river, undressed and plunged in. He swam out to the middle, steadied himself and glanced along the grey raining surface of the water. The sky was a dripping sponge over the river which had begun to swell. All the arid dusty watermarks of drought on the trees and bushes were disappearing as if they, too, had been rubbed away leaving a clean but cracked slate, a web of broken lines nature had no desire to erase. These were salutary reminders of the displacement of the past, the basic untrustworthiness in every material image as well as in the conception of a supporting canvas. Were it otherwise the immaterial creation of freedom would have been banished for ever, and no one would ever dream, in all perversity, of seeing it.

Fenwick held his breath, dived for a long spell before coming up and swimming in again. As he dressed he recalled the concrete, half-hallucinatory drama of midnight. He found himself concentrating on the most insubstantial models and witnesses. These obsessed his mind (even more than the presences of Weng and Stoll who had formed a circle with him around Chiung) and he could not banish them, as he remembered them, standing on the stelling between himself and the clearing on the bank. Who, indeed, were they? It was reasonable to assume they included Van Brock and Jordan. But who were the others he had seen when he flashed the light of his thought? True, he had not given it a moment of reflection, at the time, and afterwards, in any case, there had only been

Van Brock and Jordan, no longer appearing, as it were, strung out so emphatically and sombrely against him. He turned over the mental roll-call of names. Bryant was absent and had not yet returned. This was incontrovertible. Perez was away. This, too, was a fact. There had been no one else sleeping in the camp last night who could stand in a row beside Van Brock and Jordan. It was a circumstantial riddle which made Fenwick aware of his disabilities. Facts were, perhaps, always obscure in the end. Could he be sure of even the two men who must have been standing along there, away from Chiung, Weng, Stoll and himself? Could he swear that the couple were not a conspiracy of spirit and emotion? There were many important things to do this morning, but these questions filled his mind to the overwhelming exclusion of all else. He would question the crew.

The rain kept on drizzling and the forest now began to splash long monotonous teardrops, separate and collective. Fenwick drank his morning coffee and decided to question Jordan, first. Did he know whether anyone had entertained any friends last night at the men's resthouse? Jordan did not know. He also looked unwilling to find out. Fenwick had shrunken deplorably in his (Jordan's) estimation. Such a question would have been unnecessary if Fenwick had always accepted Jordan's sound advice. Why, the state of affairs that had happened (and which owed its origin to Fenwick's own insecure liberal ideas) would never have had the opportunity to occur. One would never be worried to ask who entertained whom, if one always left people's private morality or immorality alone so that it never materially affected the order of government. It only became necessary to survey the role of vulgar intimacies when one's public area of duty was disordered by a conscience in nature one tried mistakenly to view. Jordan did not think a social expedition should ever be so cornered that it had to discover who kept company with whom. This was always the beginning of the end of oneself and everything. An open invitation (surely this had now become clear) to the ghosts of

447

chaos under whatever name they paraded. Not only distress of conscience. But the immortal foul sisters – hope and progress. Jordan had no illusions. He knew how cruel these relations could be, whatever their duration and life. Why did Fenwick question him now? It was like trying to find a way of securing Pandora's box after it had been dismantled. No one could recall the plagues let loose. Or like bolting the door of the stable after Pegasus himself had flown. No one could repair the damage which had been done. Perhaps he had always known it (even in the most successful of times) though he had been able to conceal the ultimate self-sacrifice and rent in himself. It was useless questioning Jordan, Fenwick knew. The man had done nothing save grumble improvidently like a woman. And Fenwick had been forced to put a reckless construction on everything he had said. He found he had grown better now at reading the constitution of another man's lips – since the time he had confronted black Poseidon and learnt of the nameless spiritual disease which confounds all nations and functions, save one undying art of community, alone, the profession of incurable diagnosis.

Fenwick questioned Van Brock. The latter was pensive and stricken as if he had been half-wrecked by malaria. The balloons of cheeks he normally possessed had been pricked, almost overnight. His habitual air and expression – self-indulgent and self-satisfied – had been sucked down into the pool of his eyes. The foul ague he had experienced intermittently for some weeks (and which he had had very badly, long ago, and thought he had killed for good) had become inward and enormous like a gale, all at once, shaking every conception of duty and existence.

He mooned over Fenwick's question, wanting to banish his inquisitor before another full onslaught descended on his senses. Had he had any visitors from the river last night? He did not think so though the night was confusing and confused in his mind. He had rushed down to the stelling like a man in a dream when Fenwick had cried out. . . . He awoke to the summons, sweating profusely. The agitation and the wind of fever in his blood had temporarily stopped. Someone had been sponging his brow. God knew who it was. He had been dreaming of home. The obscure village of his boyhood (a small number of black inhabitants) – Dartmouth the name was, situate on the Arabian coast some miles from the end of the public road where Charity stood.

He told Fenwick he remembered the someone now. It was his grandmother who had been sponging and scolding him. He had become terribly filthy in the process of recovering her old wedding-ring – made of pure gold – which she had nearly lost. He had bathed in an open sewer and had been fortunate, indeed, to find the gold he was searching for in the bed of such a swamp. Dartmouth was a poor village as everyone knew. (No wonder gold was counted as more precious than life. And yet, sometimes, it was not the gold alone but the memory of the giver which illumined a gift.)

The village looked out over the receding brow of the foreshore, so often wrapped in the long Atlantic surf which succeeded in flattening itself out into a huge towel on the ground. There was always this waving flag of naked battle between the sea and the land, mother and son. From birth the village had struggled for survival against the lap of the sea. Each new frantic mouth that opened for nourishment spat out again its own juice, the harsh milk was too bitter to swallow. Sometimes, nevertheless, it could be overwhelmingly sweet. There was the rainy season when the village benefited from its station and situation between the estuaries of two rivers, the Essequebo and the Pomeroon. Then the water along the coast was abundantly good to taste. It could be drunk, with almost carefree abandon, by animal and plant. In the dry season, however, one was grateful for every wall and erection against the sea. The mouths of the rivers had grown into tongues of salt and fresh water threatened to become dearer than dirt, dearer than the earth one walked upon. For this reason, more

449

sacred and compelling than any other, perhaps, the ritual of waste and disposal sometimes littered the ground and turned into a festival.

Before sunrise, the villagers emptied the urine in their nightly pots into a quagmire and swamp. It was as if the sea that had been excluded by walls now rose within them.

After sunrise, they trudged to the oldest wells of their faith to tease every dripping measure of incorruptible sweetness from the bowels of the earth.

The ritual of waste and the purest consolation of being had become wedded to the fibre of their natures. To have abandoned it would have been to lose the contradictory spirit of gold. . . .

Van Brock had taken his ailing grandmother's chamber-pot and poured its golden contents into the quagmire at the back of the land. The air was always unwholesome in the early morning, just before the stars fell from keeping guard. . . . He returned to find the sick old woman transfigured by anxiety. Daylight was fast approaching and she began bemoaning the loss of her ring. The stick of her finger had grown so dry the ring sometimes slipped off between the pillow of daylight and the sheets of night. Occasionally it fell and rolled across the floor of noon or morning and her grandson had to hunt in every crevice of time for it. . . . She could no longer contain herself on this occasion and she rose from her bed to look everywhere. Vertigo rushed upon her, leaving her desolated and ill and chattering all over as if every pore in her body cried out for the lost direction and fellowship of youth.

Had she swallowed the ring from her finger and passed it out? Van Brock was horrified by her every tottering question. Had he seen it? Had he heard it? Van Brock thought he remembered something but how – in God's name – could he be sure? Something had looked like gold in the lantern light. He had distinctly not given it a thought. Coming to think of it – he had heard a faint sound. The devil knew whose call it was he had heard in the dark. The voice of wailing rock, the immortal shiver of a diamond, the groan that sometimes splashed out of a bucket of sound. He had not given it a thought, seeking merely to do his duty and return home.

His grandmother was the oldest most troublesome woman in the world, he felt. She forgot everything (save her most stubborn ring of possession) and was inclined to lose everything. The doctor from Charity had warned her to lie still but she kept fidgeting. Van Brock sometimes prayed to himself that she would die and leave him in peace. Every old cow or horse in the fields had to die, sooner or later. Sometimes he felt that if she died he would be incapable of grief. In fact he would rejoice. Yet – in spite of his wisdom and conceit – he knew he would grieve in his bones. Of late he had tried to tread upon all speculation or wonder in fetching wood, water, cooking, going off – half-way to Charity – to do an afternoon's job in a road-mending or sea-defences gang. He had been unable, however, to crush the feverish limb of thought. Who was his grandfather? Would he know him if he saw him? No. He had to confess he would not. His grandmother had once instructed him that her husband (his grandfather) was a Dutchman who had owned a plantation in the Pomeroon. Grandson Van Brock, however, did not entirely trust this story. He had heard from another ancient villager that his grandfather was a simple pork-knocker who had been drowned in the nameless falls of the interior, not the sea, this time, where the white Dutchman was said to have gone down, but the black rivers of an obstinate heartland. It was he (the simpleton) who had sent the lump out of which the circle of gold was formed. . . .

The stories told were equally visionary as childish and common-or-garden, and Van Brock could not help suspecting that the ancient mind of his grandmother was wandering from pole to pole. She spoke of her only child and daughter (Van Brock's mother) who had died when a son and a grandson was born. She spoke of her daughter's husband (Van Brock's father) who had run away into the bush for good. She mixed up her grandson's father (her daughter's runaway husband) with her own husband, the boy's maternal grandfather (who possessed the twin heads – Dutchman and African).

Sometimes they were all one undivided column and person, sometimes they were two, sometimes they were three, a trinity so singular and real it vanished into obscurity. It was impossible to tell where it stood. One thing was certain. The old woman was the fourth, the only living ancestor he knew. He clung to her and yet was so exasperated by her, he wanted her to die and melt into the ground with all the rest. . . .

He tried to console her but no one (not even her grandson) could replace the loss of the ring. He promised to work and buy her another. But this made no impression upon her. She was blind to every reason, every promise, every suggestion, every plea to consider what she was doing, to return to her bed, lie still, wait, see. She was blind to everything save the bond of love. The ring (however skeletal, even primitive and obscene in its generation) was everything and everyone she knew and desired. She could not bear the decapitation of memory. Van Brock grew angry and abused her. She collapsed. The cords in her neck loosened. The grey dusty hair grew dim. Her dribble turned into the agony of sweat. Not another murmur of protest. Not another motion of desire or disgust. . . . She was dead. . . .

Van Brock descended into the grave pit even before she did, searched for the ring and restored it to her finger as a dutiful high priest at the wedding of memory. Was it an ancestor of life or of death he had created at that moment? He was obsessed with the self-indulgence and ordure of love as with the ghost of glory.

Bryant and Catalena arrived soon after the inquisition of Van Brock had ended. Fenwick knew as soon as he saw them that something dreadful (it was the first expression he deciphered on their lips) had happened . . . Poseidon was dead . . . God was dead. . . . This was the dreadful annunciation. The oldest cage of impotency, they knew, had been splintered. The

ancient cords had been broken of verbal and material
inapprehension. . . . An angel of polemic and absurdity would
have shouted for joy – instead of weeping helplessly in the way
Bryant and Catalena did.

Everything one thought or discovered or brought to light,
Fenwick declared, was instantly plastered with the slime of
spiritual parody, the parody of a universal and uncapturable
essence. They must be careful not to lose a viewless conception
in a deformed relationship. . . . The pure paint of love scarcely
dries on a human canvas without a modicum of foreign dust
entering and altering every subtle colour and emotional tone,
which affects the painter as well as the painted property of
life. . . .

Bryant was insane with love and grief and nothing Fenwick
said – however wise or invaluable – could console him. It was
his fault he kept insisting – the death of his "grandfather" and
the abduction of Catalena. He had killed the old man beyond a
shadow of doubt. All he wanted was a blessing from him, a
declaration of kinship, but this greed for affection had sown
the seeds of tragedy.

He had set out, light-hearted, to fulfil his mission, yesterday,
arrived at Poseidon's, and found only Catalena there. Perez
was by the riverside at the gauge. The old man had vanished
but Catalena said she knew where he had gone. She had
followed him when he set out, begging him to protect her. But
he had driven her back, telling her – in his grotesque, uncertain
way – to remain with her brute.

Perez whipped her, night and day, pointing out to her that
she was responsible for Fenwick's decision to fire him, and that
unless she was able to put this ruling into reverse before the
time of departure, he would murder her.

Bryant found himself unable to withstand her. His greed for
ancient remembrance and love possessed many dormant
signals, now coming to primitive life, beauty as well as lust.
Catalena was the model of his compulsive derangement, a
living projection and vessel, nevertheless, to offset the last

impending signal of all, which was to be a god's death. If he had known this, would he not have abandoned her to be crucified, and turned back from the future?

It was a profound riddle to test one's imagination. Catalena had arrived, Fenwick knew, on the mailboat, *Andromeda*. Half-priestess, half-prostitute. Had Andromeda not been saved by Perseus and his perennial agents in history around the globe, around the centuries – had she been left to suffer death, would history have regarded her rock as the true cross, the true death of the gods?

It was a question no one was permitted to frame or answer at the time. Least of all Bryant. All he or anyone could do was help her to write a little fable or note of action. Not too rigid an invention, something elastic and malleable that time would work upon and expand in another's governing brain and heart. Something calculated to fire and console a husband's imagination, give him all he desired in the poor companionship of the present. Allow him to betray her and himself. Make him think she had gone to a higher authority (Fenwick, perhaps) to beg for the paltry wage he needed. Not to beg for mercy for herself, at all, but cash for him. Fool. How she hated the devil she had married, hated all the misery she had embraced. She would do anything, beg anyone, lie with any man to ensure for herself a flying start. Perez would never understand the deception until it was too late to be less than grateful. By then he would be gorged by the employment he wanted, too gorged to care whether he had made her into his and everyman's mercenary whore. Money or life! That was the motto instilled into her by the beast.

Mad to hope she would change. Sufficient if she managed to escape. Bryant wanted her. He saw she could be anything to him, do anything for him . . . She would take him first to the place where Poseidon was hiding. . . .

They raced down the ladder of the house, came quickly to a thrusting trail, winding and thrusting ever forward until the ground ceased to roll.

The Reading

They were both watching each other, longing for the consummation of their hopes. It was an anxious predilection and an uneasy truce. She knew he was already looking through her to the end of a blind trail. He knew she was looking inward upon herself, on her peculiar cross and predicament and soul of unreason, without which she would never have ventured to travel with him. It was the kind of relationship which could prosper since the future was its only design. However much they could be fulfilled in each other now, even desperately fulfilled in the present, they were entangled beyond the insecurity of pleasure. . . . Bryant suddenly fell on her with this thought and possessed her with the utmost resolution and vigour. . . . He had been dreaming of her for a longer time than he cared to admit. From the moment he plotted to find room in the river for her. Long before she herself actually knew. And now it was as if every wily condition – enforced or involuntary – of life and absence was justified in an act of impossible union. . . .

It was afternoon when they came to the clearing where Poseidon and the rebels had congregated: a wide opening in the bush (surrounding the usual black cave and hut which symbolized the region) had been trampled by horses and cattle. The smell of pitiless dung seized their nostrils like a devastating over-ripe sourness. Catalena was disturbed. She wanted to turn back. The truth was she had never ventured beyond this consuming barrier, a deterrent fired in the artifice of her lung by the human herd to discourage her visit from another world. On the other hand it was the scent an indefatigable huntsman would pick up and follow across time. If not Bryant now, Weng later on or the jungle police of another civilization. There was no astronomical prison of escape for anyone – man or beast – across the centuries or through the bush of space. All were doomed to see themselves die to the basest as the loftiest motives of conspiracy. . . . And this would be the devouring turning-point (time itself would be unable to follow) beyond which the angelic counsels of war and the nobility of devils could not go for it would possess no self-created road or direction to be traversed and dismantled by those who sought to escape, and those who desired to follow. . . .

Bryant urged Catalena to push on into the smell of the earth. . . . The trees fell away into a close ring around them, and they marched across the clearing, brilliantly lit by the afternoon sun like a dying fire. Poseidon and a dozen men or so were seated in a circle before the door of the hut. They had cooked a meal on the ground, the last grains of which they were eating. Bryant was torn by the desire to run forward and embrace the old man but the thought of the woman at his side restrained him. . . . Poseidon sprang to his feet. He appeared to rebuke every feeble, impotent nerve in his body. . . . He swallowed his last morsel of food, and with a shout, plucked a rod from the ground. . . . His entire demeanour was terrible as he advanced on Catalena. Why had she disobeyed him and insisted on returning like a miserable spy, bringing one of the surveyor's men with her, the same devil who had persuaded him to take her in along with that monster, her husband? They were all intent on betraying his authority. It was clear. If he did not act now she might be the soul of his downfall. She had secreted herself in his house to learn all she could and now here she was to flout her brazen-faced plans. . . . He jumped forward, his stick uplifted to strike every peril. . . .

The attack was so unexpected they were almost paralysed with astonishment, the seated disciples on the ground as well as Bryant and the woman. Catalena was the first to turn and run in wild panic. A drooping horse stood in the clearing, a mare that sensed her coming and lifted her head out of a bucket of grass in which she had been nibbling. The girl tripped and fell, half-rose, full of terror, almost clasping the animal's indifferent hoof. Poseidon was fast approaching with the raised pole, exasperated and transfigured. In one timeless enduring instant he appeared to lose all fumbling enfeeblement. The indomitable ardour and strength of years rediscovered their furious potency, the most frightful lover of age. He knew he would live for ever in the minds of his people. . . .

Bryant, who had succeeded in overtaking and confronting him, leapt up to take the blow across his chest, doubling his sharp fists as an involuntary precaution. He would not have hurt the old warrior for all the world. But the speed of his arrival and intention was beyond the ancient one's eye. Poseidon stumbled and fell, in his race, of unequal body and spirit, on the cruel knuckles of the one who loved him best, the grandson he had begotten in the dreadful apotheosis of history. He half-crumpled, as if he had suffered a vision and a stroke in the midst of incredible exertion, blinded by blood in his nostrils and eyes. His head struck the rim of the bucket on the ground and he lay on an animal of shadow as if the horse had kicked him until he fell bleeding under her. Crimson stars spattered Catalena's dress. She lost consciousness. . . .

Soon after, an hour before nightfall, the old man's grey body was laid out like the ashes of a fire the sun still lit. His followers were so amazed and dumbfounded by the bitter, treacherous hopelessness of it all, they no longer desired to wait to take the steps they had planned against the science of the invader. He (Fenwick) was far away, it seemed, at this instant, but two representatives of his dominion were in their hands. Let them make an end to all waiting and planning for an accursed ultimatum, *now*. Bitterness had become their only treasure, the bitterness which instructed them to abandon everything, every plan of action, which paled into meaningless insignificance beside the overwhelming emotion of helpless hate. It was useless to dream that they could contain their own decisive lot any longer, in the leaderless crisis in which they were involved, and since they were incapable of doing so, nothing in the world had ever truly done so, or was genuinely able to do so.

In surrendering to the eternal and broken cage in themselves, they were surrendering to the open violence of time all the choking cup of horror to come, the last remaining dregs of themselves, which once drunk and endured now in the terror of the present, might be incapsulated out of a material future and hardening helpless function.

They decided the man and the woman they had made prisoners must be put on quick trial in the light of dawn. Two messengers of the jury were despatched before nightfall to collect certain instruments: instruments of self-torture as well as the combined will of judgement over themselves.

For it was equally the trial and inquisition of themselves (each one laying bare himself in his heart) as of the prisoners they held. The great judge of themselves was dead, and they alone could judge the relics of security or insecurity he had left. Long before dawn or midnight the consciousness of the trial commenced, even before the two messengers of the jury had returned with the instruments and presents of tradition and law they wished to demolish from around them since these no longer contained them. As the night wore on the woman felt the shadows of terror in freedom around her, clutching and abandoning at one and the same time every straw of her limbs in the wind. The fire of desire that had been lit emphasized the black void of the night and the black face of the judge, godless now as well as godlike, lying mute and uncreated amongst them. Their formless outcry stirred not even a quiver on his lips, neither imitation nor resonance, and the fire that flickered within and without his countenance, streaked him only with the premature coming of the dawn, the false or early dawn dubbed upon the cheeks of men. It signified the lie in their hopes as well as the creation of a jewel of light without self-evident generation or action.

The shadows that wept drank in the flying spirit streaming on his brow like the dregs of their own stumbling agony. They groaned because in reality there was nothing there they could catch save an immaterial depth of reflection. The false material day had not yet come and life itself was absent from him and –

it seemed – from themselves. There was nothing running there at all on the ground save the bitterness of alien reflection. How could they sustain themselves in the shadow of pure nothingness, the empty ritual of counsellor and counselled, judge and judged?

The wraith of a woman they had captured in Poseidon's dying breath felt the unwholesome fingers of the night lifting her sleeping dress as she lay still bound and helpless on the ground. She screamed for the first time, it seemed, in life's own dream. The shadows fled and ignored her. But they drew in again with kisses (which were not yet kisses) the caress of dead lips, moist as the slavering tongues of beasts. She screamed again to repulse every foundation in a monster of self-knowledge to which she was allied from the very beginning, equally real as unreal, artifice or folly as well as misery and cunning. There was only the drooping shadow of the mare whose tail fondled her breasts with the masquerading brush of pleasure.

Nothing stood between her and them save the ribs of Bryant. Watching him in the firelight she seemed bound to him and yet formless as ever. They had stripped him in their fury and he pleaded with them. He told them he loved the black shape lying on the ground. It was the condition of universal freedom, the broad base of countless beings. He sought to protect the woman and himself since it was the last tribute he could pay the memory of ancestor and judge whose uplifted stroke should be transformed into the nerve of progeny in their imagination. The old man dreamed (why should they argue otherwise?) of protecting his race, a race of phantoms, the pursuing and pursued, more the latter than the former. The miscalculation of death should not turn to rape or folly in themselves, to the rending of every living potential witness. . . . Bryant prayed and fought that they would reduce the sentence of self-repudiation they wished to pass on the woman and on themselves – to be locked together in the light of the strange jewel that crowned the dead god's brow. His plea fell on deaf ears for they saw her as the seed and helplessness of their own growing disaster they had in their power to end once and for all. . . . She writhed ceaselessly to free herself until in breathless exhaustion she stopped, spent and shuddering as if her limbs were the strings of homunculus. The judges of her illegitimate conception were falling towards her to rape and construct her into the new model of their woe, withdrawing again, returning over her, backwards and forwards like a pendulum of indecision. Only their shadows touched her but she screamed for help with witless abandon. No one heard her or answered her as far as she was aware, save that she seemed to hear the distant conjunction of other limbs dressing in the borrowed darkness overhead. She was cold in spite of the naked fire (with ague or delirium) praying crazily that some one would wrap her in the dead man's garments, anything to be born to survive. . . .

It was an hour or two past midnight and the first drops of rain fell, then ceased and withdrew even as they tasted the sacred skin of the fire. The wind's black appetite, in the lungs of the void overhead, remained unabated, even when breathless, scattering a few more starry drops on the woman's frame and the fire's dress, and storing up an impending drizzle and fall.

Instead of covering her with Poseidon's rags several hands held her and stripped her. When naked she was thinner than they had expected (as if all her wild bravado was of hysterical slight moment). She might have been still half a child and appeared in one light indestructible as gleaming ivory, and yet, in another glimmer of consciousness, weak and full of supplication, the rarest matchsticks of beauty, tipped with one secret brush of shadow to fire a man's lust. They lifted her and flung her down. The shining reflection running over the dead man's lips reached out and touched her mouth, flickering, with the same expiring breath as when he had fallen under the horse's hoof. She screamed, anticipating brutal nails on fingers of darkness, stripping her further and cutting her again, slicing into every tip of her body to the dice of bone in her blood until her flesh would quiver as if it had been plucked out of a shell. . . .

Nothing protected her now, she dreamed feverishly; she was a naked spirit indeed without constellation or cover, form or condition. Nothing save the ridiculous light of compassion. But who knows what trump card falls out of a man's hand at the last moment and clothes his thought? *Something* held them from killing her. They were gambling amongst themselves. To whom did she first belong? That was the question. Could they settle it with the flick of a card – the queen of their hearts? Or would they double it by marrying her to the jack of spades who would first lie on her? Who held the joker's hand which stood in Fenwick's coat? Would he arrive now as he had done before? Her delirium mounted. She would not have understood the thread of connection if she had seen Chiung standing there like every loser over the fabric of his winnings. . . . And yet someone (whether she knew his nameless coat or not) stood over her to save her in the light of unconditional circumstance. . . . She tried to focus her eyes but he vanished, leaving a picture framed in the place, the wild twins who had haunted Chiung and Fenwick and the crew that very night. . . . Poseidon's company knew them as the two members of the jury they had sent to collect the deeds of the law (aged papers signifying grants of land, licences of occupancy, mortgaged freehold, the instruments of their leases . . .). They had sent them on this errand a nightfall ago. Now they had returned but it was not merely the intervention of their arrival which saved the woman's life. It was the news they blurted out as they fell panting and breathless on the ground. News that provoked in the group of men the greatest consternation and alarm and turned them away from their victim. An uproar of questions seemed to come from the dreaming past, the chaotic present, and an inquisitor who split everyone's skull to survey the depth of crucial interlocution. (She understood little as Fenwick fired question after question at her: she was hardly

461

able to stand and keep the raining eyes of the morning open. What time had the messengers arrived? he asked her, putting two and two together. His questions invoked the conscience of the night within her.)

Why had they hit the tide-reader so hard on his head to strike him dead, the black company were demanding of the twins. This was the tale the messengers had told. Were they sure of this? Yes, they were sure, dead sure. The facts were plain as anything. They repeated their story, a little less winded now, but still clutching a stitch in their side. . . . They had stopped under the stelling, thinking it was Fenwick they saw. They wanted to make a quick pound or two from the fool. It was a stupid whim to have followed, a freak of circumstance. They had discovered it wasn't Fenwick at all. They had tried to make the best of a bad bargain with the man they found there. At first he seemed reasonable and obliging. Then he insulted them. Afterwards he cheated them. . . . They waited until he thought he was safe and then they crept upon him in the dark and beat his brains – twice as hard as they had actually intended – stone-cold. They felt his heart quickly. It had stopped. The cheater was dead. They remained riveted for an eternity to the deck of the stelling. Then they fled. . . .

And now it was all over. At any moment Weng and his men, followed by the jungle police, would be on their heels. The trial had ended. The dead judge was agreeable to everything even to being abandoned in panic by his followers who were frightened men. Because of these reasons, which had become part of the irony of judgement, the sentence they wished to read was taken out of their hands and rendered invalid. At the selfsame moment that they were beginning to execute a picture of the void in themselves, their world was peopling itself afresh, against their will, against their bitter intention. The phantoms moved in their mind, they could hear the furies of persecution and prosecution approaching, phantoms they had summoned by misadventure and involuntary will. What manoeuvre could they adopt to stay the action they had so foolishly set in train the very instant they needed to bind or ban every man? There were none they could discover save flight. Time no longer stood to allow them to dig a hole in which to let their prisoners down beyond anyone's reckoning; and then time too was required to seal it up so that no one would dream it had ever been opened. Time not only to seal the earth so that it would look as if it had never been touched but to open it again, in broad daylight, before formal witnesses – as if for the first time – in order to put stinking Poseidon in a bed over the runaway lovers for all eternity, stinking to heaven until the witnesses of his descent were unable to look into the bottomless pit.

A desperate resolution and yet so simple to perform once time stood and waited and did the most bitter bidding, holding back the present hordes of men. Time for Bryant and Catalena to appear to run and make swift love on every trail across the earth; while Fenwick grew to believe they had put their foot and escaped upon another rung in the secret ladder. The land was the mystery in which he would never chart where they had vanished. . . .

Who would suspect anything when the followers of Poseidon had turned so sensible they were yielding all their holdings and immovable possessions to be vested in the state or in the grave? Let the foolish lovers fly into nothingness while time stopped to bring witnesses to the burial of God enclosing the instruments his disciples had vainly possessed – the apparatus of the law they once honoured. It was childish to contemplate this unaccomplished funeral (where the dead would have buried the dead), Fenwick knew, rebuking every phantom in himself. The law could not be buried, nor given to the dust. There were always copies and current records (since mankind began) of the covenant time would have stopped to imprison. No one could force a void in the spirit of the law even with an act of humility or the surrender of one's land and property. Least of all by damming the ghost of responsibility. Time should have known better but it always seemed so ignorant of its own nativity or asylum or prison-house. And yet it would have prided itself on knowing *now* (if in stopping to read it had successfully executed) what no one else could dream to know . . God's grave over emptiness, over the unacknowledged wedding of man and woman, the unacknowledged burial of man and woman. . . . Time was prepared to bind its possessions above these unknown relics and over no other origin and abyss of itself. . . . It was an unendurable sentence which had been entertained, and which needed universal strength in execution that neither the dead nor the living possessed. . . . The instant the prison of the void was self- created, a breath of spirit knew how to open a single unconditional link in a chain of circumstance.

Fenwick was dreaming a very strange dream: it seemed that an inquisition of dead gods and heroes had ended, an inquiry into the dramatic role of conscience in time and being, the dangers of mortal ascent and immortal descent. The one chosen from amongst them to descend was crying something Fenwick was unable to fathom but the echoes of annunciation grew on every hand and became resonant with life. . . . In our end . . . our end . . . our end is our beginning . . . beginning . . . beginning. Fenwick awoke. It was the dawn of the seventh day.